The Historical Novel Prize was founded in memory of Georgette Heyer, by Bodley Head and Corgi Books, in 1977. Rhona Martin's remarkable first novel won the award in competition with 150 entries.

Rhona Martin was born in London. Her father came from South Dakota, and her mother was a descendant of the Bishop John Hooper who was burnt at the stake for his religious beliefs by 'Bloody' Queen Mary.

She studied art and the history of costume at the Bristol Academy of Art and worked for a time as a theatrical designer. She emerged from marriage with two daughters and a desire to get back into the entertainment world, and then worked in a disco and in cinema management. Five years ago she changed to secretarial work in order to have more time for writing. Gallows Wedding is the result.

RHONA MARTIN

A dark novel of witchcraft and forbidden
love set against the backdrop of religious
upheaval in Henry VIII's times.

ROMAUNCE
Cirencester

Romaunce Books

1A The Wool Market Dyer Street Cirencester Gloucestershire GL7 2PR
An imprint of Memoirs Publishing www.mereobooks.com

Gallows Wedding: 978-1-86151-545-2

First published in Great Britain in 2015
by Romaunce Books, an imprint of Memoirs Publishing

The address for Memoirs Publishing Group Limited can be found at
www.memoirspublishing.com

The Memoirs Publishing Group Ltd Reg. No. 7834348

The Memoirs Publishing Group supports both The Forest Stewardship Council® (FSC®) and the PEFC® leading international forest-certification organisations. Our books carrying both the FSC label and the PEFC® and are printed on FSC®-certified paper. FSC® is the only forest-certification scheme supported by the leading environmental organisations including Greenpeace. Our paper procurement policy can be found at www.memoirspublishing.com/environment

Typeset in 10/13pt Palatino
by Wiltshire Associates Publisher Services Ltd. Printed and bound in Great Britain
by Printondemand-Worldwide, Peterborough PE2 6XD

For my daughters

CONTENTS

PART I

Cradle of Fire

1

Their eyes held across the limp figure on the pallet. Fear filled the tiny room like an ominous rumble of thunder. Tibby blessed herself, glad for the first time that the child she had just delivered was not hers.

Tom dropped his head in his hands, the rushlight glinting on his foxy hair. The baby kicked feebly, gave a gasping squeal and began to breathe.

'Oh, no!' he groaned. 'I hoped it were -'

'Sh-sh!' warned Tibby fiercely, glancing at Margery's pale face and shadowed eyes. She pulled herself together, cut the cord and bound up the mother. Then she began rapidly to collect up her things.

'Where you going?' Tom looked up, his old young face anxious.

'Home!' she muttered briefly. 'You don't think I'm stopping here. They'll say I "touched" it. You know I didn't. You saw me put the pearl-wort under her knee. Who's going to believe me? It's always the midwife's fault...'

Tom started up. 'How do I know you won't tell!'

'Tell? Why should I tell? I'm in trouble same as you.' 'You don't understand.' He grabbed her shoulders to make her look at him. 'There's been no baby born here tonight.' She frowned, uncomprehending, until he added slowly, 'Not born alive, that is.'

Tibby stared. 'Tom -you cannamean-' It was a cross, to be sure, but crosses were to be borne. Poor Margery ... her firstborn! She said, aghast, 'Dunna do it, Tom.'

Tom's voice shook. 'I got to, Tib. You know I have.'

''But Margery-'

'There'll be others. It won't be so hard for her again. I'll make a birthing stool so they come easy. You'll see, it's for the best-' He spoke eagerly, trying to convince himself as much as her. 'Better now than -'

'Tom ...' a voice came feebly from the shadows. 'What is it?' After the months of waiting, the punishing hours of labour, was there a girl or a boy ...

' Witchmarked.' Tom said it bluntly; the baby was quiet, so he added, 'Born dead. Dunna look. I'll bury it outside.'

'No, Tom!' Tibby snatched it from him and it set up a healthy cry.

'It's not dead!' Margery tried to struggle upright on the blood-soaked ruin of her bed, 'Give it here!' She reached out for it and then, bewildered by their reluctance, she began to cry exhaustedly. 'I want my baby,' she begged weakly, pitifully.

'You canna do it, Tom!' Tibby put a stout arm about the weeping girl. 'Here's your baby, dunna you fret yourself, 'tis a fine bonny girl. Only - 'tis witchmarked, like Tom says, and right bad.' She glared fiercely in his direction. 'But we anna going to let him do away with it!'

'Oh, no!' sobbed Margery, her head bent over the puling infant. 'My baby - not my baby!' She rocked back and forth, hysterically clutching the child, and abruptly lost consciousness.

'There!' scolded Tibby, triumphant. 'Now see what you done.'

Tom looked helplessly from one to the other. He was beaten.

He could override one woman but not two. Not when one was his Margery. He knelt awkwardly beside her. 'Marge, love ...' She moaned and her eyelids flickered. 'Dunna take on so, you know I wunna do it, not if you say No ...' They rubbed her hands and feet until she returned to them. At last Tom said, 'Well, Tib, what we going to do, then? Cut it out?'

Margery held the baby tighter and looked at them with frightened eyes.

'No use,' declared Tib, 'things like that do always grow again. No, all you can do is keep your big mouth buttoned tight and hope nobody sees. And stop scaring the daylights out of this poor girl!'

Tom coloured angrily. What right had she to tell him how to treat his wife?

'That's all very well.' His tone was surly. 'I anna having no imps suckled in this house-'

'Oh, Tom, how could you!'

'Old wives' tales!' snapped Tibby, trying to control the prickle that was running up her own spine. 'To say such a thing about your own flesh and blood!'

'"Tain't my flesh and blood. 'Tis a changling for all I know, and none of mine. I'm telling you, the first time I sees-'

'You won't see nothing, you great stupid lump. Weren't you there all along? How could anyone change it under your very nose? Talk sense, can't you!' Tibby's voice was sharpened by concern for her patient, whose lips were again turning colour.

'Not someone - something,' Tom muttered darkly. Tibby silenced him.

'If you're so lily-livered best get out in the woods and dig up some rowan saplings. Plant 'em in a circle round the house and keep her inside. They won't cross that. Not imps nor witches nor spooks nor nothing else. And give her a good name.'

'I thought to call her Nan,' put in Margery timidly. 'Like the Rose of Hever,' she explained.

'The King's whore!' roared Tom, jerked out of his fantasies. 'Over my dead body!'

'Now, now, Tom,' soothed Tibby, 'that's no matter now. But Nan's no good. You want a good strong Christian name. Mary or Martha or such.'

'Them's no good. I heard tell of a witch called Mary and two called Elizabeth.'

'What then?'

Tom thought for a moment. 'We-ell ... if you want to keep the witches off a cow, you ties a switch of hazel to her tail. Never know it to fail. So it's Hazel, I reckon. We're like to call it Hazel.'

'Hazel,' repeated Margery, tasting the name. She smiled for the first time. 'I like that, Tom. That's pretty. We're going to call her Hazel.'

'Yes, well...' Tom felt his surliness melting. 'You got to rest now, Marge. You got to get strong again.'

Margery's eyes shone softly, and Tib nudged her, chuckling. 'Strong enough to start the next, he means!'

Tom had had enough. He got to his feet and his tone was truculent.

'I'm bringing the goat in, now. She'll be catching her death out there.'

'Oh yes, bring the goat in,' jeered Tibby, recognising her dismissal; she added tartly, 'Be sad indeed if the goat got wet. Much more of a matter than a firstborn child ...'

Tom said sourly, 'We got to feed a baby. The goat feeds us. And you'll be expecting your birthing price, no doubt.'

'No!' said Tibby, her face hard and square as a man's. 'I've not been here tonight. I'll take no payment. Just don't you let me hear of no harm coming to that child.' She called goodnight to Margery from the doorway and followed him out to where the goat was tethered. It stood shivering and dull-eyed, with the night rain streaming from its coat.

'There,' exclaimed Tom, 'it's started already! The goat's going sick!'

'Duckpuddles!' snorted Tibby, edging away. 'Mind now, don't you let me hear ...'

'All right, all right,' muttered Tom, untying the animal to lead her indoors, 'but you'll see ...'

His words were blown away by the wind and Tibby did not catch them.

'What?' she shouted back over her shoulder. His voice followed her, rain-tossed, down the hill.

'I say no good's going to come of this - you mark my words!'

Tibby did not answer. She had done her job. Delivered living child and seen it and the mother safe. And yet - she shivered with more than the pre-dawn chill. Disturbed and uneasy, she stumped off into the night.

2

The fust in the cottage was becoming unbearable. The sun sucked steam from the thatch, drove a dagger of light down the chimney, and drew an oily sweat from the paper windows. Margery stirred restlessly as the odour of the rosemary and wild garlic in their pots joined the fume from the floor to assail her queasy stomach. She threw off the single cover and touched the back of a hand to the face of the girl beside her, then smiled, finding it healthily cool. Then she moved her hand lightly over her own swollen belly. Her brows drew together as she thought she felt a gentle contracting of the muscles.

The girl turned towards her, mumbling drowsily, and then in the middle of a yawn said sharply, 'Mother!' Suddenly alert, she added, 'You going to birth it today?'

Margery relaxed with a sigh. 'When the apple's ripe 'twill drop. Nothing we can do to hurry it. Still, the sooner the better, I suppose.' She heaved her unwieldy body to a sitting position and sat smiling at her daughter, rubbing the small of her back to ease the cricks before making the effort of getting to her feet.

She was no stranger to pregnancy now. In the fourteen years of her marriage she had borne eight children and four of them had lived and thrived. She sighed; three were gone from her now, Jody to a blacksmith and the others God knew where, and no one could say if she would ever see them again. But not this one: this one they dared not sell.

They had planted their saplings of rowan and they had hung a crucifix about her neck and they had called her Hazel to keep the witches at bay. They had prayed - at least Margery had - as devoutly as they had hoped; perhaps it was not really what it seemed, perhaps it would disappear as the child grew, perhaps ... But it had not disappeared, and it was all too clearly v/hat it seemed. And the woman so marked stood surely in the shadow of the rope. If only Tom ... with an effort, she turned her mind away.

If only Jody could have stayed at home! Fie must be twelve now, brown-eyed and russet-haired like Tom, almost a man himself ... Jody would have known the best thing to do about Hazel. But now there was only herself, hampered as she was by the coming babe, to keep Hazel safe. And the danger grew daily. Sooner or later someone would catch her, strip her for his pleasure, and afterwards - would he denounce her as a witch and see her hang? Who could tell... if she disappointed or resisted him ... she was barely grown, scarce out of her childhood. Yet watching her move about the darkened room ...

'Hazel, put your shift on - don't wander about with that thing showing!'

'There's no one here but us.'

Margery glanced uneasily behind her. 'That's all you know.'

Mischief bubbled in Hazel and she stooped, one hand extended, as if she were calling hens.

'Here - pretty, pretty, pretty! Here - pretty, pretty-' Then she saw Margery's face and hugged her impulsively. 'Oh, Mother - you dunna really think I'd suckle the Devil! You know I'd fly a mile from anything with horns - I canna even abide cows!' She laughed, 'I'll put something on if it worries you, but you're so easy teased!'

Margery watched her leaning into the heavy press where their few garments were stored. That'll be the next to go, she thought. If we can find someone to buy it ... How she hated having to sell the things Tom had made. She thought of the spinning wheel that they had clung to up to the last; they had used it with pride and with love, and parting with it had been painful.

Hazel put on her shift. Then she took Margery's old gown that had become too small for her, carried it to the door, and shook it hard in the fresh air, blinking at the sunlight.

'It gets tighter every day,' she complained, squeezing it down over her budding breasts.

'Slack it off, then. Come here, I'll do it for you.' Margery let out the lacing to ease her, then patted her on the rump. 'Remember, now, don't call the Devil, not even in fun. You never know what might be listening.'

Hazel aired Margery's own clothes and handed them to her, and smiled as she dragged her fingers through her hair.

'I'll lay fresh rushes before the baby comes. This floor smells like a midden.' She picked up the water bucket and went out.

Margery dressed slowly. She felt tired this morning. Perhaps it was a good sign. The sooner the birth was over the better, for they could not move until it was. And they had to get on the road before they had nothing left to sell. She looked around her at the familiar place and felt the tears rise ... Oh, Tom, why did you have to fight them when they took our bit of land! We'd have kept body and soul together somehow, with the carpentry, with something, we'd have managed without it one way or another ... but when the others from the village came, off you had to go hotheaded to throw your life away! You always were the wild one. I should have known you'd never die in your bed ...

She sighed again. Looking from the door, she could see Hazel stepping out in the morning sunlight with a bucket in each hand. The yoke was too big for her and sat awkwardly on her immature shoulders. How could anyone think evil of a harmless child? And yet - who had lived quieter than old Nanny Webster, who wove the finest cloth for miles around? And they had hanged her only last summer, and burned not only her loom, saying it was enchanted, but her cat and her tame hare along with it, swearing that they had all been consorting with the Evil One. The old woman was speechless with shock. The cat died without a sound, muffled in its bag, mercifully stifled by the smoke perhaps. Only the hare screamed long and dreadfully, 'letting the Devil out'. Margery winced, remembering the sound.

Now the whole problem of Hazel fell on her shoulders alone; all because Tom - she checked her thoughts. Tom was Tom, God rest him, and could only have been what he was. It was up to her to find safety for the girl before she began to be what she was - whatever unnatural thing that might turn out to be.

She was kneading up dough for a loaf when the thought touched her like a chilly hand. Why had Hazel said 'I'd fly a mile'? Why not 'I'd run a mile' - like anybody else...

She beat the flour from her hands and went out of doors to get warm. She sat on the wall in the sun and closed her eyes. Holy Mother, she prayed, Holy Mother, let the baby come soon!

Hazel sat on the brink of the well to rest after the long sweat of winding up the buckets. Summer was well on and the water was low. She drew deep breaths of the sweet air, savouring the scent of wood smoke drifting towards her from the village fires.

They were the only ones using the old well now that the new one had been sunk in the village. It had become her favourite place, a lone and secret refuge where she could listen to birdsong or watch the tawny squirrels flicker in the highest branches of the oaks. Often she would come up here alone to think her thoughts, or to escape the wrath of Tom when the

9

goat went dry, and the place was a balm to her spirit. She would sit in silence and watch while a spider built a web, and go away refreshed. But not today.

A figure was slowly winding its way up the path from the village to their door. She leaned forward, catching sight of a snowy wimple crowned by a broad-brimmed hat. Only the midwife wore such things, even without her basket with its white cloth she could be recognised by her clothes. If Tibby was on her way it was time for Hazel to go back; she always helped with her mother's confinements and had a soft spot for Tibby, knowing instinctively that her gruff voice and rough manners meant nothing. She felt a warmth from Tibby that she had never known from Tom.

Hazel pushed back the hair from her damp forehead, shouldered the buckets, and started walking back.

Tibby reached the newly built sheep wall that divided Margery's cot from the rest of the village. This was the wall, she reflected, that had started all the trouble, putting boundaries where they had no right to be and putting honest folk out of their homes. Now Tom was dead, and others beside, and Margery only remained on sufferance. As soon as her child was born her cottage would go too, to make yet more pasture for the encroaching sheep. And from what Tib had heard from the travelling apothecary, there were others yet worse off in other parts; some landowners were evicting whole communities to make more grazing lands. Tib did not know what the world was coming to. Time was when the lords of the manors had cared what became of their tenants, but not now. They cared for nothing any more as long as their rents rolled in. She sighed. Cursing fate was not going to help Margery or Hazel. No time today to stop and get her breath, her errand was too urgent. She caught sight of Margery stooping to gather herbs and called out to her.

Margery straightened her back carefully.

'Why, Tibby, I haven't sent for you yet. What brings you?'

Panting, the old woman sank down on a stone.

'I had to come.' She mopped her face with a fold of her skirt. 'Where's the girl?'

'Gone for water,' said Margery with a sinking of the stomach. She looked searchingly at Tibby. 'Why, what's wrong?'

'Trouble, and like to be more trouble. You must get away now and take her with you. No time to wait for the baby. There's talk in the village and no time to be lost.'

Margery sat down weakly beside her. 'Oh no, Tib! I can't bear any more - how can I take to the road like this?'

'Take to it you must,' said Tib firmly, 'or tomorrow may be too late. You don't know the way they'm talking down there.'

'But who's talking? What about? I don't understand ...'

'About the plague and that Dickun's wife. Seems she saw a hare dancing in the moonlight outside her cottage last night and this morning he's took with it. They say she's vowing someone brought the sickness to Dickun - some witch in the shape of the hare.'

Margery looked at her despairingly. 'But there's always plague in town in the hot weather, always has been, always will be - nothing to do with witches! Someone must have come this way from the town and brought it on their clothes.'

'You try telling that to an angry mob!' said Tibby sagely.

'But even then, what's it to do with us? Has someone found out about Hazel - Tib, you haven't told?'

'God's truth and I haven't, and I don't know how you can say such a thing, and me holding my peace these many a year! Maybe nobody knows, all I'm saying is there's some funny old talk going on. People a-gathering in little groups and a-muttering away and a-looking up here towards your place. I dunna like the looks of it so I come to warn you. They'm frightened, Margery, and when folks is frightened they starts to look around 'em for a scapegoat. Maybe they're telling themselves if they gets rid of Hazel the plague'll go away. I always did think as you kept her too much apart - as good as telling the world there was something wrong about the child. And you never can tell what folks is going to think with the Old One looking over their shoulder. Seems like it comes between them and their wits. So best thing is, you get stirring and get you both on the road.'

'Today?' Margery said unhappily. It was one thing to know you had to go, another to actually start the journey.

'Now, this minute!' Tibby said flatly. 'And don't sit there wringing your hands, woman, get you ready and on your way while there's still time. Innocent she may be but there's nought going to save her once they see what's there to be seen.'

Tib got up and started to pull her to her feet. She was used to taking charge in emergencies. There might be a time and a place for sympathising but this was assuredly not it.

'Wait, Tibby ...' Margery's eyes went suddenly out of focus, as if she were listening to something inside herself. 'I - I can't,' she faltered, and the eyes she raised to Tibby's were appalled.

'You're not-'

Margery nodded, holding her breath, and then she let it go in a long sibilance, her eyes dismayed.

'I can't take her, Tib. What am I going to do?'

They stared at each other, hands locked. Tibby thought fast. 'Can you manage to deliver yourself?'

Margery hesitated, biting her lips. Then she nodded. 'It's not the first. I've got the birthing stool.'

'Good, then leave everything to me. I'll take her to my house and take the way through the woods; won't no one think of looking for her there. I'll keep her there till you can go your ways together. Don't you fret now, just get on and birth that suckling. Lie up for a little and then come as soon as you can.'

Margery agreed weakly, trying to conquer her doubts.

'How will you get her to go with you? She'll not want to leave me.'

'I'll think of something, don't you fret. Now come you in the house.'

Margery stumbled in getting to her feet; Tibby steadied her and led her indoors where she busied herself with preparations for the birth. She got out the birthing stool that Tom had made, low and backless, with stout arms for gripping and a hollow seat to permit the passage of the child; she dusted it and rubbed it over with the bunch of herbs she always carried in her basket. She moved the little pots of rosemary and garlic from the hearth and set them on the window-sill to discourage the plague from coming in. She brought in firewood and lit it and set the cauldron over it to boil. She dropped in a handful of dried foliage and threw another into the fire. Then she went to the press and took out the worn but carefully folded linen that had served all Margery's babies. The familiar herbal odour filled Margery's nostrils, reminiscent of so many such occasions with Tibby in attendance. Watching her bustling about in the firelight's flicker, it did not seem possible that all the old familiar life was gone, that disaster hung over them and nothing would ever be the same again. Well, there was nothing more that she could do now. She closed her eyes and gave herself over to her labour.

The sound of footsteps took Tibby outside again.

'Set down them buckets, Hazel, and come with me. I want you to fetch back a simple for your mother.'

'A simple? Why? Is she sick, is she took a-bed?'

She started towards the door but Tibby intercepted her. 'She's well enough. 'Tis just some of my raspberry-leaf tea she's wanting, to speed her labour. You'll fetch it back for her a sight quicker than I could, your legs is younger than mine. That's unless you've a mind to stand there all day dithering.'

Hazel set the buckets down slowly. 'Where is she? Why can't I see her?'

At that moment Margery appeared in the doorway, leaning against the jamb and peering, dazzled, into the sunlight.

'I'm all right, Hazel. Go along with Tibby.' Her hand, out of sight behind the door, gripped the edge of a beam to steady her; she raised the other one partly to ward off the glare and partly to shield her face from Hazel's experienced eye. If the girl saw she was in labour no device of Tibby's was likely to drag her away.

'Mother, are you sure?' She was hesitating, her suspicions already aroused. Margery felt another contraction building up.

'Of course!' she snapped. 'Now run along and do as you're told. What a girl it is for arguing, to be sure. Get you gone !' She turned back into the house, not trusting herself further.

Hazel stood uncertain for a moment. Then she yielded to Tibby and followed her away.

Margery leaned her back against the wall and slowly sank to her knees. Now that she was alone she could give way to her tears and they rolled unhindered down her cheeks. She longed to call Hazel back; she wanted to roll back the years and seek the comfort of her own mother again; she wanted Tom, rough and uncaring as he had often been; anyone, just so she was not to be alone in her extremity. Most of all, she wished with all her heart she could have kept Tibby with her.

Something was telling her that alone of all her children since the first, this one was not going to be born so easily. Something was going to go wrong with this birth and she knew it.

Tobias Kemble, preacher, apothecary and travelling quack, produced the parchment from his pouch, unrolled it with a flourish and held it high above his head.

'See for yourselves!' he invited his audience, knowing well enough that none of them could read. They shuffled their feet uneasily, not wanting to call attention to their ignorance. 'It says here,' he continued, pressing his advantage, ' - and this, mark you, is her true and attested confession - that this foul witch, Mother Waterlowe, being brought to judgement, and "being ready prepared to receive her death, she confessed earnestly that she had been a witch" ' - here he paused again to assess the effect of the words - ' "and used such execrable sorcery for the space of fifteen years." ' He lowered the scroll and dropped his voice to a confidential level before continuing. 'Fifteen years, my friends! I wonder if you realise what this means. It means,' and here he raised his voice again, 'that for fifteen long years this wicked woman was working away in secret at her malicious schemes and charms, doing untold harm to her innocent neighbours, doing the Devil's bidding without anyone being the wiser!'

He rocked back on his heels, surveying the small knot of listeners which was slowly growing as he talked, judging his moment. 'Could it not be,' he challenged them, 'that there are those among you who should be brought into the light? That there are those whose innermost thoughts would not bear investigation and whose malice wreaks havoc among their enemies ... And if there is one' - a pause more telling than before - 'I say to you, if there is, then her neighbours must indeed be asleep. And if they are not asleep, if they suspect her and yet say nothing-' Deftly he shifted his gaze from face to face among them, scrutinising, accusing. 'Then they are as culpable as she! They are just as steeped in sin, just as much in the service of the Evil One, and just as ripe for the gallows! The Bible says you shall not suffer a witch to live.'

He surveyed with satisfaction the consternation he had caused. Now he would see some action. 'I say to you that he who knows of the existence of a witch and does not come forward is no true Christian and shall himself be damned! I say to you, be vigilant, for there are those among us who work evil things in secret. Has any woman among you had a babe who is hare-shotten?'

A young woman was thrust unwillingly forward from the group to stand before him, twisting her hands in her apron.

'Go on, tell him, Marian!' A chorus of voices prodded her on.

''Tweren't my fault if the hare crossed my path,' she

blubbered. 'It were up by carpenter's cottage on the way back from the old well!'

Tobias nodded gravely. 'And who amongst you has lost a child?' Several voices answered. 'Or a horse, or an ox?' The chorus swelled to a shout; soon everyone was vying with his neighbour. One had lost a sow and all her litter, another had had his horse go lame, a third recalled that his grandam had suddenly gone blind. And all were convinced, now that it had been pointed out to them, that they were the victims of witchcraft.

Kemble was hard put to it to disguise his gratification. Not for nothing, after all, had he tramped the dusty miles in search of a village without a resident priest.

'It is as I feared, ' he pronounced gravely, 'and you will be wise to seek further aid, for from what I can see there is at least one witch amongst you. I thank God that I have passed this way and can deliver you. I shall need a horse.' They looked at one another in bewilderment.

'I must ride with all haste,' he explained, 'to find one Master Lawyer Wilkins, and bring him back with me. He is a great finder of witches and all shall be done in due order and to the glory of the Church.'

'But we know who it is, master!' a dozen voices assailed him, as he had guessed they would. He was ready for them. He raised an imperious hand. The leavings of one poor villager's wife would not line anyone's pockets.

'We may think we know, but it is not for us to judge. And where we may suspect one, a trained investigator such as Master Wilkins can trace her to the nest. There will be others, I can promise you. And we shall flush them out!' Wilkins was expert in manipulating his victims into implicating those with more money. And he, Tobias, was not going to be cheated of his moment of importance - still less of his pickings, which could on occasion be rich. He saw himself officiating at the trial, basking in reflected glory, and later accepting gracefully his share of the deceased's estate. Let Master Calvin look to his laurels: the name of Kemble might also be writ large in the annals of the witch hunt.

'Brethren, be vigilant. I shall return with Master Wilkins, and then there shall be such a purging as you have never seen. God keep you. Watch and pray.'

They watched him ride away with mixed feelings. Everyone knew that something must be done, but no one cared to be the first to do it. To this extent they were glad of the restraint placed on them. It lifted some of the responsibility but also left them feeling strangely helpless. Kemble might not return for many days and in that time anything could happen. Already since this morning there was another door in the village marked with the red cross of the plague. They knew well enough where to look for their malefactor. Had not all these disasters befallen since the unfortunate death of Tom Wood? It was well known that witches sought to avenge their misfortunes on the world about them. They looked nervously towards the cottage on the hill and huddled together as if for protection, forgetting in their superstitious dread that other men had also died with Tom. Uneasily, in ones and twos, they went their several ways.

Tobias Kemble rode away from the village well pleased with his day's work. Already he was making notes for a long and elaborate trial. No doubt more than one suspect could be rounded up; Master Wilkins would charge a goodly fee from which the preacher could expect a fair commission. He was smiling as he straddled his borrowed horse. He had reckoned without Alice Smith.

3

Alice held her breath against the hot fumes of the forge, hurried through it to the back room and set down the heavy basket with relief. It had been a warm and dusty walk from the great house to the smithy, though she was grateful for the leftover food she had been allowed to bring home.

'How you feeling, Ma?' she called to the sick woman in the corner.

'Poorly, poorly,' came the reply. It was always the same, thought Alice, as the familiar rattling cough followed the words; as if nothing were left in the sunken chest but old rusty spittle and cobwebs.

'This'll comfort you,' she soothed, taking the jar of broth and tipping it into a kettle to heat.

'Best give it your father,' came the querulous voice, 'I canna. ..'

'The Lady Edith sent it for you, and you're to eat it,' Alice insisted. 'Father has the victuals for all of you, God knows.'

'He has to work for all of us, don't he!' retorted her mother, with a sudden access of strength that made Alice smile.

'That's as may be but you're having this,' and she carried the broth over to the bed where the invalid lay huddled. 'Open wide,' she coaxed playfully, trickling the savoury spoonful between the few remaining teeth. The old woman grinned in spite of herself, slurping and sucking her way through it like a baby. Not that she felt much like a baby. Her thirty-five years sat heavily on her when she had a bout like this. But her Alice was a good girl to her old Ma ...

'Here,' she mumbled, 'this don't taste of umbles, my girl.'

'Real meat,' Alice nodded proudly. 'Venison!'

Her mother started up, perturbed. ' You havna thieved it, Alice ? I don't want you hanging for me-'

'Rest easy,' Alice pushed her gently back on the bed. 'I didna thieve it, it was give to me. The cook knows all about it and why it's here.'

'And why is it here, then?' The laugh was sardonic. 'Somebody die and leave it to you?' She fell back, cackling at her own joke, until a fit of coughing overtook her.

Alice was glad of the diversion. She had her own reasons for being uneasy about the meat, and her mother had come a little too close to the truth. She took a surreptitious sup of the brew herself. It tasted good enough. And the hounds had continued fit. They were romping like children when she came away ... Reassured, she settled her mother to sleep and set the room to rights. When she had prepared the evening meal, she slipped out unnoticed to call at the back window of a cottage a few doors away.

A round, rosy face appeared and lit at the sight of her; a moment later the two girls were greeting each other in the garden.

'I canna stop long, got to be back by sundown.'

'Your Ma took bad again?'

Alice nodded, her brows furrowed. 'Can't get her to eat, only a sup or two. Brought her some broth from the kitchens today, she wouldna take but a mouthful. Fresh venison in it, too. Beautiful. But she couldna be tempted.'

Debbie's eyes widened. 'Fresh venison - how'd you come by that?'

'Well,' Alice hesitated, her frown deepening. 'Look - promise you won't tell. I mean, I'm sure it's all right or I wouldna given it her. It's not what you'd choose for a sick woman - but they all swear it wasna the meat as did it.'

Debbie's attention was riveted. 'What you talking about - it wasna the meat as did what?'

Alice looked about her, leaned closer and lowered her voice.

'It was at dinner last night in Great Hall. One of Lord Eustace's men was at the board, hacking away at his roast with the others and talking about how his horse had gone lame, when all of a sudden he falls to the floor with a terrible cry and just lies there, making choking noises, like as if something had got him by the throat and was strangling him, and not another word could he get out - and still canna, not even as much as to say what's wrong with him, poor man!'

'Go on then, what happened then?'

'Well, that's not all. When they tried to get him to his feet - well, they thought first off he'd just overdone the wine, see - they found that his sword arm and his leg and all his right side was just like a dead man's! He couldna stand, nor grip nothing, nor utter not one word. Well, then of course they said his meat must be poisoned, so they threw a piece to the dogs to find out. But they ate it and came back for more. Only,' here Alice hesitated, troubled in mind, 'only I didna see why the dogs should have it when my Ma was sick, so I asked the cook if I could bring it home. You don't think it'll hurt her, do you?'

Debbie considered for a moment. 'I don't reckon,' she said. 'Don't sound like poison if the dogs is all right. Besides, it sounds more like a curse if you ask me.'

'That's what everyone's saying,' admitted Alice, 'I just wish I could be sure in my mind.'

Debbie was less concerned with the meat than with the man. 'Who was it,' she asked, 'anyone I've seen?'

'Big Edgar. Tall, flax-haired. I tell you, Deb, I saw him as they carried him from Great Hall. Half a man and half a corpse, he is now. 'Tis frightening to see him, one eye a- glaring and the other dead as glass. A fine broad man in his prime, he was - well, you'd know him - it was him on his horse as trampled poor Tom Wood to his death on the night of the rising.'

'Tom Wood... breathed Debbie. Her expression changed. 'Look, Alice - I got to go now or I'll get beaten. Hope your Ma's better soon.'

'Yes,' said Alice, only slightly surprised. 'Best be getting back to her, I suppose.'

Debbie watched her friend out of sight. Then she picked up her skirts and ran as fast as her plump legs would carry her to the house of Dickun's aunt.

The news ran through the small community like wildfire, fanning the half-lulled fears of the morning to an uncontrolled superstitious panic. People came anxiously from their houses, hardly knowing where they were bound or what they intended. All they were sure of was that there was a witch among them who must be destroyed if they were to survive. The knot on the green reformed and grew into a mob. They reminded each other of the words of Tobias Kemble. 'There are venomous weeds among your growing corn,' he had said. 'I say to you, tear them out and cast them into the fire!' A witch - a witch - the whispers became shouts, their resolution bolstered by their numbers. By the pond on the green a gallows was soon hammered together, and around it stood a growing pile of faggots.

As the sun was sucked into its grave behind the forest, spattering the pond with bloody reflections, it was a grim party which, reinforced with small beer and armed with rope, firebrands and crucifixes, made its way up the hill towards the carpenter's cottage.

Margery was still in labour.

Her waters had broken about noon, but though the pains came hard and often, she had dragged herself from the bed to the birthing stool and sweated and strained to no avail. The instinct that had warned her that something was wrong had been unerring. Try as she would, she could not bring the child. From time to time her exhausted body gave up, and then she vomited wretchedly until the onslaught was renewed.

The fire under the trivet had long since burned out and the water in the cauldron was merely tepid. She leaned against it, weak and sweating, bathing her face with shaking hands, and slowly became aware of voices and footsteps on the path outside.

They've come for Hazel, she thought dizzily, but they're too late - she's gone ... She looked up, startled but without any real fear, as the door burst open and the four ringleaders fell in.

'What do you want?' she demanded feebly, though she knew well enough. 'I'm alone, and in childbed.'

'Why, so you are, mistress, and spawning another one, no doubt!'

The others nodded in agreement and a hostile murmur spread back along the procession that straggled up the hill. Margery looked from one to another, uncomprehending. The fresh air that had blown in with them was overpowered by the herbal brew and the hot animal stench of birth blood, and her stomach twisted again with nausea.

'There's no one here ...' she began, and then a fierce contraction forced her to her knees. Rough hands seized her and dragged her outside; her sodden shift was torn from her back; her knees and hands were skinned on the stony ground as she felt herself shoved, pulled, kicked or carried along with the mob. She saw no faces, only legs or feet, and even they swam crazily past her eyes in a nightmare whirl. She gave one long despairing scream of terror and agony as the truth was borne in upon her at last. They had not come for Hazel: they had come for her.

For the next few hours she drifted in and out of consciousness. At times she was dimly aware of being on trial, as faces familiar and unfamiliar swam in and out of her vision without registering anything on her mind. At one point in a moment of lucidity she caught sight of Marian, and appealed to her. 'Help me, Marian, you know me! For God's sake help me!' But Marian only crossed herself piously and sidled away with uneasy glances about her. At other times she thought she was at home, with Tibby in attendance while the baby struggled for birth; her flagging heart threatened to choke her, thundering in her throat and in her ears. In her delirium she thought that needles were being driven into her, she dreamed she was drowning, and awoke gasping and choking with her nostrils full of water, but by now she was beyond pain, beyond thinking, beyond fear or even praying; her fruitless labour was tearing her apart as she lapsed again and again into merciful blackness.

They gathered around to watch her, those at the back pressing forward to see her strangled breathing like a half-drowned dog's.

''Tis proof!'

'The water won't have them as renounce their baptism.'

'She's made her pact with the Devil!'

'The witch must die!'

Neighbours and gossips who had known her all her life stood by unmoved as she was dragged from the pond's brink to the gibbet and the waiting faggots. Divested of the familiar homespun, naked and contorted in labour, sweat- stained hair plastered to her ashen face, she was no longer Margery Wood with whom they had spun a yarn on their doorsteps, but a thing, a menacing, unspeakable thing, a malignant growth to be ruthlessly pruned before it overpowered them all and devoured their children.

From the chinks in her shutters Tibby watched appalled. More than once in her long life she had seen women tried for witchcraft. But always there had been some semblance of sanity in the proceedings, some honest attempt at justice in the hearing, not this unreasoning hysteria, this animal lust for blood that seemed to have taken possession of the villagers. If anyone was possessed of the Devil, it was they, thought Tib. Never had she thought to see a woman dragged from childbed and put to the torture, a woman too sick even to answer her inquisitors. This whole affair was a mockery, a travesty of justice. A hare dancing in the moonlight had passed sentence: the rest was simply a formality.

Time was when honest folk could live in peace, she reflected bitterly, and what the world was coming to she did not know. When the King himself could accuse his wife of witchcraft - aye, and put her to the sword to boot - how were simple folk to keep their heads? Time would come, and she could see it coming, when no honest dealer in simples would be safe, no herbalist, no midwife ... she felt suddenly the icy fingers of fear in her own stomach. She put the thought away from her.

She reproached herself bitterly for leaving Margery alone. For not realising who they were after instead of jumping to the conclusion it was Hazel. Of course it had been Margery! Poor girl, half demented as she was with grief and shock, hadn't she railed and screamed hysterically at everyone in sight when they brought her Tom's poor trampled body - and now that ill luck befell the village they thought she was taking her revenge. When she was removed, they believed the sun would shine again....

She could not bear to think of having left her alone. Yet reason told her that to stay would not have helped her: they would only have shared the same fate. As it was, the girl at least was safe. And Margery would have been thankful for that. She looked back at Hazel where she lay slumped on the floor, still sleeping off the effects of the posset she had been tricked into drinking. Poor child, what a world to awake to - and what was to become of her? Thank God she had been spared the sight of her mother being dragged through the streets.

A scent of smoke tickled her nostrils, and peering out she caught the sinister flicker of flame, down there on the green...

It was some way off, but she could just make it out ... yes, they were lighting the fire.

Margery hung now at the rope's end, semi-conscious, while the smoke from the green wood curled up about her. The knot, inexpertly tied, had failed in its duty and she was not dead. Her body made one last frantic effort to expel the child, it tumbled feet first onto the faggots and lay for a moment, apparently lifeless, before it gasped into a thin reedy cry. Margery felt it go, and felt the life blood gush after it in a hot, unnatural torrent.

Someone reached forward and grabbed it, slashing the umbilical cord with a knife.

'A footling!'

'A wench!'

'Devil's spawn!'

They handed it from one to another as if it were red-hot.

From the dark mists in which she drifted, Margery heard its cries and coupled them with the crowd noise and the smell of fire.

'The hare ...' Her hoarse distressed whisper was scarcely audible, strangled as she was, but those who were watching her caught it and passed it on.

'The hare ... she calls upon the hare ...' the cry went around the crowd. The man who had the baby raised it high above his head.

'You shall not suffer a witch to live - there, Devil's spawn!' he yelled, and threw the screaming infant with all his might.

In the glare of the distant fire, Tibby saw his intention, and pressed her knuckles to her mouth in anguish.

'Oh, dear God, no!' she moaned, rocking back and forth, and at that moment Hazel came stumbling towards her, drunk with sleep. 'Dunna look - dunna look!' she cried to the girl, who blinked at her, taking in only the darkness, the place, and the late hour. 'I must go to my mother!' she cried pulling Tibby from the door and wrestling with the heavy bars that held it.

'You canna go, Hazel. There's nothing can save her now!' She seized the girl and held her while she herself looked through the chink. 'Oh God!' she wailed, struggling with Hazel, who heard the faint yet lusty cry of the newborn change to a fearful screaming such as she had never heard before. She stopped moving and stared at Tibby.

'The baby!' Her voice started as a shocked whisper before it rose in horror. 'Tibby, what are they doing to the baby?'

Tibby's face crumpled suddenly, and she pulled Hazel closer into her arms. 'The poor innocent!' she sobbed. 'Oh, God save the poor innocent! May God forgive them, they've thrown it in the fire!'

The flames roared higher as the night wind caught the faggots, and a dreadful sickening odour came drifting towards them.

Tihby's breakdown was Hazel's undoing. They clung to each other, weeping helplessly.

4

In a clearing in the forest where sunlight slanted bronze through the oaks, Timothy Kettle knelt by his fire.

Work for the day was over; Joan had gone round the farms with the mended pots and pans. Now he was occupied in plucking for their evening meal the hen he had poached last night. They would need to move on tomorrow: this area had yielded all it was going to.

The two older children sprawled and squabbled in the dirt, evil-smelling but healthy, each with his own tow- coloured thatch and bright blue eyes. The smaller one came over and urinated in the fire, sending up a brackish odour and splashing the chicken Tim was cleaning. He raised a foot and roughly booted him out of the way.

'Dunna your Ma tell you nothing!' he bellowed, and the child bellowed in response, scrubbing his running nose with a grimy fist.

Why didn't Joan teach them not to piss out the fire! He rummaged angrily in the smouldering mess, trying to make it rekindle. Thanks be, at least she had taken the baby with her, slung in a bundle on her spreading hip.

Joan! How she had gone to pieces in a few short years; never a beauty, she had been raddled and aged out of recognition by childbearing and the rough vagrant life, and intermittent toothache made her a sullen companion. His own teeth were still pretty sound; he had little sympathy with a pain he had never felt. Joan, he told himself, was nothing to him now: he despised her even as he took his pleasure of her.

He looked with distaste at his children: they stank. The fact that he also stank he did not consider.

He finished his sketchy dressing of the scrawny bird, impaled it on a stake, and hung it over the fire between two forked sticks. He relit the fire and banked it with charcoal, and presently was rewarded with a bright clear glow. He lay back, crossing his knees, and rubbed the soot and chicken guts from his hands on his breechings. The chicken began to sizzle, spitting into the fire and sending out a delicious aroma, reaching the children who sidled over hopefully, like scrounging dogs. Tim glared at them warningly, then closed his eyes, chewing on a straw. Small as they were, they waited in silence. They knew their father's temper.

Tim was dozing off when the snapping of a twig brought him to his feet. Even a tinker had to sleep with one eye open in these days of beggars and outlaws; there always seemed to be someone with even less than you. Tim stood ready to fight for the cart which was his livelihood, mentally assessing his chances of coming off best.

It was only a threesome of women who approached, and the first was Joan. She was holding something in her apron and his face suffused with sudden fury. What had the imbecile woman done now'? Brought back something she hadn't been told ...

Her voice reached him ahead of her, slow and stupid like everything about her.

'Tim ...' she came lumbering up the slope, red-faced and sweating, 'I brought eggs from the farm-'

The back of his hand sent her sprawling. 'We need money, not eggs!' His foot found its mark. 'We don't never buy eggs, not never. Come we needs eggs, I gets 'em. Dunna you never learn nothing, you poor booby!'

Joan stared at him and then at the slimy mess on the front of her skirt, and comprehension slowly dawned on her broad face. 'You smashed 'em,' she said stupidly, and then with dawning anger she repeated it. 'Yoii smashed my eggs!'

'I'll smash you along an' all if you don't learn sense!' He stood above her, short and stocky, his face the colour of beetroot.

Joan was a big woman, not easy to anger, but he had managed it. She stumbled to her feet and launched herself like a lioness, yelling, punching, shrieking curses, tearing out his hair in handfuls and slashing at him with the blackened stumps of her teeth. Like wild beasts they rolled and pummelled one another, while the baby screamed unheeded in the dust of the battlefield and the children watched, hopping up and down with excitement. Clearly they were accustomed to the spectacle.

Hazel was not. Her home had been rough but respectable, and the sight of grown people, a man and a woman, brawling on the ground like animals, appalled her. She would have tried to rescue the woman, but Tibby restrained her.

'You interfere and they'll both turn on you, see if they don't,' she whispered.

'But Tib, he'll kill her!'

'No, he won't. I'll lay she's used to it or she wouldn't have started it. Land sakes, I do believe they're laughing!'

Tim had freed himself. Joan in trying to follow him had trodden on the ragged hem of her gown and collapsed face downwards, her great behind in the air. Her husband's anger had evaporated; he rocked with helpless laughter as she struggled to get up. The little boys, emboldened by his good humour, danced around the fallen monster, giggling and throwing her skirts over her head while she swatted - and missed - them, and finally weakened into laughter herself.

Tim dried his eyes and pulled her to her feet, then he appeared to notice the two women for the first time.

'Ladies . . .' He made an elaborate, mocking gesture of doffing an imaginary cap and sweeping the ground with it. 'What can I do for you?'

'We need food ...'

His face clouded but Joan put in hastily, 'They've got money, Tim.' They exchanged glances, and to Hazel's bewilderment laughter bubbled up again between them.

This time it had a curious undertone, as if they were sharing a secret, unpleasant joke.

'Step right up, mistresses,' he made a show of dusting off the ground before their feet, 'and right welcome you be, to be sure. Not often we're honoured with such fine company - not often at all - but my Joan'll make ye comfortable for the night.' He winked at Joan where she was stooping to pick up the wailing baby from where it had rolled in the dust. 'Won't ye, goodwife ?' He booted her sociably in the backside and she, assured of his good favour, grinned snaggled-toothed but happy.

Tibby and Hazel came forward not without hesitation; they had hoped to buy themselves a meal and be on their way. But with night drawing on it seemed foolish to refuse hospitality so warmly offered, dubious though it might be - and protection from tinkers was better than none at all.

Hazel said, 'Shall I wash the children for you?'

Joan stared. 'Not sick, are they?'

Hazel withdrew, abashed.

They shared the chicken, Tim tearing it apart with his hands and tossing the pieces to one or another as he thought fit. Hazel and Tibby ate hungrily; it was the first food they had tasted since their furtive slipping away from Tibby's cottage, in the grey twilight before dawn of the previous day.

Hazel had watched numbly as the old woman made preparation for the journey, rolling a few essentials into lengths of cloth for them to tie about their waists. When she saw her remove a hearth-stone and dig up a little hoard of coins, she said, 'You mustna give me your money, Tib-'

'I'm coming with you. '

'But you'll be back ...'

'I've spent my days bringing new life into the world. This is no place for me any more.' She looked suddenly so much older as she straightened herself from the hearth that pity for her displaced, for the moment, Hazel's other, less bearable thoughts.

'Poor Tib,' she whispered, and went to press her hot tear-stained cheek against the midwife's rough-hewn face.

'I'll look after you,' she promised, 'I'm strong, you'll see ...'

Tibby had freed herself abruptly, aware of her accustomed role as the tower of strength and unable to see herself in any other. As always, she took refuge in brusqueness.

'No time to waste, now,' she snapped, 'we can sit and feel sorry for each other later on. Now, get on with you!' But she had dashed the back of a roughened hand across her eyes, and Hazel was not deceived. When they crept away through the forest in the early gloom, her arm was firm and protective about Tibby's shoulders.

And so now they sat with the tinkers and shared their fire, luxuriating in its warmth now that the sun had gone down, while their feet throbbed and protested and the ache in their legs seemed to reach the backs of their necks. The meal had been delicious, dirt notwithstanding, and although their share of the single chicken left them unsatisfied Tibby, true to her word, got out her purse and gave Timothy a coin; then she thought of the children and added another one.

He thanked her obsequiously and set about building them a shelter of brushwood, covering and flooring it with bracken fronds. It was not much, he said, but would keep off the weather should it rain before dawn. He looked at Tibby expectantly and it occurred to her that for this service he hoped to extract another coin. But she felt they would need all that was left for their own survival, so she merely thanked him and pretended not to understand.

'Where you bound for, then?' he asked at one point.

'Heading for the monastery, if 'tisn't too far. We lost my son - her father - with the plague.' She crossed herself dutifully and added, 'Some time ago, no danger to you folk now - well, as you understand, there's no other help for us but there.'

Joan opened her mouth to say something but as usual she was too slow and Timothy silenced her.

'You're on the right road then,' was all he said.

As soon as they decently could, the two pilgrims struggled stiffly to their feet and crawled into their shelter.

They had slept little the night before, huddled against the wall of a ruined cottage, too hungry and too nervous to do more than rest their weary limbs and listen wide-eyed to the unaccustomed night sounds of the wild life about them. Now on the sweet-smelling bracken, the comforting sounds of humanity not far away, they both sank into instant and exhausted sleep.

'Why dinna you tell 'em?' Joan asked her husband as he flopped down beside her.

'Tell 'em what?'

'Why, about - you know. Why dinna you?'

'Shut your face and spread your legs,' said Tim.

Tim was right about the weather. They were awakened by the soft splash of rain and the sweet dank smell of it on the thirsty earth. Hazel had slept so deeply that for a moment she was puzzled to see Tibby's form beside her instead of Margery's. Then it all came rushing back to her with a merciless clarity and she could not be alone with it. But once she had aroused her companion, all she said was, 'It's raining.'

She crawled to the mouth of the shelter and looked out. 'They're gone!'

Tibby joined her and together they peered at the deserted clearing. Apart from the scar of the fire, there was no trace of Tim, his wife, his children or his cart. They had vanished as if they had never been.

They looked at each other.

'They must have gone off in the night,' mused Hazel, 'it's only now getting light. Now why would they do that?'

They were not left long in doubt. When Tibby went for her purse it was not there. The leather thongs which had tethered it to her girdle had been cleanly cut by some blade of the sharpness of a razor. Nestling in the bracken where she had slept they found a single gold coin where it had fallen. Of her life's savings, it was all that survived.

'Now we know why he built us a shelter - not from the goodness of his miserable heart at all! If we'd took off our clothes they'd have had them too!'

'They left us our shoes,' said Hazel.

'And we're going to need them! No hope of getting a donkey now. We'll have to walk every last step. Never did have no time for tinkers, dirty thieving lot -this just goes to show, you can't trust none of them! Scum of the earth, that's what they are - who else'd have robbed an old woman and a child!' As always when she was agitated, Tib let fly. She ranted on, easing her feelings, in which for the moment indignation overtopped her sense of disaster, forgetting that it was she who had thought of approaching Joan Kettle in the first place ... Hazel was not paying much attention; she was wrestling with her shoes.

'I can't get 'em on,' she protested. It was true. Her feet were so swollen and blistered that, softened though they were by age and hard wear, her shoes could in no way be coerced into covering them. 'Shall I leave 'em behind?'

'Land sakes, no! We can't afford to throw nothing away - tie 'em to your girdle or round your neck like me. You may be glad to trade 'em for a crust of bread afore we're through.'

They added their useless shoes to their burdens and tore

strips from their shifts to bind their feet for protection from the road, but before many miles they had worn into painful sodden ridges and they were glad to go barefoot. The mud oozed between their toes, comforting at first but cold and clammy; on their blistered heels it dried into cakes and cracked the skin off with it. The rain, soft and insistent, did not let up, and by midday they were drenched to the skin. Their long skirts dragged in the mud and their wet cloaks hung like dead men on their shoulders. They plodded on doggedly, in a rain-soaked silence.

Late in the afternoon a watery sun broke through. They spread their cloaks over bushes but although they steamed feebly, the trees were still dripping down on them and they did not dry out.

'Look, Tib,' said Hazel, 'if the tinkers can make a fire we ought to be able to. Did you bring a tinderbox?'

'Somewhere.' Tib began to rummage. 'But you need dry kindling for a fire.'

'Well, I'll go and look anyway...

Their effort at a fire was not what Tim Kettle would have made of it, but it cheered them a little to know that they could make one at all, and Hazel in her search for wood had come upon a grove of unripe blackberries. They devoured them, and were rewarded by griping stomach pains throughout the night.

They did not attempt to walk further that night. The only shelter that offered itself was an ancient oak, blasted by lightning and hollow in the trunk; they squeezed their way in through a gap in the bark and found within a dry bed of leaves which showed signs of occupation by other wayfarers before them. Hazel swept it out with a bunch of twigs while there was still light enough to see by, and then they sat by the fire until darkness fell.

The end of summer was near, and although the nights were not cold the dampness of their clothing was sufficient to keep them shivering through the small hours, adding to the wretchedness of the stomach cramps. At some point in her dozing, Hazel was startled to full wakefulness by a rustling that seemed to come from just above her head, followed by the fall of something soft and warm in her lap. She gave a scream that came out as a terrified whisper, and Tibby chuckled in the darkness.

'Sakes, child, 'tis only an owl has dropped you a gift.' And so it was, a repulsive little offering of those parts of a mouse for which the owl had no further use.

In the grey light of a dawn that promised yet more rain, Hazel asked, 'How far away's the monastery, do we know?'

'I don't know for certain. My sister went when she lost her man, but with her not coming back I never did hear tell. They say, though, that once you reach the river 'tis no more than a good day's walk along the bank. And if we find the river, might be there's a cottage or two will look kindly on us. I never thought to go begging in my old age but we canna see what's hidden round the corner.'

They made their way back to the road, which presently joined another, wider one, obviously more used; they were encouraged by this to hope for wayside alms, listening for approaching travellers and rehearsing what they should say. But after two horsemen and a loaded folkwain had passed them by as if they were invisible, their optimism began to fade.

There must be ways of living off the land, thought Hazel, how did the tinkers and the charcoal burners manage? 'Come we needs eggs, I gets 'em,' Tim had said -but how? It gave her food for thought on the long slow trudge that dragged on, for hour after weary hour. When they rested at last, she set a primitive snare as Tom had once showed her, using the thongs of Tibby's cut purse and a bent sapling, and setting it carefully at the mouth of a run in a bramble patch. In the morning, she called excitedly, 'Tibby, Tibby, we've caught something!'

The midwife came hobbling up to look. It was a leveret. Caught and suspended by one hind leg, it dangled just out of reach of the ground; below it was a little hollow made by the frantic scrabbling of its forepaws to find a foothold. It hung now, limp and despairing, the sunlight glowing rose and amber through its delicate ears, its sides still heaving, still quivering. Suddenly it saw them and sprang into a frenzy of activity, twisting, thrashing, clawing the air in a desperate and futile bid to escape. Hazel carefully bent the sapling so that the hare touched ground. It froze, staring at her, its pale nostrils flaring, large eyes glazed with terror, as if it could no longer move.

'Go on, then,' came Tibby's voice from behind her, 'kill it then, don't sit there looking at it.'

Hazel shook her head slowly.

'I canna,' she confessed. She was shocked at the discovery'. 'You'll have to. I'm going to look the other way.'

'A fat lot of good you are!' grumbled Tibby. 'You with your fine promises of looking after me, you set a trap and then can't kill your catch!'

But it was her hand that reached down and slipped off the noose. She'd seen enough of killing to last her a lifetime. They watched the young hare collect its wits, and then bolt crazily away, their hunger unassuaged.

'I wasna that hungry anyhow,' said Tib.

Hazel, whose healthy young stomach ached for food, looked at her in surprise. The faded eyes were just a little too bright, the hand she touched too warm. Oh God, she heard herself thinking, not that - not at this very moment, please not that...

As casually as she could, she said, 'We'd better rest today. Our feet's got to heal a bit before we can get on.'

Tibby agreed too easily, and Hazel's anxiety increased.

She made Tibby comfortable as best she could with a bed of bracken and both cloaks, watching over her with anxious eyes until noon. By then Tibby had not worsened and her fears were calmed; if it had really been the plague, it would be obvious by now - she would probably be dead. So when she drifted into an uneasy sleep Hazel slipped away to explore their surroundings.

She could not find the healing herbs she hoped for; few of them grew in forest ground, and besides she did not know what ailed Tib or what was needed. But she did find a few shreds of wild garlic, and that was sovereign for anything, so they said. She took it back to Tib who was still sleeping, a light dew of sweat upon her face. She bruised a few of the stems, spread the pungent sap where she would inhale it, and tucked the rest into her hands: perhaps when she woke she would know better what to do with it.

She watched a little while and then crept away again. She had heard the sound of water and a buoyant hope sustained her that they had found the river at last.

It was, when she found it, only a brook, little more than a woodland stream. But she thrust her raw feet into it gratefully, and after a quick look about her stripped off her travel-weary shift and held it in the running water. She looked at her stained old gown and wondered what that would look and feel like if it were clean. But Margery had never washed it and she did not dare try; instead she put it next to her skin and spread the shift to dry on the undergrowth. When she had washed her hair and body she felt refreshed. She sat trailing her feet in the stream and saw a fish flash by - a tiny one, but still a fish - and she could bring herself to kill a fish, she told herself. It would not look at her with dreadful pleading eyes as the hare had done. She spent a long time trying to catch one. It was harder than she thought.

The faint scent of woodsmoke reminded her that she must gather kindling for a fire. She stood up, gathered up her shift ... woodsmoke! That must mean people - charcoal burners, tinkers, someone with food! But she was wary of strangers now, so she moved down the bed of the stream with some stealth until she saw the faint curl of lavender snaking its way up through the branches. Rather than go too close, she climbed an overhanging branch for a better view.

She could see the roof of a cottage in a clearing on the bank further downstream. A sawing horse stood nearby, surrounded by off-cuts of timber and drifts of sawdust; a goat was tethered near the door and a few scraggy chickens scratched and crooned in the dust about its feet. The smell of new-baked bread came to her, filling her mouth with tantalising saliva; as she watched, the woodcutter's wife leaned out and set three loaves on the window-sill to cool...

It was almost dark when she got back to Tibby, who was sitting up and chafing her hands against the evening chill.

'Where have you been?' she called feebly, and started to wheeze. 'I thought you were lost.'

Apart from a harsh cough that was racking her, she seemed better. Hazel felt a flooding of relief. She busied herself lighting a fire and spread her wet shift near it to dry off. Then she produced the loaf.

'Behold!' she cried, tearing through golden crust and creamy crumb to share it between them.

If Tibby hesitated it was momentary, and a matter of form.

'It was give to you,' she suggested. Hazel, recognising the prompting in her tone, lowered her eyes and made a mental adjustment to the truth.

'I reckon it was a Godsend,' she said. Surely nobody could gainsay that.

At first light the next morning, filled with fresh bread and sweet stream water, they moved on. Tibby was pale and coughing, but at least she was on her feet; the rheumatism that dogged her was aggravated by the discomfort in which they slept and, added to the half- healed blisters on their feet, conspired to slow them down. But they were still alive, still moving, and whatever the hardships of their pilgrimage a safe refuge awaited them at the end.

The dense forest thinned as they travelled, the dappled light reaching them as though it shone through water; and although the sun slanting down through the green aquarium in which they moved still surprised the shifting shapes of deer in the early morning, the road wound at last through pleasant woodland where after a long pull uphill they were rewarded by the sight of a rolling valley. Far away in the distance they could see like a brilliant silver wire the glint of the river.

As they approached cultivated land their diet of unripe blackberries and hazelnuts was supplemented by windfall apples, shared with the slugs and birds, and such other trifles as Hazel could coax from the hand of God. But, leaving the shelter of the woods behind them, they felt much colder at night and were miserably aware of the chill of a heavy dew. They slept now under bushes, or even in hollows in the ground.

Hazel became conscious of a too-familiar ache, and groaned inwardly; she could have done without that at this time, especially as she had brought nothing with her; she had left her home on that sunny day with no thought of not returning. She tore yet another strip from her eroded shift, folded it and packed it with moss. It was rough and uncomfortable but it would have to serve. Before many miles her legs were rubbed raw.

Tibby ate a little less each day, coughed a little more each night, and still the distant river seemed no nearer. One day they looked up into a damp grey sky to see a flight of swifts flying South, unbelievably high and remote.

Tib said quietly, 'The swifts are leaving ...'

'We'll be under cover before the nights draw in,' said Hazel stoutly, though even her confidence was beginning to wane. She did not doubt that the monastery would be reached, but to set a time limit was wishful thinking and only to cheer the sick. She remembered stories of wolves, wondering if they had been silently stalked through the forest that lay behind them; she had seen nothing, but then wolves would not be hungry-yet. Even the gentle-seeming deer would be dangerous soon; when the rutting season was upon them the handsome stags had been known to kill.

She quickened her pace a little, tightening her arm about her sagging companion who seemed smaller and quieter than she had before. Despite the chill in the rising wind Tib felt hot to the touch and her skin had a constant glisten of sweat. Her impulse was to stop and rest and only dire necessity and Hazel's urging kept her on the move. Yet when they stopped at night she could not rest but tossed and muttered feverishly until dawn, when she sank into a heavy doze from which it was difficult to arouse her. When they finally reached the river she had not eaten for several days.

Slowed down as they were it took them more than a day's walk to reach the monastery. It was on the evening of the second day, as they walked with river mist rising to swirl about their ankles, that they saw the dark pile of it, massive and unmistakable, looming on the brow of the hill.

'Look there!' triumphed Hazel. 'What did I tell you-'

Tibby nodded, wordless, and patted her arm. They turned their backs on the river and climbed laboriously towards their goal.

Some yards from the gates, they stopped, uncertain. Something was wrong. Hazel stared, trying to focus her tired mind on the mystery. Where were the people - the livestock - the sounds of living, and …

'Tibby!' she cried. 'Why aren't there any lights?'

Tibby sank to her knees and tears of exhaustion coursed down her cheeks. 'You go and see, Hazel. I canna,' she said.

Hazel went and, weary as she was, a desperate fear lent her speed. Soon she was running back, calling as she came.

'There's no one there, not a living soul - and part of the place is burned down and all the Brothers are gone away-' She stopped abruptly, seeing Tibby's face. 'Tell me,' she tried to control herself, but a wayward sob escaped her. 'Oh, Tib, what does it mean ?'

Tibby knew all too well what it meant. Why had she not thought of it before?

'The King's men,' she whispered brokenly, 'they have been here.' She raised a trembling hand to cross herself. 'God forgive him, he was a great king once.'

The heavy oak doors of the lodge had been torn from their hinges, and it was into this dubious shelter that they crept with heavy hearts. It was cold comfort compared with what they had hoped for, but it was a roof over their heads and four sound walls such as they had not known since leaving the village. It seemed a lifetime since they had slept indoors. They heard the scutter of small animal feet as they entered, and from somewhere in the rafters a great white barn owl swooped past them and out through the open door to float away in a majestic silence. And to this, thought Hazel, they had travelled the many miles, with their one gold piece carefully kept as dowry! Tibby was beyond thinking at all.

The place had been stripped of everything movable, but there remained a ponderous black linen-press, empty now except for spiders, and a vast fourposter bed, the first that Hazel had ever seen. Its hangings and bedding were gone, but onto its hard base old Tibby sank gratefully, and did not move again.

Hazel lay down beside her, trying to keep her warm; from her chest could be heard a faint bubbling sound like a cauldron just coming to the boil. From time to time she muttered and rambled and once she sat up, grasped the scared girl by the shoulders, and demanded sternly, 'And who will eat my sins then, tell me that?'

Hazel stared. 'You don't need no sin-eater, you're not about to die.' The old woman stared back at her, the moment of clarity past. 'Mother,' she whimpered,

'Mother, who stands there in the corner?' She peered intently into the darkness, and Hazel wanted to scream and scream and scream ...

'Oh dunna, Tibby, dunna,' she pleaded, pulling her down again and holding her there, hiding her own eyes against the emaciated shoulder, the icy fingers of fear running down her spine.

The midwife was quiet for a while and seemed to be dozing; Hazel, although she did not sleep, lay with her eyes tight shut, for dread that she too might see the Old One standing in the corner. Presently the sick woman stirred again.

'Hazel,' she complained faintly, 'Hazel... I wet myself,' and she began crying weakly, like a child.

Hazel pulled her own garments out of the way and tried to comfort her.

'Dunna fret you, Tibby,' she murmured, 'dunna fret, 'tis no matter,' but the old woman was already drifting back into a world of dreams where none could follow her.

Hazel slept at last through sheer exhaustion.

She awoke in the pre-dawn chill from a nightmare in which the monastery had hurtled from its perch upon the hill and crushed her. She was pinned by its fall and could not move. She woke gasping and tried to get up, but she could not, she was trapped by something that held her down and she could not escape. She screamed soundlessly as she saw what it was.

It was Tibby's arm that lay across her. It was rigid and as cold as stone.

5

When her frantic struggles had freed her from the thing that was no longer Tibby, Hazel ran blindly out into the dewy meadow on bare feet, and then back, and then out again, sobbing, retching, stuffing her knuckles into her mouth, running blindly to find someone - anyone - a grown-up to tell, to ask ... and in the end she knew with a sick conviction that there was no one anywhere for her to run to, and no one to tell her what to do. There had always been someone older to take responsibility. Even on this desperate journey, though the strength had been hers, the decisions had been made by Tibby. She had no one to think for her any longer; for the first time in her life she was on her own, and she was barely thirteen years old.

She could not afterwards remember how many days she hung about the lodge where the body lay, or how she spent the time. In retrospect she could only see the swirling river mists, the summer rain, and herself alone in an empty world where she hung like a dead leaf on a twig. Once having escaped from the tiny room with its dreadful occupant, she could not bring herself to return. She knew she must make herself go back sooner or later, for her few possessions were in there and she needed them. She got as far as the door; there was a scuffling in the gloom, a glow of red eyes in the darkness and two dark shapes detached themselves from the bed and plopped onto the floor, whence they disappeared with shrill squeaks and a clatter of tiny claws. She retreated, shuddering, and resigned herself to the loss of her belongings.

She found mushrooms growing in the lush meadow within the walls. These she ate as they were, rubbing the mud off them on the long wet grass; they tasted earthy but they were there in plenty. Rest from the daily forced march revived her, and once the initial shock of Tibby's death had worn off, she began to take in her surroundings. When the sun broke through she thought she caught the gleam of distant apples over the brow of the hill behind the dead monastery. If there were apples there, there might be other comforts worth the seeking; the time had come for her to move on if she was not to live on mushrooms until she perished in the winter cold.

But before she left she must make herself go back into the lodge; in it were the knife and tinderbox on which her survival might depend - her old cloak too, and the discarded shoes into which her feet must somehow be forced before the winter.

She stood about outside for a long time trying to overcome the nightmare feeling that still clung to the place. It was only Tibby in there, she reminded herself, Tib who had never been anything but good to her, who had left her home for her sake and paid with her life for her kindness ... and who lay unburied because she, Hazel, was too weak and cowardly to do for her what was needed. And there was another thing ...

She went away and returned with a fallen branch and a handful of mushrooms. Now she had another reason for going in, a better and less selfish one; but, try as she would to shame it away, the fear was still there as she stepped up to the doorway and the yawning darkness behind it.

The branch was too heavy for her to do much with, but she swung it noisily against the door frame and then heaved it in ahead of her to scatter the rats, rushing in after it before they should have time to return to their grisly meal. The thought of them running across her bare feet in the dark made her flesh creep.

First things first, she thought, and stepped boldly up to the bed she could faintly make out. The crumpled mushrooms in her hand were now damp with sweat. She held them at arm's length above the figure on the bed, and said shakily, 'I eat thy sins, I eat thy sins, I eat thy sins -oh, Tibby, dunna haunt me-' and crammed them in her mouth which had dried so much that she could not chew.

The room was full of the nauseating odour of rotting meat and she had to muffle her face with her skirts to keep from vomiting. Had the words been right - she did not know, she could not remember what the sin-eater had mumbled over Tom. For good measure', she repeated, 'Dunna haunt me, Tib! I ate your sins, I done what I could ...' and then she choked on the mushrooms and could say no more.

The barn owl, angry at the disturbance at midday, glared down at her with smouldering amber eyes, and a stirring in a corner reminded her to hurry. She groped and encountered her shoes, half eaten by the rats, but the knife and the tinderbox were not to be found.

Tibby lay as she had left her, one arm outstretched, but Hazel's own cloak had been drawn up over her head, hiding her face.

Someone had been there before her.

She hesitated, bewildered. But she must have the cloak. She pulled at a corner and it began to slide down over the body.

The old woman had died with her eyes open: lying as she did on her side, they had slid after death from their sagging lids, and now they lay in a glassy unseeing stare upon her cheekbones. The memory of awaking in that ghastly embrace shattered Hazel's fragile composure; when the room was filled at that moment with a long heavy sigh, and the sound of a harsh, dry cough she was seized with such horror that she ran blindly from the place. Still clutching the cloak, she fled, tripping over the branch, blundering past the startled sheep that had followed her in and now stood munching with a blank white face, and did not stop until her headlong flight was arrested by a bundle of rags that caught her in its arms. A cheery voice rallied her: 'Ho now, doxy! What's up, then - is the Devil after you?'

She found herself looking into the weather-beaten face of a merry little man' no taller than herself. He was indescribably filthy and he smelled worse in life than Tibby did in death. But he was human, and he was alive. She flung her arms around him and burst into a flood of tears.

The little man disengaged himself and sat her down on the grass to recover, while he grimaced and capered on his one leg and a crutch as if she were a child to be amused out of her tears.

'Who are you?' she asked him. 'Where did you come from?'

He swept a greasy cap from his balding head and flourished it. 'The Lord Abbot at your service!' he chuckled. 'And as for where I came from - out of my mother's womb, I suppose, the same as you unless you be a changeling!' and he rolled about laughing at his own joke until Hazel said, 'I meant where do you live?'

'Why, here in the monastery, of course. Where else?' Dear God, thought Hazel, he's mad. She got to her feet. 'Well, I give you good day, then.' She hesitated, smiling uncertainly, and added, 'My Lord Abbot.' She started to move away.

'My Lord Abbot! My Lord Abbot!' he crowed, gambolling about delightedly, then suddenly bounded after her and seized her ann. 'Come along, my young mistress, you're expected, you know.' He drew her along towards the ruined building, reluctant but curious. He laid one finger alongside his nose and winked. 'Oh yes, I knew you'd be coming. The old lady told me so.'

Hazel stopped, and he cackled knowingly.

'Oh yes,' he persisted, tugging at her arm, '1 know she's dead, and some little while,' he pinched his nose with two fingers, 'but when I see one dead lady,' he paused for effect, 'not a rich lady, mark you, and travel-stained withal, and two pairs of shoes ...' he grinned into her face, 'I know we shall have a little visitor before long.'

She looked at him with new eyes. Perhaps he was not as mad as she had thought.

'Was it you ...

He nodded, suddenly sober. 'Running from the plague, was you? Well, that's life, my pretty.' He pinched her chin in a grimy paw. 'No more tears now, here we are at the door.'

He released her and disappeared with astonishing agility through a gap in the wall that once might have been a window. She followed him into a room not much larger than her cottage at home. But there the resemblance ended. Where rushes should have been was a floor paved with massive plates of stone, and from the walls sprang slender columns to arch and soar and meet above her head, so high, so dizzying that the stars painted between them began to drift before her eyes and she staggered to save herself from falling. It had the feeling of a church, but where the altar should have been was a pile of rubble and the beautiful stained glass of the windows lay in glittering fragments on the floor.

'My private chapel,' he giggled, 'and now a conducted tour of the Abbey.'

'I thought it was a monastery,' she said, stepping carefully over the head of a broken statue to pass into the next chamber. It was vast, reeking of soot and scarred by fire, and its lofty roof was open to the sky.

'Abbey - monastery - 'tis all one. This was the library. Here's where they burned the books, more than a thousand of them, so they said. Can you read?' Hazel shook her head. 'No more can I, except to write my name. But the Brother Chronicler, he was a learned man. Wept fit to break his heart when they burned his books. All his life's work and many another's before him - but what then, say I, where's the loss of a scroll no other man can read? 'Tis all the same in a hundred years by any road you travel.'

Hazel sighed.

'And all this was the King's men, Tibby said.'

'The King's men, aye! But that the King knew everything they did - that's another matter. I doubt they had orders to pocket the Abbey treasure to their own use, or-' he broke off abruptly. His mood changed and when he spoke again it was in the role of clown that she had come to expect of him.

He took her through an endless succession of rooms and outhouses: through the dairy, the brewery, the looming rooms, the guest house, the wine cellars and the dormitories, all empty and shrouded in the dust of long disuse, and yet all exuding an indefinable atmosphere of peace.

At last they came to the refectory. The reredos still stood in its centre, its dogged iron legs disappearing into the stone-flagged floor in a scuffle of wood ash.

'Couldn't shift that,' he chuckled, 'bolted to the floor, that is! And here's where I hold my court.'

'Your court ...' she repeated stupidly. She couldn't make him out; she was sure he was not the Abbot, and yet ... his little brown eyes were mocking her.

'You are pleased to make fun of me, sir!' she said crisply.

The little man burst out laughing.

'Lord bless you, child, what else should I do, and I the Abbot's fool these many a year! His Patch I was, and would be still if they hadn't given me the Abbey to myself. But so they did, and if that don't make me the Abbot you just tell me what does.'

He led her to a window from which they could see a rolling stretch of green parkland reaching to the river. Beyond it the fitful sun caught the wet thatched roofs of a distant village.

'I can remember when the peacocks strutted these lawns, and the Brothers' voices sweetened the evening air,' he went on dreamily, 'aye, and the days of plenty when no one was turned away.'

They were silent for a moment, each remembering his private loss. Then he turned towards her and spread his hands in a shrug, his clown's humour restored.

'And now there's only me to entertain the poor. And here, as I live and breathe, I hold my court.'

'I see,' said Hazel thoughtfully, 'but why do you stay here all alone - with your court, I mean,' she added quickly at the look in his eye.' Surely you could join a great house - or even join a band of players?'

He parted his rags to show her the stump of his leg, dreadfully mutilated and incompletely healed so that she had to look away.

'Who wants a Patch with that?' he said simply. 'A Patch with a missing leg is a broken toy. But an abbot, now...' He dropped his rags back into place and processed down the length of the refectory with all the pomp of the papal church. Despite his disability he had a wonderful gift for mimicry. 'No, it's better to stay here among the Brothers. Lived here all me life, I have. Well, nearly - there's a while to go yet with a bit of luck.'

Among the Brothers ... Haze! shivered. Was his court made up of ghosts?

'What happened to your leg, Master Patch' - again the warning glance - 'my Lord Abbot?' she humoured him.

'Nothing - I forget...' He was evasive. At that moment Hazel's attention was diverted by something else.

A blind man was coming up the rise from the village, a filthy bandage tied across his eyes and a long stick held in both hands slowly probing out the ground before him.

The Lord Abbot smiled.

'Here comes the first,' he said.

They watched the man as he walked towards them over the long grass into the setting sun. As he felt the shadow of the Abbey fall upon him he took off his bandage, slung his stick over his shoulder and after a quick glance around him stepped out smartly, whistling jauntily.

'He can see!' exclaimed Hazel.

'As well as you,' agreed the Patch, 'but who would give him alms if they knew that? Hard hearts make dishonest tricksters when men cannot work.'

Hazel was not so sure. She could remember the villagers barring their doors in fear when sturdy beggars like this one arrived. They fell upon the village like wolves, demanding charity, extorting by threats what they could not get for the asking. Because they came in packs the Headborough and the constable could do little to deal with them. They picked off the odd one here and there and had him whipped as a discouragement to the rest, but the beggars were not put off and their coming was dreaded by dwellers on outlying farms. She looked nervously at where in the distance three more figures were climbing the hill.

'Come along,' said the Patch. 'Time to light the fire.'

She went with him obediently to collect wood and although she opened her mouth to protest when she recognised Tibby's tinderbox, she prudently shut it again.

The beggars trickled in by ones and twos: an old woman with a crooked back which miraculously straightened as she entered. A younger woman carrying a baby which she tossed carelessly into a corner. Hazel gasped. But when she ran to save it she found it was nothing more than a deceptive bundle of rags. There were two more fake cripples, and then a man who really had no legs and had to propel himself along by his arms like some grotesque insect.

Of the many who gathered round the fire in the course of the evening, only he and three others were what they seemed to be. One of these had a leg covered in weeping sores from foot to knee; one was a young woman whose blank eyes gazed out over the head of the wan little girl who led her. The third was a man whose hands had been chopped off at the wrist.

'Caught thieving,' explained the Patch in response to Hazel's shocked inquiry. 'Lucky to be alive - they mostly die of the fever or bleed to death.'

She noticed that these few were treated with respect by the others, but it was a deference that set them apart. Being honest beggars, they did not belong.

Those who had been able to beg or steal food threw it into the cauldron over the fire in the reredos, filling the place with a delicious aroma. Those who had no food dropped a coin onto the floor. Everyone contributed something, however small. Hazel, having nothing to offer, hung back and tried not to listen to the rumblings of her stomach.

The Patch drew her forward into the circle around the fire.

'Tonight you're the guest of the Abbey.' He looked meaningly around the motley of faces. 'Tomorrow you go with the others and learn the profession.'

She learned to beg her bread in the company of Bent Meg, the crone with the crooked back. Meg knew every house and its possibilities. If the goodwife was generous, well and good; they accepted what she gave and left her in peace. If not, Meg would keep her arguing at the door while Hazel, as the younger and more agile, had to slip out of sight around the back and forage for what she could conceal. After a first sharp lesson in obedience from Meg, it was rare for her to come back empty-handed, and every few days they returned with their spoils to the Abbey where the Patch held his court. The blue woodsmoke rose and curled into the vaulted roof, mingling with the scents of mellowing stew and unwashed bodies; sometimes a skin of cider would pass from mouth to unsavoury mouth, and then Hazel would listen drowsily, warm and relaxed, as friends greeted one another and exchanged news, the glow of firelight flickering on their faces. At such moments she put out of her mind the terrifying price of being caught; Meg, she persuaded herself, was old and experienced, and knew how to keep her safe.

One evening a pair of well-dressed men came in, greeted the Patch and tossed a gold coin on the ground. Then they withdrew to a comer, where they were joined by a woman in a flamboyant gown.

'Coney-catchers,' said the Patch to Hazel, jerking his head to where they sat counting out coin and laughing between themselves. 'Wouldn't believe what tricks they know to part a fool from his money! Still, each to his trade, I say - who knows, I might come to playing the Abraham myself if times go hard.' And he elbowed her ribs, inviting her to share the joke.

'Playing the Abraham ?' she repeated, mystified.

'Acting mad,' he explained, 'going out on the road with straws in the hair, pleading, "Please, kind sir, I'm a poor lunatic, been in the madhouse-"' he broke off, his eyes glowing dangerously. 'Who says I'm mad?' he snapped.

'Who dares insult the Abbot!'

Hazel was alarmed, but the others clearly knew how to deal with the situation. Two of the nearest jumped to their feet, seized a third who was innocently chewing on a bone and hustled him outside.

'He is gone, my lord!' they assured the Patch, who sat down, mollified.

'Quite right, quite right,' he muttered. Then he added magnanimously, 'Let the fellow come back. Poor creature, he does not know what he says.'

The third man, who had already returned, exchanged grins with his companions, and the Patch turned to Hazel as if nothing had happened.

'We don't live bad, on the whole,' he said, 'but you should have been here in the old days. Why, I can remember when I was a child seeing a whole ox roasting on that very fire, me and another boy, one at each end, turning the spit and the good Brothers merry at their wine - not small beer and dog's meat like we live on now.' He smiled, but his little rheumy eyes had gone far away, and the strange glow had not quite died out of them. Hazel noticed that everyone was careful now to address him as the Lord Abbot.

Presently he disappeared from among them without a word. Later, when the others slept, she thought she could hear him shuffling along the passages on his one foot and his crutch, talking to someone whose voice she could not hear.

'What is it with the Patch,' she asked Bent Meg one day as they walked, 'is he really mad, or what?'

Meg blessed herself hastily.

'You don't want to go saying things the like of that,' she said crossly, 'and don't you go asking him no questions neither! If he likes to think he's the Lord Abbot that's up to him and none of your worryings.'

'Yes, but ... I mean, what happened to his leg? I asked him once and he said he didn't remember - how could anyone possibly forget a thing like that?'

The old woman stopped and straightened up to look at her.

'Sharp, aren't you? Better watch out you don't cut yourself. Well, I'll tell you what I've heard and you can sort it out as best you can. Some say the Abbot was a cruel man and wont to torment his Fool when 'e didn't please him, and this was what happened to the Patch's leg; that when the King's men took the Abbot away the Patch was dancing alongside, all a-crowing and a-laughing like, and the Abbot was so angered he seized a sword from one of the soldiers and struck his leg off. But I don't rightly believe that.' She stood still, musing. After a moment she bent to pluck a barley stalk and chewed on it. 'The Father Abbot was a kindly man, they say. I don't somehow see him doing a thing like that.'

Hazel waited, pretending to look for a barley stalk. Presently Meg went on.

'Course, me being new to this manor and not hereabouts when it all happened, can't rightly tell as you might say. Then, there's them as says when they came to take the Abbot he changed raiment with his Fool and let the Patch go to the gallows in his place, and this 'un here's the real Abbot all along. But then that don't seem likely neither. He don't look or talk like my idea of an abbot - though not having seen one never, can't rightly be sure of that neither.'

Meg lowered herself on to a milestone and sighed deeply.

'Maybe the other story's the right one, who can tell? There's always someone ready to make mischief about them in high places ... and yet...'

Enthralled, Hazel prompted, 'What's that then, Meg?'

Meg looked about her and lowered her voice to a confidential whisper.

'Well - and you keep this to yourself, mind you, one word and I'll have the hide off you - they say - and, mark you, I'm not one of them as says it, 'tis only what I've heard - but they say as the Patch is the Abbot's natural son by one of the village wenches.' She sat back, surveying Hazel's shocked face with satisfaction. 'Yes, they do indeed. And they say that when the Abbot defied the King's order to give up his monastery he knew his head would answer for it, and he told the Patch for the first time who his father was. They don't say why; maybe there was something he wanted him to have or to do when he was gone. Who can say?

'Anyways, to cut a long story, when the King's men came they didn't close the Abbey and take the Abbot away decent like a prisoner or such. No, they burned the library, sacked the place, and dragged the old man out and struck his head off right there in his own front yard. And when the Patch tried to save him they cast him down before the horses, one trampled his leg and another kicked him in the head, or so they say. Not deliberate maybe, just all a-milling and a- jostling in a small space, and the fellow went under just the same.' She tapped her forehead with her finger. 'He's never been the same since, they do say. Sometimes he knows who he is - clear as you or me - but then ... start him thinking about the past and he's away with the angels...' She blessed herself again for good measure.

Hazel sat silent. Aye, but that the King knew all they did ... At last she said, 'That's true, isn't it, Meg? You believe it's true, don't you?'

Meg looked uneasily about her, aware that she had said too much. 'I don't know no more than you,' she said crossly. 'If you've no better to do than listen to idle gossip I can pass on what I hear, and that's all. I'm saying no more. And don't you never ask no more questions of the Patch, you hear me, not never!'

'I never will,' promised Hazel, swallowing a lump in her throat.

Autumn was upon them; the sun had returned for long enough to dry the crops and harvest was under way. Everywhere could be seen the figures of reapers in their broad-brimmed hats, stooping with swinging sickles up and down cultivated strips and open fields.

'Soon be Harvest Home,' chuckled Meg, '"tis a good time for us. Reckon we stays here till after.'

'Only till after?' asked Hazel with a sinking heart. She had hoped her wanderings were at an end. 'What happens then?'

'Why, we moves on, of course. Can't beg for ever in the same place. Folks gets used to us and don't give no more. Only natural!'

She sucked at a tooth reflectively, treating Hazel to a speculative look, as if she were assessing her potentialities.

'Maybe 'tis time to try the city again.'

'Why the city?' Hazel put the question with misgivings. Whatever its shortcomings, she only felt at home in the country. The city was to her as foreign as the moon.

Meg was evasive.

'Mm . . . 'tis better in the winter,' was all she would say.

Afterwards, Hazel mentioned the conversation to the Patch, and he laughed.

'She means to sell you to a trugging-house,' he said.

'Whatever's that?' she asked him.

But just then a diversion was created by the harsh, strident clack of a leper's rattle.

Everyone stopped what he was doing to listen: hands full of food poised half-way to hungry mouths, words froze in mid-syllable, such was the dread inspired by the sound. The Patch got up, dipped a broken crock into the cauldron, and carried it full of the steaming pottage to set down outside for the unfortunate to consume at a safe distance. The others sat in an unhappy silence, knowing it was a fate that could befall any one of them.

A shout of laughter reached them from outside.

'Why, Poxy Tom, as I live and breathe!'

The Patch and the newcomer, an undersized man with a disfigured face, came in together, arms entwined, swinging the rattle above their heads, and the whole assembly joined in the merriment.

'Don't be feared,' said Meg to the shrinking Hazel, ' 'tis only scars from the pox. He's no more a real leper than you are, but folks is so mortal scared they never gets near enough to find out! Makes a good living, Tom does,' and she hobbled over to greet her old friend.

Hazel shook her head; she was beginning to feel that nothing could surprise her.

She looked on unmoved nowadays while young babies were bandied about from hand to hand, leased out to total strangers for a day's begging, even sold for a few pence to lonely old women at cottage doors. She grew hardened to the sight of the man with the raw leg touching up his sores with the rough edge of a stone before setting out on the day's business.

Little by little, she had gleaned something of their histories.

Some were ploughmen put out of work by the encroaching sheep pastures. Some were ex-soldiers who had been disbanded where they stood without jobs or pay or any means of returning to their homes - even if they were sure of a welcome there after many years away. A few were too crippled to work and at least one she had seen had the blank face and unintelligible speech of the mentally backward; he was regarded with a mixture of superstitious fear and ridicule tinged by compassion. He was tolerated and fed for a few days and then he went out to gather mushrooms and did not come back. Women were few and for the most part old, widows of the poor or physically handicapped in some way. One had suppurating ulcers around her nose and mouth and was almost blind.

'Is that leprosy?' whispered Hazel to Meg, and was answered with ribald laughter.

'If you've a fancy to finish your days like Nan you just stay with Bent Meg!' the Patch teased her, and Meg shook her stick in his direction.

'Don't you believe it, my pretty, old Meg'll look after you,' she cajoled, 'never you fear,' and her stick prodded the Patch in the ribs.

'Aye, that she will!' returned the Patch, laughing with her.

Hazel looked from one to the other with the feeling that they were sharing a joke at her expense. It was longer than usual before she dropped into an uneasy sleep, troubled by dreams in which she and Meg, with dead eyes hanging on her cheekbones, tramped endless roads, rasping the leper's rattle as they went.

6

Harvest was coming in, the villagers preparing to make merry. Corn dollies were fashioned by loving hands and woven into rick-ends to guard the crop; in field after outlying field the last sheaf was made into a corn-baby and carried home in triumph on the wagon with the harvesters. The last to come in was the Home Farm, because it was by far the largest and therefore took longest to cut.

'That's the one for us,' Meg told Hazel, 'the Lord of the Manor's crop, and right open-handed he is when the harvest is a good one. Throws open his barn and the leavings of the Harvest Supper to the poor, he does, and his good lady gives alms to all that come. Very pious, she is; no doubt she wants our prayers to help the crops.'

'Maybe she's just kind,' said Hazel, feeling that such cynicism amounted to ingratitude.

'Nobody's just kind!' Meg scoffed. 'They either wants our prayers or they pays us to go away. We'm a bad smell under their noses as they'm glad to get rid of. Only natural.' Hazel sighed. Was she to spend the rest of her life as a bad smell under somebody's nose ? Then she remembered. 'What's a trugging-house?' she asked.

Meg looked at her sharply.

'Been talking to the Patch, have you? Asking questions again, I shouldn't wonder. And what for do you want to know about a trugging-house, my lady?'

Hazel faltered, 'He said you were about to sell me to one.'

A smile spread itself like oil over the old woman's face. 'Well, now ... and suppose I was, what would that be for you to worry about? A nice comfortable life in a house and no work to do, just entertaining the gentlemen; fed, you'd be, and sheltered, why 'tis a fine life for a comely wench as knows what she's about. Virgin, are you?'

'Of course!' Hazel was indignant at the question, failing to see its connection.

''Tis well.' Meg made a private adjustment to the price she intended to demand. 'They'm very fussy, you know, won't take just anyone. A very lucky girl you are, having me to look after you, there's a-many would like to have your chances.' She looked at the puzzled girl to see what effect her sales talk was having. 'And don't you go boasting to any of the others of your good fortune, neither,' she added craftily, 'very jealous, they'd be. Stick a knife in your back as soon as look, I shouldn't wonder.'

Hazel walked on, somewhat mollified if not entirely reassured. But somewhere in the back of her mind there was a doubt that she could not as yet formulate. All she knew was that it seemed just a little too good to be true.

The doubt kept returning like a nagging fly, and she in turn nagged Bent Meg.

'Will you be staying there with me?'

'Not I!'

'Why not?'

'Too old and ugly.'

'For what?'

'For entertaining. Be still, now. Can't talk uphill, 'tis only natural.'

When they reached the Abbey gates Hazel stopped. 'Don't reckon I know how to entertain, whatever that is. Will you teach me so's I know what to do?'

'You don't need no teaching, they'll soon tell you what they'm after,' Meg said testily; then with an abrupt change of tone, she added, 'But I'll teach you to cut a caper if 'tis worrying you.'

If the child thought she was going to sing and dance for her living, so much the better, Meg reflected. But she would find a few choice words to say to that interfering Patch when she saw him ...

Spider, the legless man, was resting in the shadows of the archway, and as Hazel passed he leaned forward.

'Psssst -doxy...

'What ails, Spider, want me to help you along?'

He shook his shaggy head that always looked pathetically too large for his docked body.

'That old crone'll try to sell you if you don't watch out. You wouldn't be the first to go out of here with her and never be seen again.'

Hazel shivered. 'She says 'tis a good life and I'll be happy there.'

'In a trugging-house?'

His tone of derision confirmed her misgivings. On an impulse she sat on the ground beside him and told him everything. He listened gravely, picking at the dead skin on his calloused hands. At length she finished: 'The worst is, I canna get anyone to give me a straight answer about a trugging-house. They just laugh and don't say nothing.'

He said, 'If you're wanting a straight answer and no fooling, you'd best ask Nan - you know her, the one you thought had leprosy. She'll tell you all you want to know and more, that's where she's been most of her life, and cast upon the road when she was no more use to them. You ask her, she'll tell you. And if you don't like what you hear... stay away from Bent Meg.'

Hazel sighed and went in search of Nan.

That night she ate her meal with Spider and when Meg approached she flew at her.

'You're a wicked, wicked old woman and I'll never go out with you again! Pretending to look after me and all the time - now I know why they laughed at me, poor simpleton they must have thought me! You don't care nothing what's to come of me, no more than you'd care if I was took up and hanged for stealing for you. Just dunna you come near me again, not never, you hear, I dunna belong to you and if there's any selling to be done it's me as is going to do it!'

Meg tried in vain to beguile her.

'Now, now, doxy, you'm got it all wrong, 'tis only their fun they'm having with you-'

'I anna got it wrong, you old witch, I know what you did to Nan and the others and you anna going to do it to me!'

Spider watched her storming, cheeks blazing, angry tears glittering on her lashes, and wished he had legs. He wondered for the millionth time what it would be like to have a real woman instead of solacing himself alone in the sweating darkness.

"Tis enough,' he murmured, 'sit down and eat your supper.'

Meg hobbled away, muttering, and presently angry voices were to be heard in the passage outside.

' - 'tis no bad life for a wench, they'm fed and housed, ain't they, 'tis better than the road! If she stays here these ragamuffins'll have her for nothing.'

'You should have come straight out with it - I never procured for anyone without I got the girl's consent. These children aren't yours to sell - and don't tell me it's for their own good or out of the goodness of your heart because we all know better - it's to put hard coin in Bent Meg's poke and for no other reason.'

Meg put on the whining voice she used at cottage doors.

'A poor old woman 'as to eat, Patch, and I'm too old to do it for myself. My back ...'

Their voices died away. Hazel glanced uneasily at Spider who was leaning towards her with smouldering eyes. She got up and moved away.

'Is it true, Patch?' she asked unhappily when she saw him next.

'Is what true?'

'Why, that the men'll have me if I stay here.'

The Patch spread his hands in a whimsical gesture.

'You should have come when the Brothers were here. Twenty pence they used to pay for a single night.'

He sighed, reminiscing. Hazel looked at him.

'The Brothers? You mean-'

Patch nodded. 'And the Father Abbot - he paid best of all! Part of my job, as you might say, to keep them supplied.

Ask anyone in the town, they'll tell you. Used to keep their daughters for me, they did, knew I paid the best prices...

The odd look was in his eyes again and she thought, It'll just be his wanderings. Suddenly he turned on her.

'Nobody goes finding a fine young wench for me!' he accused her.

'N-no ... my Lord Abbot ...' she faltered, taken by surprise.

He looked at her long and hard, as if what she said had puzzled him. Then he smiled.

'Get me mixed up with the Abbot, do you, doxy? I'm only the Patch.'

Hazel gave up.

'But, Nan, what am I to do?' she pleaded. 'Seems wherever I go I'll end up on my back.'

Nan laughed shortly. 'That's life,' she said laconically. She was weary and sick and her life had made her cynical; she did not really care about the fate of a stranger. 'Go with Meg if you've a mind to.'

'I couldna!'

A wan smile flitted across Nan's ravaged face, recalling the remnant of beauty.

''Tis not so bad,' she mused, 'not all the time.'

'But I never did it and I'm a-feared!'

'Saving your maidenhead for some great lord, are you?' The cutting edge of sarcasm tinged her voice and then she seemed to repent it for she added more gently, 'Well, have you anything else that you can sell?'

Hazel said diffidently, 'I'm young - and strong. I could work ...'

Nan shrugged emaciated shoulders.

'Get you to the farm, then, maybe they'll let you help with the harvest.' Then as Hazel slowly moved away she called after her, 'And when that's done you can take your chances in the greenwood. Between Black John and the stags I give you till Michaelmas.'

Hazel walked away, disconsolate. But she had not gone far when Nan called her back.

'I don't mean to speak you rough; you hurt my pride.

Look,' she raised her skirts to show her ulcerated thighs, 'you don't want that. So if you've a mind for virtue, well... Find you a strong lad and wed him. He'll keep the others at bay.'

Before dawn the next day Hazel was waiting in the field for the harvesters.

It was the last remaining to be cut and the ripe corn rattled in its husks in the breeze of daybreak. It was like someone whispering, she thought, and wished she could hear the words. She stood listening, the rags of her cloak pulled tight about her in the early chill.

Somewhere a blackbird piped, loud and brilliantly clear in the dark trees. Another answered and presently was joined by thrushes, finches, linnets, all the birds who had slept long enough and couldn't wait for the day to begin, so that long before the sky lightened the air was full of their clamour and sparkling with excitement. Not far from her, a hedgehog settled in for his day's rest; she could hear the rasp of his spines as he sought the most comfortable position, and at length his contented snores.

As the first pearly light of dawn lay along the horizon, she heard the reapers coming. One was singing under his breath; the children chattered and called to one another and their noise startled a cock pheasant who rose with a whirr and a flash of bronze into the sunrise.

'Ask Jem, he's Lord of the Harvest,' she was told, 'but it's too late by rights.'

Jem was a burly man with a sunburnt face on the far side of the field.

'Jem,' bellowed the speaker, 'here's a beggar maid wants you!'

It was a shock to Hazel to hear herself referred to as a beggar. She had not thought of herself as one of them, only as being with them. She straightened her clothing and tried to comb her hair with her fingers. With what dignity she could scratch together she said, 'I want to help with the harvest.'

He looked her up and down appraisingly, then spat on the ground.

'No,' was all he said.

Hazel turned away, head high, cheeks burning.

'Wait!'

She halted, looking at him defiantly over her shoulder.

'Work today if you've a mind. You'll not be paid but you mun come to Harvest Supper. Take or leave it.'

He turned to whetting his sickle and she went to join the others. No one seemed interested in telling her what to do so she watched the others and tried to do the same, gathering and stacking behind the reapers as they moved up and down in rhythmic rows. She soon found it was the hardest work she had ever done. Within an hour her back was creaking and she was soaked with sweat in the humid heat of the day. Between the tall stalks the midges swarmed hungrily, and insects she had never seen before came out of the grass and bit her. Before long she was thirsty, and realised she should have brought water with her like the rest. They took long cooling swigs from their skin bottles but no one offered her a drink. She must really look like a beggar, she thought, humiliated.

Just as the sun reached its zenith and she was wondering how much longer she could go on, everybody stopped and sat down. They took out bundles of bread and cheeses, and skins of cider, and codlings, and again she was the only one without. Embarrassed, she tried not to watch them eat until someone said, 'Ain't you got nothing?'

She shook her head.

'Well, go you over there where the childer are sitting. Might be you'll get a bit of cake.'

She made her way over to where a woman had arrived with a basket and was handing out something to the children, who crowded round her like sparrows. As Hazel drew near she looked up, frowning.

'Big child, aren't you ? Cake is for the little 'uns. They get it instead of pay.'

Hazel squared her shoulders. 'I anna getting paid.' She swallowed her pride and added, 'I'm mortal hungry ...'

A tiny boy beside her looked up, grinned, and offered her his handful of cake. The scent of it reached her, spicy and full of fruit. She wanted to snatch it from him, to cram her mouth full, to gorge herself on its richness ... 'Eat it quick,' she said, not trusting herself, and turned to go.

'Hang on, hang on,' said the woman with the basket. 'Nobody said as you couldna have a bit, not so far as I've heard. Sit you down, not go gallivanting off.'

It was plum cake, the first she had ever tasted, and she wondered enviously what manner of rich folk could have such daily fare. She picked up the crumbs from the ground and was licking the last flavour from her fingers when she realised that the children were laughing at her, mimicking her movements. She blushed hotly and returned to her task.

The day went on, and on, and on ... It seemed to last forever. Cart after cart loaded high with the bright corn went off in the direction of the barn and still the work went on. But at last the solitary sheaf stood alone in the middle of the field, the women clapping their hands in rhythm while the men threw sickles at it from a distance, no one wanting the bad luck that went with being the one to cut the last sheaf.

The children rushed about excitedly, trying to catch the terrified rabbits that had taken refuge in the diminishing stalks and were now being flushed out by the threat of the sickles. As they emerged the dogs gave chase, yelping wildly as they raced for cover. A rabbit blundered into Hazel's legs and she picked it up, trying to soothe the frantic ticking of its heart. But it wriggled free and went careering away across the stubble. She watched it, indifferent to the jeers of the boys who had seen her let it go.

As the sheaf fell a cheer went up. Work was over and the rest was celebrations.

Hazel had often watched from a distance the Harvest Home rituals; but she had never been part of it before. Now she was caught up in it, carried along, swept forward on the tide of excitement. Tired as she was, she found herself romping with the rest, running behind the garlanded wain as it rumbled around the village, laughing and shouting back at the throwers of water who drenched them and the load for good luck. She seized a handbell from one of the others and rang it wildly, extravagantly, until Jem, deafened by the noise, reached down from his perch on the load and took it from her with a grin.

'Can I come up there?' she asked him.

'No - only me and my lady, here!' He put a playful arm round the last sheaf where it sat beside him dressed up like a human in women's clothes. His mood was quite changed from his working one, as if he had put on a different face.

'She looks lovely,' yelled Hazel above the din, and he nodded and ducked as another bucketful of water hurtled towards him. He blinked the water from his eyes and returned, 'Should be fine crops next year!'

She nodded, eyes shining, and went on capering happily alongside. She knew now where she wanted to be, and only wondered that she had not known before. She was going to stay here on the farm, and work, and be part of this life she had tasted. Her bones knew it and her muscles rejoiced, lifting her small weight as she skipped and jumped. No more problems now. And for the first time in her life she was playing.

In the barn a long table groaned under the load of whole sides of bacon, enormous flesh pies, stacked loaves of fresh-baked bread, mountains of fruit cake and apple pies the size of cartwheels.

They all thronged in, pushing and jostling through the garlanded doorway, carrying the corn doll to enthrone her on her special chair. She looked like a mad queen, Hazel thought, impassive above the crowd with the wayward corn stalks sticking through her hair.

When everyone was inside at last, the babble of voices dropped to a murmur; as time passed by it rose again to a happy uproar. But the food stood untouched, the barrels of ale unbroached. What were they waiting for?

Faces turned from time to time towards the door, as if someone else were expected to arrive. Little by little she edged her way over until she could see out.

Up the hill towards them a little party of horsemen was approaching. As they drew level with the barn they reined in, and she saw that behind them were four men trotting with a litter.

'Lady Edith ... the Lady Edith. She has travelled many miles to bless our harvest.'

The murmur started at the door and travelled back through the people, spreading a hush in its wake.

The litter was carefully set down and the curtains drawn. From between them appeared a pair of feet in gold-embroidered slippers; the feet hesitated: out of nowhere came garments and straw to make a dry path through the mire. Then and only then the feet were followed by their owner, a woman past her youth wearing a high-necked gown of sober black velvet, which her waiting-maid was anxiously trying to keep out of the mud. With it she wore the old-fashioned French hood once worn by long-dead Queen Anne, a gold crucifix on a handsome jewelled chain, and the pallor of incipient pregnancy.

To Hazel she was a dazzling sight, a vision of magnificence that passed her so close she could have reached out and touched, and her grubby fingers itched to explore the velvet. As she passed, something else seemed to come from her towards Hazel; something dark and unhappy, chilling her for a moment like a cold shadow cast on a sunny day.

As if she too sensed it, the Lady Edith paused a moment in her progress, and looked about her before moving on. But whatever she felt, her pale face with the blue-circled eyes betrayed nothing as she progressed to her appointed place.

There, at the head of the table, she spoke the grace in a cool, flat voice, and asked a blessing on the crop and the harvesters. Then without further speech she departed, the people falling back on either side to let her pass. A gracious nod to Jem, as Lord of the Harvest, was the limit of her contact with them, and it came to Hazel that she had not exchanged a smile with anyone.

She must be too grand, she supposed, shrugging off the chill that had fallen upon her as the cheerful hubbub broke out again. She wondered if the same dampening influence had been felt by the others. Certainly they seemed relieved to be rid of the restraint.

She edged her way back to the table, where everyone was pushing, shoving, laughing, shouting and cramming their mouths with good things, happily relaxed now that their benefactress had gone and left them to gorge in peace. Fat farm women cut up the pies in juicy chunks and the men used their knives to carve thick slices from the steaming meats; the cider and the ale were flowing and soon the barn rocked with song.

A piper tuned up and was joined by someone with a tabor, and dancing was soon under way, joyously abandoned and slightly tipsy. Hazel watched, a tankard of cider in one hand and a slab of apple pie in the other, and knew beyond doubt that this was where she belonged. She wanted to be really one of them - not an outsider as she now was, let in on sufferance - to be part of this farming life that was richer and more rewarding than anything she had seen in her enclosed life with Tom and Margery. She was ashamed of her time with the beggars and wanted to wash it from her life. And here were boys and girls of her own age ...

Flushed with ambition and the rosy glow of cider she rushed up to Jem and pleaded breathlessly, 'Master Jem - oh, Master Jem - can I come and work on the farm and be here always? Oh, please, Master Jem!'

Jem laughed uneasily, his ruddy face even ruddier than usual. He was drunk; but not drunk enough not to have his wits about him. He was not about to be responsible for employing a beggar on the Lord's demesne.

'Lor' bless you, child, 'tis not all Harvest Home, ye know! And I get all the hands I need at the Hiring Fair.' Then, seeing perhaps that he had kicked away her dreams, he added, 'But you're a right little worker, I'll give you that. Come back next summer and ask for me. I'll not have forgotten you.'

He turned back to the argument he was having with a shepherd, and Hazel took a long swig of her cider to wash down the lump of disappointment that had risen in her

throat. Next summer ... he might as well have said in a hundred years. And yet - it was there. And somewhere in the uncharted wilderness of her life a tiny light beckoned. She had only, somehow, to survive the winter.

She returned to the dancing, wishing she could join in. But

she did not know how. She could only stand and watch, her bare feet shuffling in the dust of the barn in time to the music, supping at her cider to give herself something to do. One day, she reminded herself, she would be back. And then she would learn. She would be dancing with the others on equal terms.

Her eyelids began to droop after the long hard day, and her muscles ached everywhere. But this day was never to lose its magic for her. She looked back on it afterwards in a golden glow that was not to be forgotten. The dust beaten up by a hundred feet hung in the air in an incandescent haze and settled in a thick layer on the leftover food that was destined for the poor. Tomorrow it would be taken to the gates in baskets and given to all who came. Bent Meg and the others would no doubt be there for the handout. But she, Hazel, would not be with them. No doubt she would have to beg her bread again - but not this bread. Her share of this harvest supper had been well and truly earned; today she was no beggar but a farm worker. This day, so special to her, was hers by right, not by charity. And next summer she would return.

One by one, the lanterns and torches guttered or were borne away. The weary crept to their beds, the drunk slept noisily where they had fallen. Soft sounds of pleasure came from the darkling hay as another generation of harvesters was begotten. Hazel slid into the sleep of the slightly inebriated on the earth floor of the barn.

Around dawn, she was awakened by the ravening appetite of the fleas out of the hay. She stretched and scratched and tottered outside into the daylight. Men were already at work in the barnyard and Jem, a stranger now and feeling the effects of last night's ale, passed her with a sour look that told her more plainly than words that her stay of leave was over.

She drew her ragged cloak about her and moved off towards the road. Her head thumped and banged and the light hurt her eyes. Her stiff limbs protested at the renewal of movement but she marched blindly away with head held high. Some day she would be back, and then ...

As for the present, she did not know where she was heading or what she intended as she tramped the earth road to the village. All she was sure of was that she was not going back to the Abbey. She felt a wave of revulsion towards the beggars and their way of life that would not let her return. She passed through the early-morning streets and on towards the country with no more on her mind than the sound of a lark suspended like a jewel on the high clear air above her.

The turning points of life are rarely heralded by fanfares or resounding claps of thunder. It was by the merest chance that in passing the smithy she glanced in through the dark cavernous doorway and caught sight of a familiar tousled yellow head.

She stopped walking and planted herself squarely, hands on hips, prepared to do battle.

'Tim Kettle,' she yelled, 'you give me back my money!'

7

Joan squatted by the fire, roasting chestnuts. It was good to have someone to do the fetching and carrying while she ate nuts and Tim hammered away at his pots. The children were out of the way and even her toothache had taken a holiday. She drew a long drowsy breath spiced with the scorching husks and the wet dank leaves of autumn, and tried to imagine what it was like to be Queen Catherine and have an army of servants.

Tim's foot brought her back to reality.

'They'm afire, you stupid bitch!'

'King Henry wouldn't do that,' she reproved him mildly, unruffled by the fate of the chestnuts.

'King Henry!' snorted Tim, and returned to his tinkering. He had long given up trying to make sense of his wife's remarks. 'No more he wouldn't,' he muttered to himself. 'Put your fool head on a pike, more like. Best place for it, if you ask me.' Presently he raised his voice again, 'Where's that wench got to anyways?'

Joan was still chewing over her new idea. It wasn't very often that she had one.

'Not if I was Queen, he wouldn't!' She nodded knowingly, pleased with her piece of deduction. It wasn't only Tim who knew how to think.

'If you was Queen!' Tim gave a shout of derisive laughter. 'If goats had wings, more like! Got a good eye for a wench, has old King Hal - five down and one to go. Don't catch him bedding the likes of you, old missus, even at his age!' He chuckled away to himself. Then he repeated his enquiry. 'Where's she got to?'

If there was a connection in his mind, Joan was too slow to see it.

'Who - Queen Catherine?'

Tim threw down what he was doing and went to look for himself. Tramping through the woods, his mind was not running on Joan. It was running on a sturdy, brown-legged girl with the soft bright eyes of a wren and a long tangle of hair. A girl who could sit quite still while he coaxed a wild young animal to eat from his hand, a girl who....

'She got her foot in a hole - got her foot in a hole!'

The boys came rushing at him up the hill, shouting excitedly, unaccompanied.

Tim was jerked back to reality.

'What ails her, canna she walk?' he snapped, then in anger, remembering the money she had been sent to collect, 'Where've you left her?'

This girl was no daft Joan. With the money for his work in her pocket, she might be off. It was the old woman's gold she had come back for and clung like a leech. He'd wasted breath reminding her of the outlaws living in the greenwood, of Black John, Grey Willy and the 'Baron' of Long Coombe - but she knew well enough who had cut the old biddy's purse and she clearly meant to stick until she got it. You had to laugh - but she wasn't getting away with it. . .

He roughed up the bigger boy to get the information he needed. She was about a mile back, limping slowly behind them. She would be about where the greenwood dipped to swallow the road.

'Is she, now,' Tim said thoughtfully. He released the boys

and sent them back to Joan. He was smiling as he started out to find her. Now here, he was thinking, was an opportunity ...

Hazel saw him coming and groped into her pocket.

'I anna stole your money, if that's what's worrying you.' She knew well enough he hadn't walked back merely to help her.

Tim grinned engagingly - at least, that was the effect he hoped for.

'As if I'd think such a thing.'

His protest was as genuine as her reassurance. They both knew that it was only lameness that had stopped her. He took her arm and steered her towards the trees.

'Where we going?' She hung back.

'Woodcutter's cottage.'

'Now? My foot hurts,' she protested.

''Tain't far.'

'You go. I'll wait here.'

'You got to come and all, see where to take the pots back.'

She looked at the darkening wood. 'No, Tim - you tell me tomorrow. I dunna want to.'

He gripped her arm, his patience exhausted, and thrust her before him with a swift glance up and down the road.

'You do as you'm told, mistress,' and Hazel had no choice.

'There's no path,' she complained. 'How will we find the way?'

'Path's through there,' he said gruffly, his voice hoarse and his heart thumping with the way his thoughts were turning. The girl tripped on her swollen foot and he had to grab both arms now, forcing her forward in front of him, hustling her faster through the undergrowth as she struggled to be free. Now, with his goal in sight, his need was becoming urgent. He must get her well away from the road if he was not to be interrupted ...

Hazel fought frantically to free herself. She was pushed relentlessly forward - further and further into the forest, struggling, sobbing - branches and brambles lashing her face, Tim's unsavoury breath burning hot on her neck. At last he released her, throwing her to the ground. Kneeling above her ...

It was just as she had feared. There was no path. No clearing. No woodcutter's cottage. Only herself, helpless on her back among the nettles. And Tim, his eyes bright and hungry, tearing with fumbling fingers at his clothing.

For a long time afterwards, Hazel lay still. Bring your knees up, her mother had said. But she hadn't been able to. He had knelt across her, pinning her legs. And she hadn't been able to move; not even when he had torn his way into her with a pain like a blunt knife, and the panic screams muffled by his horny hands had crumpled into helpless, futile sobs. She rolled onto her face and cried quietly in the crook of her arm, and when she looked up he was gone.

Now she was beginning to shiver, and it was growing dark. She must try to find her way back to the road. She blew her nose on the end of her shift, and then dried the mess between her thighs. She made out the stain of blood in the fading light but that she had heard of and it did not frighten her. The other substance must be seed, she supposed, faintly surprised to realise it was liquid. She had always thought of seed as something dry, like corn. Seed.... A new shock wave brought her to her feet. Suppose there should be a baby! Distractedly she tried to calculate the days to her next flux. She had lost track of time and couldn't be sure. She could only watch the face of the moon, and hope ... she could jump up and down, and make water, as she had seen others do ... As she went through the ritual, she noticed that she was bleeding. Perhaps it was a good sign; if her flux started now there could be no pregnancy. She jumped harder but it hurt too much; she had to give up.

First things first, and she must find her way back to the road. At least the worst had not happened; he had not stripped her bare and discovered the mark. Slowly and painfully she began to pick her way, guided by the smashed brushwood and brambles. It hurt her to walk, and not only from her foot.

It was dark under the trees, and the brambles seemed to have sprung back to life already. She dared not call out for fear it might be Tim Kettle who answered. She peered through the branches and saw with dismay that the sky itself was darkening. And now she was afraid. She pushed on desperately, she had to get away from this nightmare place, the whispering gloom and the trees that caught and dragged at her as she forged blindly through them. She was trapped. She couldn't see. And very soon she knew that she was lost. She wept hopelessly, leaning against a tree.

Someone was calling her name from a long way off. She stood very still and listened, wary as an animal: the days were gone when she had run trustingly to anyone who called. Presently the voice came again, and relief buoyed her up as she recognised it.

'Joan!' she cried, and flung herself recklessly towards a tiny point of light that bobbed in the distance.

She came crashing out of the undergrowth to bury her head on the broad grubby bosom that was suddenly the best thing she had seen in her life. Joan put down the lantern and enfolded her, she made clucking sounds like a shabby, comfortable hen, while Hazel could only sob, 'Joan - oh, Joan!' over and over again. She was incapable of putting into words what had happened to her.

Joan said, 'Tim said you were lost.'

Hazel only clung and nodded wordlessly because she did not know what else to say.

It was late when they returned to the encampment. The boys were already asleep by the dying fire. Tim was there, rolled into his sacking and snoring rhythmically. She made a wide detour of his body before huddling to rest uneasily on the far side of Joan. Even the sight of him set her shuddering.

In the days that followed she limped about the camp, unable

to tell her troubles even to Joan; Tim's wife, she knew intuitively, must be the last person to know. Withdrawn and unhappy, her inside aching and unpredictable, her sleep slashed with nightmares, she held her tongue.

Tim himself, after a startled look of disbelief at seeing her back in their midst, seemed as nervous and uneasy in her presence as she was in his, and their avoidance of each other became mutual. Yet still she lived in fear of him. She no longer allowed herself to be sent on errands with only the children for protection; she found some excuse every waking minute to stay close to Joan, who was pathetically pleased to find herself unexpectedly the object of so much attention.

'The poor little dell's been afrighted,' she confided to Tim. ''Tis my belief as she were set upon.'

Tim grunted, and took himself off to deliver his own pots, leaving Joan only faintly surprised at his docility. He was not docile at all. He was alarmed to find her less stupid than he had thought. And he was wondering how much longer it would take her to arrive at the truth.

Hazel lay still with her eyes squeezed shut and told herself yet again that she was not going to be sick. It was no good. She had just reached the point where her breathing grew light and her mouth began to fill with saliva when the children ran thumpingly across her, and she barely made it to the bushes. It was always the same just lately. Every morning found her retching and gasping while her knees shook and her palms grew clammy and she only wanted to die. Every night before sleeping she had to select a hidden place in which to vomit.

Tim looked at her sourly as she emerged, pale and sweating. How long before Joan tumbled to the fact that he had got her pregnant? Her mind worked slowly enough, God knew, but it got there in the end. And then watch out. She was bigger and heavier than he, and when aroused, more savage. If she got her hands on the knife she would probably kill him.

Hazel dragged herself to the fireside and sank onto her haunches. He leaned towards her.

'Why dunna you go!' he growled through clenched teeth, glaring fiercely.

'Give me my money and I'll go.'

The positions were reversed now; she had the upper hand. He had more to fear from her than she had from him and they both knew it. She smiled.

'I hanna got your money!' he exploded, and stumped away muttering obscenities. His notions of getting his way did not extend beyond bullying. And how could you frighten someone with nothing to lose?

Joan had toothache again. She was rarely without it but this time it was worse than usual; the pain ran along her jaw into her ear and up behind her eye, which closed promptly so that she couldn't see. It made her feel like banging her head against anything in sight. The children were cuffed at more frequent intervals, and consequently bellowed more persistently. Tim received short shrift, and even Hazel, for whom she had a softer spot, was meeting with her share.

'If you dunna let up we'll all be in the Bedlam!' roared Tim. 'See what you can find for it in the market tomorrow!'

Long before daylight they were rattling and clanking on the long road to the town. Hazel was feeling better as the sickness began to ease. She had drunk her cup of heated river water this morning and had managed to keep it down. Tim was in lighter spirits too, having a good stock of new pots to sell. As the feeble sunlight straggled through the trees it glimmered and bounced off a handsome copper vessel he had finished only yesterday. The children kept out of reach, darting and chattering like magpies. Only Joan trudged solemnly, silent and sullen, stunned by her pain.

They were joined by others going to town to sell their wares, women with baskets of eggs, of apples, of round slab cheeses, even of chickens. One sturdy farm-wife passed them in long strides carrying a pole on her shoulder with two live geese tied by their feet to either end. From time to time they cursed their fate with flailing wings and harsh screechings, but their energies were soon exhausted and they dangled dejectedly upside down from the pole. A cockerel was tightly clamped under the woman's other arm, but he seemed to have submitted to his destiny; at least he was the right way up.

The market square was already bursting with people. In the shed, the scales were set up and an argument was in progress between two farmers. Pigs, goats and horses were changing hands and a fair crowd was gathering.

Tim stopped the handcart, and set about arranging his wares to show to advantage.

'Go and find a herbalist,' he threw over his shoulder without looking up. The two women went, leaving the children absorbed in scrambling under feet and wagons in search of broken fruit.

Edging past a knot of women they caught the warm delicious smell from the open bakery, golden with bread and spiced with apple pies. Hazel looked hopefully at Joan, but saw it was no use. Joan was unmoved by anything but the longing for release from her toothache. At the foot of the market cross the vendors were setting out their goods. Baskets of pumpkins, of beans, of pears, round pats of golden butter, small brilliant red crab-apples and glowing quinces. Among them they found the herbalist, a bonny woman with the face of a scrubbed apple. She sat on a milking stool among sheaves of dried lavender, heliotrope, thyme and a basket of dried lizards.

She looked penetratingly at Hazel before turning her attention to Joan's swollen face tied up like a pudding in a cloth. She sorted out a large onion, and a few tiny wizened black objects that looked like dried-up insects.

'Now, you boil the onion,' she instructed, 'then take out the middle and shove it in your ear as hot as you can stand it. That'll take the swelling down. Keep it there, mind! And these,' she fingered the little black things, 'these are very special. You take one, you put it in the hollow tooth and you bite on it. Keep biting on it till the pain is gone. Never mind the taste.'

Joan opened her mouth to protest at the price but the rush of cold air to the tooth silenced her and she paid up with one of Tibby's gold coins. It had to be Tibby's, thought Hazel mutinously. Who ever paid for a tinker's work with gold! She scowled but said nothing.

The herbalist misconstrued.

'They're very dear,' she explained, 'I can't grow those myself, have to buy them and they come from overseas. Cloves, they call them.'

Hazel nodded, disinterested. Joan pocketed her change and bit gingerly on one of the cloves, her face a battleground between hope and dread. A hot spicy scent mingled with the rank smell of the abcess on her breath as they turned to walk away.

The woman called after them, 'And what about you, my dear - raspberry leaves? Something to ease your labour?'

Hazel froze. She dared not look at Joan. The first she knew of her reaction was the blow that sent her sprawling.

'You slut!' shrieked Joan. 'You been bedding with my Tim!'

She was less than half-way to her feet when another thump sent her crashing amongst the herbs and simples. The herb woman screamed. There was confusion of movement - shouting and scuffling - Tim's voice - Joan's face distorted with fury - the flash of steel in her upraised hand - and then something thundered into her head that knocked the world from under her. She fell down through darkness into nothing.

The light faded from a wintry sky. The last of the sheep had changed hands and the stallholders packed up their wares and took to the road. Little straggles of people and farm carts wound away into the distance. One by one the windows of the houses around the square glowed with light.

Grey shapes began to move among the evil-smelling rubbish under the stocks while a down-at-heel dog pursued them half-heartedly, its mind more intent on feeding than on ratting. Three hens scratched about for something to eat, strutting daintily on their clumsy feet and crooning to each other like gossiping housewives; the dog wheeled nervously and started at every sound. The three prisoners in the stocks, cramped and chilled, tried to ease their aching limbs.

Joan was blubbering. Tim swore at her from time to time and rattled at the boards that held them; each time he did so they pinched a piece of skin on Hazel's neck.

She sat in a stubborn silence. Her head ached and his voice went through it like a rasp. Her arm was hurting her too but she could not turn her eyes to see what was wrong: her head, hands and feet were on one side of the boards and the rest of her was on the other. At some point during the endless day, unable to contain herself, she had urinated helplessly where she sat. She wondered whether the others had done the same. None of them had had food or water since daybreak, and the wafts from the bakery had been unendurable. She had even tried to catch the few whole fruits with which they had been pelted but she had soon given that up. The rotten fruit merely burst and ran down your face and the wholesome, being hard, bounced off leaving only bruises.

The dog fled abruptly, the rats and the chickens scattered as the constable came noisily towards them in his wooden pattens, clanking his keys.

Three pairs of eyes lifted hopefully at his approach. But there were still a couple of bystanders and he kept them in suspense while he delivered his long lecture before he would release them. They squirmed in frustration. With relief so near the last few moments were unbearable.

.. and don't let me catch you in our town again. You tinkers are a disgrace to the community!' he concluded pompously.

The locks were off at last.

Firecrackers danced along Hazel's spine and she could barely straighten her back. The Kettles were already starting another row. Tim would be the winner, she thought, and they would go in search of the cart before the children. She snatched up a broken apple and hobbled away in the opposite direction.

Not until she was a mile outside the town did she realise that she was being followed.

8

Hazel stopped, her whole body attuned to the task of catching the faintest sound. She could hear nothing but the rustling leaves, the soft whisper of evening breeze in the branches. She stood still, a chilly finger of fear caressing the nape of her neck. She concentrated her eyes on the gloom behind her but she could make out nothing. Yet the sensation of being watched was inescapable. She stood, irresolute; should she go back? Whoever it was was between her and the village. Yet the farther she wandered ...

She took a few more steps away and then turned suddenly, hoping to surprise a movement. This time her ears caught a few pattering steps. Not a man, then ... a wolf? The last thing you must do with a wolf was to run. That would arouse its killer instinct even if it was not hungry. Your only chance was to stand your ground.

'Who's there?' The fierce challenge came out too timid to frighten anyone but herself.

It was answered by a low whine. A dog! Only a dog. No ravenous enemy but a potential friend. As she moved back towards it, it fled.

'Here, boy!' she called. It started towards her, then veered away suspiciously as she stretched a hand towards it. She knelt on the ground, and after much coaxing and whistling, it came, the dog she had seen foraging in the debris of the stocks. Nervous and half-starved, it grovelled and flinched at her every movement. Even in the darkness she could tell that it was no beauty and it was far too cowed to offer her any protection. But it was company, another living thing to share the lonely night to come. She stroked its rough gritty coat and fondled its flea-bitten ears and hoped it would stay with her.

But when she took a handful of its scruff to lead it along with her it cringed to the ground. It rolled on its back and lay there, grinning sycophantically, frightened into idiocy. It was afraid even of her.

She sighed at last and moved on, leaving it where it lay. There was no more she could do to reassure it and it was beginning to snap hysterically. A pity, she thought, but there it was.

Suddenly with a whoosh it passed her, frolicking crazily around her skirts and yelping excitedly. It returned to her again and again until it was clear to her that she was accepted. They walked on together towards the greenwood.

Heartened, she began to think about the future.

So far she had merely been running away, retreating from the Kettles as much as from the hostile town. Just the same, return was impossible. Her hold over Tim had been blasted in the market place, and she knew she had little hope now of recovering Tibby's gold. It was a lost cause, at least for the time being, and as such must be put away. Her road lay no longer in the direction of the Kettles.

The town had even less to offer; begging from door to door was poor profit on your own, and to live by trickery like the coney-catchers you had to have a partner. And anyway, she was banished. An outlaw, she thought, and smiled to herself, conjuring up a picture of a female, ragged, pregnant Robin Hood. She could still go back to the monastery. Bent Meg could have little use for her now - but then neither had anyone else.

The only one there who had seemed to care about her was the Patch, and he had appeared to grow madder by the minute. How much of his madness was the faking of the Abraham Man, how much was genuine? She had never been sure. Perhaps even he, didn't know. The last time she had seen him he had confided in her that the Abbot was lying in state in the lodge. He was arranging dead flowers in something held in his hand, which she recognised with nausea as one of Tibby's shoes . . . His sanity hung on too slender a thread to offer her any safe refuge. The unknown future, she decided, was preferable to a return to the past.

There would be nuts and berries enough in the woods at this time of the year; for the moment in any case her appetite was quenched by the events of the day. Her left eye was closing and a dark stain marked the painful area of her arm. The knife must have caught it before she was knocked unconscious. Joan had been ready to kill her, she thought with a shiver. She wondered briefly who had saved her but it made no difference now.

With her new-found companion she made her way across the moonlit common and on through the wasteland. Were there really wolves in the forest? She did not know. But she knew well enough that there were wolves in the world outside. And she had seen enough of people to learn that she had less to fear from rutting stags than she had from rutting men. What was it Nan had said? 'Between Black John and the stags I'll give you till Michaelmas.' And Michaelmas was nearly here. Be that as it may, her need tonight was rest. Tonight she would recover. Tomorrow she would make what plans she could.

After the noise and sweat of the town, the ancient stench of the ordure under the stocks, the forest was blessedly peaceful. It smelt of bracken and blackberries and dried leaves. Vast tree trunks swept upward on all sides to fan out like the vaulting of a roof, so remote and lofty under the evening sky that the stars seemed caught in their branches.

The two of them tramped on patiently, in silence. The deeper into the forest they penetrated, the warmer seemed the air, the drier the ground, as they left the dewfall behind them. When they could walk no further, they curled up and shared their warmth and their fleas until the morning.

'So this is where you got to!'

The woman's voice crashed in on Hazel's dream. Joan! The knife! She wakened in a flash of alarm and started up violently, casting about for something with which to defend herself.

'Don't panic, no one's going to hurt you!' The woman laughed, not unkindly. 'Poor creature, it's not to be wondered at, after yesterday.'

Hazel shaded her eyes against the sun and looked at her searchingly.

'Oh yes, you've seen me before. At the market, with my herbs, remember?'

Hazel remembered. Those herbs had been the start of all the trouble.

'I see you've got my dog.' Hazel looked around to see the animal slinking out of sight. Her heart sank, and she said reluctantly, 'If it's yours, you'd best take it, then.'

'Lor' bless you, child, I haven't come for the dog. I was sorry for you, what with a day in the stocks and everything. This morning I find you not a mile from my own cottage door. So I ask myself if there's not something I can do.'

'Don't you think you've done enough?' said Hazel bluntly. 'You and your raspberry-leaf tea!'

The woman looked at her sharply. Then she smiled back. 'That was what I meant,' she admitted. 'I felt as I'd got you into trouble I owed you a good turn, so to speak. That's why I was keeping an eye open for you. And talking of eyes, that's a beautiful black one you got there! Come on to the cottage and I'll dress it for you - and your poor little arm.' She leaned down to help Hazel to her feet; though ageing she was strong and her arm was welcome. 'I've simples enough at home to put you right as a trivet.'

'I - I canna pay,' Hazel faltered.

She could not have said what held her back, but there was something. The herb woman was kind enough - perhaps too kind. Was that it? Others had offered her help and there had always been something behind it, something to beware of. Except, of course, Tibby; but then Tibby had known her and Margery all their lives.

'You needn't pay. Like I said, I owe you a good turn.'

Her arm was around Hazel's waist, gently drawing her along, her voice warm with the promise of good firelight and friendly talk.

'The dog-' she protested feebly, for it was nowhere to be seen.

'She'll have gone along home on her own, she knows her way from here.'

'She seems frightened of you.'

'Not of me, no! She's a timid creature - and my Hal's a bit noisy about the house. He shouts at her when he's a mind to and she runs off. Always comes back, though. What's there to be frightened of in me?' She laughed. 'My, but you're a suspicious child! Though I daresay you've been treading a stony path, so I'll forgive you. Just stop your fretting - take your luck where you find it, that's what I always say. Come on, now, let's see you looking happy. What do you suppose I'm about to do, chop you up and eat you? There's not enough meat on you for that!'

Hazel looked up into the rosy face with its merry eyes and was beguiled in spite of herself.

'I'm sorry,' she said. By way of reparation, she added, 'I'm Hazel.'

'And I'm Mother Cropper,' smiled the woman, 'and I reckon now we're friends.'

They strolled along companionably. Mother Cropper asked,

'And what have you been doing with yourself till now - besides bedding with the tinker, I mean ? You don't look like the likes of them to begin with.'

Hazel coloured. 'I hanna been bedding with the tinker, for a start. It wasna like that at all. Joan was good to me - I wouldn't have betrayed her.'

'So how did it happen, then?'

She hesitated. Then decided on telling as much as was wise to tell; of her loss of home and parents and her subsequent life with the Kettles, but avoiding the Abbey and her mother's dreadful death. When she came to the memory of the rape, she began to stammer. Mother Cropper hugged her and said quickly, 'There, there, don't distress yourself. I can tell well enough what happened.

You poor child, and not a soul you could talk to. Never you mind. All you need now is a bit of sympathy, a bit of comfort, and you'll be right as rain. I daresay we can find you a little corner by the fire.'

Hazel's eyes brimmed. For a long time she said nothing. She simply nodded and returned the hug.

They arrived at the cottage at last. It stood in a little clearing in the heart of the greenwood, its doorway framed in honeysuckle that climbed on up to battle with the brambles for possession of the thatch. Its one window, protected by shutters, gave onto a patch of ground grown thick with herbs. Hazel could smell lavender, heliotrope, thyme and many others which she could not name. Above all, from the interior of the cot, a savoury odour of meat came to greet her, reminding her stomach to awake and clamour for food. Trying to ignore it, she said, 'Why do you live so far away from everyone else?'

Again, the quick, penetrating glance from Mother Cropper. 'Well, it's my Hal, you see. Woodcutting's his trade so we have to live near the trees. And I've plenty of room to grow herbs and make remedies and a nice bit of privacy to do it. We like our bit of privacy, do Hal and I.' Hazel was silent; it seemed to her odd that if they cherished their solitude she was welcome as she appeared to be. At that moment the cottage door opened and a man stood framed in the doorway. He was tall, raw-boned and young enough to be Mother Cropper's son. He challenged them with, 'What we got here, then?'

Mother Cropper answered quickly, and her tone sounded hasty, defensive.

'Just a poor wench I found lost in the greenwood - with child, she is.'

He had seemed about to give tongue but at the words 'with child' he closed his mouth abruptly, and the two of them exchanged a glance that Hazel could not read. Then, 'Come in, my dear, and take your rest by the fire,' he said, his eyes dead as stones, ushering them inside. He picked up an adze, tossed it into the leather sling with the rest of his tools, shouldered a massive axe, and was gone.

Hazel sat sipping her ale while Mother Cropper bathed her arm.

'Not too much of that till I finish,' she was warned, 'or you'll start the bleeding again.'

'I'll be careful,' she said. 'Was that your son?'

'What of it?' The rejoinder was sharp, and immediately it was softened into a joke. 'Why, don't I look old enough?' 'It wasn't that,' Hazel was embarrassed. 'It's just -well, I can see he'd rather be on his own. I think, when you've finished, I'd best be moving on.'

'You take no notice of him. Men have their queer little ways but he'll get over it. And where would you be moving on to, may I ask? And without even a bite of that lovely stew in the cauldron? You stay where you are, my child, until it's cooked. That won't be till sundown, so there'll be a bit of nice bread and some cheese to keep you going until then. I'll warrant you haven't eaten since yesterday.'

Between rest and warmth and good cosseting Hazel began at length to relax. This was a one-room cottage like Margery's, and as such it felt like home. The furnishings, the spinning-wheel, the woodman's tools all added to the illusion, and as the day wore on she felt almost as if her wanderings had never been. Only the awareness of the baby within her reminded her that this was not so; yet in a strange way even that seemed natural.

At dusk, the man returned. Silent, though not openly hostile, he took his meats with them, and when Mother Cropper produced some wine - 'I always keep a little drop stowed away for a special occasion' - he mulled and spiced it for them all to share. Hazel felt her eyelids drooping, trying to keep awake on the hard straight chair. The next she knew she was being carried upwards and carefully lowered on to warm gentle hay. She heard vaguely the buzz of their voices in the room below. At one point they arose to a sudden crescendo.

'I tell you it's a boy,' insisted the woman's voice. 'I'll make sure of it tomorrow.'

She wondered briefly why it was important. And then she was asleep.

The night's sleep restored her and she awoke fresh. She shook the hay from her clothes and hair and lowered herself down the ladder to help her new friend with the chores.

Hal had gone out early and Mother Cropper was scrubbing his trencher in a bucket outside the door.

'Hazel, help yourself to bread and ale,' she called over her shoulder.

She found the ale easily enough, hanging in a skin by the open window. The bread was another matter. Tall cupboards flanked the window, but they were not filled with food. They revealed a strange assortment of bowls, knives of varying shapes, and little hammers with the heads rounded off. She recognised the jar of cloves, and a basket of dried lizards she had last seen at the market. There were strange substances in jars that she could not identify; and at the dark back of the cupboard her hand met a board, quite small, with what felt like a lump of something plastered to it. Carefully she drew it out. What she saw made her stare in horror. It was a frog, nailed by its paws in the form of crucifixion, its mouth gaping.

She started and almost dropped it as Mother Cropper appeared in the doorway.

'What have you got?' Her voice had an edge which was quickly sheathed in a smile.

'I - I was looking for the bread,' Hazel said. It was too late to pretend; better to brazen it out. 'I found this.' She held out her hand and the woman took the frog from her, glanced at it and tossed it aside.

'That's my Hal again,' she said confidingly. 'Not partial to animals, he isn't - specially vermin. Gets a bit carried away sometimes - has his funny little ways, as I said - well, gets a bit queer, you know. Always been the same, ever since he was a baby. Tell you what, my dear. Best not to let him know you found that. Ashamed, he'd be, to think you knew about him. Well, he don't mean to be cruel, it's just his little way. Upset you, did it? Some folks are frightened of frogs, I know, but it's quite dead now, it can't hurt you. Not about to faint, are you? Here, come and sit down a minute, you look quite sickly.' She bustled about cheer fully, found the bread and poured ale for Hazel and herself. 'There, now.'

After a moment, she got up, rummaged in a corner and came back with a needle on a long piece of thread.

'Now, we'll just make sure the baby's all right.'

She placed a stool under Hazel's feet and held the needle suspended over her body. After a time it began to swing as if a breeze had caught it; then it started to move in a circle, gathering momentum as it went.

'Ah-ha!' muttered Mother Cropper to herself.

Hazel looked up. 'What does that mean?'

'That means the little fellow's doing fine.'

Something from last night stirred in Hazel's mind. Something from the edge of sleep ...

'Is it a boy, then?' she asked.

Mother Cropper's round eyes opened wide and innocent. 'Now, my dear,' she protested, 'how in the world would I be knowing that?'

The rest of the day passed uneventfully. Mother Cropper seemed eager to initiate her into the arts of herbal cures, and spent the morning explaining the uses of the bunched herbs that hung in fragrant tassels from the roof- beams. Lavender, wild garlic, the common cooking herbs, rue, bergamot, with these she was familiar. But there were others - tansy, saffron, mountain flax, even violets - at whose uses she could only guess. And she almost certainly recognised a bundle of hemlock half obscured in a corner. A tentative enquiry brought a close-lipped reply.

'Can't run before you can walk. Ask no questions, you'll be told no lies.'

Hazel felt strongly that the old woman had something to hide. She would have to tread carefully and hold her tongue. Maybe poisonous herbs were used in medicines. .. if not, she had better look the other way. It would be madness to throw away food and lodging unless she had to. Besides, this trade she had a chance to learn must be prosperous - these Croppers lived better than anyone else she knew. And armed with that, she need never starve again.

She thought long and hard whilst pounding cloves and peppercorns with slow, inexpert hands. It was one thing to appear conveniently blind: quite another to be so. After supper, she resolved, she would stay them out and investigate the mysterious cupboard; she had her pretext ready. She was rested now, and wanted to stay up to enjoy the company of her hosts. But in the event, plied with good food and the richly spiced wine, she was once more swallowed by sleep, and found herself again being carried up to the roof-space.

The same thing happened night after night. She was never able to stay awake for long enough to snatch a moment alone. Yet always after the first heavy drowse had worn off, she became aware of a buzz of voices in the room below. They droned and tangled with the threads of her dreaming, making little sense. Yet she was left with the impression that on occasions there were more than two people downstairs.

Once she thought she heard knocking, and the muffled sounds of someone being bundled inside and hushed in urgent whispers. Curious, she crawled through the hay to where she could peer down unobserved.

Three figures were huddled over the table. In its centre she could just make out something bright: a mirror - but no, it shone black as jet in the fitful light of the dips.

Mother Cropper seemed to be gazing into it, murmuring in a disembodied voice.

'-and beyond the water-'

Her voice stopped abruptly. Her overturned chair rasped the rushes and Hazel ducked swiftly down behind the hay. The woman could not possibly have seen her, nor had anyone else looked up - but clearly she had known she was being watched.

She lay still, heart thudding. A foot creaked the first rung of the ladder. She shut her eyes. Should she try to regain the hollow, still warm, where she had been left - could she roll there without a give-away sound? There might be time-

It was too late.

Her nostrils caught the goatish reek of Hal Cropper just in time to save her from starting at the violent nudge that assaulted the small of her back.

She made no sound. Another rough shove sent her rolling. She kept her eyes closed - not too tightly, eyelids relaxed - desperately feigning sleep.

She stopped. Spreadeagled. On her back.

He was scrutinising her face - he had to be ...

She waited for the sound of his going that would release

her. Would he never move? He was waiting - waiting to trap her ... She could not lie motionless forever and he knew it .. . she felt a sneeze building up. She willed herself not to give way to it, her eyes began to ooze, her nose to dribble, her throat was filling. She must either swallow or sneeze - either would be her undoing - at last it was too much.

An almighty sneeze broke loose and her body jerked violently upwards to an inevitable collision with the man crouched over her. No one was there.

She sat for a moment, confused, before she realised her mistake. Of course he wasn't there. He had no need to wait for her to betray herself. She had already done so.

When he had shoved her and she had not moved, he had known that she was faking; a real sleeper would have been awakened - at least would have stirred, mumbled, moved away- and she had not. He knew. And he had said nothing- why?

Even more disconcerting, he had vanished from her sleeping quarters without her knowing it. If he could do that, he could appear in the same way ...

The silence below was broken by whispers and she heard Mother Cropper say guardedly, 'More tomorrow-'

More what? The sound of the door opening, someone going out. That must be it: more talk tomorrow. Or was it?

Was it more wine, perhaps, to make her sleep longer? What was happening down there that she was not allowed to know about? Uneasy with questions, it was a long time before she slept.

In the ordinary light of the next morning it did not take her long to attach a meaning to 'more tomorrow'. She had been knocked out by drugged wine before. But why? Since Mother Cropper was prepared to share her wise woman's secrets with her, what more was there to hide? It was hard to believe that she was coy about her relationship with her son - if son he was. She treated him quite openly as her lover and her every look warned Hazel to keep her distance - as if she hadn't had enough of men! So, there had to be something else ...

She sighed. She didn't want to find something that would mean she had to go on running. She wanted to stay here, to sit tight and eat well and keep a roof over her head until she was delivered. She dreaded the thought of walking the road, of scratching to live on nuts and roots, of facing her labour alone and leaving a stillborn child in a lonely ditch. Perhaps the old woman was a poisoner. Perhaps she did dabble in the black arts . . . All she asked was not to be involved; to be allowed to turn her head and pretend she did not know. Suppose she went to Mother Cropper, said to her just that? It would be madness. Her every instinct warned her so. And yet-

'You know, don't you?'

Mother Cropper's voice made her jump guiltily.

'Know-what?' she stammered, playing for time to think.

The woman smiled confidingly. 'Why, that we're two of a kind, of course.'

Hazel swallowed. This was the last thing she had expected. 'We?'

'You and me. You never thought I could see into the future, too. Not till last night, that is.'

'Last night-' Hazel's throat felt dry and her voice came with difficulty. She floundered out of her depth. 'What do you mean, "too"? I canna ...'

The smile deepened approvingly. 'That's a sensible girl to keep her own counsel. "A still tongue keepeth a wise head," like they say. But you don't have to keep no secrets from me, my dear. I know what you are. You'll have the Mark on you somewhere, I've no doubt.'

Hazel held tight to the table edge while the room wheeled around her. The persuasive voice continued.

'We could do much together, my dear. I with my knowledge, you with your natural gift. We could have power. Power....'

The woman's face was transformed. Her eyes glowed dark and hollow, became caves, prowled by strange and fearful desires that Hazel could not read.

'1 - I dunno ...'

'Not yet.' Mother Cropper gazed through her to something beyond, something that renewed her youth. 'Not yet, but you will. They fear us, the lowly ones, because we have the power. They fear us and hunt us, but they cannot harm us.' She held up a hand to silence Hazel's protest. 'Not us, not the real ones, only the fools and the pretenders. We are stronger than them. Stronger than anyone....' She leaned forward, her whole body seemed to pulsate with some excitement from within herself, and she began to rock faintly as if to its rhythm, her arms clasped tightly around her body, to and fro, to and fro, absorbed in her own emotion, as if no one else were there. Hazel crept away, leaving her still rocking, her eyes still rapt, and moved towards the door. She wanted air, space, to think, to know what to do. She felt trapped, endangered, closed in upon . . . With her hand on the latch, she turned back.

Mother Cropper was watching her, her eyes dark with secrets.

'That's right,' she breathed, and waited, as if she were coaxing an animal. Hazel stood immobilised for a moment. Her instincts told her to escape into the open air. Her feet began slowly taking her back towards the woman in the chair.

'What do you want?' The challenge was meaningless. Even as she spoke she was extending her hands, palm upwards, as if robbed of her will.

Mother Cropper did not take her eyes from Hazel's. It was as if they were locked together like wrestlers. 'That's good.' Her voice was low, even, soothing as a draught of mandrake. 'You hear me when I call. We make a start.'

9

A dazzle of light pierced Hazel's eyes and drove like a long sharp knife into her throbbing head. Painfully, she turned away, wondering why there was light at all in the dark loft she was used to. She groped for the hay and met only rushes, the stone edge of the hearth. Her mouth felt sour, her stomach twisted evilly. The child lay within her as if dead. With an effort, she swallowed back the acid water that welled up from her throat and lay still.

She was not in the loft. She was downstairs. And she was not alone. She forced her reluctant eyes to open a crack; the Croppers were sprawled on the floor, the empty wineskin beside them. Hal slept face downwards, half obscuring the woman, who in an attempt to escape his weight had twisted her head sideways and was snoring. The others ... where were the others? What others, what was she thinking of? But there had been others. She closed her eyes and drew deep breaths, trying to clear her mind.

There had been others. And there had been ... things. She did not want to dwell on them. But they had happened just the same. The things ... and people. And animals, pitiful and patient, lacking the wit to run away ... her mind cringed away. There had been much in the past months that was nauseating.

She had floundered through it like a horse led blinkered through a fire until it had finally culminated in the nightmare of last night. The Sabbath. The word brought it all shrieking back to her, she rolled her face onto her arm and tried to find refuge in sleep. There had been pleasure, too. Acute and new to her. And a sensation of floating, of drifting on the air... And bound up with the pleasure, something she did not want to remember. The floating, flying - yes, the feeling of flying - that had been all pleasure. Even now she felt slightly unstable, as though the earth were tilting under her, tilting and gently swinging.... only now there was a queasy undercurrent, anything but pleasant.

What had happened last night? It was difficult to separate memories from dreams. She remembered the flying ointment concocted from the red and white spotted toadstools she had thought to be deadly. Stewed and distilled and compounded with dormouse fat. She remembered her hands and feet being anointed with it, then her thighs and between her breasts, and how the movements had become more intimate, more caressing, as she had found herself more and more helpless to resist, her eyelids drooping as though drugged.... her thoughts veered and swayed. She was again naked astride the broomstick, the caresses mounting to tension, the tension to excitement, the excitement to a white-hot urgency until her body shattered into slivers of fire and ice and she was flying, flying through the night air with her spirit singing for joy among the stars ... this was magic indeed. She could see music, hear the vibrant throbbing colours of fire ... every fibre, every nerve in her thrummed in response ...

Hal's voice jagged her awake.

'Wine!' he demanded hoarsely. He groped for the skin and sucked at it noisily, then threw it away in disgust.

Hazel kept her eyes shut. She did not want to talk. She wanted to sort out her thoughts.

Mother Cropper's voice said, 'Hold your noise, can't you. My head aches.'

So does mine, thought Hazel, determined not to be roused. Now it was all ugly again, dirty and disgusting, like the backside of the Goat. The Goat! She remembered now, the creature neither animal nor man - what was it? She did not know or want to know. Only to blot out the past months as though they had never been, to return to some sort of normal life, even if it meant starvation. Last night had finished her. Enough was enough.

After last night, it was no longer possible to persuade herself that their 'magic' was a harmless make-believe; whatever the results, the intent was malignant, earnest, evil, the practices unspeakably foul. She felt dirtied. Even the remembered joy filled her with shame and disgust, tied up as it was with so much her mind recoiled from. She had been drifting in the tow of a powerful tide, warmed and fed and housed, living easy, without effort. Now, abruptly, she glimpsed the rocks ahead. She must go. She would bide her time until the moment came. She had not really been watching for it until now; it was bound to come. When it did, she would slip away - and she would take the dog with her, before it had its pups. They could look elsewhere for the brains of the newborn they wanted for that charm of theirs! The wretched animal should have her pups in the peace of the greenwood. There was time yet; she would make her plans and when the time was ripe, she would go. She was stronger now, after the months of good food, and her time was not yet. Spring was near, and she could survive a few weeks out of doors; if Joan Kettle could bear her children under the skies it must be possible. In the last resort she could still find shelter at the Abbey. Pier decision reached, she felt better. She lay quietly in the darkness behind her eyelids, making her schemes. Contentedly, she dozed, and the room darkened.

From time to time she was aware of sounds about her; Hal got up muttering, and made water in a corner. She heard him lumbering drunkenly about the room, overturning stools and barking his shins. Then he subsided again, she heard them both drinking, belching, mumbling . . . and then silence. He had evidently found another skin of wine, or perhaps cider. Whatever it was put them both back to sleep and Hazel was left in peace.

'She thinks it's the dog...

The cackling laughter echoed through the silence.

Hazel's eyes flicked open. She raised herself a little to listen. No sound. No movement. Her companions lay like fallen trees. She lay blinking in the darkness. What had she heard? Someone had spoken, laughed - or was it a dream? She leaned over and peered into Mother Cropper's sleeping face. It was smiling faintly. Which one of them had been dreaming? Had she caught some mysterious echo of the other woman's dream? She shivered. That laughter had been frightening. Derisive and sinister, it had torn like a cry of alarm through her doze. 'She thinks it's the dog ...' She stared into the darkness and her mind slowly cleared, her thoughts coming truly into focus for the first time after months of drugged sleep, self-deception and confusion. What was it that was so important about the dog? It was pregnant; they wanted its pups for their repulsive work ... the brains of the new-born ...

'She thinks it's the dog ...'

She froze into full wakefulness as the pieces of the puzzle clicked together. Mother of God, she must get away! There was not a moment to lose! For the first time she was awake while her captors slept: it was a chance she would never have again.

Her instinct was to get up and run, to fly in panic from this dreadful place. She had to force herself to move slowly, slowly, as she edged towards the door. Every moment was an agony of suspense. At any perceptible sound or movement they might awake. Sweating with fear, she manoeuvred her awkward shape across the rushes until her hands found the wood of the door. She pulled herself to her knees, leaning against it, groping with moist fingers for the latch, praying that the bar was not in place across the door. She released the breath she had been holding as she found the bar leaning free against the lintel. Next to it was something that moved, threatening to fall. Quickly, she caught it, exploring its shape in the darkness. It was the broom. As she laid it down she noticed a stickiness on the rounded nub of the handle. She sniffed her fingers. Flying ointment! Disgust scalded her as she recognised the source of her fantasies of last night. Now she had anger to add to her fear. She found the latch, held it still to avoid its telltale rattle, and eased herself to her feet. It was not easy to work her thickened body out through the door without opening it to the point where it creaked, or letting in a rush of cold air to arouse the sleepers. Still holding the latch-bar, she raised it carefully clear of its cradle and pulled the heavy door inwards. It swung, reluctant but mercifully quiet on its hinges, wide enough to allow her to squeeze through. Fresh air blessed her face, filling her with new life. She stepped towards freedom-

'And where do you think you're going?' rasped Mother Cropper's voice.

'Air,' moaned Hazel, and thrust her fingers into her throat to make herself vomit. She brought up nothing but the sound was convincing.

'Come back to bed,' growled the woman.

'Coming,' Hazel moaned again, and waited.

Now Hal was stirring. She heard him mutter something and lunge to his feet. She could never out-run him. She glanced about her in desperation. Nearby was a bunker he had built for storing wood. The next moment she was inside it, jammed between the hard logs and the lid. Her heart thudded so loudly she was afraid they could hear it from outside. A spider ran out of the bark and across her face. She willed herself not to move.

They were both up now, blundering about the clearing, muttering and cursing.

'She's gone-'

'What woke you?'

'Heard her.'

'I heard nothing.'

'Heard her thoughts, blockhead! She knows-'

'Why didn't you bar the door?'

'Why didn't you?'

Hazel wrenched her mind away from her surroundings, the box, the spider ... Instead she concentrated fiercely, pretending she was out in the open, running through the woods on the path that led back towards the town. She imagined herself panting, the soft ground thudding under her feet, the tree roots bruising her toes, brambles tearing her skin, the weight within her jolting, aching ...

Mother Cropper's voice said, 'Wait - wait, hold your noise!'

'Whasamatter?'

'I'm getting something ...'

The effort of concentration brought the sweat out on Hazel's forehead. She felt the heaviness of her legs, her dragging feet, the breath tearing through her in great sobs.

'After her! She's running back towards the town.'

She stifled her elation and kept the picture strong in her mind - a branch slashing her face -stumbling, recovering - struggling on again ... As if at a distance she heard their voices calling drunkenly to each other, the dog barking excitedly at the end of her rope, their sleep-laden footsteps blundering noisily through the undergrowth.

Until the sounds had long faded she held clear in her mind the image of herself exhaustedly running towards the haven of the town.

Without conscious thought, she climbed out of the bunker, eased her cramped limbs, and set off in the opposite direction. As she passed the dog, silent now with nose on paws, she slipped off the rope tether over its head. Its tail beat twice. Without a sound it rose and followed her.

10

The first time that hunger forced her to do battle with the dog for possession of a rabbit, she hardly knew what to do with it when she had won it.

It was still warm, still an animal. She had nothing with which to skin it and no means of cooking it. She could not eat it fur and all as the dog would. She shut her eyes, hooked a finger in a tear in the skin and pulled. It was much tougher than she expected, that soft furry pelt, but eventually she got it moving. When it was reduced to meat she opened her eyes again. She pulled the loose skin up over the head so that the face could not reproach her.

All the time the dog watched her, ears pricked, head swivelling from side to side in an agony of suspense. It was her rabbit. But the courage to go and take it back had been beaten out of her long ago. She whined, made little feigning rushes towards it only to wheel away at the last moment. Finally she dropped her head on her forepaws and drooled hopelessly.

Hazel glanced up and caught her eye. She looked at the slimy red mass in her hands and tasted a tentative finger. The smell and taste of raw blood turned her stomach. But if she lit a fire....

She got it going and turned to pick up the rabbit. It was

gone. The dog came grovelling towards her, beating the ground with her tail and licking satisfied chops.

She accepted her loss philosophically. But the next time a rabbit arrived she was ready with a sharp stone and a fire. This time she gave the dog as her share the parts she felt were uneatable, in the hope of coming to a workable agreement. It was hard to tell whether or not the plan bore fruit. Rabbits continued to arrive from time to time and she did not have too much difficulty gaining possession of them; but as often as not the hunter returned to sleep off a full belly by the fire, having clearly devoured the spoils single-handed.

But there were berries and roots, of which she at least knew now which were safe to eat. And her time with the tinkers stood her in good stead, for it had taught her something of survival in the wild. She could make a fire without the tinderbox she had once thought indispensable. She could wedge a burning brand in a crevice of rock and have light. She had learned to eat squirrels, hedgehogs and even snakes. With her total lack of implements she was living in the Stone Age, but she was living.

March had come in with late flurries of sleet that had briefly turned to snow, drifting in veils between the gaunt branches of the trees. Only a few flakes had penetrated to where she and the dog had set up house.

After leaving the cottage, she had made for the brook and waded up it through the icy water, leaving no track that could be followed. She had been well rested after the long sleep and had plodded ail night and much of the day, the dog following patiently behind her. At a point where the stream forked, she took a tributary that splashed down over rocks and followed it uphill to its source. Here she sat down on a boulder and did some thinking.

Shelter she must have; water she could not leave too far away. She looked up the towering rock face for some niche into which she could creep for the night, something to keep her hidden from wind and wild beasts until she could contrive something better. The rocks stood in bald rectangles as if hewn for building by giants and then abandoned. In the crevices grew saplings of birch and hazel, and long strands of bramble entangled the brushwood. Dusk was falling. She heaved herself wearily to her feet and began a systematic search of the outcrop.

She had all but given up hope when she found it. A narrow opening, concealed by a straggling bush, into which the dog plunged, disappeared, and bounced out again wagging her tail. Hazel leaned down and peered in. She could see nothing. She picked up a stone and threw it. It seemed to travel a fair way before striking rock. She came out and searched about for dry wood. When she had a brand burning she returned to the opening, leaned in and thrust the light before her. Inside, the cave opened out into a chamber big enough to stand up in. The floor was dry and sandy. Cautiously she went in.

Outside the frosty dusk was gathering; a cold mist rose from the ground and blurred the edges of everything. In the cave the smoke from the brand hung in the roof and sent the insects scurrying to their cracks. The air was warmer in here, but it smelt musty and she could see in a corner a little pile of bones. For a moment she hesitated. Then she thought of the alternatives. Suppressing a shiver, she set about making a fire.

Here, with bracken for a bed and the dog for company, she stayed. She petted the dog, talking to it, curling up with it for comfort at night, hoping to attach it to her by affection, realising that although she depended upon it very heavily it had no need of her unless she could create one. Since it seemed to have no name, she called it Scrambler, and after a time during which it would look about with every expression of interest to see who was being called, it finally got the idea and began to answer to it. It was a friendly, lolloping, feather-headed animal, and though she had no illusions about its value as a guard-dog she found its company reassuring.

All the time her body swelled inexorably. When she had stopped being sick in the mornings she had hoped briefly that it was all a mistake; but she knew she had been deceiving herself about that as about so much else. All the signs were there, and if there was one thing she knew about it was babies. What would become of her when it was born she dared not think about. Her mind shied away from it like a frightened animal.

The diet was not the best for an expectant mother. But it was excellent for Scrambler, who grew sleek and glossy. As spring sent a prickle of green through the underbrush she grew restless and absented herself for longer and longer periods. Finally she did not come back at all.

Throughout the first day Hazel waited. She called, 'Here, pretty-pretty-pretty-' She broke off abruptly as. memory jolted, hearing Margery's reproach. 'Here, Scrambler, come along, girl!'

She whistled. She searched as far afield as she dared without losing her bearings on the cave. Perhaps the dog was lying up somewhere, injured. If she could find her, and bring her back … but she found nothing.

When darkness fell she built a fire in the mouth of the cave, to guide the dog home. And for warmth. And as a barrier between her and the forest outside, which was eerie as it had not been before. She fell asleep still hoping for the dog's return.

The next day, her stomach grinding with hunger, she went in search of food. But there was nothing. So deep into the forest had they penetrated that she could gather nothing but a handful of nuts. Where Scrambler had gone for rabbits she did not know. She must have roamed for miles.

By evening of the second day she was desperate. Scrambler had been her protector, companion, provider - her mainstay. Without her she could not survive. Her anxiety was so deep that she could not rest. She walked miles without hope or purpose while the baby, as starved as she, thrashed despairingly. She found herself talking aloud, crying helplessly, 'What am I going to do? God help me, what am I going to do?'

She remembered the wooden crucifix that had hung around her neck throughout her childhood. She had stitched it into her bodice to protect her from the Croppers, concealed between two folds of the material. She found it now and ripped it free, falling on her knees with it held before her.

'Please, please, help me! Show me what to do. I didna want to do all them horrible things - they made me - I ran off as soon as I could - please help me, please!'

What she was hoping for she hardly knew. When darkness drove her back to the cave she flung herself down in an angry storm that matched the wild wind roaring and crashing in the branches above her.

'What's the use! You dunna care, you dunna care about me, you dunna dare nothing! Nobody cares about me, not even the dog!' She sobbed and flailed the earth with her fists. 'Help me, somebody help me - anybody, help!'

When her hysteria abated, she sobbed herself calm. In the quiet she seemed to hear her own voice distantly ... 'Here, pretty-pretty-pretty ...'

At last, cold and drained, she sat up. She scrubbed her nose with the back of her hand, and numbly kindled a fire. Crouching over it, she knelt bruisingly on the crucifix and with a gesture of impatience she picked it up and flung it away from her. What was the use of it - a useless ornament? It had not helped her against the Croppers. Stupid to think it could help her now.

'What's the good of praying?' she said aloud, and the sound of her own voice startled her. 'There's nobody up there listening.'

She asked herself what Tom would have done in her situation. Tom would have felled trees, built a house, set traps - she could do none of these things. And Margery ... Margery would have prayed. 'When all else fails, God will provide.' Fine provision he had made for her, thought Hazel bitterly - they said that even the Devil took care of his own. He listened, you could be sure of that - you only had to look at the Croppers. Oh, yes, he listened all right, crouching in his corner, grinning in the dark, waiting ...

She got up and went to look for the crucifix. It was gone. After a perfunctory search she gave up and returned to the fire, where she sat hugging herself unhappily. What did it matter, anyway?

'All right, have it your way,' she said wearily. 'And if you're so clever, let's see what you can do!'

She knew she was talking to nothing. In that moment of despair she did not believe in anything. There was nothing to help her but herself.

Outside, the wind had dropped, leaving a hush in which the falling of a leaf could be clearly heard.

She lay listening to the night sounds of the forest with a new and tingling awareness. The coughing cry of a fox sounded unexpectedly sinister. The shuffling of a badger in the bank brought her upright with apprehension, jerking her out of the uneasy sleep into which she had slipped.

She retreated to the rear of the cave and pressed her back up hard against the wall. After a time she dozed again.

She awoke in the certain knowledge that she was being watched. She was lying on her side facing the mouth of the cave and as she looked a trickle of fear ran down her spine. The mouth of the cave was filled with a dark shape.

She lay motionless, trying to analyse the outline. She made out the shape of ears, a muzzle, hackles faintly raised ... it was not a wolf. The glimmer of false dawn showed that the coat was smooth and densely black. It was not her dog. It was not, she thought with a chill, like any dog she had ever seen. There was something un-dog about it; something sinister in the way it watched her in absolute stillness. Its presence was overpowering. Its eyes did not glow fitfully like those of an animal in the shifting light. They burned into her, blazing with a sulphury yellow like the eyes of a demon.

Her hand flew automatically to where the crucifix had lived. She remembered with a shock what she had done. Holy Mother, she must have been mad!

She drew in her breath with a gasp - and in that second the creature vanished. She did not hear it go; there was no familiar patter of paws - one moment it was there and the next it was gone, leaving her in a cold sweat of terror.

She scrambled again to where she had thrown the crucifix, frantically searching the earth with her hands. She must have been out of her mind! To have called upon the powers of darkness - and she witch-marked, and with Tibby's sins upon her as well as her own! And after all she had learned with the Croppers!

'Forgive me,' she heard herself babbling. 'Forgive me, take me back...

It was nowhere in the cave. And when she looked out into the forest she shrank back. It no longer seemed vast and empty but populated and menacing, filled with a darkness that crowded in on her, a silence she could have reached out and touched.

The fire had died down to a whisper of ash. She dared not go outside to get more wood. She propped herself upright against the rear wall of the cave and sat there, wide-eyed and shivering, until the sun came up.

With the first light she pulled her rags around her and went out. There were no fresh tracks near the mouth of the cave. No animal could really have been there, she reasoned with herself. With the sunlight dappling down and the trees filled with the fish-wife chatter of birds, it was easy to tell herself that last night's horrors were a nightmare ... But dog or no dog, if she stayed in the forest alone she would die. She went to the spring and filled her stomach with water. It was better than nothing to stave off hunger pains. Then she set off downstream, determined to put as much distance as possible between her and the cave. She reasoned that if she followed the stream, since the dog would not go far from water and the town lay on the river, she was bound sooner or later to come up with one or the other; either way she would soon have company, and no one would recognise her without the tinkers. She strode out bravely in the encouraging light of day. With her skirts held high and her bodice-laces at their furthest stretch she waded all day along its meandering course; at nightfall she was hungry, exhausted and still alone. And she was still in the heart of the forest.

With the lengthening of the shadows her uneasiness returned and she was thankful that at least she was a long way from the cave. But she must find some sort of shelter for the night.

She clambered out of the stream and spent a moment contemplating her feet, pale and pearly from the water, quite a new colour. Then, keeping the sound of water within hearing, she went in search of a hiding-place. The ground here was flat, soft and peaty and devoid of rocks. But in a clearing she found a wych elm. It was very old and leaned at a crazy angle. But its trunk was some twelve paces around the base and might well be hollow. She dragged a fallen branch and swung it against the trunk, to test for the right sound and to flush out anything that might be lurking inside it. It would do, she decided. Any refuge was better than none.

The light was going fast. Wearily she hauled herself up to where the tangle of branches writhed about like a mad woman's hair, and peered down into the dark interior. She could see nothing. She broke a long twig and reached down with it, listening for a response. Any nook in the wild, she had learned, was likely to be lived in, and while she was resigned to sharing with squirrels and spiders she was not about to try conclusions with an adder. There was nothing there. She sat where she was for a moment, resting and looking about her. In the morning she would continue her quest, but for the moment she could go no further.

There were traces of old fires in the clearing. Charcoal burners, perhaps? Or even the Kettles - but she would be safely out of sight. An owl floated silently across the clearing. The moon rose through the branches of the wych elm like a fish in a net.

With the last of her energy she knotted her girdle round a branch and lowered herself down the hollow onto a bed of leaves. She fell asleep at once.

It was the cock that crowed at midnight that awoke her.

Tumbling out of the confusion of sleep she thought at first that it was morning. Her heart leapt up at the sound. She must be near the town. She sat up. Her head swam as if she had not slept. She looked at the patch of sky at the mouth of her hiding-place. It was still dark, faintly silvered by a shaft of moonlight. No dawn-struck bird was piping; nothing stirred. She must have been dreaming ... she settled again to sleep. The next second she was bolt upright.

Something had brushed against the outside of the tree.

The black dog! It must have followed her all day, eerily padding on its silent feet through the forest. She listened, so intently, so fiercely that she seemed to feel her eardrums stretching in the silence ...

She caught other sounds. Faint movements, and a blurred whisper of voices. The whispering grew to a murmur, rhythmical and slow. And the voices were human. Carefully she groped for the dangling end of her girdle and inched her way without a sound up the sloping inside of the trunk, hauling up her bulk until she could spy unseen between the branches.

Below her she made out a bare back shining with sweat, a faint glimmer of firelight. Then other limbs, other bodies, naked and pale in the moonlight, moving with measured tread in a slow circle. She recognised the design drawn on the ground, the five-pointed star within it, the bare feet careful not to step outside it. She was aware of the excitement of the men as two old women with dangling breasts lifted a third, young and beautiful, to lay her on a bench. And there was the man-goat - stepping forward from shadow, throwing back the long cloak that was his only garment, covering the girl where she lay in the sight of all. The murmuring became a rhythmic chant that grew faster and louder as tension mounted and the pace of the dance quickened. It reached a deafening crescendo and then abruptly stopped. The man left the girl and stood with arms outstretched.

Hazel heard words, responses that reminded her of church. She saw candles burning that gave no light, and the dog, its black flanks coiled under the bench where the two had lain coupling, and where an older woman now lay stretched. She saw a black rooster tied by its feet, a knife and a dish. She saw the man-goat take them up.... the bird crowed forlornly before its cry was abruptly cut off... its wings beat frantically.... there was blood everywhere. Hazel felt sick. The woman was catching in her hands the blood that splashed down over her body and drinking it. She shut her eyes....

She wished she could escape and not have to witness this horror but she was helpless. She dared not move. She hung there with her eyes closed trying to blot it out. But the sounds that reached her told her all too clearly what was going on a few feet away.

She knew well enough what she was seeing. Here was the memory to which her mind had said No. There could be no more persuading herself that it had been a dream; here it was in its ugly reality, with no drugged wine, no flying ointment to blur its bestiality, the initiation rite in which she must herself have taken part.

After an eternity everything went quiet. Still she lay there, sweating, promising herself all manner of things she had no hope of fulfilling. At last she opened her eyes.

What they met made the hair stand up along the crown of her head. On a level with her own, through the lunatic branches of the wych elm, she was looking straight into the eyes of Nanny Webster. The face was blurred and indistinct as if seen through water. But it was Nanny's, of that she was dreadfully sure.

She had watched her hang for witchcraft and would never forget it.

PART II

Beltane

1

The boys heard the rumour while they were struggling to erect the maytree. They left it where it fell and ran off to find out, with the children who had sprawled and scampered over the grass falling in behind them, scattering the grazing geese.

The cat sunning its belly on the miller's doorstep was rudely tumbled off by the mill-wife running to tell her son, who was helping with the hobby horse.

Housewives who had been at their baking since dawn beat flour from their hands and hurried to ask each other if they had heard the news. The little boys turning the spit on the green forgot their task and earned themselves a clout for letting the ox burn.

The voice of the crier rang through the town, bringing the people out of doors in a flurry of pigs and chickens to join with the garlanding girls and rush squawking and chattering through the littered streets. Dogs romped everywhere, yapping excitedly, and one rangy sand- coloured bitch, her dugs pink and saucy, went courting a replacement of the two dead pups she had dropped and dispassionately eaten in a thicket in the woods.

Lumbering in search of her came Hazel.

Heavily pregnant and with a night of terror behind her, she

wandered into the cauldron of the town without any awareness of what was going on or even of what day it was.

A group of children ran past, almost knocking her over.

'They've caught Black John - there's going to be a hanging!' they shouted to her as they passed on their joyful errand of spreading the news.

Hazel stopped. A hanging. If there was one thing she could do without this morning, that was it. She had never been able to relish a hanging as she was supposed to. She always felt for the wretch jerking and choking at the end of the rope ...

Anything was better than another night in the greenwood, though. She could never go back there now. She seemed to spend her life running away. Bent Meg, the Kettles, and now ...

Desperate, she moved on into the town. People jostled her, their wooden pattens bruising her bare toes. She had to fight to keep her feet, to save herself from going to the wall where sewage oozed through the garbage in the gutter. A pig, savage with excitement, its little red eyes glowing with anger, ran along in their midst squealing and grunting, slashing at bare legs with its tusks until two men seized it and threw it over a wall.

Everyone seemed to be going the same way. She found herself carried along in a stream of people, livestock and snapping dogs to become one of the crowd that packed the market square.

The accusing finger of a gibbet jutted from the upper storey of an inn and under it a scaffold was being hurriedly knocked together.

Hazel mistrusted crowds and felt trapped in the square with its overhanging buildings. She tried to turn back but was pushed relentlessly forward by the press of people. She looked around her at their faces alight with anticipation, the children bobbing to get a better view. The stocks and the market cross were black with people who had climbed up there. They clustered like flies, jostling for position. And all to watch someone die. She was nauseated.

The rumble of a cart over cobbles brought a roar from the crowd. In spite of herself she craned her neck to catch sight of the victim.

She saw a lion of a man who stood a head and shoulders above his captors. Even with his arms lashed with rope to his sides they were having trouble to hold him. He buffeted them with powerful shoulders like a bull shaking off terriers, not in fear but in fury against the restraint of their hands.

He was still fully clothed even to his boots. It would take more than two of ordinary stature to strip him - they would wait for his boots until he was dead.

'Who is he, what's he done?' she asked someone beside her.

'Black John, the outlaw - hey, did you see that!'

A youth had climbed up the side of the cart to spit in the big man's face. To a roar of approval one of the men hit him hard enough to send him spreadeagling backwards into the waiting arms of the crowd.

The woman next to her turned and said something but her voice was lost in the uproar.

Hazel turned her attention to the man who was starting his climb to the gallows. He was quite old, she thought, nearly as old as her father. He had Tom's fiery spirit, too. No bullying rabble was going to intimidate him. What a waste, she was thinking, to do away with such a man.

'Are they really going to hang him?' she shouted against the noise.

'Aye, right enough,' the woman beside her shouted back, then she grinned toothlessly and added, 'Unless you've a mind to marry him!'

'Marry him?' Hazel stared.

'Never heard of a gallows wedding? It's May Day. If some wench wanted him they'd have to let him off. All very well for him, though. They wouldna spare my Tom and he only poached a deer. Still got his Nan and her little one. Her mother turned her out, see.'

Hazel felt a stab of envy. Some girls had all the luck.

'I've heard of Black John,' she said thoughtfully.

'Who ain't? A name to frighten babes with, is that! Look, there's the hangman with his black hood.'

Hazel said, 'But aren't they going to wait and see if anyone'll save him?'

The woman burst out laughing. 'What, marry Black John? The wenches is all mortal scared of him!'

'I'm not afraid!' declared Hazel without thinking.

The laughter spread. Before she knew what was happening she was seized and hustled to the front. Fear, then excitement and a strange elation swept through her as she realised what was in their minds. They thought she was offering herself as a bride for Black John!

Out of the frying pan into the fire! She beat helplessly at the shoving hands that pushed her ruthlessly forward, and yet - To be married, to belong somewhere. No more nights alone in the dreadful forest - and this man was far less frightening than the Croppers. Her mouth dried and her heart banged like a drum. She was vomited out from the throng at the foot of the gallows. She picked herself up from her knees. She heard herself say loudly in a voice she did not recognise, 'I claim this man from the gallows!' In a flash of inspiration she added, 'I carry his child.'

The man on the gallows looked at her briefly. What did he see? A stray cat come in from the woods? Pregnant, half-starved, flea-bitten, the eyes in their shadowed sockets luminous with want. He was on the point of death and he did not care. He turned away.

The crowd caught his muttered words and tossed them about on gusts of laughter.

Hazel strained her ears.

'What did he say?'

'He says he's got enough troubles!'

They repeated it to each other, enjoying the joke. Even the hangman relaxed, his shoulders shaking. Black John was a rare one, to be sure - good for a laugh to the end.

To Hazel it was a slap in the face. She blushed hotly, but the pitiless hands pushed her forward. They were going to have their fun, one way or the other. A hanging or a wedding, it didn't matter. Either was splendid entertainment for May Day.

Whistles and catcalls broke out.

'Don't you want your bride, Black John?'

'Here's a fine young wench for the price of a good scrubbing. Better than a rope's end any day!'

Someone grabbed a handful of her long matted hair and combed rough fingers through it.

'Look at these beautiful tresses!'

'O-oh, dunna!' she cried, but they were getting into their stride. They teased and jostled her without compassion.

'Maybe he'd like her better clean - let's get a broom and sweep her!'

'I'll warrant he's got a broom of his own would do the job a treat!'

This evoked a roar of laughter and they tweaked aside her ragged skirt to show her swelling shape.

'Too late - some wag's done it for him, that's never his!'

The crowd rocked with laughter. This was great sport. As good as a bull-baiting. They hoisted her up protesting and shouldered her up level with where the wretched man still stood with his head in the noose.

His eyes stared straight before him. His mouth was grimly set. He looked smaller and very much alone. Suddenly she understood. He had steeled himself for the rope and all he wanted was to be left alone to go through with it.

She hated them all for tormenting him and herself for being

fooled. They had no interest in letting him go and she had merely become their dupe.

Blazing, she struck out blindly at bobbing heads.

'Put me down! Let go, put me down! Dunna you have no shame to make such a mockery?'

Her voice rang out with such authority that they put her down. Grudging but shamefaced they released her and stood back, sniggering. Still sparkling with anger she straightened her draggled clothes and drew the shreds of her dignity about her. The man's face was above her eye- level now. All she could see was his boots, expensive and fine and obviously stolen. You couldn't help who wouldn't be helped. Best to salvage her pride and go.

'So be it, if that's how you want it,' she flung up at him, 'you die your way and I'll die mine!'

She turned on her heel and charged blindly into the crowd. Taken by surprise, they parted to let her through. She marched away unseeing, her head held high to contain the tears of humiliation stinging the backs of her eyes.

Black John watched her go, his attention captured in spite of himself. There was something about her, a quality of indestructibility, like that of an ant...

She was half-way across the square when the voices reached her, telling her to go back. She thought mutinously of refusing but she was given no choice. She was dragged back and bundled up willy-nilly to stand beside him on the scaffold.

It was a fearful place to be. She marvelled at his calm. He towered above her, massively built, sloe-eyed, black- bearded and altogether terrifying. Hazel found her courage beginning to slip. She had been teased, tormented and bandied about and what she wanted most was to escape and have a good cry. But she was desperate. There could be no turning back.

'They say if you wed me they'll let you go,' she said quickly before she could change her mind.

His bold eyes swept her up and down, undressing and assessing her at his leisure.

'So you'd wed me, would you?' Was he laughing behind that beard? 'Not afraid to wake and find me on your pillow?' Then, as she said nothing, 'Turn about then, let's have a look at you.'

Suddenly she was nettled at his independence, his arrogance. She crossed her arms tightly across her bosom and a bright spot flamed in the centre of either cheek.

'Beggars can't be choosers, sir. That goes for us both, I think!'

The crispness of her tone took him by surprise. The fierce eyebrows shot up and he laughed disarmingly.

'Why, so it does, mistress! We're neither of us any great catch and that's the truth!'

Fresh laughter broke around them like a boisterous sea. She flung him a furious glance but she had to look upwards to deliver it and it lost its potency. She had lost control of the situation and did not know how to recover it. Her nails dug into her palms. She drew deep breaths to calm herself.

'Untie me.'

Hazel closed her eyes to blot out the ocean of faces. She felt a rough finger gently brush away the angry tear that had escaped onto her burning cheek.

'And what do they call you?'

'Hazel ...' her voice was inaudible. Someone thumped her in the back.

'Tell him your name, girl!'

Black John's voice thundered out, 'Let her be!'

'I'm Hazel,' she blurted.

She felt her hand swallowed up in one of his.

'Then, Hazel, I'm pleased to wed you. If you'll be so kind.'

The rest of the day was a nightmare of noise, exhaustion and forced gaiety.

The hangman loomed over her, his eyes slits of brightness in the hood that hid his face. He held out his hand.

Money! Why had she not thought of that - he had to be paid and she had nothing. She looked blankly at him, despairingly at Black John. He gave her ankle a sidelong nudge with his boot, glanced meaningly downwards....

She made a pretence of going up her skirt to get her nonexistent purse, and under cover slid her hand down between soft leather and the hard warmth of his leg. She came up with a little leather bag full of coin.

'Give him fifty,' he muttered, 'I'm not worth more.'

Hazel hesitated. Fifty was higher than she could count. She tipped a handful of gold pieces into the waiting palm and the fingers closed over them like a trap.

She glanced in uncertainty at the man beside her. He appeared to shrug one eyebrow. Then he took one more piece from the purse, to use as the marriage token. She clutched it in her hand throughout the day. Whatever the outcome might be, it was her own. Not money, this coin, but special. Her wedding gold.

The ceremony was scant and derisive, like something in a mummers' play, their hands symbolically joined by the hangman's rope. Afterwards Hazel was thankful to be handed down from the scaffold - but instead of reaching the ground she found herself with Black John in the cart. The ox was unharnessed, and with men between the shafts they rumbled off.

' Smile!' urged the man beside her under his breath.' Look happy or they'll tear you to pieces!'

'What does it mean - where are they taking us?'

'We're May King and Queen for our sins. And what it means is that having cheated the gallows we have to supply the entertainment. If we ran for it now we'd never get out alive.'

He was grinning, bowing extravagantly, waving his arm in

acknowledgement of the shower of flowers that pelted into the cart. Hazel swayed.

'Cheer up,' he admonished her, 'you look as if you could do with your share of the roast!'

She wrenched her face into a smile, leaning back against his arm that was all that kept her on her feet. But it was all right. In a while this would be over. And he was strong and dominant and on her side. She glowed with the warmth of not being alone.

The cart nudged slowly through the winding crowded streets. In some places Black John had to lower his head to avoid the jutting upper storeys. There must be rich people in towns, Hazel thought, to have upstairs and downstairs in the same house. She tried to picture the inside of a cottage with another on the top....

The men had set up the maytree by the time they arrived. They were taken from the cart and enthroned overlooking the green. She was thankful to sit down though she had almost forgotten how it felt to sit in a chair. This one was hard and upright and sharp with the hawthorn with which it had been trimmed for the occasion. She gripped its thorny edges to steady herself, dizzy from hunger and the unwanted child that still stirred feebly within her.

Through endless hours she sat shifting her weight from one numb buttock to the other, while the interminable May games took their course. She smiled until her face ached through the wrestling, the races, the tug-o'-war, the bullbaiting, the cock-fights ... After them came the Mystery Play and after that the Morris dancing, and still she waited giddily in the hot spring sun, tormented by the smell of the roasting beef.

Her head ached and she drooled. She could think of nothing but the meat. She watched in an agony of suspense as one after another strolled up to the carcass, slashed off a piece and went away eating.

She must have been forgotten. Or she was not to be given

any. Or perhaps no one would think of her until there was none left. She dared not leave her chair. She sat transfixed, watching the little flares of the dying fire as the fragrant juices dripped onto the hot embers. If she could just have the drippings ...

Black John's voice boomed out beside her from time to time, cracking jokes with the crowd. Keeping the laughter going and the good humour, keeping them both alive. She closed her eyes, trying to forget her hunger.

'Here - catch!'

A chunk of hot meat landed in her lap. She fell upon it like a wolf, tearing at it with her teeth, the rich juices running between her fingers, making unconscious animal sounds as she devoured it. She could not get it to her stomach fast enough.

She became aware of sudden quiet. Then an outbreak of laughter. She looked at Black John. He was leaning back in his chair, watching her with amusement, his own food unheeded in his hand.

'No one's going to snatch it from you,' he said.

Shame flooded her, souring the taste of the food. She finished it very slowly and in silence. Afterwards it lay in an uneasy lump in her stomach, but she grimly kept it down. Roast beef was too rare in her life to be relinquished lightly.

Cider and ale were flowing freely and the mood of the revellers grew rowdy as the sun went down. The young drifted away in ones and twos. At least, thought Hazel thankfully, there would be no more sleeping in the woods. Her man had gold and now he was pardoned. She remembered the harvest fruit cake, the insides of houses she had glimpsed on their journey from the square. She was a wife now, and would have a home. She would have an oaken chair like her granny's, and one day even a bed of real goose feathers ... her eyelids drooped in the glow of cider and a heavy meal.

'Don't fall asleep.'

She glanced at the man beside her. He reclined among the

mayflowers, a wineskin in his hand, a ruddy glow on his cheekbones above the dark smudge of his beard. To all appearances he was relaxed and slightly drunk. But all the time his black eyes moved, alert and watchful, assessing everything that moved, like those of an animal sensing danger.

'Why?'

Her question was stupid and she knew it. She had guessed the answer before it was out.

'We must get away from here and the further the better. I've no intention of playing Jack-in-the-Green.'

She shivered. The May King of ancient times who had been sacrificed to the crops! She protested, 'They dunna do that anymore.'

'You are too trusting.' He gestured towards where a drunken brawl had broken out. Already a knot was gathering as the knives began to flash.

Hazel's heart sank.

'Must we go tonight?'

'There's a long walk ahead.'

'Oh, no!'

'Oh, yes.'

'Where are we to live then?'

'In the greenwood, where else?'

'Oh, not the greenwood!' She was ready to weep, her golden bubble pricked.

'Stay here if you like. I am going.'

Her chin set stubbornly.

'Oh, no,' she said firmly. 'I'm going with you. I'm your wife-' His eyes rolled upwards and she bit back the rest. 'But why,' she pleaded, trying a new tack, 'why does it have to be the greenwood, why do we have to hide?'

Anything but the greenwood, anything ... He threw away the wineskin and stood up.

'Because we can't stay here and live. Neither one of us after today. When Eustace hears that they let me go he's going to tear this place to shreds.' He leaned forward and pulled her to her feet. 'I'll see you safely out of the town. After that you must fend for yourself.'

2

They crept away in the deepening dusk, hoping for the diversion of the fight to cover their disappearance.

They meandered liked homing lovers through the nearby streets but once out of sight of the green Black John strode out towards the wasteland.

Hazel followed silently behind him, her dreams forgotten. It had become so normal for her to be trudging through the dew to nowhere that she had given up her hopes without a struggle and with barely a sigh. She missed the warmth of the fire in the evening chill. That was all.

After a perfunctory glance behind him to see that she was following, her bridegroom took no more notice of her than if she had been a dog trotting at his heel. He strode ahead in a morose silence, only stopping from time to time to cup his hands to his mouth and emit a long piercing whistle. Then he would stand listening for a moment before going on again.

'Why do-'

'Sh-shl' he silenced her, and struck off in a new direction.

'I'm cold,' she complained.

'Walk faster,' he shouted back, and she pounded after him.

Around and around the wasteland they went, back and forth and across and across while her legs ached and her stomach muscles creaked. She dared not lose sight of him.

If she feared him, this man of whom she had heard nothing good, she feared the darkness more. After an eternity, he said, 'He must have strayed. I'll find him when it's light.' 'Find who?'

'Black Man.'

'Your henchman?'

His laugh was the crack of a whip.

'You could say that. My horse.'

'Your horse!'

She could not believe it. For a horse she had been dragged over the heath, stumbled through brambles, exhausted herself....

'Who needs a horse in the greenwood?' She thought of the gold in his boot. 'You could buy another.'

His look withered her.

'You do not buy another comrade-in-arms. You live together, you die together-' He made a little gesture of impatience, 'You wouldn't understand.'

Hazel sighed. 'I'll help you find him in the morning.'

He seemed not to have heard her. He was off again. Plodding breathlessly behind him, she called, 'Why do you call him Black Man?'

She was not really interested. Secluded from animals throughout her childhood, she was nervous of horses. But she was desperate to establish some contact with the man who was ready to stride off into the darkness without her.

'My father called him Black Prince. But princes are treacherous. He's Black Man now. It's all one to him, I daresay.'

The conversation was exhausted. She had no breath for more. It was as much as she could do to keep him in sight. He went charging on with his swift long-legged gait while she panted behind him, forgotten. Finally, 'Please ...' she pleaded, catching at his sleeve.

He stopped, peering into her haggard face in the moonlight.

'You're tired out.' He sounded surprised.

She could only nod, her teeth chattering with cold and exhaustion while she got her breath. He took off his doublet and hung it around her.

'There's shelter nearby. You can sleep.'

They moved off, he leading her with a hand on her shoulder.

The promised shelter was two walls of a ruined cottage that the shepherds had used at the lambing. It reeked of sheep and the shreds of thatch still hanging were filled with the tiny sounds of fieldmice. Hazel scratched about for wood and laboriously kindled a fire. As she stooped over it, breathing on the flame, it was abruptly extinguished by a boot.

'Do you want to tell the world where we are?'

She looked up at him. From where she crouched he looked as tall as a tree.

'It's warmth,' she faltered, 'protection ...'

'You have me.'

She could not read his expression. She stood up, uneasy in his presence now that they were no longer on the move. She did not know what he expected of her, and he had the right to expect ... everything. And he had a fierce animal vitality that disturbed her. She waited for him to say something. He said nothing. Sweating with nerves, she said, 'Sir, if you - if you -' She did not know how to go on.

Still he said nothing. She shut her eyes and blurted, 'I- I'm with child.'

He nodded. 'Take your ease, mistress. I do not bed with-' he paused, selecting carefully the word, 'children.'

Hazel caught his sardonic tone and her cheeks flamed. She would almost rather he had raped her.

He stretched out to sleep with his hand on his knife, his back against a wall. She lay down primly against the other one. But she could not sleep.

Every animal that stirred in the darkness was for her the black dog. If she opened her eyes she dreaded to see again

Nanny Webster's face in its watery shroud. Little by little she edged her way over to lie beside the mountainous body. Intimidating though it was, it was warmly, reassuringly real. Very carefully, for fear of waking him, she knotted the end of her girdle through his belt. Satisfied that he could not leave without waking her, she relaxed at last. When he turned and threw a drowsy arm across her she huddled into it gratefully, thankful he had not awakened....

A flicker of amusement crossed his face before he slept.

She awoke in the chill of dawn. She was alone.

She struggled to her feet and hurried out to look for him. Far across the wasteland she caught a glimpse of a white shirt. Was it he? She still had his doublet. Clutching it she stumbled over the rough grass, calling his name. But he was too far away to hear her. She sobbed. Then the long piercing whistle reached her and she stopped abruptly, her panic turned to relief which was quickly succeeded by anger.

He was still searching for that cursed horse! To find it he had left her alone and gone off without a word - no warning, nothing! Wait till he came back! If he came back ... She pushed on again, calling louder.

Again the whistle. This time, though faintly, she was sure there was the answering whicker of a horse. Black John shouted something in the distance. Another whinny. Then unmistakably the far-off thunder of hooves, and out of nowhere it appeared, the biggest blackest horse she had ever seen or imagined, a mountain on four hooves.

He came careering out of the haze, a black colossus, wheeled sharply as he saw John and then came frisking up, gentle as a kitten, tossing his great head and shaking his mane in a frenzy of greeting. There was a moment's exchange between them and then horse and rider came cantering towards her. She smiled, her anger evaporated, and tried not to flinch as they bore down upon her, shaking the ground she stood on. Black John was smiling as he waved a brace of rabbits over his head.

'Breakfast!'

'How did you catch them?' she asked, astonished.

'Found them. You have to know where to look, of course.'

'Shall I skin them?'

'Not now, no time to eat. One for you, one for me.' He dropped one down to her but made no move to dismount.

'I thought you'd gone without me,' she said.

'I had,' he said wryly. 'I suppose you want to come with me?'

She took hold of the bridle.

'I got to come with you. I'm your wife.'

'My barefoot bride,' he acknowledged. 'And you can ride a horse, no doubt?'

'Yes,' lied Hazel. 'And dunna you mock me, neither!' 'Don't say dunna. It betrays your origins.'

'I'm proud of my origins!'

He twitched the reins out of her hand. 'Go back to them, then.'

'I canna!'

He leaned forward in the saddle, confidentially. 'Look, child, don't be foolish. You can't come with me in your condition. Go home and ask your father to take you back.' 'My father's dead.'

'Your mother, then.'

'I canna - you don't know what happened-'

'I know well enough. Do you think you're the first little girl to be turned out of doors?'

He fished in his boot and tossed her down his purse. 'You can keep the doublet,' he called back as he rode away.

She flung the doublet after him, screaming, 'I took you for a man - you're not, you're nothing! Nothing, d'you hear me! I saved your life and this is how you repay me - you're nothing!

Nothing!' and she threw herself face down in the heather, sobbing with rage and disappointment.

She was making too much noise herself to hear the throb of returning hooves.

'Get up!'

It was a command, sharp and uncompromising. She obeyed it.

'Well, madam! If you come with me you come on my terms.'

He reached down and grasped her under the armpits, lifting her, gross and awkward as she was, and dumped her none too gently on his saddle-bow.

A shaft of pain shot upwards through her body, rekindling her anger. She did not waste her energy on his face which looked invulnerable. She doubled up a fist and brought it downwards with all her force. A fraction from its target it was arrested. A hand like a' steel shackle snapped shut about her wrist.

'What -would you!'

For a second they glared into each other's eyes. Then to her amazement he laughed.

'Don't you know you could cripple a man like that?'

'You hurt me!' She was still defiant, her eyes glared back unswerving. He gave her a little shake.

'It wasn't meant.'

He settled her more comfortably but did not release the murderous little fist.

'Feral cat!' he chided her as he captured the other one.

And so they rode, he chuckling to himself, she sitting stiffly with imprisoned hands staring fixedly at Black Man's ears.

Hazel fumed for a while. But eventually her condition, the warmth of the day and the lullaby motion of the horse prevailed and she slept.

Black John glanced down at her nodding head and smiled. He released her hands and tipped her back against his shoulder. It was a feral cat indeed that he had by the tail, lost in the wild and gone savage from neglect. But spirited, oh yes. Poor little cat.

That evening he judged they were far enough from the town to build a fire and roast their rabbits by it.

'So you're not afraid of me?' he said, as he sat with his hands spread to the blaze.

'I'm not afraid of any man,' declared Hazel stoutly. Perhaps if she said it loud enough it might be true. She added, 'It comes of having nothing to lose.'

'An interesting thought,' said John. 'Come, help me with my boots, they haven't been off for a week.'

He had to show her what to do. No man of her acquaintance had ever owned a pair of boots. She stood with her back to him, his foot between her knees, and pulled while he shoved with his other at her backside.

'I don't think much of that,' she informed him, puffing.

'Never mind,' he said, massaging his feet, 'let's see what's accumulated.'

He upturned them one at a time, emptying out the contents. There were gold coins, pieces of jewellery. Hazel said, 'How can you walk with all that in your boots?'

'I don't walk.'

She giggled. 'No wonder you need a horse.'

'Only a fool keeps all his riches in one purse,' he said, turning over his loot. 'Here's a ring for you. Wait - you don't want that.'

He was working at it, trying to remove something. 'The fat fool,' he muttered under his breath. 'There, I have it!'

He handed it to her, tossing away something into a corner. She scrubbed her hands on her skirt and took the ring from him. It was big and only fitted on her thumb. Its rich gold dazzled her, the great purple stone glowed in the firelight like a drop of blood.

'Is it really for me?' she breathed. As an afterthought she added, 'What was that you threw away?'

'Never mind. The ring is yours. I thought it would go with your gown.'

She glanced at him sidelong. He was gibing at her again. Did he think she went clad like a beggar for fun? He tossed her food as if to a dog and looked away while she ate it. He had not even troubled to note her name - if he addressed her at all it was as Ivy, May, Holly, Ash - anything but Hazel. It was too much.

'It's not kind of you to make fun of me,' she said soberly. 'I had a good home once.'

The humour left his face like a light going out. His tone had the bitter blackness of congealed blood.

'Aye, mistress,' he said bleakly, 'and so had I!'

All the next day he was gloomy and silent, his teasing mood gone. At first light they were on the move, but it seemed to Hazel that they were taking another direction. The following day they doubled back again.

'Where are we going?' she asked, bewildered.

'Nowhere. On the move, out of sight.'

Back and forth across the same terrain they went, never using the roads yet keeping them under surveillance. They ate well. Whatever they needed Black John produced after an absence, short or long. 'The road is my larder - and my treasury,' he said. They lacked for nothing but they wandered aimlessly, never stopping in the same place twice.

'It's a pointless life,' said Hazel.

'You had a better, no doubt?'

She ignored the taunt and sat trying to hug her knees. They seemed to go further out of reach every day.

'If I had your riches,' she said dreamily, 'I'd have a farm. I'd have a bit of land somewhere - somewhere nobody knows me - and put down roots.' She shivered. 'It'd have to be far, far from here.'

He glanced at her, but said nothing.

'We could have a place of our own,' she said coaxingly, 'and I'd work with you on the land-'

His laugh lashed her. 'Forget it, mistress. I'll keep the gold and you keep your dreams.'

She flared, 'You'd rather go on killing people - that's what you do, isn't it?'

'What did you think they were hanging me for?'

'And the man who had my ring - you killed him, too.' 'He didn't need it where he was going.'

'But he wasn't going there till you sent him!'

He shrugged, 'We all go sooner or later - I just helped him on his way. No doubt he thanked me for it - he'd spent his life trying to buy his way in - sh!'

His hand on her arm held her silent. 'Look down there.' From where they sat the road was visible at intervals. A young man was passing along it, travelling alone in the gathering dusk. Without a sound, John got to his feet.

'Hope he's said his prayers,' he observed, 'I like the cut of his doublet.'

She knelt with closed eyes and covered her ears as she had done before. Don't let it happen, please don't...

She was not sure for whom she prayed; for the doomed traveller or for Black John's safe return, her own continued protection. For all her efforts not to hear, the gasping cry reached her ears. It usually did.

He came back arrayed in the doublet.

'How like you that?'

'It smells of death,' said Hazel.

'You'll get used to it,' he said.

In the morning it took her all her willpower to rise. She had lain awake most of the night trying not to recognise what was going on inside her. By morning she was forced to accept it. The day she had dreaded, the day she had tried to shut out of her mind was here.

'Come on!' Black John was impatient, already on the horse.

'Coming....' she answered, clinging clammy-handed to a tree. Somehow she had to get up on the horse too. If he knew what was happening he would leave her behind. She took a few unsteady steps before her knees buckled.

He looked at her piercingly.

'Dear God, the child's giving birth!' He swung himself down and caught her as she stumbled. 'Lie down, you can't ride like that.'

'No, no, take me with you, it won't be for hours yet!' She clutched at his sleeve, desperate. 'I won't be no trouble, I promise!' She did not know what to say, how to hold him. 'Dunna leave me behind, please, oh, please!' She began to cry hysterically. He slapped her face.

'You - stay - here!' he said slowly and emphatically. 'You lie down here and behave yourself. Don't move from this spot.'

His tone was exasperated. He shook off her clinging hands, remounted and was gone.

3

For a time the tears and the labour pains came thick and fast. Then they both ceased. Hazel waited. Nothing happened. She dried her eyes and tried to think what to do.

She could either stay where she was and sweat it out or she could make her way to the road and try to get help. The pains might come on again before she found anyone, but she stood a better chance of being found out in the open. She decided to walk.

It was not easy scrambling down the tussocky bank to the road but she managed it and began to walk slowly and rather carefully along the track. It was deserted at this early hour. She consoled herself with the thought that there was all day for someone to discover her plight. The first person along would surely help her.

After more than an hour of faltering over the ruts she heard the thud of hooves and looked behind her. Two riders were approaching at a canter. She waved and called to them. To her dismay they spurred their horses and passed her at a gallop, disappearing in a thunder of dust while she stood gaping after them. Anyone would have thought they were afraid of her.

She kept walking, though it was becoming difficult. The exercise was having its effect and the pains were beginning again, slow and strong, the sort that meant business.

A preacher came by on a donkey. As he drew level with her he looked about him uneasily and pulled down his velvet hat to hide his face.

Hazel reached out, caught at his reins. Something like panic showed in his pale eyes.

'Help me!' she begged him.

'No, no,' he shrilled, 'I know you and your man - I've nothing for you - let me go!'

He thrashed at her arms until she let go and the frightened donkey bolted, taking with it the last of her hopes.

She stood forlornly in the dust of the road. Of course no one would stop for her. They thought she was bait for an ambush! A pain stronger than before assailed her and she bent forward, hugging her stomach. An angry shout alarmed her as she straightened up. She looked up to see Black John galloping towards her.

'You little fool - what do you think you're doing?'

Fury was in his face, in the fierce swoop of his eyebrows. She lurched towards him in an orgy of relief. She had never been more thankful to see anyone.

'You came back,' she said wonderingly as he dismounted. 'I thought-'

'I told you to wait!' he thundered. He picked her up and swung her into the saddle. 'I had to break cover to find you. In future you do as you're told.'

Hazel clung to the saddle-bow and tears of reaction streamed down her happy face. It was the first good thing that had happened to her and she could hardly believe her luck. She reached out a tentative hand to touch his rough black curling hair.

'I'm sorry ...' she whispered.

He glanced up from where he walked below her, leading the horse. He seemed to be laughing.

'My fault, no doubt - since I said you were too trusting. Never mind now, save your strength.'

They made their way back quietly to where they had spent the night. He lifted her down and laid her gently on the bracken bed.

'You must have it here,' he said. 'Can you manage?' In answer to her unspoken question he added, 'I'll wait with you.' He stretched out on the bank beside her.

Hazel nodded, feeling a new confidence warming her. She was not afraid of pain, only of being abandoned. Somehow things would be all right. She smiled up at him. He grinned.

'I've not played midwife before. No doubt you'll be able to tell me what to do.'

She nodded again, 'I'm one of eight.' She felt it was her turn to be amused. She had known strong men to blanch and faint at a birth. Tom had always found pressing, business elsewhere. She tried to relax as another contraction built up.

'There's nothing to do yet. Just rub my back,' she said.

When it had passed, 'I must walk the horse, he's lathered,' he said.

She closed her eyes contentedly. This time she knew he would come back.

The day wore on and the baby seemed no nearer. Black John withdrew at intervals and returned with this or that - a rich mantle lined with fur which he spread over Hazel, drowning her in unaccustomed luxury; a skin of wine that was even more comforting. Its warmth crept through her like a benediction.

She grew weary and her back felt ready to break; Black John rubbed faithfully hour after hour.

'Doesn't your arm ache?' she asked him.

He shrugged an eyebrow. 'No more than your back.'

Dusk fell, bringing out the scent of bluebells. He stretched out beside her with a sigh. 'Don't worry about me, just get on with having your baby.'

She knew how he must feel. She could remember long tedious hours of waiting with Margery while the sun beckoned and nothing seemed to be happening in the stuffy room.

'I'm sorry to take so long ...' she whispered, turning her face towards him.

He smiled faintly. 'I wasn't going anywhere.'

Some time the next morning the labour gathered momentum. The pains became longer and stronger with less breathing space between. She could no longer lie quiet but began to move restlessly, her face shining with sweat. Little groans were squeezed out of her despite her efforts to be stoical.

'Oh - and my mother used to shuck 'em out so easy!' she panted between spasms.

Black John lifted a strand of damp hair and pushed it back off her face. 'So will you when you've had eight,' he said.

Hazel's eyes rolled upwards as she filled her lungs for the next assault.

Soon she was thrashing helplessly, aware of nothing but the fire in her belly that breathed and glowed, blazed and died down like the rhythmic breathing of a demon.

'Tyburn must be like this!' she gasped.

Black John wagged his head.

'Aye, mistress - you're over young for this caper. This will teach you to go bundling in the hay!'

He tried to think how to help her but he only knew about mares. 'Try pushing,' he suggested.

She tried and it helped a bit but not enough. Nothing was enough, nothing really helped. She was desperate - she couldn't do it - she was trapped in a sea of fear and pain for ever ... her mind was fogged. In it was the idea that the dreadful black dog had somehow got inside her and was savaging its way out - she must get rid of it - she must-

'I canna - I canna-' her voice rose hysterically 'Help me-'

Her body was splitting in two - she could feel it tearing! Her hands reached down towards the source of pain.

John seized them before they arrived at where something glossy was appearing between the quivering thighs.

'Now-now - up on your knees - that's my brave girl - it's nearly done-'

There was a convulsive movement, a rush of bloody fluid. Hazel with a gasping sigh fell back in an exhausted heap. She was still not clear in her mind.

'There goes my waters,' she said weakly.

She heard John's exultant laugh.

'There goes your son!' he said.

Hazel lay still for a moment. Suddenly her eyes brimmed. She blinked, sniffed and struggled up to look at her baby.

He lay where he had fallen, limp and shattered from the long ordeal of birth. His eyes still closed, on his minute face an expression of faint bewilderment, he had been dropped from his place of safety into a hostile and chilly world. His tiny lip puckered and he cried, his voice rising frail and impotent among the bluebells.

She reached down and gathered him up, a pathetic wet scrap of humanity.

'Oh, dunna ... dunna cry!' and she burst into tears herself.

Black John stared at her, nonplussed. Why weep when all was over and the baby safely born? Well, women were women - even little ones. He shrugged philosophically and drew his knife.

Hazel heard the lisp of steel and caught the flash of light on the blade. A memory sprang like a wolf spider from the darkness of her mind and she screamed. She had not wanted the child that had been laid upon her like a curse. She had spent fruitless hours jumping from trees, bathing in icy waters, trying to make herself swallow poisonous berries ... but that had been before, when it was just a lump in her stomach. Now she saw a face, hands, eyes, minutely human, an individual who was at the same time unbelievably her own. She saw a knife poised above him, saw him in peril -

'Dunna kill him!' she cried. Then she caught the eyes of the man and saw she had been wrong.

'Do not,' he corrected her icily. Unsmiling, he turned the hilt towards her hand. 'Here. You do it - you cut the cord.'

'I - I'm sorry,' she stammered.

'No,' he said stiffly, 'you are right to trust no one.'

Well might he call her a feral cat, thought Hazel wretchedly. A hand had been stretched to her - and she had savaged it. She had deeply insulted him, this strange man who was full of contradictions. There had been warmth between them, the beginnings of friendship - and she had destroyed it. She averted her eyes and did the only thing she could. Diffidently, she handed him her baby.

After a hesitation that was barely perceptible, he took him from her. He made a neat job of the umbilical cord- surgery of a sort being his trade - wrapped up the squealing infant and handed him back to her. He disposed of the afterbirth and went to the brook to wash his hands.

When he returned, Hazel was sobbing quietly, her head bent over the baby.

'What is it?' He stopped abruptly. 'Is he dead?'

She shook her head. The little boy was sleeping, his miniature fist crammed into his mouth, his crinkled eyes tight shut. But still she sobbed. She felt a hand on her shoulder, heard his voice soften with concern.

'Are you in pain?'

She tried to stop but she could not, it seemed that she must weep for the rest of her life. She reached out a groping hand, her head bent over the baby. The words when they came were ripped out of her.

'My mother ...'

The memory she had locked away had broken free at last to drown her in grief. Her sobs came deeper, more painful than before.

Black John kneeled down and drew her, baby and all, into his arms, and cradled her without words until the storm had passed. After a long silence, he said softly, 'Better now?'

She nodded and drew a deep sigh, pressing closer against his shoulder. Lying there, feeling the strong slow beat of his heart, hearing the vibrations of his voice, she felt strangely at peace. Her sorrow had expunged itself and left in its place an inexplicable lightness of heart.

'Poor child ...' He took a fold of her gown and clumsily mopped at her tears. 'Take heart, you're young. Some day you may find your bit of land and a pretty lad to go with it.' He sat her up, smiled wryly. 'Meantime you must make do with me - a bloodstained ruffian old enough to have sired you.' His expression altered. 'I don't really kill babies. Only Godfearing citizens do that.'

Hazel encircled his neck and mumbled into his unkempt beard, 'I know, I could cut out my tongue! Oh, I know you were a good man once!'

He snorted, 'And you were once a plump domestic tabby, no doubt! See what it's brought us to.'

She drew back to look into the dark forbidding eyes and saw for the first time how they bubbled with mischief.

You're right, she thought, I'll get my bit of land. But I don't want no pretty boy to go with it - I want you. She heard him saying, '... we must get you to bed.'

'Mm-mm,' she murmured drowsily, hugging her secret to herself where it glowed like wine within her. She sighed again, and said happily, 'I'm thinking perhaps you'd best set me down. I'm bleeding all over you.'

The woman was finishing her meal, mopping the trencher with a piece of bread, when the thundering started on her door. She sat still. Very still. And prayed. It was not answered: the hammering came heavier and more insistent. No one she knew would knock like that.

'Who is it? Give your name!' she stalled, looking about her for some weapon with which to defend herself. Her voice was unsteady as she added, 'Is that you, my son?' She hoped that if the intruder thought her son was expected he might leave her alone.

The knocking started again. The man outside was losing patience.

'You know me, mistress - open your door if you don't want it broken down!'

There was a movement as if the words were about to be put into practice.

'Black John!' It was a frightened whisper that escaped her. Bracing herself, she went to open the door. 'Why, Heaven save us, what have you got there?'

Black John was just raising a booted foot to kick in the door as she opened it. Encumbered as he was, he all but fell into the tiny room, filling it to overflowing with his enormous presence.

'A stray cat and her kitten,' he said shortly. 'Where's your bed?'

He eased his burden down gently while she hovered with the light. What she saw made her suck in her breath with a sharp hiss. The thin bedraggled girl lay limp on the straw, her face ashen under its tan and her arms wound tightly about a newborn infant.

'They say you're a woman for simples. Take you these two children and nurse them well. Look to the girl - she's bleeding overmuch.' He straightened his back and threw a handful of coin on to the table. 'There's gold for your trouble - double when I return if they're safe and well.'

She looked at the gold. It was more than she had ever seen before. She passed the tip of her tongue over lips that had suddenly dried.

'I hope they don't die on me,' she said, glancing uneasily towards the pallet in the corner.

'So do I, mistress.'

He drew his long knife and thoughtfully inspected the blade. He turned it this way and that, regarding his reflection, testing its edge with his thumb. The woman watched it like a rabbit watching a stoat,

'So do I indeed.' He put away the knife and smiled unnervingly. 'For your sake,' he added softly.

He left her to her thoughts and returned to the bedside.

'Mistress Ash ...'

The heavy eyes flickered open and focused on him with difficulty.

'Child., I'm going.'

Hazel's head swam and her eyes filled. His face was a blur in the darkness.

'Dunna leave me ...'

He picked up her chilled hand and warmed it in his. 'I must. We've lingered too long hereabouts already. You'll be safe with this woman, she knows I'm not to be trifled with.' The hesitation was barely perceptible. 'When you're rested I'll come back for you.'

She knew he would not come back. She would have to go and find him. If she died tonight she would never see him again. She closed her eyes and the tears ran scalding down her temples.

'Stay till the morning,' she pleaded.

'With Black Man standing out there like a beacon fire, telling the world where to find me? No, I must go -it's safer for us both. Without me no one knows you, and the woman here won't talk.'

He made to stand up but she clung to his hand. She swallowed her tears and tried to be sensible.

'When will you come for me?'

'Soon.'

'Promise?'

Again the hesitation. 'I promise.'

He would not come. Desperate, she played her one useless card. She knew it meant nothing to him. She was whistling in the dark.

'Remember - I'm your wife ...'

The last time she had said that he had taunted her. She kept her eyes closed, waiting for the jibe. Smiling, pretending not to remember ...

She felt his fingers gently pinch her chin.

'Eat up your meats and grow strong,' he said softly. And then the darkness claimed her again.

She drifted helplessly on the borders of consciousness, never knowing if she slept or waked. Dreams and fantasies dragged her mercilessly into their mazes, her ears rang with chanting and voices whispered just out of hearing. The familiar scent of birth herbs confused her and she thought she was back at home with Margery. The black dog with the sulphurous eyes bounded in, tail wagging, and dragged off the newborn infant with its teeth. When she tried to pursue it she found herself bouncing and floating, drifting like smoke on the wind. Between nightmares she felt herself packed and bandaged and gained the curious impression that her head was lower than her feet. The baby ... where was the baby?

The whispering grew at intervals. Words penetrated her mind and tangled with her dreaming.

.. zimat..

'Sesamie de laponie ..

.. set it to sun in the dog days ...'

.. sure it's not baptised?'

The baby ... where was the baby? She struggled to rise, moaning, and was pressed back down, while something bitter was trickled between her lips. Then silence. Then more dreams ... more chanting ... where had she heard it before?

The whispering grew again, excitedly. Grey Willy ... Grey Willy ... the name kept nibbling at the edge of her consciousness ... she was walking with Grey Willy to the Abbey and he was lacking a leg . . .

'No matter - the left or the right...'

'We can use the teeth ...'

She was walking with Grey Willy and it was dark.... dark under the gallows where a corpse was hanging ... time had shredded the flesh but in the mouth the teeth were still firm. She had to work and work to loosen them ... they must have the teeth ... suddenly the jaw gave way and she fell down, down, down into darkness ... A sheep bleated distantly, again and again. The bleating stopped and warmth enveloped her ... smelling of blood - and of something more ... of sheep ...

She seemed to be floating to the top of a deep still pool, coming up slowly towards the light. She lay still a moment before opening her eyes. Someone, a woman, was saying, 'There, what did I tell you - works like a charm! Take that to John Farmer for his sheep. We can roast up the carcass for meat and cheap at the price.'

Hazel frowned. Something about the voice troubled her.

The speaker came and stood over her, peering into her face as she opened her eyes. As her vision cleared she found herself looking into eyes she recognised.

'Welcome home, my dear,' said Mother Cropper.

4

'Don't look so scared, my dear,' said Mother Cropper, 'you'll be right as a trivet in no time. It was touch and go for a little - but there, you're a strong young thing and I have a trick or two up my sleeve.' She smiled, 'I knew you'd be back.'

Hazel swallowed. Her voice came as a harsh dry whisper, 'Where's - my baby?'

'Here he is.' He was held out to her, tiny and rigid in his swaddling bands. 'Thriving and fair as an angel - never think it to look at him, you wouldn't!' The woman's chuckle had a sinister undertone.

She felt her hands and feet turn cold.

'What - what have you done to him!'

In her weakness, her anxiety, she grabbed at him and pulled him over on top of her so that he set up a wail.

'Dunna, dunna cry, my darling,' she cradled him, weeping, 'I wunna let 'em hurt you ...'

She felt him taken from her; her arms had no strength to hold him though she tried.

'Not yours, my dear. Belongs to the coven, he does, like you and me. Not wise of you to run away, it wasn't - not wise at all. Not when the Prince of Darkness has marked you both for his own-'

'No, no ...' Not the witchmark ... Here pretty, pretty ... she heard her own voice calling through the woods ...

She tried vainly to rise, to reach her son, who, his mouth a small square of protest, his body quivering with rage, was held just out of reach by Mother Cropper.

'Oh, yes! Like mother, like son and as plain as ever I saw. A natural for the charm, and unbaptized... She picked up a knife from the table and slit the swaddlings over his chest. She held him before Hazel's eyes, still squalling, his skin like any other baby's, overly pink and scaling in places. But there was one significant difference. There were three tiny nipples instead of two.

Hazel felt her mouth opening in a scream. All that came out was a long choking gasp. Her hands flew to her throat. She tried to say, 'He's mine and no coven shall have him! I'll call him Angel and keep him safe - his name's Angel, you hear! Angel ...' She struggled and gasped and it was like a nightmare. She was trapped in a screaming silence. In her throat was an empty void, air that whispered and said nothing.

Mother Cropper smiled and moved away.

'That'll keep her quiet, won't it?' she cooed to the bawling babe.

What did she mean - had she taken away her voice? Was there really power in her to do such things? Hazel gathered her depleted strength for one last effort to make herself heard. She filled her lungs, doubled her fists and screamed ... there was not a sound. Futile to tell herself that she did not believe such things; in a tiny corner of herself that had not changed since the beginning of time, she knew that she did.

She burst into helpless sobs. And even her weeping made no sound.

For days Hazel was too weak to do anything but drift in and out of sleep, waking only to suckle the babe or attend to her body's needs. And when her strength began to return she was careful to betray no sign of it. Biddable and docile, she lay in the straw with closed eyes, secretly flexing her leg muscles under the covers.

Reasoning that not even the Croppers would dare to try anything while Black John lurked in the neighbourhood, she swallowed everything that was spooned into her mouth in the hope of quick recovery. For the moment there was nothing she could do but drowse in the firelight; the baby slept beside her like his namesake, his silvery fuzz of hair glowing like a halo.

The whispering had stopped now that she was conscious. But in time, as she hoped, they grew careless and she began to pick up words when they thought she slept. But there was little to be gleaned from her eavesdropping. A meaningful glance here, a word there….

'… we wunna dare …'

'No, but after …'

'…no use until…'

There was an atmosphere of suppressed excitement. Even Hal's brooding presence seemed to catch fire; he took to looking sidelong at where Hazel lay with the baby and flicking his tongue between his lips like a lizard. The tension in her stomach tightened in response, but she was careful to give no sign. If she were to escape them a second time, she would have to be even more cunning than before. It was no good, she thought sadly, pinning her hopes on Black John.

But she must at least pretend to expect him back - if only because Mother Cropper could read her thoughts. She turned restlessly on the straw and tried to think about something else.

She was wakened by a feeling rather than by a sound. A feeling that warned her to listen behind closed eyes to the voices, tense and low, that buzzed in the room. The whispering again!

'… the left - 'tis better, the Devil's hand …'

.. squeezed the blood out -every last drop…'

'… but the brains and swaddlings, we canna wait…'

'... miss the dog days ...'

'.. . sure 'tis not baptised?'

'Sh-shsh!'

For a time she could distinguish nothing. Then the voices gradually mounted again until she could make out a few words.

'We darena - suppose he comes back ...'

'Sh-shsh!'

Again the voices died, and again climbed back.

.. a thousand crowns on his head...

. more than he'll pay me for them - I'll not be the loser!'

.. but they let him go ...

'Aye, but that was never intended, he gave 'em the slip...'

'The Lord Eustace hanged ten burghers of the town for that...'

'A costly lark!'

'... larking at the Hop Bine with Bess! ... tonight's the chance . . . the Sheriff.'

'. . . enjoy it - 'twill be his last. . .'

And who, thought Hazel with an irrelevant stab of jealousy, was Bess? No wonder he had not come back for her. For a moment she thought bitterly, Let him be caught, what does he care for me! But it was only for a moment. The next she was scheming frantically in the darkness under the sable cloak he had stolen for her.

She lay still as death as she heard them move towards her, felt the light of the dip glowing through her closed eyelids. She forced herself to imagine sunlit meadows, children gathering flowers ...

'Sweet dreams,' murmured Mother Cropper. 'She's soundly off till morning.'

Hal grunted. 'Suppose she wakes while we're gone?'

'Suppose she does, blockhead! What could she do - too weak to move and no tongue in her head - besides, what the ear hasn't heard the heart won't grieve over - not till it's too late!'

Hazel drew a deep sigh and turned over away from the light!'

Hal muttered, 'She's asleep all right. Best lose no time.' The light that had almost undone her moved away. The door opened and closed once, twice . . . and there was silence. She reached out for the baby. He was not there.

In the windowless closet at the back of the Hop Bine that served Bess as a living space, Black John relaxed with a tankard of ale and a platter of squab pie. It was long since he had slept under a roof and the smell of oozing rushes was less than tempting, but Bess was a roisterous bedfellow who would more than make up for shortcomings. Good old Bess ...

He would be away betimes, though, well before dawn. A thousand crowns was a great deal of money. It might prove too much temptation even for her. His gold shone bright but Eustace's might well shine even brighter - there was so much more of it. He knew to the penny how much - who better! - it should change hands someday, by God, though it cost him his life ...

He stretched out his long legs and eased off his boots. Tomorrow he would spend a while ridding himself of Bess's vermin. Then perhaps go back to see how the girl was faring with her babe. Mother Cropper had an unsavoury reputation. He would find a better lodging for them, and see them provided for before going on his way. She deserved that much. There was a fearlessness about her that appealed to him, a tough determination to survive - the quality of indestructibility that had struck him that day in the market place. She was not afraid of him. It was refreshing to a man at whom the women he bought looked fearfully, and escaped as soon as they dared. Had things been different.... but there was little fun in a spitting vixen gone domestic with her cub. Besides, when he achieved what he must, it would be with no village Juliet beside him.

A commotion in the tavern broke in on his thoughts. He started up and struggled into his boots. The Sheriff's men! A thousand crowns was a dazzling sum and he had left his illusions far behind him.

Without a sound, he moved over to the door and eased it open a fraction. Squinting through the crack he could make out the forms of Bess and the taverner bending over something on the floor by the outer door. The guests had gathered round and he could see nothing but their backs.

'Fainted clean away-'

'Fair drownded with the rain-'

'Alone on such a night-'

'Scarce more than a child!'

'But a fine fur cloak - and rags beneath, I swear!'

Black John swore softly. He saw his night's entertainment disappearing over the horizon and felt a moment of exasperation. Could this turbulent wench never stay where she was told?

They were lifting her, bringing her to the fire.

'Bring wine …. mull it good and hot...'

Bess in her errand passed near him and he hissed to catch her attention.

'Hsst! Bring her here. In here'-as she paused, surprised - 'discreetly, mind.' He flattened himself to the wall behind the door and waited.

Hazel was sitting up now. She looked at Bess, bright and brassy, leaning over her and offering wine, and something in her look assured her that rumour had been right. Her eyes asked an urgent question of Bess; her answer was an almost imperceptible movement of the head. Black John was here. She must find him. She could think no further than that. She sipped the hot wine, drinking in new life. Bess was talking to the guests.

'I'll take her to my bedchamber, she can rest there.' She turned to Hazel, 'Come, can you stand?'

Hazel got carefully to her feet. Her legs did not want to hold her but they would have to. A moment of darkness threatened her; she blinked it down, leaning on Bess's arm. The men crowded round on the pretext of helping, eager to touch the two girls. Bess expertly fended them off, laughingly careful not to offend her customers. At the door to her chamber she excluded them.

'How now, gentlemen! Not in milady's chamber!'

' 'Twouldn't be the first time, Bess!' they reminded her, and she returned with a wink, 'Aye, but one at a time and not before the children!'

This earned a roar of good-natured laughter and they made their escape.

'Well - and what now?'

Black John's voice, edgy with impatience, took Hazel by surprise. She had not expected to find him so easily - or so plainly displeased to see her. Even had she regained the use of her voice she would now have lost her tongue. She looked desperately from one to the other, unable to produce a sound. She was bitterly aware that she intruded; she did not need John's look to tell her, or the difficulty with which Bess suppressed her laughter.

She had been a fool to come! Her anger rose to meet his. She choked down a sob, shook her head, and glaring at them both turned and blundered towards the door.

'Not so fast!' His arm barred the way. 'Did you walk all this way just to see what I was at?' His voice mocked her, 'What, not one word?'

Bess took the light and held it higher. 'John - I don't believe she can.'

Hazel turned to her, jealousy forgotten - what did it matter? If Bess understood she could help her... and somebody must. Someone must make John understand, and she could not. She looked pleadingly at Bess.

'What's the matter, love?' Bess asked gently, her coarse, kind face perturbed.

'Has that old witch cut her tongue!' John's voice was sharp. He turned her towards him and peered into her face. She shook her head, opened her mouth obediently to show him.

'What old witch?' asked Bess.

'Mother Cropper,' he tossed over his shoulder, and turned again to Hazel, his tone modified. 'Child, what is it?'

Hazel made a cradling movement of her arms, managed to mouth the words 'My baby-' before her face crumpled. Then she was sobbing helplessly in Black John's arms.

'There, there ...' He patted her heaving shoulders. She heard him say to Bess, 'She had a baby. It must have died.'

She raised her head. He was looking past her. She reached up her hand and turned his face towards her, shaking her head. 'The woman-' she mouthed at him. He frowned, uncomprehending.

'What's she trying to say?' he said to Bess. 'It looks like "woman"

Hazel turned to Bess and mouthed again.

'It is "woman",' Bess confirmed. 'John! Did you say Mother Cropper?'

'What of it?'

'Did she steal it?' she demanded of Hazel, who nodded frantically. 'That's what she's trying to tell you - the old witch has stolen her baby! Oh, the poor, poor girl ...'

Hazel was passed from John's arms to Bess's. In the man's face fury gathered like a brewing storm.

'I paid that old besom to look after them. If she's tricked me she shall answer with her life!'

'John, where are you going?'

'Keep the girl hidden - I'll be back. No heathen granny defies me and gets away with it!'

Before either of them could stop him, he was gone.

By the light of the dip in his woodshed, Hal Cropper ticked off the ingredients on his fingers. They were all there, waiting for the last essential two.

The swaddles would stink. They could be left to the women. The brains - that was his speciality. His tongue flicked lizard fashion over his lips. He picked up the fine chisel, reached out for the mallet-

His first thought was that someone had punched him in the kidneys. Then, as he turned to face his attacker, pain tore through him as the blood gushed out. Another blow, to the stomach, ripping upwards . . . red flooded his eyes ... a hot salt slime bubbled from his mouth ... agonisingly, he vomited . . . the chisel fell from his fingers as he buckled forward, clutching at his spilling guts ...

Black John leaned past him to the table where the baby lay, its thumb rammed far into its mouth, minute fingers curled over its nose. He touched it and it wailed reassuringly. He picked it up, stiff and awkward on its swaddling-board, and wiped a bloodied hand on its coverings. He buckled the damp wriggling bundle, still protesting, into his doublet and turned to go. As he did so he came face to face with Mother Cropper.

She stared at him for an instant. Then she looked past him and saw Hal, still twitching and shuddering on the ground.

She ran to him, her anguish wrung from her in a dreadful cry, kneeling beside him, trying to cradle him, locked as he was in his death spasm.

'Oh, my Hal - my Hal...' she crooned, rocking back and forth. 'I'll get him, I'll get him for this, I will, if it's the last thing I do ...'

Black John paused with his hand on the door.

'A son for a son,' he said evenly, 'a fair exchange, I think!'

He left her kneeling there, keening, her eyes fixed on him like those of a basilisk.

'Dear God,' whispered Bess, 'the Sheriff's men!'

Holding the lantern high, she went out boldly to greet them.

'What cheer, gentlemen! Not often we see you here for a merry evening.'

The sergeant shouldered her aside, striding past her into the tavern. She turned to one she knew by sight.

'On duty, is he?'

'Aye, we all are. Pressing duty, too.'

'Why - who are they after?'

The man lowered his voice. 'Black John, no less.'

Bess feigned astonishment. 'Not here?' She forced a laugh, 'He'll surely not hide in such a public place!'

'Ah!' The man looked knowing, self-important. He inclined his head slightly, as if imparting something confidential. 'According to information laid...' He straightened up with an air of satisfaction.

Bess rewarded him with the round eyes he expected.

'There now! Well, I never!'

'Aye - claimed the reward, they have. But mark you,' his hand slid down to slyly pinch her bottom, 'if you was to be able to point him out to me, no reason why you shouldn't be the one to benefit. What do you say?'

'Well ...' Bess sounded dubious, 'I dunna swear as I could. What sort does he look like?'

They moved inside where the taverner and guests were being roughly put about. Bess pointed to where a fat merchant was trying to conceal his bulk behind a high- backed settle.

'Would that like be him?' she whispered to her companion. The men were pounding about, thumping on panelling, opening chests, overturning tables in their frustration. Women were screeching, the taverner's dog snarling, barking and wagging his tail by turns, the horses in the undercroft stable whickering and stamping excitedly at the noise. Suddenly the sergeant noticed the little door behind the chimney-breast. Resolutely he moved towards it.

Bess grabbed the arm of the man beside her.

'Dunna let him go in there - 'tis my bedchamber!'

'No way of saving it, I fear. We have to search.'

'But there's a sick woman in there. We think she has-' She reached up and whispered in his ear.

His eyes widened in horror.

'Sir!' he sprang forward, whispered in the sergeant's ear. The hand that had lifted the latch let it drop. The face turned colour.

Bess said urgently, 'Promise you wunna say nothing - we'd have no custom here if it leaked out. We'll have her out and buried before the dawn.'

The sergeant quickly pulled himself together.

'It seems we have been misinformed. Your pardon, gentlemen, for this disturbance.'

They were gone even faster than they had come in. Bess heaved a sigh of relief. They would not be back here for a day or two. Thank God they had not barged in and found the girl in there with her sable cloak and sporting a bishop's ring - they'd have known soon enough that all they had to do was wait!

'What did you tell 'em that cleared 'em out so quick?' Robbie the taverner stood akimbo, his round red face surprised. Bess pushed back the hair from her face.

'I said I had the Sheriff in there with his breeches down!' Her laugh was greeted with a roar of approval. Nobody loved the Sheriff - or his men. In an atmosphere of instant good humour they set about restoring the overturned furniture. Robbie cut a large hunk of pie.

'Give this to the little lass,' he said, 'she looks half starved.'

Bess pushed open the door to. her chamber and was astonished to see Hazel contentedly nursing her baby.

'Well done, Bess! Come in quietly,' said Black John.

'It's no good, John,' Bess held up the dip and peered into Hazel's face, 'it's my belief Mother Cropper put a spell on her.'

Half an hour of patient coaxing had produced not an

audible word. Hazel looked fearfully from one to the other; at the mention of the dread name she began to tremble.

John opened his mouth to roar 'Nonsense!' but one look at Hazel was enough to tell him she believed it. Bess believed it too! From the tail of his eye he could see her crossing herself, an automatic if incongruous gesture of self-defence. He was a man and a soldier. He believed what he saw, and not always all of that. He had not seen the Cropper woman casting any spell. But he had seen hysteria before. He had seen men in battle lose their speech, even their sight, for a time. It always came back.

Hazel was trembling violently, her eyes dilated wildly. He drew her to her feet and held her warmly against him. Her heart was racing like a frightened rabbit's.

'There now,' he murmured soothingly, stroking her back, 'There now . . .' as if he were gentling a mare. 'So the old ratbag magicked you, did she?' He said it quietly, seriously, meeting superstition with superstition.

Hazel looked up and drew a long hiccuping sigh. He felt her begin to relax. He held her closer, slender and pliant, like a young plant. Her trembling diminished.

'Well, I have a magic too.' He tilted her chin and brushed his lips over hers. He let his tongue go briefly in search of hers and was aware of the swift intake of her breath, the instinctive movement to follow as he drew his mouth away. Her heart was beating fast again. But differently ... He smiled into her half-closed eyes. 'And mine is the stronger,' he said. He winked across her shoulder at Bess, who turned away half laughing, knowing all too well what he meant.

'You must go,' she said.

Hazel smiled dreamily. Black John was her strength. If he said it would be so, it would be so. She was not going to be parted from him again.

'Yes,' he said in a businesslike tone. 'We must go. I would not have Bess here get her neck stretched for me.'

He guided her through the concealed niche at the back of the closet through which he had entered. She found herself below in the stable among horses, tack and hayracks. Outside she could hear the plash of falling rain. Black Man, startled from his drowsing, was saddled up in the dark. Hazel, taking no chances after twice being left behind, held fast to his bridle with one hand and the baby with the other.

Bess had followed them out. Black John leaned down from the saddle and put something into her hand.

'You have not seen me, Bess - you understand. And my thanks to you.'

He reached down a hand to Hazel, who put the baby into it. He took the damp bundle reluctantly and thrust it back at her as soon as she was mounted.

'Why not leave them with me?' suggested Bess. 'You'd travel faster alone.'

John hesitated. Hazel held her breath, wishing Bess to Hell. Bess waited, her mind full of things she dared not ask. Then he said, 'They come with me - we'll pass as travellers.' As Bess opened her mouth, he added, 'I have my reasons.'

His heels thumped Black Man's sides and they were away in a cloud of spray, leaving her to her reflections.

She stood for a long time, thinking. Black John had never to her knowledge taken a woman with him before. Why did he now? And such a one! She was a bit of an overblown rose herself, perhaps, but that one ... a green bud scarcely showing colour! If he wanted a woman, why not take a real one, why not herself who could show him some pleasure? Her resentment cooled as she thought of life as it must be on the road. Not for her the rain-wet night with a newborn babe - you wouldn't catch her out there! Hers might be a hovel to some but at least it was shelter. And then, there were the men and their money ... even John himself, darting in and out of her life like a kingfisher over a muddy pool. He could be a charmer when he wanted, right enough. But she wouldn't trust herself to one such as he - not she, she was no fool. 'I have my reasons,' that was what he had said. And dark enough reasons they would be, if she knew anything.

Bess pursed her lips. Then she tossed the gold piece in her palm and returned indoors.

5

Hazel lay back against the remembered warmth of John and let the world slide away from her. She did not know where they were going and she did not care. Cosy under the sables, she did not even feel the rain.

From time to time during the night she stirred, settled the baby more comfortably and drifted off again. Each time she awoke and pressed her head against Black John she felt the answering pressure of his arm. A tiny glow of peace inside her grew and prospered. When at last the sky lightened she was drowsing.

John reined in and looked about him with a practised eye. In another day he would be out of his own territory and into Grey Willy's. And Grey Willy was dead. He weighed the time they had been on the road against the likelihood that they were being followed. He made a rapid assessment of the terrain.

The greenwood through which the road wound was thinning to the familiar pattern of wasteland with its felled timber, its trees stripped of their lower branches by hook or by crook for firewood. There would be a village not far away which was best avoided. In the growing light he could see sheep like spots of fungus on a green hillside, a whisper of woodsmoke rising from a chimney out of sight.

The horse's head drooped and he wandered a few paces in search of grazing. John clucked to him, turning his head towards a wooded gully away to the left.

It would serve them well enough. It had a stream of fresh water and plenty of cover. He left the girl to sleep, his knife and doublet with her. An unarmed, shirt-sleeved traveller was hardly likely to be taken for an outlaw. Leaving Black Man cropping the lush grass of the little valley, he went on foot to the farm to buy food.

No more robberies for a time, he thought. No blazing a trail for the Sheriff's men to follow. The gold in his boots was more than adequate for their needs. They would travel by night, keeping out of sight by day, and Eustace would find him vanished off the face of the earth. Until the time was ripe. He smiled to think of Eustace stamping up and down the Great Hall, scattering the hounds. Crashing his fist down on the long table where they both had dined . . . maybe he would take out another ten burghers and hang them - what would be would be. They would be rid of him soon enough one way or another ...

The girl slept long into the morning and awoke looking refreshed. When they had eaten, he said, 'You're rested?'

She nodded.

'Then keep watch while I sleep.'

He stretched out, his head in her lap, squinting up at her as she shuffled to find a comfortable position. He dozed, her hand light on his hair.

At some time during the afternoon he felt her move and opened his eyes a crack. She leaned forward over him to pick up her baby. She had one breast uncovered. It hung close to his face, small, rounded and creamy where the line of tan faded out. At its tip a single drop of milk trembled like a pearl, or a tear. He clenched his teeth on an urgent desire to displace the nuzzling babe and press his own mouth there. He closed his eyes again. But sleep was gone.

Presently he got up, stretched, and went for a walk.

He was gone so long that Hazel, growing anxious, went to look for him. Rounding a bush she stopped, hardly able to believe what she saw. She suppressed a smile and stepped back out of sight.

With his back half-turned to her, using his murderous knife and intent on his reflection in a puddle, Black John was trimming his beard.

They moved off into the setting sun, avoiding the village and heading as far as she could judge south-west.

Black Man, bred to carry a knight in armour at full canter, plodded on tirelessly mile after mile, carrying them both. Hazel lost track of how long they travelled or how far, it being the least important thing on her mind. All it meant to her was more time, more distance between her and the past. She had John. She had her baby. Her world was complete. Day by day her taut nerves relaxed.

The heavy forest through which they moved thinned, and they came out into sunlight over rolling downs. The days were hot, the nights fragrant. The sky glowed after sundown like a green pearl. By day it was filled with scudding clouds that blew and billowed and built fantastic castles above their heads, scenting the air with rain that never fell.

'They come off the sea,' said John, and left Hazel wondering. The sea was something outside her experience.

Safe from pursuit now, they rested a whole day by a river bank. Hazel spent the time in weaving a basket of rushes to hold the baby. John watched her, chewing on a straw, while Black Man rested and grazed the rich pasture of the riverside. When evening fell and they did not move on Hazel wondered if this was where they were destined to stay. But at daybreak they were on their way again.

The rolling landscape flattened to a wild moor patched with heather and studded with gorse, the bright yellow flowers startling against the blackish thorn of its foliage. Here the black horse lifted his huge head and snuffed the air, his nostrils flaring, and whickered softly with pleasure.

'He smells the sea-wrack,' said John, leaning forward to pat the massive neck.

Hazel too sensed a difference in the air, though she could not put a name to it. Brackish, it was, and somehow - yes, damp. Then the wind changed and it was gone again.

Mist rose out of nowhere as the sun went down, crawling between the horse's legs, writhing about them in ghostly shapes as they moved. Black John was walking to stretch his legs, while Hazel rode alone, the baby in his cradle lashed to the saddle. She felt exposed and uneasy on her isolated perch. An eerie bluish glow came and went somewhere over to her left.

Grave lights! She shivered. No telling if they were safely far away or drawing nearer ... She shrank as a wreath of mist licked her face. The supernatural threatened her again, it was all around her, pressing in on her. She reached a timid hand towards the dark shape of the man walking ahead.

The horse, sensing her fear, stopped and blew noisily. He stamped a nervous hoof and flicked back his ears.

John swung himself up behind her.

'It's all right,' he said to them both in the same tone. He took the reins and clucked with his tongue and the animal moved forward, his confidence restored.

Hazel crouched against him and felt better. Tom would have jeered at her fears, but he showed no sign. He rode on with eyes fixed ahead in fierce concentration. But she suspected it was bogs and not demons he was watchful for.

Towards dawn, the mists began to glow with a rosy incandescence. Then abruptly they were out of them into daylight, the moor burning lurid behind them in an angry sunrise, as if it resented having let them escape.

Before them was something that Hazel had never imagined.

All along the skyline for further than the eye could follow shone an endless shift of colours; of blue, of green, of purple, of every nameless shade in between. And over this the brilliant light bounced and glittered like jewels in the sun.

She stared, entranced, not believing what she saw. It was - a silk scarf crusted with diamonds. It was - a dawn sky crammed with stars. It was-

A hand cupped her shoulder.

'There, Mistress Ash - there's the sea.'

She flung him an excited glance and scrambled down from the saddle. She started running towards where she could make out a huddle of thatch in the dip of a valley and far beyond it the bobbing masts of boats. It really was water, then, all that vast expanse of it! She had not thought there was so much water in the world. She wanted to go and plunge her hands in it, to feel its wetness, to convince herself. But though she ran till she was breathless it came no nearer. It retreated tantalisingly before her, always just below that dazzling horizon.

Black John came up with her in a creak of leather and a whiff of horsy sweat. He was laughing.

'It's a long way yet, you'd better ride with me!'

He hoisted her up and urged the horse to a canter. She joined in his laughter and threw an impulsive ami about his neck.

Her joy was infectious. The old horse felt it along with the sea breeze in his nostrils and moved his great bulk as lightly as a colt, his mane and tail streaming out behind him along with the girl's long hair. The man felt it, tossing the blackened years behind him as he headed for the beaches of his boyhood.

The canter romped to a gallop. They all went careering madly over the sweet grass in the morning air.

The sun blazed down. By the time they had picked their way down the little gully to the beach they were soaked with sweat.

'Come,' said John, 'let's drown our vermin in the sea.'

Hazel looked up from where she was sifting through her fingers the fine silver sand that she had never seen before. He was drawing off his clothes. Was she to do the same? She hung back, pretending not to understand.

'Come on,' he prompted, tweaking at her gown. She blushed. 'What- so shy? I've seen it all before, remember.'

But then it had been different - then it had not mattered if he thought her ugly! And now, when she had just had a child ...

He was laughing at her, standing beside her naked and unconcerned. She loosened her laces and drew the gown off over her head, keeping her back to him. But his eyes were on the sea as he waited, hand outstretched. She stole a sidelong glance. He was magnificent even now, she thought from her ripe age of fourteen years; how he must have looked when he was young, before the scars of battle marred his hide! Over his rib-cage she could see where a heavy blow had left a permanent hollow. Down his right thigh ran a seam in which she could have laid two fingers. But he was lean and muscular as a sleek scarred animal.

She discarded the ludicrous remnant that had been her shift and felt the cool breeze tickling her skin. It set her tingling with a strange excitement. She took his hand and ran with him to the water's edge.

She would not have thought that mere water could make so much noise. It roared and howled and hissed over the sand, and reared up in great green rolls that came smashing down towards her. She could feel the drumming of it under her feet like a giant trying to come up from underground. Intimidated, she would have turned back if he had not dragged her in after him.

It was cold! Mother of God, it was freezing! It gripped her feet like icy jaws and she felt the cramps running up under her insteps. She gasped and tried to free her hand but he would not release it, he drew her inexorably with him out into the waves. The water was up her legs now, and he looked back laughing as she jumped up and down trying to keep its freezing fingers from her crutch. Then a tall wave came and drenched them both, forcing the air from her lungs in a shriek of shock, of excited laughter, of delight... the next moment they were playing in the shallows like two children, laughing and thrashing up the water into foam. John dowsed his head to rid himself of lice and Hazel tried to do the same. She came up gasping and choking, her nose and eyes full of water and her wet hair plastered to her face.

'Try breathing out!' he shouted. He looked at where she held one hand just under her left breast. 'What's that you're hiding?'

She shook her head and danced away from him, the hand still in place. He gave chase. They splashed out of the water and up the beach.

He was the stronger and swifter but she was the more agile and had given him the slip several times when he finally tripped her and they came down together, laughing and breathless on the warm sand.

The laughter stilled suddenly. Was it her heart that beat so wildly - or was it his? The hand was still in place. He laid his over it, his fingers brushing her breast, lingering over the taut nipple. His thumb caressed her palm ... he lifted her hand.

'What have we here?' he said softly.

Hazel felt his breath as he spoke. Droplets of water ran from his hair and fell upon her face. Once more she was helpless on her back with the weight of a man above her. His shadow was between her and the sun. But it was a delicious terror that gripped her.... her eyes were closing. She thought she shook her head but she was losing the power to deny him. She could think of nothing but the time he had kissed her so briefly and then had seemed to forget. Now he was close again. She longed to feel his mouth ... she must escape him and run away ... she began to tremble. She could not look at him ...

'Who's this one for?' he was whispering, his mouth brushing hers.

Her lips formed the words against his, "'Tis for the Devil...'

Only his eyes laughed. 'Then 'tis for me.'

His kiss lulled her mind to sleep. His mouth travelled over her, his hair brushed her skin. Her arms drank him in, ecstatically ...

Far away along the beach came a small penetrating voice.

'Your child is crying,' said Black John.

As Hazel walked unsteadily back along the sand to her small demanding son, there was just one fear in her mind concerning John. It was no longer that he might one day take her by force. It was that he might never take her at all.

John looked at Angel, fed now and back in his cradle.

'He stinks,' he remarked. 'Can't you do something?'

Hazel took the knife and carried the baby to the water's edge. She carefully cut away the swaddling bands that Mother Cropper had put on him, stiff and sodden with everything he had passed since his birth. They had been convenient enough for travelling but she did not like them. None of Margery's babies had been swaddled - though the neighbours had whispered that she kept them alive by witchcraft instead of by warmth. When she had cleaned him gently, she wrapped him in the cleanest part of her shift and laid him back in his cradle. He stretched his cramped limbs and began to kick. Something that might have been the germ of a smile flickered briefly across his face.

Hazel looked with distaste at her own discarded garment. It had not been off her back since last summer. It was stiff with the dirt and sweat of months. She felt so clean and fresh from her bathe that the thought of crawling back into it was depressing. With a sigh she bent to pick it up. It was twitched out of her hand.

'Leave it. Just wear the cloak.'

He put it about her shoulders. Its sable lining caressed her from neck to heel as he helped her to the saddle.

He tossed away the travel-stained doublet he had murdered for. He hung his precious boots across the saddle and swung himself up behind Hazel, riding barefoot and shirtless under the sun as they headed up the steep gully away from the beach. But his knife was still secure in his belt. He was still Black John.

Black Man was beginning to tire at last. To ease him John dismounted, leading him at an ambling pace while Hazel rode with the baby, talking to him from time to time, letting him pause to graze.

As the sun reached its zenith Hazel could no longer stand the heat inside the sable cloak. She let it slide little by little to her hips, telling herself that John could not see her, walking ahead as he was. But she kept a fold across her belly to hide the stretch marks of which she was so conscious. He had seen her before, she reminded herself. And felt the touch of her, as she had of him ... the memory was intoxicating. Her eyelids drooped. She gave herself over to the dizzying contact of their skin from breast to knee ... a warm sensuality glowed in her like wine, heightening her perceptions. She was aware of the unaccustomed touch of cool air against her body, of the tremor of her full breasts with the movements of the horse. She closed her eyes and let her mind drift back to the morning.

A touch aroused her. He was walking beside her, his arm brushing her leg. Although he did not appear to be looking she felt his eyes like a hot caress sweep over her. He said nothing. Presently his hand touched her ankle. His fingers encircled it lightly, then roamed over her bare foot, enfolding, fondling, exploring it as if he would learn its contours. She spread her toes in an access of pleasure.

The horse, now that he had ceased to urge it on, came to a standstill. John's face was against her thigh. He turned his open mouth against it. Her hands came down of their own volition to entwine fingers in his hair. Slowly he raised his head, eyes kindling. She leaned down towards him as he reached up ...

The baby whimpered unheeded as she slid from the horse's back.

So the road was open. Black John smiled thoughtfully into the sunset.

'What cheer, Mistress Ash?' He spoke softly as the sleeper on his shoulder stirred and sighed.

'Wahtchyer ...' she whispered back.

She rubbed her cheek against his skin. Her world glowed like an opal. Oh, my love, my love, my darling ... my love ... the words had come tumbling out of her as her body dissolved into a shower of light. Weeping and laughing, she had covered his face with her kisses. Now she slept. The afterglow throbbed itself out of the sky.

John's own release had been swift and hot and he returned her kisses with something like tenderness. Hazel in her inexperience had taken it for love. It was the biggest - and the happiest - mistake of her life.

John had been silent for a long while, his brows drawn together in deep thought.

'Why,' he mused at last, 'would a hanging corpse have one hand missing?'

Hazel shivered.

'Grey Willy ... the left or the right,' she whispered. The sun lost some of its heat.

'Grey Willy indeed,' he affirmed. He turned to her, his face lit with interest. 'What do you know of it?'

Hazel felt her throat constrict. 'The C-croppers had it.' 'What for?'

'I - I dunno.' Strange how the mention of their name had set her stammering.

He took her chilled fingers in his and rubbed them warm. 'Forget it,' he said. 'Just idle curiosity.'

Hazel searched her memory, eager to please him. 'Something about the dog days,' she said, 'and setting it in the sun.'

'Of course - the Hand of Glory!' He slapped his thigh. 'No doubt they thought to make their fortune with it.' 'What is it?' It had a horrid fascination. She flinched from being told yet could not keep herself from asking.

'A candle - for thieves. They claim that when it's lit in a house no sleeper can awaken. They light the fingers: one, two, three, four - presto, the house is theirs! Or so they believe. No doubt Grey Willy sees the humour of it, having been a villain himself.'

'It's horrible ...'

John glanced at her sidelong.

'Your voice is shrinking,' he said, 'time for a little more magic.'

Afterwards, as they lay quiet, he said, 'We spend the summer by the sea. How like you that?'

'Oh ... yes!' she breathed, the Croppers forgotten. How good life was now! Angel was thriving. Black John was hers. And now this - she had not known such happiness existed. Each day dropped like a present in her lap.

Abigail sat spinning by her cottage door.

As always when the breeze was not too sharp, Little John had brought out her spinning wheel and set it down in the garden where she could warm her bones in the sun. Let others boast of their roses down in the village! You couldn't have everything and she had the sea. It wasn't everyone who could sit among the lavender in the lee of the wall, and look out over the nodding heads of sea-pinks to that blue expanse. On a clear day you could see the lacy shapes of tall ships with the distant prickle of sunlight on their canvas.

It was a good enough place to end one's days in. They were lucky still to have their home since the Master was lost and so many changes made ... but there, they had somehow been overlooked and thankful to be so. Or perhaps someone had remembered her kindly ... she smiled into the brightness of the afternoon. The spinning wheel whirred slower and she drowsed.

Time slipped away from her as she sat between waking and sleeping, lullabyed by the distant whisper of the sea. In her mind's eye she saw for the thousandth time her darling as he rode at the head of his men, tall and proud on the great black horse that had carried him to war and had never. - brought him back. How strong he had seemed, how full of confidence with his life stretching out before him - every inch the leader of men. Yet to her, as always, the babe she had nursed, the wayward boy with the wit to charm her when she most needed to be stern ... The sky had gone dark when they told her. A desert had yawned in her life that even her own Little John had never quite been able to fill.

How the sad old ghosts came crowding back when she sat alone like this. Her lost one ... aye, and his lady mother. So gentle, so fragile with her pretty brown eyes ... and now there was only that usurper!

She bridled at the thought of him. Anger dispelled her melancholy and she sat up, eyes flashing, and set the wheel whirring savagely.

'Good day to you.'

She had not heard the man's approach. She looked up sharply, her thoughts still hot. Who dared come tramping to her cottage door? Some ruffian of the new Lord's, no doubt, with that wild hair and unkempt beard - and shirtless to boot! No respect for her grey hairs or her intimate connection with the old family - that counted for nothing now, she supposed. What was the new generation coming to, she'd like to know!

'Who's that?' she demanded. 'Who comes here?'

She peered at him fiercely, trying to identify the towering stranger who stood, almost diffidently, at her gate. And yet... there was something familiar in the way he stood - something in the voice -

'Abby?'

The smile, though tentative, was unmistakable. She rose, her vision blurring. She took an unsteady step towards him.

'Master John - oh, my Master John!'

He vaulted the wall in the old familiar way and caught her as her knees gave way.

6

Hazel watched downcast as John picked up the old woman and carried her indoors. They were no longer alone. Theirs had been a one-to-one relationship, two against the world; she was not ready to share it with anyone else. Dejection deepened into resentment when he failed to call her in but left her sitting forgotten on the horse outside.

She picked Angel out of his basket and held him close for comfort. Black John was the limit of her horizon: she had foolishly imagined herself to be the limit of his. Now she had to accept it was not so. But it was too soon.

A young man came out of the cottage and took Black Man by the bridle. He stood awkwardly waiting, until it dawned on her that he had come to unsaddle him. She dismounted and walked away along the path, not knowing what else to do. She was still outside, alone and unmissed, when the sun went down.

She had walked along the cliff and she had walked back again. She had fed Angel and winded him. She had cuddled him to sleep in the soft fur of her cloak. And still John had not come out of the cottage.

It was growing cold. She sat on her feet on the donkey of the spinning wheel and longed to go inside where the lamps were lit. She could not swallow her pride to creep in as unnoticed as she had been left outside. Stubbornly she waited while her resentment slowly collapsed into depression.

Once more the cottage door opened and she started up. But it was only the same young man come to bring in the spinning wheel. She walked away quickly before he could speak to her. She went on walking without looking back. She felt unwanted and desolate.

'You tended the horse - what did you do with the girl?' Little John shuffled his feet, embarrassed.

'She like - went off, sir.'

John swore under his breath and went out to look for her. His eyes picked her out at last in the fading light, a forlorn little figure on the cliff edge outlined against the sea. She sat motionless, cradling the baby and hugging her knees. He walked on down the cliff path towards her.

Hazel heard his approaching tread and shrank a little. What if he were angry at her wandering off? She pulled herself up. What had become of her? She, who had not feared his killer knife, now fearing his displeasure! She breathed deeply and tried to think what to say now that the moment was here.

He sat down beside her on the grass, not speaking. At last she said lamely, 'I was watching the sea-'

'-and fell asleep,' he finished for her.

She raised her head and stared hard at the glowing sky. ''Tis a grand cottage,' she said lightly, 'real glass in the windows.' She could not say any more.

'Good Cornish stone,' he assented. He added in a different tone, 'I'm a lout. I don't deserve you.'

Hazel wrestled with herself and at last smiled grudgingly. 'No, you dunna.'

'You should beat me more often.'

She knew she was being cajoled but she didn't care. He had left his fine friends to come and find her. She laughed and rubbed a hand across her nose. How could she be solemn with this idiot grin breaking out inside her?

He stretched out on the grass and gently rubbed her back.

'We sleep in a bed tonight. How like you that?'

She turned to look at him, eyes shining. She had foreseen herself alone with Angel on the desolate moor.

'Us-in a bed?'

'You and I - of course.' He regarded her lazily. The movement of his hand was slow and sensual. She felt her bones dissolving.

'Like proper wedded folk?' she said shyly, her hand going to the gold coin strung about her neck.

It was his turn to laugh. The sound crackled out like the splintering of ice.

'Please God better than that!' he said.

He led her into the cottage and she stood abashed, not knowing what to say.

A bright fire burned in the ingle and the old lady, neatly gowned in homespun, was bringing new bread and cider to the table. Something that smelled very good was sizzling in a skillet.

'Sea-food,' said John appreciatively. 'Come to the table, child. Abby, this is Hazel.'

She bobbed in deference, waiting for him to add 'My wife'. Instead he turned to her and said roguishly, 'See - I remembered your name.'

She sat down awkwardly, trying to balance the baby and at the same time hold her cloak together to save displaying her nakedness underneath. John laughed.

'She has no clothes, Abby. No doubt you can fit her up.'

'Of course, my lord.'

Hazel's eyes flew open wide and were rewarded with a warning look from John. She noticed that their hosts stood back and did not join them in the meal. She was aware too that though Abby's eyes were warm with love while they rested upon John, when they fell upon her a shutter seemed to come down. A bland mask of politeness, disguising - what? She ate her meal in an uneasy silence, looking for guidance to John, from whom none was forthcoming. By bedtime she was smouldering.

'Who is that old biddy?' she whispered fiercely.' "Lord" this, "lord" that - dunna she know what you are ?'

His voice beside her in the darkness was coldly restrained.

'As you once observed, I was a good man once. Are you so eager to disillusion her?'

Hazel wrestled to find the words.

'It's not that so much - it's how she looks at me, like I wasna there. And I feel it the worse because we've took her bed.'

'I take her bed - not you. It's what she expects.'

'But why -why? Is she a servant or summat? What's she to you?'

'My childhood nurse. Now are you satisfied?'

Hazel fell silent, struggling to comprehend. Nurses were for childbed. Though there had been Tib. Presently she said softly, 'Perhaps she dunna like me because she's jealous.'

'Perhaps,' he drew her towards him, 'and don't say dunna.'

The promised treat of sleeping in a bed fell somewhat short for Hazel. She felt enclosed and in need of air and awoke at intervals during the night while John slept soundly beside her. By morning she had decided there was much to be said for the wild grass and the stars - and solitude with your man. She was embarrassed when Abby walked unannounced into the room, nettled when she addressed her sole remark to the still unconscious John.

'I trust you slept well, Master John ?'

Hazel sat up and smiled sweetly.

'From owl-drop to sparrow-fart,' she said.

Happiness had come to Abigail in her declining years, filling her home and spreading to those around her. Her beloved

'Young Master' had returned from the dead, and all was about to be as it was before. With difficulty John restrained her from running to spread the news. His return must be kept secret, he persuaded her, until he was ready to arrive officially and in the proper style. He had no heart to tell her that he was come like a thief in the night, that a bootful of gold stood between him and destitution; no stomach to speak of the price on his head - still less of the part he had played in putting it there. She fussed over him like a hen with one chick. For the moment he was content to let her have her way.

Her son's meagre wardrobe was raided to find him clothes while the boy stood by, frizzy-haired and amiable, pleased at the return of the master he too remembered.

But Little John's pleasure was in his mother's delight. His eyes saw deeper than hers and he felt only pity for the ravaged man he barely recognised. Even when his mother had cropped the wild mane, tutting over the iron-grey streaks that shone on the once dense black, even when she had reduced the beard to her notion of a gentlemanly style, she could not bring back the man who had ridden away. But, mercifully, she did not see it. To her he would always be the boy she had reared and no change was apparent to her.

With loving pride she produced a ruby earring she had treasured through the years, and held it to his ear. He turned to the girl, laughing, 'How like you that?'

Hazel, feeling more of an outsider by the hour, felt a tingle of jealousy.

'I dunna,' she said flatly. 'I dunna like you dressed up like a popinjay!'

'You preferred Black John, no doubt!' His voice had an edge to it.

Hazel held her ground. 'At least he was an honest rogue.'

The exchange was over Abby's head. But she was not to be left out.

'It would not be what she understands,' she said purringly, and had the satisfaction of seeing Hazel's colour rise.

'I'm well aware of what she understands,' said John shortly.

Abby withdrew. She accepted Hazel as a whim of her master's. If she was startled by the appearance in her kitchen of a girl wearing nothing but a gold ring and a sable cloak she was careful not to show it. It was not for her to comment on the eccentricities of her gods. He might bed with a dozen girls if he'd a mind to. She would never be the one to ask a question. She fed the girl and clothed her, and combed out her tangled hair as she would have cared for a lap-dog he had brought in. And that was all.

She took possession of the golden-haired Angel and crooned over him. She was entranced - to have a baby to care for again, and such a bonny one!

Hazel, apprehensive for her secret, snatched him back.

Abigail's deference to John did not extend to Hazel and she lost no time in saying so. Her authority was not to be flouted by any village wench. She had forgotten more about babies than Hazel would ever know. The child needed swaddling, she asserted firmly. He was being cooled for the grave.

Hazel was adamant. The baby was hers. He was not to be swaddled without her consent. 'The wrappings of an unbaptised child ...' the words still haunted her mind. She could not forget. She clutched him fiercely, spitting defiance while Angel yelled in protest.

'Feral cat!' chided John, half amused, half annoyed that she must tangle with Abby. 'Can't you lend her the child to sweeten her old age?'

'He's mine, I'll not have him swaddled!'

'Swaddled - unswaddled - what does it matter? Profit from what Abby can teach you - learn how to care for a high-born child - ' He stopped abruptly as if he had said too much.

Hazel softened. He must be thinking of the children they would one day have.

'I dunna want him swaddled,' she said pleadingly. She went over and whispered in his ear, 'I'm feared of her seeing the mark.'

'The mark!' He was scornful. 'It's nothing - a quirk of nature. Which he gets from his mother, 1 think.'

She coloured. It was the first time he had alluded to it and she wished he had not. Not here in front of others.

He ignored her discomfiture. He took the baby from her arms and handed him to Abby.

'It's nothing to be ashamed of. Don't be foolish.'

She knew it was going to sound silly. Especially to him. But she had to say it. Wringing her hands, she stumbled, 'I tried to tell you before ... they say 'tis for the Devil!'

She was totally unprepared for his reaction.

'And I've told you before -' he seized her, stripped her gown to the waist, and tossed her up, laughing - 'that 'tis for me!'

Hazel struggled free, her face an angry scarlet. She gathered her clothing in one hand and delivered a stinging slap with the other.

'You dunna do that to your wife in front of servants!' Abigail gasped. She opened her mouth to put the upstart in her place but before she could speak the offender had been hustled from the room.

Little John said, 'You got to allow him a sin or two, Ma. He's had it rough, I reckon.'

Abigail pulled herself together.

'He's the Master,' she said firmly. 'He beds where he chooses. But that little baggage, to give herself such airs! Wife, indeed! As if he'd wed with the likes of that, even if he could!'

'I dunno,' Little John chuckled. 'I reckon he'd have more pleasure of her than he's like to get out of-'

It was his turn to have his ears boxed. Abby rounded on him.

'You keep a civil tongue in your head for talking about your betters! And keep your thieving eyes off your master's piece -

I've seen you look at her, don't think I haven't!'

He grinned, 'A fellow can look, don't mean nothing. Though I'll say I wouldn't say no to his leavings when he's done.' He ducked to avoid another clout. 'Come on, now.' He put an arm about her shoulders, joggled her affectionately, 'You know I won't do nothing to upset him.'

He refrained from pointing out that John was not his master, that he had nothing but his futile dreams of revenge. His youth was behind him. Maybe even his title was not really his anymore, though to them he would always be Lord John. Hard-worked fisherman though he was, given the chance he would not trade with him. If he found comfort in coupling with a beggar in a ditch, who would want to rob him of it - he had little else to hope for,

God knew. But Abigail lived in the past and must be humoured. She was too old to be forced into facing facts.

'I promise I won't look at her no more. All right?' Abigail was somewhat mollified. 'And not another disrespectful word about - you know who.... '

'I promise.' That would not be difficult. She rarely crossed his mind. He shouldn't think she often crossed Lord John's ...

'That's better,' Abby smiled, reproof tempered with indulgence. He was, after all, her son. 'You could get strung up by your thumbs for saying less.'

'Oh-ah,' he replied absently. He wasn't worried about his thumbs for the moment. He was thinking about the girl Hazel. She didn't seem to be the sort to 'give herself airs'. What had made her say such a strange thing?

'Wonder what he told her,' he said musingly.

His eyes met Abby's. She had been thinking the same thing.

Hazel was sobbing distractedly.

'I was good enough for you with the rope around your neck, now you're ashamed of me!'

John paced the floor, exasperated. 'You talk like a fool.' 'Then tell 'em we're wed!'

'No!'

'Why not - why canna you tell 'em?'

'Because I do not choose.' He rounded on her, grasping her roughly by the shoulders. 'Do you want me to tell that poor doting old creature that I had to be rescued from the gallows? Is that what you want?'

Hazel shook her head, unable to see for the tears.

'Just tell her we're wed. Just so she treats me right. She won't talk to me, John. She thinks I'm some kind of whore. I can see it in her eyes every time she looks at me.' She covered her face with her hands and her voice was muffled. 'My mother brought me up right. I anna like that.'

'I know,' he sighed. 'Spare me your respectability.' Why couldn't she be what he had taken her for? Emotional ties were the last thing he had use for.

'Please tell her,' pleaded Hazel. 'Please…

'Have done!' he snapped. A squirming conscience made him irritable. 'I'll tell her to treat you better. Be satisfied.'

'But I'm your wife-' she wailed.

The same old theme. He had heard it once too often. He pushed her away.

'Who would have married anyone who fed her,' he reminded her brutally.

It cut the more deeply because it was true. She hit back.

'And you'd have took anyone to save your neck!'

A smile tugged at the corner of his mouth.

'Touche!'

The term was lost on Hazel but she understood the smile. She scrubbed her eyes and looked up into his brooding face.

'Dunna be spiteful. I love you now.' She reached up to press her damp cheek against his, 'If you was to put me away from you I'd die.'

She had handed him a weapon. He thrust it home.

'In that case,' he said very clearly and precisely, 'you had best be very careful what you say to Abigail.'

Hazel drew back. It was a moment before she fully understood what he had said. She stared, unbelieving.

John straightened up to his full height. His hand fell so heavily on her shoulder that it made her jump.

'Your first lesson in life, small Hazel,' he said soberly. 'It's not he who is right who wins - it is he who holds the sword.'

Hazel went early to the shore, and she went alone.

No use hoping for John to go with her now, even if she had wanted him to. He spent less and less time in her company and she was left more and more to her own devices. She spent long hours on the shore collecting and discarding pebbles, seaweed, shells, poking about in rocky pools to see the tiny spiderlike crabs go scurrying for shelter. It never failed to interest her but she wanted to share it with John. And he was almost always missing on some mysterious errand, from which he returned elated or downcast but with never a word to tell her where he had been.

Today she had not even looked for him. Today she wanted to think.

There was too much about their coming here that she did not understand. Why was he, a homeless outlaw, received like a king in this outlandish place? Why, if it came to that, were they here at all? She knew him too well to believe he had travelled so far just to say Hello. And there was Abigail herself - why was she not allowed to know that they were wed? Knowing John, there was more behind it than consideration for the old nurse's feelings - she knew him to use people as ruthlessly as he trod on grass. And if he had really come to see Abby, why did he disappear for days on end? The way things were, the old lady saw even less of him than she did herself. And if Abby was not meant to know about her, why had he brought her here?

She was not grass, she told herself. She would not be walked upon and never know the reason why. There were things she needed to know - that she had a right to know. And she intended to find out. Where did he go when he did not return all night? A woman somewhere ... a sharp blade twisted within her at the thought. What if it was not only Abby who must not know? What if there were someone else, someone who meant so much to him that he could not keep away?

Surprises had come thick and fast in her life and she had learned to take them in her stride. But this was bewildering in a different way. Questions writhed in her mind like snakes, and at the bottom of it all there was something wrong. It distressed her to watch him changing day by day before her eyes. If only he would talk to her.... But he never did.

Far off by the water's edge she could see Little John at work on his boat. She paused, thoughtful. She had promised not to talk of these things to Abby.

But nothing had been said about Little John.

He looked up as she approached and she could see that her presence embarrassed him. Was he in the secret?

Perhaps he foresaw the questions she was longing to ask.

'Mornin', Mistress Hazel,' he mumbled, obviously hoping she would pass on by.

She sat down on the sand and began to draw a pattern with her finger.

'Why do you call me mistress?'

He did not answer.

'I'm younger than you, you know.'

'Oh-ah,' he made a pretence of looking for a tool. 'Yere 'tis!' and he moved round to the far side of the boat.

'Why do you?' she persisted. 'Is it because I'm your master's wife, did he tell you to?'

If she could discover what he had said to Little John she might find a clue. She might learn if it was Abby who was being deceived - or herself. He was silent.

'Well, answer me!'

She was gnawed by the feeling that everyone knew more than she did. What was it that he didn't want to say?

'Little John!' she yelled at last in frustration, 'Tell me!'

Little John put down his tools and straightened up. He looked very large and not very happy. She said, 'I'm sorry. I shouldna shout at you.'

'Tha's all right, Mistress Hazel. I understand. But I treats you with respect, don't I? In't you satisfied?'

Hazel sighed. She could not complain of his behaviour. But it was not the point at issue.

'Now my Ma,' he went on, 'I know she's a bit sharp. But she's old. You have to forgive her. She don't stomach such goings on. Now me, I'm different. Don't matter to me what folks do.'

He had not answered her question and it came to her that he was not going to answer it. There were none so dull as those who wished to be. But she had one last try.

'No,' she agreed, and slipped in quickly, 'specially married folks, eh?' It was not exactly a question but it certainly invited an answer. She waited vainly for him to agree or contradict. He bent again to his task with a big show of diligence. He whistled between his teeth. She could feel him waiting tensely for her to go. She was wasting her time.

Exasperated, she marched off up the beach. She would have this out with John himself. But when she reached the cottage he was not there.

'Where's John?' she demanded of Abigail.

'Master John went out,' replied Abigail, carefully emphasising the word 'Master'.

'Where did he go?'

Abby's mouth folded in a prim line.

'Not for the likes of us to ask.' She was bent on putting Hazel in her place.

'Didn't he leave me no message?'

'Now why in the world would he do that?' A gleam of

triumph lit Abby's eye. Her hands folded smugly across her apron.

'Because I'm his wife!' Hazel wanted to shout at her, to wipe the holier-than-thou look off her face. But the words were forbidden. She had promised. It was not to be endured! Goaded beyond speech she went out.

The day of endless waiting wore slowly away and still he had not returned. Her anger turned to anxiety. Had he left her? Black Man was missing. It would not be the first time ... But not now, surely - not now that they had become lovers? Even if there were someone else, he must surely have said something, let fall some hint... but she was not sure of anything anymore. She kept taking herself for walks, telling herself that when she returned he would be there. But she came back again and again to the same sinking of the stomach.

Dusk fell. The sea howled up and down the beach. The seabirds ceased their mewing and settled on the rocks. And still she was alone.

Little John came in for his supper and she contrived to get him alone.

'Where is he, Little John? Dunna pretend you don't know.'

'Why not ask him yourself when he do get back?'

'But suppose-' She broke off, unwilling to betray her misgivings to Little John. Was he assuming - or did he know that John was coming back? How could she ask him? She began to pace the floor in her agitation.

Little John said, 'Why don't you go to bed and wait for him, Mistress Hazel? Like as not he's only up to the tavern with his friends.'

'Friends - what friends?'

'Why, I dunno.' The big fellow shrugged his shoulders, his face blank and innocent.

If he's with some woman, thought Hazel-

'Where's this tavern, then?'

'Why, only up on the road apace. Just a few miles away.'

'Take me there!'

His jaw dropped, 'Mistress - I can't do that!'

'Oh, yes, you can!' she said firmly. 'You take me there now.' She saw a bland mask of obstinacy settle over his face and searched about for a means of moving him. 'Now,' she repeated, 'or I'll - I'll-' in a flash of inspiration - 'I'll tell him you raped me!'

'Mistress Hazel,' he was aghast, 'you wouldn't do that!'

'Try me,' said Hazel, picking up her cloak. 'Come on!'

She bundled him out of the door. She felt better now that she was doing something. Whatever happened was better than lying awake with her stomach in knots.

'I reckon he'll have the hide off me for this,' grumbled Little John as they trudged through the darkness.

'He won't know unless you tell him. Scratch my back and I'll scratch yours.'

'And what about my supper?' he remembered.

'Your mother'll keep it hot for you. Give her something else to think about,' said Hazel grimly. They completed the journey in silence.

'He's here, look.'

Little John raised an arm in the direction of the monstrous shadow that moved near the lighted windows of the inn. Black Man raised his head and blew them a greeting. Then he went back to his grazing. Hazel said, 'Stay out of sight till you see me safely inside. Then you can go'

Little John stared. He'd never known another young woman like this one.

'But how will you get home?'

'That's not your problem. If you dunna want to be seen go and hide yourself.'

He scratched his head. Then he did as he was told. He watched her as she smoothed her hair, walked up the path to the inn and boldly knocked on the door. A burst of noise reached him as she disappeared inside. He was grinning to himself as he started back. The master had better look to it, he reckoned. He'd met his match in this one if he ever would.

'What is it, innkeeper?'

Black John's voice dominated the hubbub from the inner room. It was unmistakable with its suggestion of restrained power. A lion on a leash. She said quickly, 'That's him. Let me by!'

'Not so fast, mistress!'

The smell of sweat and stale beer was overpowering as the man's arm was raised to bar her way. She tried to duck under it, unsuccessfully.

A fair-haired man dressed in velvet came forward.

'What goes on here?'

The innkeeper told him and he seemed to enjoy the joke. He called back over his shoulder, 'Here's a fine young wench says she's come to fetch her husband - sounds like you, Pengerran!'

A gust of laughter flooded out to engulf her.

'What - will you carry him home in your apron, mistress?'

'Bring her in here-'

'Let's have a look at her-'

The innkeeper was elbowed aside and she found herself pulled forward, sucked into a whirlpool of heat and noise. And there in the midst of it was Black John.

He sat sprawled in a chair near the fire, a tankard in his hand. One booted foot was propped insolently on the table on which lay the remains of a roasted haunch. The small room was filled to overflowing with men in rich clothes. But even on his own he would have filled it. His presence was so overpowering that despite his homespun shirt and borrowed fisherman's hose he dominated the assembly. He did not even need to stand. Their attention was held by him without any effort on his part.

He eyed her lazily as he had from the gallows.

'So, my little cat comes padding after me. Have a chair, my very inquisitive small Hazel.'

These men were all laughing at her. Her cheeks burned. But she stood her ground.

'I dunna want to sit. I dunna like this place. I come to ask-'

'Sit down!' It was the warning roar of the lion. With one finger he pushed her backwards into a chair. She clutched at its bobbined arms to save herself. He was on his feet now, towering over her. She trembled. But she was not going to give in. Not for this had she trudged the long miles. She swallowed, 'Come away, John. Now - I got to talk to you!'

'All in good time.'

He jerked off her girdle. Before she knew what he was about she found herself tied into her chair. Furious, she struggled to be free.

'Let me up!' she blazed. She lashed out with her feet. 'I'll make you pay for this, you see if I don't!'

He threw back his head and laughed, 'You hear that, my friends? I shall be made to pay!'

'What shall we do with her, Pengerran - pass her around among the company?'

The fair-haired man lurched forward to a chorus of beery approval. John sent him reeling with a good-natured shove.

'I keep my own house in order, with all due thanks. As for you, madam-' he grasped Hazel's face in one hand. He was still smiling, putting up a show for his friends; but she felt his anger in the pressure of his fingers. 'You find too much to say,' and he stopped her mouth in the most effective way.

It was a kiss without tenderness, brutal and contemptuous. As if he had thumbed his nose at her, there in the presence of his friends. It completed her humiliation as nothing else could have done. She met it with clenched teeth. She suppressed the traitor flame that tried to lick through her and her eyes blazed back defiant into his. But she was beaten.

Before she could recover he had bound a kerchief across her

mouth. He released her with a gesture of disdain, bruising her back against the carved wood of the chair. Then he lifted it with her as easily as if it were a toy, and set it on the table amongst the food.

'My mascot, gentlemen.' He presented her with a mocking bow, 'I give you a toast. To the best of all bedfellows - a mute one!' He wagged a maddening finger under Hazel's impotent nose. 'No more interruptions, now. Not another word.'

She shut her eyes to escape their ribaldries. But she could hear them all around her. She seethed. But there was nothing she could do.

John's voice said conversationally, 'You were saying, March?'

She peeped between her eyelids. He was back in his chair by the ingle. A man with long silvery hair glanced uneasily in her direction.

'Little pitchers have long ears, do they not?'

Her interest was awakened. What were they discussing that she should not hear - what might she learn if she listened carefully? Then John said something beyond her understanding.

'Si nous parlons français elle ne comprend pas.'

Her eyes popped open. They met his and she shut them again fast.

'Eavesdropping?'

His tone unnerved her. She shook her head.

'Remember, curiosity's a great killer of cats.'

She felt suddenly afraid. She wished she had not come. She was relieved when his attention was diverted from her by someone saying peevishly, 'See here, Pengerran, we haven't all spent years in France. Let's have a language we all understand, for God's sake!'

'Latin, then. We all have Latin, I think?'

There was a murmur of assent. It sounded a little like something she had heard in church. But like the prayers, she could make nothing of it. There was not even a name or a place name she could recognise. Their voices droned on and on. Sometimes they were urgent, sometimes raised in argument. They talked without ceasing while her back began to ache and her head to droop. There were no more jokes, no smiles. Whatever they said, it must be deadly serious.

She wondered unhappily what John would do with her when they had finished. She knew now she should not have come. Her foolish jealousy had led her to blunder in on something better left undiscovered. Something so secret that they had to use foreign words to discuss it. France - Latin - her head was spinning. But one thing was fast becoming clear to her. This man she had married was anything but what he seemed.

She awoke stiff and chilled in the grey hours of the morning. The stuffy room was heavy with male odours and stale drink. John was untying her. He was not smiling now. There were dark shadows under his eyes and his face was drawn and grim.

'So, small Hazel,' he said. 'The time has come for you and me to take a little walk.'

7

Hazel struggled breathlessly up the slope with Black John's hand relentless on the nape of her neck.

She had toyed with the idea of making a run for it but she knew she could never escape him on the open moor. She dared not ask where they were going. In any case, she knew. He was taking her out to a quiet place to kill her.

She thought of Angel. Why hadn't she stayed with him? What would become of him now? She had allowed herself to be lulled into thinking that Black John had changed his nature. She had known him for a villain and a murderer - how could she have let herself forget! It was too late now to be wise. She was going to die.

How would he do it? She had not seen him with his long knife lately - but he might well have been wearing it today among his fellow conspirators. She could not look behind her for the pressure of his hand on her neck. But perhaps it was better not to know. She stumbled on blindly, her heart thudding and her legs going numb.

Why were they climbing, climbing - to some high place? She choked on a gasping cry as the answer came to her - the cliff! She tripped on her long skirt and fell face downwards in the grass. His hands grasped her arms and she was yanked to her feet. Below her she heard the sea and the mewing gulls. Already she felt the jagged rocks, the awful drop through the air ...

'Oh, no, dunna!' she sobbed in terror, digging in her heels as he tried to turn her away from him. She clutched frantically at his shirt. Eyes shut, teeth clenched, she told herself that if he threw her down she would try to take him with her. The cloth ripped out of her hands. Her feet found nothing ... she held her breath ...

She heard his voice, dispassionate, saying, 'Be still! There now - look over there - you see it, that great house-'

She swayed as he set her down. Her eyes opened sightless and slowly focused on his face. If he knew what had been in her mind he gave no sign. He released her and she sagged to the ground.

'I have rushed you too fast,' he said.

Hazel's head reeled. Everything thumped up and down inside her. Her body rebelled and she twisted away from him to be sick.

Impassive, unapproachable, he waited for her to recover. She cleaned her face with handfuls of wet grass while she got her breath. She was too stunned to cry. He was holding out his hand to her.

'Get up.'

Her knees had turned to jelly. He had to help her onto her unsteady feet. She clung to his arm as if she were drowning and her eyes searched his face, gaunt and savage in the raw light of dawn. Please, they pleaded. Please ... She wanted comfort, reassurance. It was not enough to be reprieved. She wanted to know that she was forgiven, wanted to turn back the clock and find again the man she had thought she knew.

'John,' she faltered.

What were they doing in this wild place? What could have driven them to stand here like strangers, she with the fear of death in her heart, he with God knew what in his?

'John,' she whispered again.

'Have you finished?' he enquired coldly.

Anger flared in her. He despised her for her display of emotion, he who was so cool and arrogant. And she had dared to embarrass him before his friends. Her feelings' were of no account. She flung away his hand.

'I hate you!' she blurted, and went stumbling away from him across the heather, her arm across her eyes.

She did not hear him until he was upon her. She knew a moment of panic as he threw her to the ground and then she was returning his kisses with a passion that exceeded his. Her brush with death had inflamed her hunger for life and afterwards she was left trembling. His face drooped breathless against hers at last and she held him for a long time in silence, her fingers still knotted in his hair. It was a moment not to be ruined with words.

When they had drowsed in the early sun, when she had felt his dead weight upon her stir and sigh, she whispered, 'I didna come to spy on you. I thought you was with a woman.'

She felt him smile.

'I've been faithful to you all summer. That's a folly quite new to me.'

Resentment flickered that even now he regarded her as a joke. But she said evenly, 'And you forgive me?'

He raised his head to look at her, half mocking, half serious while the shreds of dawn still clung about them.

'So it would seem.'

She smiled, and ran a careful finger along his coarse black lashes. He brushed away her hand and added, 'I should have remembered that children are curious.'

'I'm not a child!'

How could he say that when he had just used her as a woman!

'You are to me. Be glad of it, it's your safeguard.'

She didn't believe him. She was drunk with success and didn't know where to stop.

'I love you as a woman,' she insisted.

'You don't know what you say.'

His face darkened abruptly. He got up. The spell was broken.

They stood on a high place looking down, and saw across a valley the grey craggy pile that looked more like an outcrop of rock than a fortified dwelling.

Here were no gracious acres, no deer park, no lily-starred moat. Here was a fierce living wrung from a grudging land. A place of tearing gales and the scent of rain. Of towering white thunderheads over granite cliffs, of shipwreck and green death in icy water. And here was Black John in his natural setting. Here she could see he belonged as nowhere else.

'My land,' he was saying, 'my home!'

His knuckles showed white and his voice was harsh. The eyes he turned on her were dark with anguish. She thought, He cares more about this than anything else in the world. More than me . . .

". . . driven off like a wolf from my own gate, and that usurping bastard takes my place!' He rounded on her, barked, 'You think that's right?'

'No,' she said quickly. 'No.' She repeated in a faraway whisper, 'Your home ...'

Did the squirrels still flash amber in the sun... were there still houseleeks sprouting in the thatch, protecting the house from lightning - or was it all grazed now by the wretched sheep? 'Sheep eat men,' she had heard Tom say. And yet she owed her life to one - she wrenched her mind away. It sickened her to think of it flayed of its skin and still alive.

He saw her expression and misinterpreted it.

'Don't pity me, help me. Help me get it back.'

'If I can,' she said dubiously. How could she possibly help

him - how could anyone? It would need an army to take such a house.

'You can help,' he said, watching her. 'There's a thing to be done that only you can do.'

Pleasure, pride, misgivings jostled in her for possession. Did he think she was a witch after all and could work miracles? If he did, when she failed as she must. . . He was still watching her. Faintly, sardonically amused.

'You don't understand ... how should you? Sit down, it's a long story.'

He passed her a wineskin from his belt as she sank obediently onto the long grass. When she passed it back he took a long swig and gestured with it towards the stone castle.

'I was born over there. Abby's cottage, the tavern, the village, all the land around for miles -all mine. By right. By inheritance from my father through his father and away back for as long as time. There was a John Pengerran when Vortigern was king. There was never any doubt cast on our ownership. Our right, our honour - unassailable as our walls. But my father raised force after force to fight the King's battles and by the time of my birth our fortunes were crumbling.

'He was shrewd. He betrothed me in my cradle to the daughter of a lifelong friend - and one of the richest dowries in the land. With her came the manor of Buxford and its revenues. No - hear me out! So far so good and given peace we might have prospered. But when the King came to the throne he was as greedy for France as his father had been for gold. My own father died in the year that I was twenty and it fell to me to scrape together what force I could muster in the service of the King.'

He paused, his mouth drawn tight and bitter across his teeth. The words came as if bitten off one by one, 'It was a futile - costly - bloody - waste of time. We were cut to pieces - good men like Little John, not even knowing why they were there, butchered on the field like cattle.'

John fell silent, seeing again the burning gunmetal sky over France. The stench and the agony of wounds broiled by the sun. The fear-voided urine of men and horses. The drone of flies. The thirst and the retching. The death rattle, and the silence that said too much. At last he went on, 'The survivors went to the galleys, I suppose. I never saw any of them again.'

Hazel shivered. She had heard of the galleys. Chained to the oars, the prisoners were. And if the ship went down they all drowned like rats in a trap.

'But not you,' she said thankfully.

His eyes came back to her from a distance.

'Not I!' His mouth had a wry twist. 'I was lodged in comfort in my captor's house. Carried from the field on a litter - eventually - as befits a prisoner likely to be worth a ransom. One of the old school, that Frenchman. And he had patience, to give the devil his due. Year after year he waited. Fed me, housed me, healed my wounds. He saw it as an investment, I suppose. He even tended my horse in the hope of extracting a few more francs. Such a valuable destrier, he said! But time soured his hospitality in the end. And when he realised the laugh was on him it warped his sense of humour.

'" It would appear, *mon ami*" - I can hear his voice now - "that your family no longer requires your presence. Perhaps you should go home and find out why."'

'He set you free?'

'No doubt that is what he called it. He knew what he was doing. To kill me would have been a breach of chivalry. To turn me adrift in hostile country with nothing but my horse - that was different. That disposed of me neatly without a spot on his honour. He kept my armour and all my weapons. Even my father's sword. One day I'll have it back and spit him with it!' His laughter rasped her nerves. 'Don't look like that. All men are alike. I killed the first barehanded and took his knife - I have it still.

'After that it was easier. I hacked my way through France to Calais. I had enough gold by then to be able to take ship.'

He paused, looked at her reflectively.

'You'd think my troubles would be over then. That once in England I'd find myself among friends. You would be wrong. No one is eager to rally round a failure. The soldier who returns victorious is a hero. The vanquished is at best an embarrassment. So it was beg or butcher my way back to Buxford. I've lived on my wits ever since.'

He waited for her to say something.

'Why so silent?'

'How many have you killed?'

'How many?' He shrugged. 'God knows. Does it matter?'

Did it matter! How had she come to love a man so bloody, without conscience or compassion - she who could not bring herself to kill a rabbit? She shook her head and sighed. It was too late. Something in her expression nettled him.

'You need not look so pious. Your father was no different - he'd have killed if the chance had fallen to him.'

'He wouldna! No more than I would!'

'Don't fool yourself!' His eyes bored into her. 'Anyone will kill under the right kind of pressure. When it's kill or die - you kill!'

She glared back, silent and mutinous.

'The trouble with you,' he told her, 'is that you've seen nothing of life. Born in a bottle and never seen out of the neck.'

Hazel gasped.

'I've what!' She was up on her knees, blazing with indignation. 'Now just you listen to me, Master Wonderful Black John - because I can tell you a thing or two about life as you don't know! Let me tell you there's more to life than rattling knives and clanging about in armour like a tinker's cart! And there's worse ways of dying than by the sword. I anna crossed the sea like you and I anna been in battle, but I bet you never starved through the hunger gap like me-'

'Through the what?'

'There - you see! You dunna even know what it is! The hunger gap, my well-fed friend, is when you've ate the last crust and the last berry and the last withered apple and the bit of pig you tried to save's gone so sour even the rats won't eat it. It's when you're waiting for something - anything - to grow big enough to harvest. Because when there's a lot of you to one little strip you canna grow enough to put anything by. Just enough to fill your bellies if you're lucky. And when that's gone there's nothing to live on but the fat on your bones. If you anna got enough of that you die. Not quick and clean but slow and miserable, a little bit every day. It's when the old folks gets thinned out, and the sickly children. It's when my brothers had to be sold 'cause we couldna feed 'em no more. Night after night I'd hear my mother crying. And that's just the hunger gap. On top of that I seen my mother and her baby killed, I seen a poor old fellow gone off his head 'cause he lost a leg and couldn't remember how. I seen a woman dying slow on the road covered in yaws she got in a brothel. I seen.... too much. I been raped and beaten and put in the stocks. And I had a baby which is more than you can do! So you get on with your butchering if that's what you've a mind for. But dunna you never - not never again - tell me as I've never seen nothing of life!'

Her eyes challenged his. For a long moment his stared back, gritty as jet. Then slowly the lines at their corners crinkled into humour. A corner of his mouth twitched. He got to his feet and offered her his arm.

'We'd better get back to your son,' he said 'Forged of such mettle he should be a great man someday.'

As they walked her head began buzzing again with yet unanswered questions. If he had meant to explain things to her he had only succeeded in confusing her still further. If this was his home why had he gone to Buxford? Why was he locked out - surely a man could go home even if he had lost a battle? She sighed; it was her own fault. It was she who had distracted him by starting an argument.

'Did you ever find out why the ransom wasn't paid?'

His laugh was derisive.

'Oh yes, indeed. I found out all right. They told me I was dead.'

'Who told you - Abby and Little John?'

'No. Long ago when I first arrived from France.'

'I dunna follow you ...'

'I heard it in a tavern. I was near home and yet unrecognised. The passing of time, I suppose. Added to the fact that I was the last one they expected to see. So I stayed in the shadows and asked a few questions. A French courier had brought news of my death but he had never been seen to leave. He had died of the plague, they had heard, and had to be quickly buried. They had thought it strange because no one else had caught the plague that year. It was a nine days' wonder and soon forgotten. They talked of the price of wool. Of the doubling of rents whenever a lease fell in. Of the new Lord of the Manor and his tyranny. I took to the greenwood. The rest you know.'

'But - I still dunna understand. How could there be a new Lord - and why couldn't you go home?'

He stopped walking and turned to face her.

'Because my sorrowing widow' - he wrapped the words in venom and spat them out- 'who "loved me as a woman", having inherited all to the last blade of grass, wed herself within the month - to my own cousin Eustace who'd stayed cosily at home.'

He fished in his belt-pouch and thrust into Hazel's hand a faded miniature. Through the pale stiff conventions of the artist's work, she recognised the pious martyred face of the Lady Edith.

'There she is. My whey-faced whore. My lady wife!'
He turned on his heel and went striding on.

8

Hazel stood still and felt the life drain out of her.

'Come on,' he called back, 'what are you waiting for?'

She groped for words inside herself. Found nothing. He halted and looked back.

'What's the matter?'

His voice had an edge to it. She tried to pull herself together.

'You . . .' she stammered, 'but I - we-'

He stood, faintly irritated, on safe ground while she floundered in a morass of doubts and fears. Her voice broke, 'Oh, please, wait-'

He came briskly back towards her. Impatient and - yes, defensive. A boy caught out in a prank.

'What now?'

It was more than an enquiry. A challenge. She raised stunned eyes from the miniature.

'You said - your wife ...'

'Yes.' He added lightly, 'What of it?'

He smiled. He was going to brazen it out. With a knife in her belly she was expected to laugh - as he would himself. She made an effort.

'I didna understand. You never said-' Her voice trailed off.

He shook his head over her in mock despair, 'Oh, Hazel, Hazel

He laughed, spread his hands in an eloquent gesture, 'Did you think a man reaches my age still unwed?'

'I - I - but we are wed!' she insisted hopelessly.

He shook his head again and took her gently by the shoulders. 'Real marriages are not entered into so lightly. But it served us both at the time.'

Hazel clenched her teeth against their chattering. He drew her unresisting into his arms.

'You're cold as a stone,' he said.

She stood numb and unresponsive, thinking, What becomes of me now ? She didn't belong here. She didn't belong anywhere. And somewhere there was a woman with the right to banish her ...

'Child, how you tremble!'

She was quivering, thought John, as Black Man had quivered when the pike had pierced them both. He held her hard against him until the spasm passed. Then he released her.

'Come now, enough of this.'

'What happens now?' Her voice was taut and shrunken. It gave him a moment's uneasiness.

'What should happen?'

'To me. What happens to me? What am I to do?'

'Do? Nothing. It makes no difference to you. I keep my bargains.'

'Bargains!'

Is that all it is to you, even now! 'Tell her I've got enough troubles ...' As if I hadn't enough without I had to love you . . .

She must have said it aloud, for he said, 'It was a fair exchange, a life for a life.' He added levelly, 'I never asked that you should love me.'

Hazel pulled hard on the muscles of her chin to keep it steady.

'No,' she matched her tone to his. 'Be fair - you didna.' She lifted her head and stared straight in front of her. 'But I do just the same.' It was all she had. He was not going to take it from her. 'Now, let's go.'

She thrust her hand into his, unsmiling. She forced her legs that seemed to have lost their bones to move one in front of the other, walking in a void. She moved blindly, pulling on him to follow. He hung back.

'Hazel, child-'

'No!' she said, desperate. 'Talk of something else.' Her thoughts were too painful to share. She wanted to sort them out in peace. Alone.

He fell in beside her, his only answer the pressure of his fingers.

She said with unnatural brightness, 'You knew my father, then?'

'No. But I live with an ear to the ground or I wouldn't live long.'

'And my mother?'

Instantly she regretted it. At this of all moments she could not speak calmly of Margery.

He nodded and deftly turned the subject. 'Do you know what they say of you in your home village?'

They would have names for me in the village. And for you. They would come at night with their pots and pans and make rough music under our windows....

'Did you hear?'

'Yes - no. What do they say?'

What does it matter, I can never go back there now. Why didn't you kill me....

'... you flew away with the midwife on your broomsticks. Are you listening?'

She nodded mechanically. He was doing his best to help her, in his fashion. She had a fleeting vision of the Patch capering on his shattered leg to charm her out of her tears.

'They told me you were seen against the night sky, your

eyes glowing green like a cat's and the lightning crackling from your hair.'_

If only we had ... if only we had flown away ... what good can ever come of this now?

'You're walking far too fast,' he said. 'Slow down, you'll exhaust yourself.'

'I'm all right.'

I must exhaust myself. I want to be too tired to feel anything. Too tired to know if I'm dead or alive. Too tired to care.

'Hazel-'

'No!' She said it sharply because it was the second time. No - not now, don't be kind to me now. Don't undo me - let me keep my pride.

He pressed her hand briefly and let her have her way.

They could hear Angel screaming long before they reached the cottage. Hazel's breasts, taut and aching, responded with a brimming of milk. She started towards the cottage door, thinking gratefully of the relief of his sucking. Then she remembered Abby. Abby must have known this all along. She stopped. She could not face Abby now. Not yet. She stood confused and wretched, not knowing what to do. She took one step and was unable to force herself further. A warm enormous hand enveloped her shoulder.

'Wait here,' said John.

She heard Abby's voice railing inside the cottage and his cutting across it, deep and incisive. And now at last the tears came, heavy and silent like blood from a wound. She stood there blinded by them in the warmth of the sun. Why couldn't you have been mine like I thought...

She took the baby from the hands that proffered him and took refuge in the barn. She sat down with him in the straw.

Black Man had hardly appeared to notice her until now. Now, of all times, he came plodding after her. Sensing her distress as she sat struggling for self-control, he lowered his head from its church-tower height and blew softly, wetly down her neck.

Little John came back into the kitchen. His gait was stiff and his eyes accusing.

'Summat's up with Mistress Hazel.' He spoke to his mother but he looked straight at John. 'Breaking her heart out there in the barn, she is.'

Abby straightened her back and dried her hands on her apron.

'While I'm in here washing linen for her child!' With mounting colour she turned towards the door. 'I'm going out there to give her a piece of my mind.'

She found her way barred.

'No, Abby,' John said quietly.

She squared her shoulders.

'It's not right. A strong young wench to sit feeling sorry for herself while an old woman does her work. You know it's not right, Master John.'

'But you are not going to give her a piece of your mind.' His voice was even, without anger. 'You will give her the same respect as you give to me.' Abby bridled but he went on relentlessly, 'Or as you give to the Lady Edith.'

'The Lady' Edith is a lady!'   ,

'And Hazel is a fine brave girl. More honest than the rest of us put together. Now sit down.'

Abby stood her ground for a moment but his authority defeated her in the end as it always had. She buttoned her mouth up tight and went back to her washing.

'Suppose he's told her,' commented Little John when he had gone.

Abby looked up crossly.

'Told her?' She had not the patience for puzzles. 'Told her what?'

'Why, that they're not proper wed, of course.'

Abby snorted. 'She must have known that all along.'

'Not yesterday, she didn't,' Little John asserted stubbornly. 'Yesterday she was trying to tell me she was his wife. And she believed it - I'd stake my life she did.'

'Then she must have deceived herself.' She did not want to learn that her idol had clay feet. Somebody, somewhere was making a mistake. She tried to ease the crick in her neck. 'She's nobbut a child - he wouldn't do such a thing. Not my Master John!'

'Oh, Ma!' he burst out in sudden exasperation. 'You think the sun do shine out of his arse-hole! I tell you he deceived her, he give her some cause somehow to think she was wed to him.'

'Humph!' said Abby painfully. She added grudgingly, 'Poor little maid - if it's true.' She dried her hands for the second time, and suddenly seemed to realise what he had said. 'And don't you use such language to me!' she shrilled.

'Men! Scoundrels, the lot of you! Get yourself out of my kitchen so I can work!'

She seized a broom and drove him out of doors. Then she bent to her sweeping, swallowing angry tears.

Tired out in the homely straw, Hazel had cried herself to sleep. Black John stared broodingly down at her where she lay, the damp hair flung across her face, the eyelids swollen and the mouth pathetic.

In the crook of her arm, her nipple still in his mouth from which ran a tiny trickle of milk, slept her baby. His forehead and nose were toasted golden by the sun. His stomach bloated, his knees drawn up, he resembled nothing more closely than a tadpole. From time to time a faint grin of wind twitched across his face and the spasm caused him to spread startled fingers. Then they slowly curled again into a bud of sleep.

John watched in silence for a long time. Then he sighed heavily and turned away. He crossed the barn without a sound and went out into the sunlight, pulling the door behind him. Why could not pale useless Edith have given him such a son?

Hazel presented herself at the evening meal with a freshly

scrubbed face and her long hair wet from the sea. She was calm and cheerful as she removed her trencher from its place beside John's and set it down by Abby's and Little John's. It was not intended as a slight to him. It was to spare herself the need to tell Abby in so many words that now she 'knew her place'. That she was as much a menial as they. That she was here on sufferance.

Abby looked at her in surprise. John said sharply, 'What's this? You take your meats with me.'

Hazel said pleasantly, 'That's for Abby to say. I'm her guest now.' She did not say the rest. But it hung in the air. Abby was watching her with a new expression.

'You sit where you please.' She hesitated. 'Alongside the Master if you've a mind to.'

'And what does the Master say?'

He rose. With a half-mocking bow he indicated the place beside him. It was an invitation, not a command. Hazel looked again at Abby.

I don't belong here, said her look. I don't belong anywhere; if you offer me this right I shall hold on to it...

Abby looked steadily back.

'I reckon your place is with him,' she said. Then she twinkled unexpectedly. 'From owl-drop to sparrow-fart,' she added.

Hazel moved sedately to the place beside John. He seated her with a courtly gesture, noting her straight back and lifted chin. In an impulse he picked up her small roughened hand and kissed it.

It was a salute to valour, nothing more. But her eyes flicked upward, hoping ...

Abby's met them and read what was in her heart. Then they met John's and saw what was in his.

'Master John,' her faded eyes clouded and her voice shook with reproach. 'Oh, Master John, how could you!'

John stabbed a warning glance at her. She was looking at

him as she had looked when he was seven. When he had chopped one leg off a rabbit to see if it could run on three.

'Bring the meats.'

It was less of an order than a shot across her bows. Abby obeyed it. He distracted Hazel by chucking her under the chin. He did not intend her to intercept that look. With his plan so near to fruition he could not afford a hitch.

'Did you love her?'

She had been lying wakeful. When the gleam of his eyes in the darkness betrayed his wakefulness the question was wrung from her.

'Love her?' He dragged his thoughts back from where they had been wandering, 'Who?'

'Her.' She struggled to frame the words. 'Your - your - did you?'

Do you still? Is it that house you can't bear to lose - or her?

'Did I love her?' He turned the words over thoughtfully, as if the idea were strange to him. 'My dear child -' he raised himself on an elbow, regarding her quizzically.

'Wives - are not for loving but for getting heirs. They come with the land, like the tenants. A wife performs her duty, a husband his, and both are lucky if they're even the same age. One expects nothing else. Such things - they are a matter of property, of inheritance. No, a man may love land, sons, heritage, horses' - he touched her cheek - 'even a wench or two. Hardly a wife!'

He lay back, smiling at the bizarre idea. Hazel turned her face against his shoulder. Love me, love me ... it was like praying. You said it in your mind where no one could hear and hoped for it to happen. I thought I was your wife ...

As if he had heard her thoughts he said, 'You surely don't envy Edith?'

She swallowed, saying nothing. But she knew she did. She

wanted to be something permanent in his life. Something not to be lost or left behind. And a wife was that.

John held her gently, 'Don't cry, my chuck. I'll take care of you, you'll see ...' When all this was over he would see her right. Find her some fresh-faced country lad and set them up in a farm on the estate. Nothing but the best. But what to say to her now? He had never learned to take pleasure in inflicting pain as some men could. He was indifferent to it, cynical. But he preferred the merry Hazel he was used to. After a moment's thought he tilted her face towards him.

'When I lie with you, it is not to get heirs.'

Hazel smiled in the darkness. That at least she felt to be true. For her this loving had a poignancy she had not known before, shadowed by a parting she could not as yet foresee. When it was accomplished she still clung to him.

'I love you,' she whispered, her throat constricting.

'Sh-sh,' he murmured, his lips against her hair. They slept, their bodies still joined.

'Don't look like there's going to be much leavings for the likes of me,' Little John grinned at Abby. 'Look there,' he pointed to the beach below where two figures stood out sharply against the sea.

John stood waiting while Hazel came running towards him along the strand with a long streamer of seaweed blowing back like a banner from her hand. Her hair was whipped across her face by the wind and her skin shone with sea-spray and a peachy glow of health. He caught her and swung her off her feet.

'You're laughing again. That's good.'

'You got to laugh,' she said, 'the other's a waste of time. And besides,' she fixed her gaze on the violet horizon, 'just because you love someone doesn't mean they owe you something. I been thinking about it. You give, you dunna look for payment.' She stared hard at the sea. Say you love me back ...

'So, no more tears?'

She shook her head. Not where you can see them. 'Life's too short.'

A violent shudder ran through her. John felt it.

'What's the matter?'

'Nothing,' she laughed unsteadily. 'Someone trod on my grave.'

He eyed her thoughtfully as they strolled at the water's edge. It really was a quite unusual girl. A pity if it had to be thrown to the wolves.

The summer days strolled peaceably one after another. John came and went as unpredictably as ever, and with time she learned to await his return with something like equanimity. The sea was bright, the gulls wheeled overhead. Abby no longer wanted to slap her down. It was not in her nature to be downcast for long.

Today she planned to take Angel down to the shore and let him kick his brown feet in the creamy foam in the sun. The days were shortening, and she wanted to make the most of them.

She followed John out to where he was mounting Black Man. She stood squinting up into the light, smiling him on his way.

'Give the baby to Abby,' he said. 'You're coming with me.'

9

'Where are we going?' asked Hazel.

'Trooping the colour.' His mouth twitched at the corners. They rode on, he grinning into his beard and she with her eyes full of questions.

It was good to be riding with John again, good to have him to herself. She sat quiet for a long time, enjoying the sunlight and the romping wind, the familiar rhythm of the horse. They were travelling steadily inland. At the summit of a high ridge he reined in.

'See there,' he said, pointing, 'from here you can see the sea on both sides of Cornwall.'

She looked. It was true. A faint blue ribbon in the distance shone on either side of them.

'What is this place called?'

'Foxhole,' he said.

'Is this where we're bound for?'

He shook his head. 'I wanted you to see it,' he said. He urged the horse on and they were on their way again.

Hazel wrestled with her thoughts. At last she had to give them voice.

'This that you want me to do - it's to help you get back your house?'

He nodded.

'And' - she hesitated- 'her.'

'It's the land I want. When I am the master I'll dispose as I think fit.'

She said thoughtfully, 'Just the same, you're asking me to cut my own throat.'

'Silly child!' he rallied her. 'You've never seen such a man as I could find for you - handsome, young - one of your own kind-'

'I do my own choosing, thank you.' She could not bear to hear more.

John headed her off. 'Don't you want to avenge your father?'

She considered. 'My father never liked me much. I reckon he mistrusted me.'

'Mistrusted?'

'Aye! He was afeared - because of the mark. Tib said he wanted to kill me when I was born.'

'Hm-mm,' said John. He wasn't doing too well. He tried another tack. 'Your mother, then?'

'Dunna talk about my mother,' Hazel said quietly. 'You anna fit.'

His quick look was a warning.

'I'm sorry, John, I love you as you well know. But you anna fit.'

She said it so mildly, so soberly. She went on, 'Anyway, revenge never does no good. It only makes more hatred and it canna bring nobody back.'

'You don't care to be rid of Eustace?'

His voice was sharp, his expression inscrutable. She said, 'I never said that.' She wanted to tell him that she did not have to embrace his cause to want to see him win. But she couldn't find the words. She said, 'I'd help you anyway.' He relaxed. 'And you'll do anything I say?'

A nagging fear that had been at the back of her mind found its expression.

'I won't have to kill nobody?'

'You won't have to kill.'

She smiled, relieved.

'Anything,' she promised.

They came at last to a stony castle not unlike Pengerran. It was gaunt and forbidding and struck a dank chill into the bones. Horses were tethered to a ring in the ground inside the curtain wall. John tethered Black Man among them and led her in through a towering door. In the great hall a number of men were gathered, some of whom she had seen before at the inn. The silvery-haired man was there, and seemed to be playing host to the others. But this time there was no laughter, no cheer. Their faces were straight and gloomy. A murmur of conversation stopped as they came in.

John said without preamble, 'Look well at all these men. Look long and hard at each until you know his face by heart. One of them will bring you a message one day. It is vital that you recognise him.'

Hesitantly she moved among them. His tone no less than his words made her uneasy. She stared dutifully at each face, trying to commit it to memory. How could she be sure of so many, having seen them only once?

'I'll try,' she said doubtfully.

'You must do better. Lives will depend on it.'

She looked at him, startled. Did he mean his life? Disturbed, she redoubled her efforts. But the harder she tried the more all their faces seemed to merge into one.

'And you, gentlemen, mark well this girl. She will be older when you see her next and the young change rapidly.'

So she was not to bear the responsibility alone - she was thankful for that. But what was he talking about? As always, everyone knew but her. Frowning with the effort of concentration she peered into the face of the silvery-haired man. He smiled.

'Well, now, you will remember me easily enough. The only gnarled old stump in a forest of saplings.'

Hazel blushed, not knowing what to say. He touched her cheek with a finger dry as paper, and whispered confidentially, 'Don't look so worried, child. It may never happen.'

It struck her as a very strange thing to say. She smiled diffidently and passed on, her thoughts whirling.

One by one, the other men got up and left in silence. John followed them out. Hazel turned to go after him.

'Stay,' said the silver-haired man, 'a little wine?'

She paused, uncertain, while he filled three goblets and held one out to her. The second he lifted towards her and drained in one gulp. He refilled it immediately and gestured towards the one still on the table.

'For our friend outside,' he said. 'Oh, he'll be back.' He followed her anxious glance. 'I suspect you're far too valuable to him to be left behind.'

Hazel felt she should be pleased by that. But there was something not quite right about it, something double- edged. He was still regarding her with his gentle worldly eyes, his knowing smile. He was too subtle. She preferred people out in the open.

'You're not his friend?' she asked bluntly.

His smile deepened, 'And if I were not?'

'I should warn him,' she said. Instantly she knew she shouldn't have told him that. It was foolhardy to invite enmity from one who stood between you and the door.

The old man chuckled approvingly. 'Bravely said, my child! But you need not worry. I was his friend before his birth and I'm too old to change my loyalties. But the Pengerrans are a hard race for a tender young thing like you. How in the world did he persuade you to it? Eh?' He lowered his voice conspiratorially, 'Come, tell an old fellow a secret. What does he promise you to do it?'

Hazel drew back. She felt the angry colour prickle along her cheekbones. She had not forgotten her humiliation at the inn.

'I don't understand you, sir.' Tom had always held that old virgins grew bawdy. Did it apply to men as well?

He laughed, 'Come come, now! No need to pretend with me, it's a simple enough question - what does he offer you?' How dared he, thought Hazel.

'Do you think I can be bought!' she snapped.

The old gentleman sobered suddenly. He looked at her hard for a long moment, his expression unreadable. Then he gravely bowed to her and held out his hand.

'Forgive me, my dear, for a blundering old fool. I should have known better, of course.' He drew her unwilling hand through his emaciated elbow and led her towards the door.

'Come, I have something to show you.'

Hazel swallowed her resentment. For John's sake she must not quarrel with his friends though God knew some of them provoked her to it.

They walked slowly across the drawbridge into the outer courtyard while he told her of his old man's dream of planting it as gardens in the days to come. They must make a strange pair, she thought; him in his musty finery that reeked of a bygone age, she in her homespun that Abby had made, the first new garment she had owned. And here they walked arm in arm in the sun, like a lord and his lady strolling through their park.

On their way back they stopped at a little door within the portcullis. It opened rustily, tearing down a curtain of cobwebs. Peering inside, she could see a collection of weapons in varying stages of decay. The dim light glanced over halberds and swords and in a corner a wilting suit of armour rusted, its headpiece yawning eerily between its feet.

Her companion rummaged inside and emerged with something heavy and metallic which he was attempting to polish with a piece of cloth. He wrapped it and handed it to

Hazel, who almost dropped it because of its unexpected weight.

'What is it?' she asked wonderingly.

'Call it-' he hesitated. Then, with a smile from which age had not entirely robbed its charm, 'Call it a peace offering. From me to you. It's for hunting, but I daresay it could kill should the occasion arise.' He closed the door and wrenched round the stubborn key in the creaking lock, his hand shaking a little from the effort. 'Keep it for your protection. Oh, I know' - he held up a hand to silence her - 'that you have your John. But a long road has its turns and we can't see past them. So this is for you.'

He seemed well content with his gift. Hazel, feeling that something was due from her, thanked him politely and contrived to look pleased. But her only thought was how strange a thing it was to give to a girl. The gift had made her uneasy in a way she could not define.

The old man had brought his wine cup with him and now he seemed suddenly to notice that it was empty. He hurried inside to refill it while Hazel waited, uncertain, near the door.

At that moment John returned. He came striding into the courtyard. 'Where have you been?' he asked tersely.

'With the old gentleman. Look, he gave me-'

'Fitzarthur? What did he say to you? Where is he now?'

'Nothing,' she said, crestfallen. She had wanted to show him her gift. 'He went inside for more wine.'

John swore softly under his breath and plunged into the house. She heard his voice snarling, barking, worrying at someone inside, and then a crash as if something had been hurled to the floor. She heard the elder man's voice quiet and calm, and then John's at last simmering down. She listened for a while but then, unable to make out their words, she shrugged and left them to it.

'What is he up to, Black Man? Do you know?'

He lowered his gigantic head and shook off the flies.

Hazel laughed. 'You don't know either,' she said.

She showed her gift to John at last, displaying it carefully in its wrappings.

'What is it?' she asked him.

He looked at it with mild interest.

'It's a fowling-piece.' He took it from her, turning it over and about. 'Meant for killing birds - bustards and the like. Too noisy for me, it would arouse the neighbourhood. Nice, though.'

He weighed it in his hand, examined it inside and out. 'See, you put the powder in here and the shot goes there, so.' Then he took an oily rag and began to clean it.

'I wonder why he gave it to me,' mused Hazel.

'Who?'

'Master Fitzarthur.'

'Lord Fitzarthur,' he corrected her. 'He took a fancy to you, one supposes. He lost a daughter once at about your age. His only child. No doubt he's reminded of her.'

'Poor old man,' said Hazel softly. She remembered looking; back as they rode away and seeing his solitary figure at a casement. Smiling and waving, she had thought she discerned a faint forlorn movement in response. She thought of him alone in his mouldering castle. 'It's not surprising he drinks.'

John looked up sharply, 'You noticed that?'

She nodded, 'Not to say he was drunk. But you can see he can't manage without it.'

'More's the pity. It loosens his tongue and that could be a costly business.'

Hazel wished she could have asked him what he meant. She wished, too, that she could express her misgivings about this whole affair. But she was learning at last to hold her tongue. Instead she twirled a red leaf between her fingers and held it to the light to see its sunset glow.

'The summer's over,' she said wistfully.

'Yes, it's over,' agreed John.

Abby met them at the cottage door. She had been trying to console the hungry baby with her empty breast and she smiled as she handed him to Hazel. John she passed over with a frosty nod.

'Well, mistress, and what's turned your wind to the East?'

His tone was only half amused. Since the incident of the evening meal her attitude to him had subtly changed. She catered for his wants with the same meticulous care but the old solicitude was missing. What she did for him was no longer done for love. If she did it for duty, or for old times' sake - or to justify the gold he had dropped in her lap - he did not know. But she had been closer to him than his mother and it uneased him like a prickle in the shirt.

'Nothing, my lord.'

So he was Master John no longer. He regarded her uncompromising back with compressed lips. Then he shrugged and turned away. It was all one in the long run.

'Please, Abby,' entreated Hazel when he had gone. 'You'll only make him hate me.'

'Hate!' snorted Abby. 'You'd be better off without him!'

'But I couldna live without him,' said Hazel, which to her was simple fact. But to Abby it sounded like extravagance. She wanted to take this stupid girl and shake some sense into her. But it would be a waste of time. She knew that better than most, having adored him blindly for so long herself.

'Hazel!' came his voice from outside.

She was past her and gone before Abby could open her mouth. Abby sighed. No one could save her. It was far too late.

'Sss-tt! Hazel!' John's voice hissed urgent in her ear. 'Wake up!'

She took a reluctant peep. It was still dark.

'Mm-mm,' she murmured drowsily, and prepared to go back to sleep. He shook her roughly.

'Wake up!' he commanded hoarsely. 'Put this on and come with me.'

She got to her feet, head swimming, and fumbled for the tinderbox.

'No,' he said swiftly. 'No light, we go in secret. Don't make a sound.'

She struggled from sleep into the garment he had thrown her, a coarse rough sack that reached her knees and hung so loose it left her shivering. It smelt of mackerel and of Little John. A few scales clung to it and shimmered in the gloom

'What's happening?' she asked, groping towards him in the darkness.

'Never mind,' he hissed. 'Keep quiet and follow close.'

They crept from the cottage out into the night. The moon was down. Only a few stars prickled the sky and the air was damp and misty from the sea. Leading her by the hand he made his way down the cliff and along the beach.

'Where are we going?'

'Pengerran.'

'But -this way?'

She could hear the grin in his voice.

'This way!'

They plodded over sand and rock barefooted, barking their toes. At last she saw in the phosphorescent glow from the sea that they had reached a tiny cove. The sea lapped both its arms and in the depths yawned a monstrous cavern. He nudged her ahead of him. 'In there.'

She had to force herself to go in. Alone she would never have done it. Under her feet was seaweed, springy and unpleasantly alive. She imagined it moving as she trod on it. Only John pushing close behind her kept her moving. 'Ugh-gh!'

She had put her hand on something soft and wet on the wall she could not see.

'Sea anemones. They won't hurt you.'

She shivered. 'Dark as a cow's guts in here.'

'Afraid?' His tone implied criticism.

'Course not!' she lied stoutly. 'Just cold. And I can't see where I'm going.'

He hustled her along a little further and then she heard him striking flint. The light surprised her standing hunched with her fists drawn up under her chin.

'You lie - you are afraid.'

'No -no, I'm not!' She straightened herself quickly. She was more afraid of being left here alone to find her way back. 'What is this place?'

'Cathedral Cave.' He held up the rushlight and the fitful light bounced back off the dripping walls. 'You can only get in here at spring tides. The rest of the year it's under water. Look up there,' he indicated a deep fissure high up near the back of the cave, 'that's where we're going. The back door to Pengerran.'

'The back ... you anna going in there alone!'

'No. I shall have you with me.'

'But - it's madness ! We'll be killed!'

'Not the way we're going. The secret is passed from father to son. Not even my mother knew of it. We come up under the tower inside the keep. Move!' He shoved her before him into the narrow tunnel. 'In less than two hours this cave will fill with water again.'

The salty rotting fish smell of the seabed gave place to a dank earth odour. Her stomach knotted tight with a deep primeval fear of being underground. It seemed to her as she plodded behind John that life had shrunk to the dimensions of the tunnel - with death awaiting them at either end. She clutched desperately at his arm, her nails making deep weals in his skin.

'Why are we going?' Her whisper echoed in the emptiness.

'Just visiting. No more talking. We're coming near.'

The passage ended abruptly in a rocky chamber. In one wall was a great stone slab with a ring in it. Next to it was a sconce into which John put the rushlight before he extinguished it. She heard him grunting and straining, then a muffled rumble as the stone began to move.

A lighter shade of darkness appeared in the crack. They listened intently, hardly daring to breathe. Then little by little he widened the gap until they could both squeeze through.

They were crouching in a narrow shaft that pierced the thickness of a massive wall. To their left it slanted steeply upwards to end on a barred grille, just discernible in the starlight. A waft of fresh air reached them, sweet with the smell of dewy grass.

'Come,' whispered John, and drew her with him down the slope to the right, down into the engulfing darkness.

Hazel swallowed and tried not to breathe. It smelled like a drain down there. Crawling, slithering, bracing with their arms, they fetched up at last against the cold metal of another grille. The shaft was barred at both ends.

'What do we do now?' breathed Hazel.

'Sh-sh . . .' He was peeling off the fishing smock over her head. With his mouth against her ear - 'Do exactly as I tell you.'

He filled his palms with spittle and smoothed it over her body. Then he proceeded to thread her carefully between the bars. It was a painfully tight squeeze and there was little to cling to on the other side. She shivered in the unnatural chill of the place.

'What now?'

'Listen carefully. You must find the stone that moves. Can you count to three?'

'I can count to ten!' she hissed furiously. 'My father-' 'Forget your father. Count three from the bottom on this side' - he tapped her right hand - 'and pull out the stone. Behind it you'll find a lever, very old and stiff. Push it with all your strength, away from you. Now stand up.'

She straightened up carefully, pressing against the damp stonework for fear of falling. She found the stone, contrived to get her fingers into the crevices around it, and dragged it out. It was so heavy that she could not hold it and it fell with a thud to the floor below.

'Never mind,' said John. 'Now the lever.'

She found it and threw all her small weight against it. Nothing happened. It defied her as if it were embedded in rock.

'I canna,' she panted, crouching to where John's eyes were a glisten in the darkness.

'Wait,' he said. He took a grip on the bars. 'Now try.' She wrestled with it again and this time she won. She leaned sweating against the dank wall while, creaking and groaning, the grille subsided slowly into the stonework.

'My private portcullis.' He grabbed her arm and pulled her back into the shaft. 'Listen!'

Footsteps echoed along a distant passage. As they listened, they came closer and a faint impression of light began to waver in the yawning gloom below. Someone was coming towards them, carrying a torch. As the light came nearer Hazel could make out below them a windowless chamber with a single door. It was through a grille near the top that the light was coming, flickering and bouncing off the chains that trailed from staples in the wall. She looked at John.

He nodded. 'The dungeon.' His hands tightened painfully on her arms. He whispered against her ear, 'We've got to get through that door.'

The footsteps crashed like thunder into the silence. The light flared as the torch was held up to the grille and part of a face was visible between the bars.

'Don't scream!'

His hands released their hold and she felt herself catapulted into the open. She clawed the air trying to save herself and gasped as she sprawled naked on her hands and knees in the bitter slime of the floor.

The man outside gave a cry of surprise, his keys already scraping in the lock. He came bursting through the door and was upon her before she could regain her feet.

A thud and the torch went spinning from his hand. As she scrambled out of reach she saw two figures rolling together on the floor. One stood up.

'Look away,' said John, a length of chain between his hands.

She needed no second bidding, but she wished she could not hear.

'Help me,' he said, dragging the body towards the shaft. He propped it upright against the wall below the opening. 'Hold him there.'

It took all her strength to hold the man upright. With a spring John caught the sill in his hands and levered himself into the opening. Reaching down he grasped the man's clothing and dragged his dead weight up into the shaft behind him.

'Shut the door,' he told her, 'and find his keys. They're on the floor somewhere, I heard them fall.'

She found the keys, a massive bunch of iron, and stood listening to his breathing and the slow lisp of cloth over stone as he inched his way back into the tunnel. Only a man of his fantastic strength could have done it. It's nothing to him, she thought, watching the dead pathetic feet disappearing. No more than if he handled a side of beef. He doesn't think that's a person he's just killed. Even, maybe, some kin of Abby's ...

Her listening ears caught another sound. Infinitely smaller, more sinister. The sound of tiny sharp teeth ... scraping ... crunching ... bone. Bones - somebody's bones! Her palms broke out in a fresh sweat. Holy Mother, bring him back quick! People have died in this place. She gritted her teeth as something scampered over her foot.

Pressing herself to the weeping stones she tried to control her thoughts. This was the thing she had had to do. That no one else could have done. Because she was small enough. And female. Be thankful it was done. It was over now - so stop shaking. Her teeth chattered with nervous reaction and the ghastly chill of the place. The inside of a grave must be like this - damp and earthy and choked with the smells of putrid flesh ... the keys fell jingling from her hand.

'You'd better wait here!' snapped John as he picked them up.

It brought her up with a jerk. 'No - I'm coming with you!'

She hadn't an idea where he was going but the thought of waiting here alone was intolerable. Anything was better than that.

He looked at her piercingly in the light of the guttering torch. 'If you faint-'

'-you'll leave me.' She looked at him steadily. 'I know.'

His expression changed subtly. Enigmatically.

'Just don't faint,' he said.

He was already easing the door on its protesting hinges. She thought of the smock left somewhere in the shaft and made a move to retrieve it.

'Forget it,' he seized her wrist. 'No time to waste.' He drew her relentlessly out through the door and locked it from the outside.

'But I got nothing on,' she protested.

'If we're seen you won't live long enough to blush.'

There was nothing for it but to follow him.

Inching her way behind him along unseen walls in the echoing vaults below Pengerran, not knowing where or why she was going, took on the lightheaded excitement of a childhood prank. Escape from the dungeon had released her tensions too abruptly and she wrestled with an insane desire to laugh.

It seemed to her that they padded barefoot along midnight corridors like two children escapading out of bed. Her taut nerves reacted with a touch of hysteria. When she failed to notice that he had taken a step upwards, when she tripped and bumped into him it struck her as wildly funny. She stifled a soundless giggle as she clutched at him and he suppressed her ruthlessly between his back and the wall.

'Shh ... shh ... sh ...' he breathed. 'You want to die laughing?'

The moment passed, leaving her weak, leaving her melted against him in an unpredictable wave of sensuality, aware in the pressure of his arm and shoulder that he too felt the heady wine of it. Then they moved on.

There was a subtle change in the movement of air. She took a step up. Then another - and another. And then they were climbing, climbing, steep and twisting, round and round in a spiral so sharp that they seemed to be walking on each other's heads. At intervals a swirl of air warned of an opening in the wall, an access to another floor. At each one John stopped and listened before moving on.

At last he cupped his hands to her ear and whispered, 'Can you whistle?'

She nodded.

'Then stay here and listen. If you hear anything anywhere give one low whistle and keep still. What I want is in the turret room above. This is the only way out, so listen well.' He nipped her ear-lobe and was gone.

She would have listened in dread in any case. For her the darkness was always peopled with the unknown. But she could hear nothing. She could not even hear John in the room above. She wondered that anyone so big could move so silently. Was he moving - or had he been caught and killed without a sound? She stood motionless in a stillness that pressed against her skin. It was as if she had gone both deaf and blind. She stared straight ahead of her into a blackness as dense as the silence and a prickle of sweat broke out along her hairline. She thought of the black dog ...

She started violently as his hand brushed hers. For all her vigilance she had not heard him return.

'I've got it!' he whispered, triumphant. 'Let's go-'

And then he dropped the keys.

10

For a moment outside time they stood frozen, unable to do anything but listen while the heavy bunch clanked from step to step, their small noise echoing wildly around the empty drum of the turret.

'Quick!'

She was jerked off her feet as they flung themselves down the dark spiral. Running - falling - hitting one stair in a dozen - they reeled and twisted, racketing downwards - downwards - gathering speed in a desperate plunge towards the keys.

The floor hit them. They sprawled together - groping - searching as the sounds of voices and footsteps reached them.

'Run!' She heard the keys jangle under his hand. 'Run for your life!'

His grip on her arm pulled her with him - fast - too fast - her feet lost the ground - lost it again - then they were at a standstill, dancing with impatience while he wrestled with the keys.

'Jesus - why did I lock it!'

She sweated in an agony of terror while he tried three - four - there were so many on the bunch! More voices - and more footsteps - running now - a faint rumour of light bobbed and wavered at the far end of the vault. She stifled a sob. She wanted to tear the keys from his hand and try herself.

The lock screeched at last. They were inside - unbelievably - slamming the door. As a rabble of men spewed into sight John drove the key home like a knife to the groin and wrenched the tumblers over. They were safe!

Hazel leapt for the shaft. She felt herself snatched back and clamped beside him to the wall nearest the door, her mouth covered almost to the eyebrows by his hand.

'Wait!' he mouthed.

She shrank into her skin as the men came pounding up to the door outside.

There was a confusion of shouts and running feet. 'There's nobody here!'

'Get Jud with the keys!'

'They've got away-'

'No, it's a dead end-'

'Fool! They're in one of the cells!'

'Where's Jud?'

'Must have jumped him. They've got him inside somewhere-'

'Jud! Jud, are you there?'

They were milling up and down thundering on doors, shouting for Jud. Then another voice was added. Clear and decisive. Taking control.

'Take the cells one by one. Bring a ram. When you find the right door break it down. Start here!'

The noise went breaking like a roller of surf down to the far end of the vault.

'Now!' John thrust her towards the shaft.

Hazel made a jump of which she did not know she was capable and was up in the shaft ahead of John. He was behind her, hauling up the grille as she began the uphill struggle to the tunnel mouth. It clattered up noisily over its ratchets, bringing a shout of response from outside. An army of feet followed. Something heavy thudded against the door.

'They can't see us. Keep going!'

He was forging up behind her, bracing with knees and elbows, lifting her ahead of him as she fought her way up the killing slope.

'Keep going - into the tunnel!'

They fell through onto the body of Jud and combined their weights to close the slab behind them, thankful for the noise of the battering ram to drown its telltale rumble. It moved so slowly, so stubbornly - but it moved. The last they saw through its crack was the throb of torchlights, as the door splintered and the men with the ram came crashing into the room below.

There was a moment's silence.

'They've gone - escaped!'

'The air shaft! Search the grounds!'

The voices reached them blessedly muffled by the protecting stones. In a different world, they leaned panting and sweating against the slab.

'We're safe,' breathed John. 'They'll never find us here.' Hazel felt a great sob building up inside her, threatening to tear loose. She mustn't let a sound escape her. She mustn't ... only a tiny squeak, scarcely audible. Another was building up behind it she found herself suddenly pressed against John, her face muffled in his chest, her head clasped in his hard strong hands.

'It's all right. . . it's all right.'

The taut spring unwound itself. She was calm.

Almost before the noises had died away, before they had caught their breath, he was stooping to the body on the floor, tucking the keys into the belt.

'Take his other arm. We've got to drag him to the sea. He should be dead but best make sure.'

Hazel groped downward with a shiver. 'Is he bloody?' 'No. I choked him with the chain.'

Reluctantly she stooped, grasped the deadweight arm, trying not to touch the skin, trying to hold it by the sleeve. She had never touched a corpse other than Tibby's. Were this man's eyes hanging dead upon his face . . . She shuddered as the head rolled towards her.

He was unbelievably heavy. And he slowed them down. 'Canna we leave him?' panted Hazel. 'He'll never be found.'

'He must be found.'

'Must be-'

'In three days' time the sea will give him back - with his keys still on him. Drowned. An accident. A nine days' wonder how he got drunk and deserted his post - and we'll be forgotten.'

'But they know we were there.'

'They only heard noises. With any luck they'll put them down to him.'

Hazel was doubtful but she went on obediently hauling. His scheme might be full of holes but she could do no better. A new thought struck her.

'They'll miss what you've taken.'

'They didn't know it was there.'

She puffed away in silence for a while. Then, 'Would you really have left me?'

'Left you?'

'If I'd fainted?'

'I'd have killed you.'

She stopped. 'Why!' It was an explosion of indignation. To be killed merely for fainting - it was too much.

'They can have fun with a woman with a red-hot iron.'- He added with a touch of impatience, 'Come on!'

She felt herself smiling in the darkness. It was a funny kind of loving....

John said abruptly, 'Listen!'

A faint dull booming came to them. Echoing, humming through the rock.

'The tide! Come on!'

They abandoned their burden and ran, their hearts pounding.

'Once it fills the cave it won't go down again until the spring!'

They could hear it roaring and howling in the cave long before they reached it. A thrash of cold spray drenched them and with a shock of dismay they saw it boiling and curling like demented cream. As they hesitated fresh surf came romping through the cave mouth, prowling and snarling, sucking at the seaweed, gnashing at their ankles like a hungry animal.

'Can you swim?'

She shook her head, numbed with terror in the eerie reflected light.

'Then you'll have to hold on. I'll do the swimming.' He had taken off" his belt and was passing it round both their bodies, lashing them together, her face against his back. 'Hold your nose and hang on for your life. Don't breathe when we go under or you'll drown.'

The maddened sea had already half-filled the cave. It screamed and thundered and bullied and she wanted to flee before it. The thought of being plunged into it filled her with dread. She shut her eyes.

'Get a good grip - no, not round my neck! Whatever happens don't panic -and don't let go. Now!'

She felt the lifting and then the hurtling down, down ... they were falling through the icy flood, down ... down ... She was aware of the strength of muscle and of the greater strength of the sea, they were drifting backwards, sucked back against the powerful forging of his stroke, sucked back harder - faster - they were slammed mercilessly against the roof of the cave, the air driven out of her . . . then moving forward again, slowly at first then faster, faster, driving forward at a terrifying speed - she couldn't see where - she must not breathe in this icy grip. Black stars whirled in her head, her lungs were bursting, darkness roared in her ears and a hammer beat somewhere, forging jags of light through the blackness ... blackness ...

Something was crushing her ribs as the darkness lifted,

something heavy that pounded rhythmically and without pity. She choked, gasped - and bitter brine gushed from her mouth and ran from her nostrils. She remembered vaguely that she had to hold on ... and her fingers curled into sand. She tried to raise herself and was seized by a paroxysm of coughing.

'That's better,' said John. 'I thought for a moment you'd given me the slip.'

His hands supported her while she gasped and shivered and abruptly burst into tears.

'It's all right,' he said. 'It's all right now.'

He held her against him but he could give her no warmth, he was as cold and exhausted as she. Only his mouth was warm. She stopped crying. He said, 'I've done my best to drown you - now say you love me!'

She glanced at him quickly. His eyes were mocking as usual. But there was something else ... She ventured lightly, 'Say you love me would be more to the point!'

'But I do,' he said with equal lightness. He grinned and added, 'Every night.'

She leaned against him, precariously balanced between laughter and tears. He stood up, staggering slightly, and pulled her to her feet.

'Can you walk?'

She nodded, took an unsteady step and grabbed at him as her legs gave way. Who would have thought that her body weighed so much! But after a few steps it was easier. They plodded over the sand weaving a little from side to side.

John was humming under his breath. 'Sing,' he commanded her. 'It'll warm you.'

She tried and was immediately racked by coughing.

'Good!' he approved. 'Get rid of the water. Try again.'

He would not allow her to give up but made her persevere until her lungs stopped protesting and her voice rose clear. His song was some bawdy ballad she did not know. It did not matter. He kept her going by pinching or slapping the parts of her alluded to. It shortened the half- mile ordeal of the beach. But the cliff climb took the last of her strength.

John swung her up off her feet and kicked open the cottage door.

'Abby! Get up! Build the fire high and mull some cider! Quickly!'

He propped Hazel in the chair before the hearth and swathed her in the sable cloak.

'Little John, get up! Stir yourself!' A well-aimed kick to the rump reinforced his words. 'Pack some provisions and saddle up my horse.' The man growled sleepily but stumbled to his feet.

'What's the matter? What's amiss?' cried Abby in alarm. 'Lord sakes! You're soaking wet - what's happened?'

John said with exaggerated patience, 'A moonlight swim! The sea's in a nasty mood.'

Little John gave a loud guffaw as he went out of the door. But Abby, slower of comprehension than her son, threw up her hands.

'Moonlight swimming, indeed! At this time of the year with the tides at springs. And to take that child-'

'Never mind, Abby.' He gave her a gentle shove, 'Just do as I say and what you don't know can't hang you.'

They drank the spiced cider scalding hot in the bright blaze of the fire and Hazel felt the life returning to her hands and feet. Abby clucked and fussed over her as she once had over John, bathing her cuts and binding up her knees. John stood by with a faint sardonic smile. When Little John returned he said, 'Find me a smock and hosen for Hazel. She can't go as she is.'

He handed the garments to Hazel and she slowly got into them, swaying a little from the mulled cider and fatigue, wondering why she was being asked to dress when all she wanted was to fall into bed and sleep till Domesday.

'Hurry,' he urged her, 'we must be away before daybreak.'

She stared at him, unable to believe her ears. 'Oh, not tonight,' she pleaded. 'Please not now, I want to go to bed!' He looked at her, bruised, bleeding and still waterlogged. She looked smaller than ever swamped by Little John's clothes. He cupped her chin.

'I'm sorry, my chuck.' Fie leaned down and kissed her gently. 'You and I have slept in a bed for the last time.'

11

Abby watched their departure by torchlight before dawn. She kissed Hazel for the first time and said, 'If anything should happen, you bring Angel and come to me. There's always a home for you where I am.'

Hazel put an arm around Abby and pressed a chilled cheek to hers.

'You been good to me, Abby. I dunna forget.'

Abby straightened her apron and folded her hands primly. 'Goodbye, my lord.'

He cocked a sarcastic eyebrow. 'No kiss for me?'

'Kisses is for innocents. You're a man now.'

Her inference was not lost on him. His eyes skewered her briefly and he mounted with an angry twitch of the reins.

Abby watched him unmoved. His displeasure troubled her no longer. She had witnessed the corruption of her gods. They were all the same. Between him and the usurping Eustace there was not one whit to choose.

Beside her, Little John growled, 'He goes to his death, Ma. Can't you give him your blessing?'

Abby turned away. If the downfall of her idol had withered her heart it had also cleared her judgement. Her blessings were for the besotted girl who was riding away so trustingly to be crucified. She stood on the cliff and watched them out of sight, outlined against the shimmer of the sea.

Little John said, 'You'll miss him. See if you don't.'

Abby stared fixedly at the empty horizon that was slowly drowning in a blur of tears. 'Aye,' she said unsteadily, 'I'll miss him. Been better if he'd never come: back.'

Relaxed between the warmth of John and the horse and the snuggling baby, Hazel drowsed in the tail of the night.

She had played her part - not unsuccessfully as it turned out. The ordeal was behind her. As the chilling effects of near-drowning receded she felt a glow of pride. She had been included in John's adventuring, part of his plan, privy to his secret. And now, unexpectedly, she had him to herself again as they travelled through the silent hours.

'Where are we going?' she asked sleepily.

'Back to Buxford.'

Buxford-witch country! Was the coven still looking for her and Angel? She should have had him baptised while she could ... She was silent.

'Don't tell me you'll miss the sea.' His laugh was forced. 'I'd have thought you'd had enough of it.'

'I will.' She had not thought of it till now. But it was not like anything else. Its brightness in the morning, its lullaby at night. She would have liked to say goodbye, as if it were a person. She said nothing, not caring to risk his derision.

'Does it have to be Buxford?' She returned to the subject uneasily. 'I'm feared of the Croppers.'

'You'll be safe enough.'

'But why are we going - I thought it was Pengerran you wanted?'

'Both are mine. And now I can prove my identity.'

She sat up. 'With what you took last night?'

'With what I took last night.'

Suddenly it was all clear to her. She twisted on her perch to look at him, eyes shining.

'So now you can go to the King and tell him what happened! And he'll turn the Lord Eustace out and give you back your lands - oh, it's wonderful!' In her elation she forgot that a wife would be restored to him with his lands.

He looked at her strangely in the growing light. He shook his head.

'My dear Mistress Ash - if only it were so simple!'

'You mean - the King wouldn't help you? But he must!'

'You're thinking of King Arthur and his Holy Knights, no doubt! Real princes are not petitioned empty-handed. Not this prince,' he added with a touch of sourness.

Hazel was dashed. 'What was the use of taking it, then?' It seemed to her that they had risked their lives for nothing. 'It doesn't help?'

'It does help. But I must do my own dirty work. First displace Eustace by my own efforts - and at my own expense - and then prove my inheritance. Possession is nine points of the law and the King's Grace will be obliged to recognise my right - from the moment I lay my hands on the key to the coffers.'

Hazel was shocked. 'I don't believe the King's like that! Kings have all the gold in the world. Why should they want more?'

'And how do you imagine they get it?'

She thought about it for the first time.

'I don't know,' she said, surprised.

'Alas, poor Hazel! What is to be done about this innocence of yours - will nothing relieve you of it? Here, nurse your kitten and worry about something you understand.'

His sarcasm left her smarting. For a long time the silence was broken only by Black Man's plodding and the sound of Angel who was noisily sucking his thumb.

The sea mist followed them inland. As they rode into the sunrise it glowed like a pink pearl. In thickets and hedgerows the early birds fought and chattered over the ripening haws.

'It'll be a hard winter,' observed Hazel for something to say.

'I'll find you a hearth to purr by, never fear.' His tone was testy and added to her uneasiness. 'All in good time. This is only the beginning.'

'I anna worried,' she assured him quickly. But she was depressed. Where was the camaraderie of last night?

Perhaps he was just tired. And the baby was whimpering - he was not used to babies. She put it to her breast under the smock and it was quiet. She leaned her head lightly against John and tried to sleep.

As they crossed the moor a magpie flew up. It clattered straight towards them, scolding and beating its wings almost in their faces.

'Oh, no,' she cried, 'one magpie - quick, find another!' Struggling awake, she looked about frantically for a second. John was deep in thought. She thumped his ribs. 'John - look quick! We mustn't see one magpie, it's bad luck!'

He glanced about him perfunctorily to humour her. 'There isn't another. You and your superstitions! You'll be telling me next you believe in fairies.'

'You think I'm stupid!' she retorted hotly. 'You think all peasants are stupid - I'm not! It's just the things I know's different from the things you know. You know about kings and such and I know about magpies. "One for sorrow, two for joy" - we got to see two together or else turn back!' 'Turn back!' he barked. 'We turn back for nothing, and get that through your head! We're going on.'

'But we canna,' she entreated, filled with premonitions of disaster, 'we got to go back or something terrible will happen!'

He looked at her hard and cold. 'Are you turning coward?'

'No! No, I'm not, I'll do anything - die if I have to, you know that. But we got to turn back now!'

He shook his head. 'Too late. My plans are laid.' He spurred the horse to give point to his words.

Hazel said despairingly, 'Why do you have to do this harebrained thing? Why canna we live in peace with Abby and farm a bit of land-' Her voice trailed away as she saw his expression. His eyes blazed with scorn.

'Can you see me - "farming a bit of land"!'

She looked up at him where he loomed above her, his wild hair ruffled by the wind. One might as well ask an eagle to settle down to laying eggs.

'I suppose not.' She sighed unhappily, 'A pox on all magpies!'

Unexpectedly, he reined in and dismounted.

'What are you doing?'

'Ridding you of it. Since it troubles you.' He had produced the fowling-piece from somewhere and was priming it. 'Where did it go?'

'Over there.' She pointed to where it had settled on a tree. Was it wise to kill a bird of ill omen? She was not sure. But certainly it would be less than wise to warn him not to. After all, he was doing it for her. She watched him take careful aim and fire.

The fowling-piece roared. Angel screamed. Hazel cowered. And two and a half rooks fell out of the sky.

'They died of fright,' said John. 'You look as if you were about to join them.' He blew on the smoking gun to cool it, his good humour restored. 'Wait til! I see Fitzarthur!'

Black Man was waltzing skittishly, excited by the noise. John brought him under control and mounted behind her.

'Well, Mistress Ash. Can you bake rook pie?'

She forced a laugh while she comforted the frightened baby. But her eyes were drawn irresistibly to where the magpie flapped lazily into the sky unscathed. There was still only the one. And somehow their failure to kill it made it worse.

There is darkness. There is darkness and a breath-catching pain. It writhes and strangles in the head. Noises... noises like a lunatic peal of bells ... jangling ... hurting. And cold ... cold as death ...

Hazel shivered. She turned gratefully towards the warmth

of the sun that had disturbed her doze. She was glad to be disturbed. There was something in her sleeping that she did not like. But it was high noon and the movement of the horse monotonous. Angel slumbered milkily and John was silent. Almost before she had prised up her heavy lids they had drooped again and she was gone.

Why am I pressed with my face against a wall - I feel no chains? What holds me here? Try drawing back the head-ah, no - agony! Falling back - sweating - world tilting crazily - swinging - a pendulum - sickening - giddy - be still... Not a wall. On the ground. It is the ground that presses against my face. Why? Try to collect myself. I am lying on the ground and I am cold. This is not any place that I know. It is cold and it is dark ... dark ... and sleepy. That is it... I want to sleep ...

John was looking at her oddly.

'I - I was dreaming,' she said, confused. 'Did I make a noise?'

He shook his head. 'I thought you were awake. Your eyes were open.'

She frowned, trying to make sense of the strange vivid fragments that were already retreating from her mind.

'Maybe I'm wandering,' she said doubtfully. 'Maybe it's hunger. Can we stop for a bit?'

When they had eaten she watched in faint surprise as he began unsaddling Black Man. Nightfall was far off and they were still on the open moor.

'I'll be all right to go on,' she said tentatively.

He did not answer. He just went on removing bridle and bit and then piled the tack together in a neat stack. Then he rummaged in the saddlebag for the fowling-piece.

'John-' her voice tailed away.

He said nothing. Only his dark jaw tightened in a way she had come to know and her stomach tightened in response, in apprehension. She was silent while he cleaned and primed the gun. Then he laid a heavy hand on Black Man's flank and led him away out of sight across the moor.

'Oh, no! 'she whispered to herself despairingly. 'Oh, no...'

She sat listening against her will, hardly knowing if her anguish was for the horse whose trust betrayed him to his death or for the man who had to bring himself to kill him. He must have a reason, she told herself, clutching at sanity, some terrible reason to do such a thing. Why won't he tell me, talk to me - it's so much worse not knowing ... The distant roar of the fowling-piece silenced her thought. Even then she could not believe it. It must be another bad dream, she told herself.

After an eternity John came back. He was alone. A glance at his face was enough to warn her against asking questions. She picked up the baby and as much of the gear as she could carry and followed him unspeaking; he strode ahead of her in a brooding silence.

When they left the moor behind them she was exhausted. She plodded wearily, too tired to think, only finding the strength to put one foot in front of the other. She wondered numbly if they were going to complete the distance to Buxford on foot. She felt that nothing could surprise her any more.

She stood behind him in the lighted doorway of an inn and looked back across the moor, shrouded now in misty dusk. Like a graveyard. Like the door to another world. A door that was locked behind her with everything good on the other side. And Black Man ... her eyes filled suddenly, blinding her. Then she realised that John was calling her to follow. She blundered after him through the door into the foetid atmosphere of the inn, blinking to clear her vision, but it was no use. She sat on the floor with the baby and fed him and still the tears streamed helplessly down her face though she made no sound. John glanced at her sharply.

'Don't,' he said gruffly. 'For God's sake - don't. Here!' He thrust a steaming tankard towards her and she gulped down the hot liquid urgently, painfully, against the need to sob. Perhaps if she could be drunk she need not think. Perhaps ... It was long before the warmth of it lulled her mind. When it did, she had turned away from him before she slept.

An icy blow swamps the face and recedes and goes hissing away into endless voids of darkness ... that gasp tore my throat out - God! The pain ebbs slowly.... breathing heavily ... so difficult, choking, choking! There are no thoughts in this head. Only a hammer that bangs and pounds, driving out everything but pain, and there's plenty of that. Can't swallow . . . when I rub fingers together they feel wet - blood? No. Not sticky enough. Water ...

Hazel tossed and moaned. She wanted to wake yet was dimly aware that misery awaited her in wakefulness as well.

Somebody grumbled, 'Keep her quiet, can't you! Some of us want to sleep!'

John's big arm extinguished her. 'Sh-sh ...' he was whispering. 'It's all right...'

'No-' she whimpered, clinging to him. 'No - can't breathe... .' but she was drawn away, helpless, drowning, into the night.

A sound is coming towards me like the noise from a blowhole, booming, thundering, like the sea. The sea! But where - which direction? Must run, get a bearing - can't see anything in this blackness ... ah - there! The noise is deafening - run - too late, it's upon me - feet sucked from under - grab something, anything - rocky wall, grip it like a barnacle against the pull of the tide, sucking, dragging ... hold on ... hold on ... and I'm still here. Plastered like seaweed while the tide goes back to gather reinforcements. Must keep moving. Forge forward, quicker, faster, staggering through darkness, trying to run - no strength. Fighting for breath, blundering from wall to wall in some nightmare tunnel with the sea at my heels . . . what am I doing here? Never mind, just keep climbing, climbing, away from the sea. Get as high as possible. Keep going. Plod on. How the head thuds! And the neck. ... one killing pain ... feel it with the fingers - carefully. It's wealed like the neck of a hanged man! And swollen ... that's what chokes the breath ... am I hanged.... strangled? There was a girl! Naked - what a waste! What... Here comes the sea again! Run, try, run faster, rocking and cannoning - wall to wall - chest aching - and the wall turns traitor and defeats me! It turns on itself and makes a trap - a cell - a dead end! NO-O! A howl of rage and despair boiling out of me, tearing its way up through this ravaged throat. My arms have a life of their own and go thrashing about without my guidance. My head swims and my heart bursts and the darkness roars.... and my hands touch ... metal. Is it really so dark, or am I blind?

I can taste blood. There is something in my hands and it is heavy ... cold ... No, it is my arms that feel heavy, dragging from the thing in my hands that is above my head... something on the wall... a ring. Stand up, pull up by it - this ring ... It moved! Only a little, but it moved - move it more - move it - what is it ... a way out? Move it, it must be moved - and I can't! The body straining, straining, the head throbbing dangerously - and at last, daylight! Daylight - green and watery like at the bottom of a cornfield-and the smell of grass, earth, and this is not rock or earth or seashore - this is masonry. Masonry .... stonework . . . where? There is a gap where the stone was, a narrow gap and something beyond ... reach forward and look through ... some sort of shaft and the light coming dimly through a grille away up to the left - an airshaft! Pengerran! This is Pengerran, and down to the right - the other end of the shaft - that's the Tomb, where we put the Frenchman ... And now it all comes back - raise the alarm! The man - the girl - escaping! Can't shout - what then? The ring! Yes, that ring - slam it hard against the rock - like a chime - once, twice - the echoes go ringing through the stonework - that should rouse them! Not a sound. Nobody's heard ... Must climb through into the shaft, then - steady, steady - dizzy. Hands and knees, then carefully through the gap - aa-ah! Something sharp in the side - knife-wound? No, a key - the key! That's the answer - down the shaft to the lower grille, the one to the cell - clatter on the bars with the keys - someone's got to hear. First rest a moment, gather strength ... I can see light down there! In the cell, through the grille - and a shape - yes, something - looks like - yes, like a sawing-horse - and timber - splintered, big stuff, like a door maybe ... Don't understand ... but it means someone's down there working - or has been - they'll be back

... Now, through into the shaft, heave the weight through somehow ... and the body too gross, too heavy to stand upright... the effort makes me want to vomit - but at last I'm out in the shaft - steep and slippery with the damp ... have to brace myself... feet to one wall, hands to the opposite ... slowly - brace hard ... The body screams for mercy, but no quarter.... got to do it ... blackness explodes in the brain like a powder keg going up. Something hot rushing through ears and nostrils and a pitching forward down the shaft ... down, down, head first and out of control... down. Pain - terror as the grille rushes up to meet me - and all feeling fades. This is death... death... darkness ... silence ... this is death ...

She was sobbing noisily and John was shaking her roughly.

'Hazel! Hazel! Stop it -you're rousing the house!'

A chorus of voices confirmed the protest but she was out of control and babbling hysterically.

'I'm dead! I'm dead!' she sobbed, beside herself.

'Soon will be if you don't shut up!'

'Keep her quiet, can't you!'

'Hazel - stop it!'

The flat of his hard hand rocked her head on her shoulders, jolting her back to reality. She stopped abruptly, her eyes watering from the force of the blow. He pulled her against him, 'There now, it's all right.'

The baby awoke and his yelling added to the chaos. The voices grew surlier.

'My apologies, gentlemen. A nightmare - we were set upon and robbed today.'

Sympathy was instant. Someone picked up Angel and gave him suck. Hazel found a wineskin pushed into her hands and a woman leaned across and whispered something in John's ear. He smiled. Under cover of nuzzling Hazel's neck he muttered fiercely, 'For God's sake, pull yourself together. What's the matter with you?'

'I don't know.' She felt dazed, her mind a blank from which the dream had already faded. 'What was I on about?' She snuggled drowsily onto his shoulder but he shook her awake again.

'You said you were dead.'

'Dead?' She frowned, trying to catch the fugitive shreds of something ... 'I dunna remember.'

'Well, get this through your head. You're alive' - he glanced about him swiftly before he finished - 'and your name's not Jud!'

'Better this morning, mistress?'

She nodded from where she sat in the sun on the mounting block. The innkeeper smiled and went about his business.

'Here comes your man,' he said amiably.

She looked up. And then looked harder in disbelief. John was coming up the road towards her leading two horses, a cobby roan mare and a tall clumsy bay with a weatherbeaten coat. She got to her feet as he approached.

'If you wanted horses-' Words had failed her. But his look would have silenced her in any case.

'He was too conspicuous,' he said defensively. Then, 'Too easily recognised,' he explained with a taint of sarcasm. He indicated her sable cloak, 'That must go too.'

'But...' She could not bear to part with the garment she had lived in, sheltered under, given birth and made love in. It was part of her life. She took it off slowly and stood hugging it, as if it had been a living animal. 'It's my home,' she said helplessly.

John softened a fraction. 'Keep it a little longer. Then it must go.'

She clasped it tighter. He added, 'And the ring.'

The ring! The beautiful purple stone he had given her on her wedding day. He was taking back everything he had ever given her. Was she to be abandoned, disposed of like Black Man? Her early joy in adventuring alone with him chilled under a sense of foreboding.

'I dunna understand.'

'We can keep nothing to connect us with Black John.' He saw her look and smiled faintly. 'You can keep your baby.'

She said nothing as he mounted the bay and motioned to her to follow on the mare. Her sense of rejection was complete.

The journey proceeded inexorably and with each day she had less heart for it. She felt she had left the good life behind her with the sparkle of sunlight on the sea. The inland scenery with its heavy woods oppressed her and she was aware of menace in every shadow. The first crossroads to sport a gallows set her shivering. If she had escaped sinister pursuers by her flight to Cornwall it was only to find them implacably lying in wait on her return. She had known grief in her life, loneliness and desperation. She had never felt anything like the depression that descended on her now.

John became more unapproachable as time passed. He rarely spoke and never laughed and she sensed that he was drawn taut as a bowstring. He had shaved off his beard, and now she could see the lines of age and bitterness etched on his face. She saw too what it was that gave his smile its sardonic twist: a long, puckered scar that ran from his hairline down to one corner of his mouth. Without his beard, without his horse, he looked subdued and vulnerable, his familiar bravado vanished. She had never seen him so gaunt, so unsmiling, so diminished.

At night he stretched out nearby but did not touch her. Lacking the temerity to close the gap between them, she drew what comfort she could from cuddling the baby. It distressed her to know that when she lay sleepless she could no longer turn to John for solace. Her nights were troubled not by dreams but by fear of dreams, and she had lost the ease with which she had once slept soundly on hard earth. But she knew he fared no better. She would wake from sleep to find him staring hollow-eyed into the darkness.

'You're afraid,' she breathed, hardly daring to speak the words.

'Yes.' He sighed heavily, and reached unseeing for her hand. It was a change in him that frightened her.

'You - of dying?'

The ghost of a smile. 'My dear Mistress Ash - do you not know me better than that ? It is failure that I fear.'

Failure ... to take Pengerran alone would need an army, even she knew that. And he had - what? Old men in rusting armour and velvet-clad fops. She pressed his hand.

'You don't have to win for me,' she said. 'Give it up.'

'I can't,' he said, 'I'm committed. I can't turn back.'

'Why not?'

'My father's spirit would not let me rest.'

They passed through the village where she was born. She sank her head into the homespun cloak that had replaced her beloved sables, dreading to be recognised. But no one as much as gave her a second look. She wondered if the cottage still stood, tom between wanting to see it and not wanting to. Even the sight of Tibby's house gave her a twist of the heart. And she averted her eyes too late to avoid the burn scar on the grass of the green. Surely, it should have been greened over by now, she thought. Unless.... She shivered, and thumped her heels against the mare's unresponsive sides to hurry her on.

John was calling to her. She took no notice and chivvied the reluctant animal to a sluggish trot, pretending not to hear. He meant her to stop, she knew it. And she was not sure what disobedience might bring upon her from this strange new John. But even his anger was less dreadful to her than another moment spent in this place. She put her head down and rode on.

He caught her up and seized her bridle, glaring.

'We're stopping here!'

'Not here -' She turned on him, anguished and vehement.

He stared, perplexed. She could see he did not recognise the place. 'Please, John ...' she besought him, willing him to understand. 'Please not here!'

He gave her a long, searching look. Then he released her bridle and clucked to the horses to move on. To her he said nothing. And he had retreated so far behind his wall of strangeness that she could find no words with which to break through it.

She had fallen into the habit of riding behind in silence, her only view of him that uncommunicative back. It was useless for her to try to talk to him. His mind was so far away from her that she might as well not be there. But she understood at last what it was that drove him so relentlessly on his futile errand. Little John had understood too, she realised; it was the reason for the rough tenderness he had always shown him. She would have liked to go back and tell Abby that she had it all wrong, that he wasn't driven by greed or ambition or dreams of a glorious future. He had little or no hope of winning and he knew it. But his honour was at stake. His honour and his father's honour, and his duty as he saw it. And he was bound to go on though it meant his death.

She would not turn from him as Abby had done, she would never change. She might one day be the only friend he had. She sighed. She would have liked to tell him about it. But she knew her offering was inadequate. He was so tied up with land and family that ordinary personal love meant nothing to him. But one day he might come to value it, and on that day she would be there. No pale Lady Edith was going to stand in her way, the Lady Edith had everything else and she was welcome to it for the joy it gave her. She, Hazel, was going to have John - whether or not she had the right! The thought heartened her and she smiled. Small matter it had been to eat Tibby's sins - she had more than enough of her own ...

Across the circle of firelight she could feel him watching her.

He lay half in shadow, saying nothing, while she tended the baby and prepared for the night's rest. Only his eyes followed her like the silent pacing of a cat.

For a long time she avoided meeting them. He had ignored her for so long that his attention now made her uneasy. If he had something to say to her it was unlikely to be anything good.

At last he said, 'Come over here.'

She pretended not to hear, staving off the evil moment for as long as she could.

A corner of his mouth twitched and he said again, 'Come here,' and regarded her lazily, knowing she would obey.

She went to him reluctantly. He reached up a hand to draw her down.

'Sit down, Mistress Ash.' His voice was softened with overtones she had not heard since the night they left Abby. She came slowly to her knees, not looking at him.

'If you got something bad to say let's have it straight out.' She lifted her chin. 'Breaking it gentle only makes it worse.' He had been gone on one of his mysterious errands most of the day. Where had he been? Dear God, what was going to happen now?

She waited, holding her breath. He said nothing, only smiled faintly. His hand travelled smoothly to the nape of her neck, moving under her hair, caressingly. Her head arched backward and her eyelids drooped. A familiar warmth awoke in her body like the glow of wine. Her eyes closed.

'Nothing to say,' he whispered, his fingers coaxing. 'I want you, that's all. Come here to me ...'

After a time he said, 'What's the matter?'

'Nothing.' She moved her head restlessly. What was the matter? She did not know.

'You lie, something's troubling you. I know - so tell me ...'

She was awake now, cool and detached. The drowsiness and the warmth had alike drained out of her.

'I love you,' she whispered, trying to bring it back. But she was looking past a stranger to a vanished man.

His laugh was a bitter weed bitten off at the roots. 'No - Black John perhaps. And you want him back.'

She could not deny it. A single tear rolled down her temple in the darkness.

'Maybe,' he said enigmatically. 'Maybe sooner than you think.'

She woke with no idea of how long she had slept. It was dark in the forest and unnaturally still. As if its teeming nocturnal life held its breath to listen for the sound that had awakened her - what was it? Now there was nothing. Not even a falling leaf. Between the tree trunks a thin ghostly mist hovered in skeins, hanging motionless in the faint light.

She called softly, 'John?'

There was no answer. She roused herself to look about for him. He was nowhere to be seen. Alarmed, she stood up, calling to him again. He did not appear. She looked towards the horses, to see only the mare drowsing where she was tethered. The bay was gone.

Oh God, she thought. Oh God, what now? As she stood there she heard it again. The sound that had awakened her. High and cold and unearthly, the calling of a vixen. She let go the breath she had been holding ... then caught it again. A vixen - in October? No! Then what - if it was not a vixen ... Jesus - what?

Where was John? Was his absence connected in some dreadful way - there it was again! Cut short this time as if strangled. Was it human or supernatural? She strained her ears for some other sound to give her a clue. It was not far from here that she had seen the black dog. She felt sweat begin to trickle between her shoulder-blades. She shut her eyes and wished she were still asleep. Then she caught another sound, the stamp and whicker of an uneasy horse - the bay!

'John!'

She began running in the direction of the sound, calling as she went. She heard him curse from a distance and shout 'Go back!' But she was too frightened to go back. She stopped calling but she kept on running towards his voice; his, and another much lighter, much higher, a woman's that sobbed and pleaded and abruptly stopped.

She broke through the undergrowth just as the moon came out and almost fell over them. For a moment she stared and then her stomach twisted in revulsion and she reeled away to be sick.

'I told you to go back!' snarled John.

Why hadn't she - dear God, why hadn't she! She should have known ... At last she got a hold on herself and forced her legs to take her back. John glanced up at where she sagged with ashen face against a tree.

'I thought you didn't kill children!' Her voice was a stricken whisper.

'She should have left it at home!' He glared up from where he stooped to clean his knife on a still palpitating body. He added viciously, 'You wanted Black John back. Be satisfied!'

She shut her eyes, trying to blot it from her mind.

'But why this - why?'

This was utterly pointless murder. This woman and her baby could have had nothing worth stealing. His answer jerked her eyelids wide again.

'So that you can take her place.'

Her heart contracted.

'I...? Why, who was she?'

'She was the Lady Edith's wet-nurse.' In the pause that followed she felt the world go swimming away from her. 'Tomorrow I sell you at the Hiring Fair.'

PART III

The Old One

1

Hazel stood in the market place and wished that she were dead. She wished that the sun would go down and stop her head aching. She wished that the earth would open and swallow her. Or that the sky would fall and bury her. Anything -so that she could escape from standing here like a prize sow with her one normal breast exposed and dribbling milk, while the eyes of the men lingered and Angel squalled hungrily, held out of reach by John's unyielding arm. She stood staring straight in front of her, cheeks burning with humiliation and prayed blasphemously, Let me die now. Let me drop into Hell but get me out of this! She shut her eyes hopefully…

'Wake up!' He dug her in the ribs. 'The steward is coming this way.'

He moved closer to her and put his arm about her shoulders. It was done not to please her but to impress the man who would buy her. But it was his arm, dear and familiar and soon to be lost to her. In spite of herself a scalding tear forced its way between her squeezed lids.

She heard a voice beside her that she hardly recognised, a voice that coaxed and wheedled in an accent like her own.

'Here's a kind gentleman, got a good face. You'll do something for my poor sister as lost her man …'

Another voice growled something about plague.

'No, no, sir- not the plague! Do we look sickly, sir? No, fell under his oxen, he did, got his fool head kicked in - saving your presence m'dear! - drunk his skinful, he had, and there's the truth of it. Ah, now, that's a different matter, sir, isn't it, knowing we're all healthy? A fine strong girl this is, years of work in her. Just look at this yield!'

His fingers bruised her taut flesh painfully, making her wince as they expressed the milk. Then, unbelievably, they were joined by others even rougher. Goaded beyond endurance, she lashed out.

'Now, now, my girl, none of that! It's just that she's upset, sir, you understand. You'll find her docile enough with your good wife.' He imprisoned her hands and treated her to a secret glare. 'There now, you foolish child - want a good home, don't you? So be good to the kind gentleman as likely'll be good to you! Dunna you take no mind to her, sir, not herself today and that's a fact. But you'll find her a right good girl come you gets her home. Give her to your wife, will you Nurse any three babes, she could. There's right fine dugs if ever I see 'em!'

Hazel could not look at him. She stared miserably at the man in black broadcloth who was going to lead her away into captivity. Whatever she said or did would make no difference to that. He had that approving buyer's look in his eye.

She had no faith in the task that John had set her. But she was sworn to help him, and even if she were not... a little time, a little haggling, and she was sold. Angel was thrust into her arms and instantly clamped his small mouth in place, easing her discomfort and threatening to release her tears. She moved forward numbly, not looking behind her.

John watched her walk away from him with her head held a fraction too high and his bowels dissolved in pity. He stood for a moment irresolute, wanting to call her back. Wanting to say something, to tell her ... what? There was nothing he could say. He watched her out of sight, thinking that she might perhaps look back. But she did not. Perhaps she was crying and did not want him to see.

Someone jostled him and he moved away. He walked slowly, aimlessly. He could not make a move in- Cornwall until the ground had cooled. He had done all he could for the moment. The sense of urgency that had sustained him for so long had drained and left a blank nothing where it had been.

He stood still in the hustle of the market with people pushing him from all directions. Black Man was gone. Hazel was gone. Bess ...?

There was a thought. One might travel further and fare worse. He chinked the coins in his hand. They would buy him a welcome at the Hop Bine. He turned on his heel and started walking.

Bess did not notice him as he came in sight of the tavern. He could see her out at the back among the goats and the geese. As he watched he saw her pull up her clothes and crouch down among the long grass, saw her face redden as she strained to relieve herself. When she had finished she took a handful of her skirts to wipe herself clean. Disgust filled his mind. Disgust and an uninvited comparison. He could not imagine Hazel doing that.

He should not be imagining Hazel. When he realised that he had walked on past the Hop Bine he made himself go back.

Bess eyed him with no sign of recognition.

'Round the back if you're selling. Front is for customers.'

He checked. Then he turned and walked away more quickly than he had approached. He must be mad! After all his pains to go unrecognised he had been ready to walk into the Hop Bine and announce his return. Agitation speeded his stride and he walked on out of the village, unmindful of the bay he had bought to carry him. He was so preoccupied that he was still pounding one foot before the other when the first bird started to think about the dawn.

And Hazel, in the goose-feather bed she had once set her

heart on, lay wakeful, too desolate and too scorched to shed a tear.

2

A faint puling came from the cradle in the corner. Hazel hauled herself out of bed in the darkness before dawn, thinking for the hundredth time that this baby, her charge, was not going to live. Poor Lady Edith. All her riches could not buy her a thriving child.

She burrowed in the covers and took it back into bed with her; its movements were so feeble, she thought sadly. Even its sucking was hardly strong enough to ease her, she always had to put Angel there to finish off. All Lady Edith's babies died, so Sarah said. Perhaps it was a judgement on her for marrying the Lord Eustace.

Angel stirred in the bed beside her and came crawling across to make sure of his share. She smiled. He would never go lacking for the want of coming forward. She wished the other poor little thing could show some spirit. Or even the faintest wish to go on living. But the Lady Edith seemed to be the same. When anxiety had driven her to go over Sarah's head to tell her that the baby was ill, she had shown no concern. She had merely said resignedly that the Lord's will would be done, and turned back to the accounts that she was checking with the steward. It seemed to Hazel unnatural. But then everything about the Lady Edith seemed unnatural.

She was neither good nor bad, kind nor unkind. She barely seemed aware that you were there. She went through her endless daily round of supervising and organising as efficiently and as soullessly as a spinning wheel or a ploughshare and displayed just about as much emotion. Even a horse took more pleasure in his daily life than she did. Had she shown the same stony indifference to John - or had it been the other way about, had his uncaringness been the start of hers? She tried to recall what Abby might have said of her. She could not remember. Either Abby had been too discreet or she had paid too little attention at the time. It was not her concern, she reminded herself.

Angel had finished his side and was struggling to get at the other. She pushed him away and tried to settle the little one more comfortably. How could it take any interest in its nourishment all strapped up as it was? In the beginning she had longed to unswaddle it; but now it looked so fragile that she had a superstitious notion that only the bandages were holding it together. She was moved to such deep pity for the pathetic scrap in her care that she almost resented Angel's bouncing health for the contrast it made. It was so unfair. And the Lady Edith's indifference to it disturbed her. She wondered if she could really be so cold; perhaps she had known so much sorrow that she no longer felt anything. Certainly she had never known love. All those dead babies, conceived and born in duty with never a kiss for sweetening! She seemed to regard Lord Eustace with the same blankness with which she regarded everything else. Perhaps she had once been happy with John. Or maybe his charm had never been turned on her. Perhaps like two wild animals in a cage they had torn each other to pieces ...

Angel was trying again. She fended him off and tried to arouse the little one who had as usual drowsed off over her feed. If you'd been a boy, she thought resentfully, they'd have moved heaven and earth to keep you alive. Only heirs are important to these people. How it must gall them to see someone like me with a healthy son and nothing to inherit! Never again would she envy the children of the rich. Better an empty belly and the freedom to follow your heart.

She stroked a gentle finger along the tiny sunken cheek.

'Come on, wake up.' She explored the moist crease under the chin. 'Time enough to sleep when you are full.'

The baby gave a squeal of resentment at being disturbed and she squeezed a few drops of milk into its open mouth. It gagged and gurgled and a minute amount went down.

'Come on,' she coaxed. 'You dunna want to sleep forever and you will if you dunna feed.'

The baby whimpered again and patiently she repeated the process. Sometimes she had to go on like this for hours, but at least she was achieving something. There was nothing else she could do. Even Sarah said so. Sarah was in charge of the nursery and should know if anyone did. But she had only shrugged.

'Up to you to keep it alive as I see it. Don't seem like nobody else'll take much trouble. Given up, they have - well, been too many the same, never live long they don't, poor little mites. And 'tisn't as if it were a boy ... But you keep it going as long as you can, my girl. Won't be no place for you once it's gone - that's unless she starts another, of course.'

She had not answered. Someone would come, John had said. Someone she would recognise, who would tell her what to do. And lives would depend on it ... She thought about it hard and then said doubtfully, 'Surely they won't just throw me out? The steward paid good money for me.' 'Lor' bless you, money don't mean nothing to them!' Sarah laughed unkindly. 'Maybe they'll give you to the Lady Joanna for a toy - like that monkey of hers.'

Hazel had bitten back a retort. Now she sighed, and shifted in the bed, trying to get comfortable. That pain she had woken up with, that had melted as she came out of sleep ... it was coming back. It was a weird pain, low in her stomach and yet not really there - as if it belonged in some part of the body that was foreign to her. But the pain was there - Mother of God, the pain was there.

She stiffened and her eyes rolled upwards in their sockets. After a while her hands and feet began to chill, and Angel squealed in protest at finding no more milk. Presently both babies slept, one hungry and one filled. Hazel was deeply unconscious.

I never thought flesh could live through anything like this ... why can't I die... if only they'd let me die - like Ma there in the corner. Can't see her breathing no more. And her face... like crumpled rag ... And what was he to throw her life away for - come back plaguing us after all these years ... dragging us down with him? Why did they have to find that cave ... right under our cottage? You can't betray a man, let him run into a trap ... Ah - God! Another turn of this thing and I won't be no man no more ... no more ... no ... no ...

She came to sobbing, moaning with a pain or the shadow of a pain that she did not understand. Sarah was standing over her, staring suspiciously, with Kate, the young girl who helped in the nursery. As she opened her eyes, Kate crossed herself.

'Sarah, I feel like death ...' She held out a weak, sweating hand towards the two, who shrank from her. 'What's wrong?' She looked from one to the other, 'Was I shouting again?'

Kate opened her mouth but before she could speak Sarah silenced her and pulled her away through the door. Hazel heard Kate protesting in the passage outside. She could not catch her words but she heard all too clearly Sarah's reply.

'That's as may be. If you ask me, someone ought to tell the Lady Edith. Small wonder if that baby don't survive!'

'The Lady Edith dunna listen to servants' gossip!' Kate's voice was raised, 'No use you carrying tales to her.'

'Carrying tales is one thing, witchcraft is another. And that girl's possessed if ever I saw it! Talking with a man's voice, speaking with such words - what woman ever had a pain in the ...'

Their voices dwindled out of hearing. Hazel sat still. What had she done now? What had she said? She must have been dreaming again - if dreaming it was. She was beginning to wonder. If she was dreaming, why did she feel real pain? It was still ebbing slowly, leaving her weak and wretched. Sarah said she was possessed by devils - was this the price of throwing away her soul with the crucifix that night? She shivered, and huddled against her sleeping son for warmth. She wished there were a place to sleep where she could not be heard. She wished she could remember what she had dreamed ... She lay for a long time tormenting her memory. But the more she tried the further it receded. By the time she had dressed and gone down to the kitchen she could hardly recall what it was she was searching for.

'You're pale this morning, didn't you sleep?'

She took her ration of ale without answering and turned shuddering from the food.

'What's up then - not sick are you?'

She shook her head.

Someone nudged the speaker and whispered in his ear. He gave vent to a raucous laugh. He leaned over to pinch Hazel's rump too sharply for comfort.

'Don't you fret about that, my girl - I got one you can borrow any time you've a mind!'

'And mine-'

'No, mine!'

She looked up perplexed as laughter went rollicking around the company. What had she been saying? The Devil take these dreams! And that was fair enough, if the Devil sent them, let him take them away.

She sat huddled in the ingle after the other servants had departed to their work, content to leave the burden of the two babies to Sarah and Kate. It was good at a moment like this to be able to unload Angel, much as she had come to love him. Just now she felt even her own life too heavy to support.

She watched dull-eyed the little scullions scraping the pots for their share of the morning meal. It was unfair that they worked hard all day and had only the leavings. There was so much that was unfair. They were arguing now as to whose turn it was to walk the treadmill. They argued about it every morning and every morning their differences were settled in the same way. A few hearty thumps from the cook and whichever was left standing had to turn the spit. Wearily, she closed her eyes.

Dimly in the distance she was aware of the disturbance that accompanied the Lady Edith's daily progress through the house. Everything must be presented for her inspection and everything must be up to her exacting standard. No one was spoken to sharply, or even reproached. But the very absence of comment told the backslider that in that cool calculating mind a note was being made of his shortcomings. Impossible to imagine the Lady Edith ever falling short herself. She was always punctual, always immaculate, and Hazel had been staggered to find that her working day - if you could call it work - was even longer and fuller than Margery's had been.

The small commotion was drawing nearer. The little retinue had reached the shambles and would soon be in the kitchens. Hazel sighed and pulled herself together for the long climb back up the twisting stair to the nursery. If Sarah was out to make trouble for her it was best not to be caught away from her post.

Sarah and Kate stopped talking as she entered the room. She took up a comb and drew it through her hair, and confined it in a fresh white coif.

'Who is this Lady Joanna you spoke of, Sarah?'

She only asked the question to dispel the uneasy silence. The answer startled her.

'The Lady Edith's daughter - the one that lived.'

'The Lady Edith's, not the Lord Eustace's?'

They looked at each other before Sarah said, 'The Lady Edith was a widow. Her first was Lord Pengerran - him that was killed in the wars.'

A cold hand squeezed her heart.

'Pengerran ... that's not a name from round here?' 'Down the West Country somewhere. It was all a long time ago. But the little girl's his.'

Hazel smoothed her gown and pinned a fresh apron in place. She contrived to keep her voice steady.

'What's she like?'

It jolted her to hear John referred to as Lord Pengerran; still more to know he had a daughter, yet another distance to be put between them. But she had to ask the question.

Sarah said, 'You'll see soon enough, she's due back from her wedding trip any day. And don't let your tongue wag too freely or it won't be liked.'

Hazel turned to look at her. 'Her wedding trip?' She thought she must have misheard. 'But - how old is She?' 'A mere child,' Sarah's lips compressed. 'That's why she's coming back to her home for a while. Give the poor mite a little time before she starts trying to make heirs.' Sarah got up. 'My tongue's run away. Best forget what I've been saying. And as for you, my girl' - the unfortunate Kate took a smart box on the ear - 'you've no call to be gawping there, get about your business!'

They both went, leaving Haze! to her thoughts. 'When I lie with you, it is not to get heirs ...' Would she ever lie with him again? It was hardly to be hoped for, whichever way things went. She could only do her part, keep her promise, and leave the rest to fate.

She moved over to the cradle and looked down at the baby girl. Could she contrive to keep her alive for the days - or the weeks - that were needed? She had to try. Perhaps she would take a little milk now she was rested.

As she stooped to pick her from the cradle she was seared

with pain. She gasped, and crumpled to the floor unconscious.

That cursed vinegar! Every time you think to slip away and escape the pain ... They got no pity ... not even for her, poor old thing ... How her face reproaches me, like as if she knew.... but he wasn't to me like he was to her ... and I can't take no more, I can't... Oh Jesus, God! Smashing teeth is one thing, but this ... he could never have won ...

Take it away - the vinegar - the screw - I'll tell you - yes, damn your eyes - take it away, I'll tell, I'll tell you anything . . .

3

Dusk deepened into darkness.

The movements among the wreckage dwindled to a faint occasional stirring. A crippled horse waited on three legs for a dead rider to lead him home. Another raised a despairing head above a shattered body, then dropped it again in the only movement it could make. A human leg waved hopelessly, like a drowning swimmer trying to attract attention.

One by one the feeble voices ceased to call. Only the squabbling of crows broke the silence.

A light wavered cautiously at the far edge of the field. It hovered and dipped, climbed, hovered and dipped again. It was joined by another from the direction of the village. Looters were moving like monstrous carrion birds among the dead.

A body detached itself from a tangle of others, struggled clear slowly and with difficulty, and staggered a few steps to slump again onto its knees. Head in arms, the figure crouched motionless. Then the approach of a looter sent it reeling away into the night.

Dawn drove a splinter of steel along a skyline ragged with the fall of rain. It fell soft and insistent, washing the blood from the battlefield, sweeping across the moor where a solitary man stood weeping for the friends who had died to no avail.

His skin was hot and taut and yet he shivered. He did not know if he was hot or cold. Living or dying. He hardly cared either way. He was choked with the bitter ashes of defeat. He had spent the last of his strength and he had no more hope.

There was only one thing left that he wanted now. He wanted Hazel back.

He wanted her moving about where he could see her. Humming little shapeless tunes under her breath, tending her baby. He wanted her smoothness, her plainness, her black-bread simplicity. He wanted to bury his head in her lap and strive no more. To care as little as she did for the things he had fought for and lost.

'There's more to life than rattling knives ...'

He stood still in the downpour and remembered her sharply as he had not remembered her in months. He could almost see her standing there with the raindrops on her hair. And he wanted her ... to take her and Black Man and ride away over the edge of the world to whatever was there.

Black Man was lost to him, somewhere on the desolate moor. And Hazel he had planted in faraway Buxford Place, unattainable to him now'. Was she still there, waiting to admit him and his men.... victorious? That dream was lost with the rest - and Hazel with it.

And yet...

He rubbed his hands over his bloodied face and blinked the rain from his eyes. Somehow', somewhere, there must be a way ...

4

'Oh, those damned dogs!'

She covered her ears with her hands to shut out the sound. It was not that their noise was unpleasant - their voices were so carefully matched that in full cry they sounded like a chime of music. It was just that every day at the same hour they were baying away on the same old note while the manor guests in their elegant clothes cantered daintily around the park in pursuit of the deer. They never caught anything - much less killed. They were not intended to. But today the very triviality of it was too much for her frayed nerves.

The baby girl was fading.

Hazel had sat all night by her cradle, alone and helpless while the others slept, miserably trying to will her to hold on to life. It was no use, and she knew it was no use. The baby would die like the rest and another little coffin would join its fellows in the vault. There was nothing she could do but wait. She had seen too many babies die to have any hope. Doomed babies all had the same face, whether it lay in a gilded cradle or on a heap of rags. Tibby used to say the Old One put his seal on them so as to know which ones to collect.

She lowered her hands as the singing hounds and the thudding hooves faded into the distance. There was nothing she could do here. Best pull herself together and go down.

Angel had slept off his morning feed and was stirring. He sat up, blinking, his tow-coloured hair standing on end. He looked like a newly hatched chick. Hazel smiled and he grinned back at her, displaying his single tooth. She held out her hands.

He heaved himself to his knees, swayed for a moment and collapsed on his ear. His short sturdy arms flailed and he was up again and forging towards her, his eyes on her face. He hadn't really got the hang of it, she thought, but he wasn't going to give up. He would always keep patiently pushing until he got what he wanted. She watched him come plodding laboriously, propelling himself on hands, knees, stomach or whatever came into contact with the floor until he reached the goal of her skirts. He grasped with both hands and dragged himself onto unsteady feet, where he stood teetering for a second, beaming red-faced and triumphant before his knees gave way and he rolled backwards with his legs in the air.

Hazel leaned down and scooped him up and his gurgling filled the room. She laughed and tossed him up. At least he was blithe and strong!

She took him down to the kitchen with her, cradled on her hip, going down the back ways to avoid the gallery and the Great Hall, where the Lord Eustace would be hearing the plaints of his tenants. She wondered how much justice they could hope for. She could not imagine anyone winning a judgement that was likely to conflict with his interests.

She edged her way carefully down the spiral stairs that were slippery at the edges, remembering another spiral stair and the night she had flung herself down it. It seemed so long ago. Hard to realise it was only last summer. Sometimes it was hard to believe it had happened at all. John had never come back for her. No messenger had ever come and she knew now that no one ever would. After all the urgency, the secrets, the sacrifices, there was nothing. Only silence, and the slow death of hope.

From an embrasure she caught sight of the little girl playing in the sunlit pleasaunce; her little monkey was with her on his length of gilded chain, muffled against the cold in his tiny jester's suit. His wizened face looked pathetic, as if he were a child who had looked at himself in a mirror and seen an old man.

As she looked the girl glanced up, and laughed in a way that drove knives through her - Joanna, the daughter of John, who had not even mentioned her existence. But then Joanna was a girl, and women merely came with the property.

She recalled the first time she had seen her. She had heard inexpert twangings coming from the room below the nursery, and glimpsed through the open door a trim girl like a blackbird perched on a stool too high for her, wrestling with a lute as big as herself. Brows drawn together in fierce concentration, she was bent on stretching her inadequate hand to subdue the rebellious strings. The lute, its rounded back against the silk of her dress, slid coyly and gracefully to the floor.

'Poxy thing!'

She sprang down, face glowing scarlet, and seized it by the neck as if she would strangle it.

A wayward sound escaped Hazel and she found herself rounded on with a crackle of angry black eyes.

'If you think it's so amusing, you try!'

Hazel shrank back, confused. 'I couldna-'

The younger girl dimpled suddenly. 'No, you couldn't. Come here and hold it - stop it slipping off my knees.'

As Hazel leaned over the lute she saw the weals that glowed on the tender skin.

'Now,' the girl was saying, half to herself. 'This one here. And this one ... and this ... so! Oh, a plague on it, you have to press so hard!'

'Oh, dunna,' Hazel begged, seeing her wince. 'You'll hurt your fingers so - that thing's like a cheese-cutter.'

'Serves them right, they're not trying!'

'But you canna, you haven't got the strength - not till you're grown.'

The blackbird eyes hardened. 'Don't tell me what I cannot do! This thing makes music - it shall make it for me.' The delicate jaw set in a stubborn line. Then she

laughed unexpectedly with a toss of black hair, 'What did you call it - a cheese-cutter?' and Hazel had known without telling whose daughter she was.

She sighed, and went on down the stair. That had been weeks ago. It was nearly Christmas now. Life had settled into a peaceful routine. No more dreams had come to trouble her and Sarah, evidently, had said nothing to the Lady Edith. Only the imminent death of the baby kept her on thorns. When it died .... what then?

She broke her fast in the kitchen, and leaving Angel at play with the other children there, went out into the sharp cold air.

As she passed the Lady Chapel, the choristers were practising. A strain of music drifted towards her, carried by the wind. She shivered and stood listening, tense as a doe.

'Lullay, my liking, my dear son, my sweeting ...'

Someone touched her arm. It was Joanna.

'Listen,' she breathed, dark eyes shining. 'Hear how it shifts from light to shade and   back again - so beautiful ...'

'Lullay my liking, my own dear darling ...'

Hazel listened. She knew nothing of music but she heard the cool unworldly melody and thought of John sleeping hard on the frosty ground. But was he - or was he pillowed warm on that Bess's fat tits? Where was he? He was callous and cruel and every day told her more clearly that she was forgotten. And yet standing here with the music lapping the edges of her mind she felt an ache go through her as if the ice had come inside.

Depressed beyond words, she climbed the weary stairway back to the nursery and resumed her watch on the cradle.

Joanna looked up from her lute as she came in.

'Why the cloak and bundle?'

'I come to say goodbye.' Her voice was tight with misery. She could not go without seeing Joanna. She was her last link with John, and now even that was to be lost to her.

'Goodbye - why, where are you going?'

'The baby's dead.'

'So?'

'So I got to go. Sarah says.'

She reflected sadly that even Joanna did not care about the baby. Her death had been expected for so long that no one cared.

'Sarah - who is Sarah?'

Hazel met the enquiry with bewilderment, 'Sarah - her that's in charge of the nursery.'

Joanna's eyes snapped and the lute chimed to the floor.

'Wait here and hold the monkey!'

Hazel dropped her bundle to catch him as he was flung carelessly, chittering with nerves, in her direction. She managed to grab his chain as he twisted from her grasp and held on to it while he sprang excitedly up and down her skirts like a frightened squirrel at a tree.

She listened in a confusion of relief and misgiving as Joanna swept out of the room. She heard her voice go ringing through the galleries, 'Where is Madam, my mother?'

She waited so long that she was sure she must be forgotten. The monkey fretted awhile, then sat down and quietly picked his nose. Hazel grew more uneasy as time passed. Should she go? What about the monkey - should she tie him to a chair, leave him, find somebody? Should she take off her cloak, hide her bundle, stay - but where? She was dismissed from the nursery.... and where was Angel all this waiting while, was he safe in the kitchen with Kate - or was Kate dismissed as well? The thought set her pacing. Now it was the monkey who watched impassive at one end of his chain while she moved restlessly at the other.

A servant came in with logs for the fire and looked at her in surprise.

'What you doing here? The Lady Joanna be shouting for you in Great Hall!'

'In Great Hall?'

'Yes, you'd better get down there quick if you dunna want trouble, and take that varmint with you! Past ten of the clock and serving dinner they are - go on, get you down there and save a beating.'

'I was told to wait here.'

'You'll go down if you knows what's good for you. The Lady Joanna's you are now, and when she shouts, you jump! Give you to her, they have, so I hear tell.'

'Give me to her!' Indignation warmed her at the thought of being 'given' to anyone - let alone to a child, a girl even younger than herself. No one can give me "but myself, she thought hotly.

The old man looked at her shrewdly.

'Wipe off that scowl,' he counselled her. 'Got a good home here long as you behaves yourself. There's many I could name as would like your chance. Anyways, you got no choice,' and he bent his back to the fire.

No, she thought, picking up the monkey to carry him down to Great Hall, she had no choice. And Joanna, after all, was someone of John's.

Hazel sat stiffly in her threadbare velvet, waiting for Joanna to say the words that meant she could go. It might be at any moment, or it might not be at all. Joanna was like that. She must remember not to sigh. Sighing brought a glint of mischief to Joanna's eye and invariably lengthened her wait.

'When I have my first flux,' Joanna was saying, 'I shall go to live with my husband. I think I shall take you with me. How like you that?'

The phrase startled Hazel out of a daydream. 'Me-' she faltered, 'with you-' She was dismayed; how could she leave Buxford? But there she went again, fooling herself! John was never coming, when was she going to face the truth? A long year had passed since he had left her here. Yet if she went, she w ould never know.

Joanna said, 'I shall want you near me when my sons are born.' The tone was too flippant, covering a note of fear. The eyes held a mute appeal. Then it was masked as she added, 'But perhaps you would prefer to work in the fields?'

Hazel thought with pity of the beautiful child and the future that awaited her. Impulsively she seized the small hand and pressed it warmly, 'Of course I wouldna - I'll be there with you!'

For the briefest moment the embrace was returned. Then the house of Pengerran remembered its dignity. Joanna shook her off.

'I shall consider it,' she said coolly.

So like John, thought Hazel; the moment of weakness must be expunged, its witness put in her place. She smiled, remembering.

Joanna looked at her curiously, 'What secret are you hiding from me?'

'Am I allowed to have secrets?'

'No, you are not.'

'Then I have none.' She blew a kiss to the monkey. He tilted his sad face to one side and blinked slowly.

Joanna regarded her narrowly, 'You lie - I can read your face!' Then she smiled unexpectedly, 'No matter, when we go to the North to my husband there will be no more secrets for you. You shall see no one but me -not even your child.'

Hazel caught her breath. 'Not even my child?'

Joanna had quickly learned that Hazel could be punished by separation from Angel. Now, she smiled wickedly.

'We might take him with us - or we might not.'

'Oh, but please, I must have my baby - I anna seen him now for a w-'

She bit back the words but she was not quick enough.

'For a week? I know. And the last time you were bad it was a fortnight. I can stop you seeing him for as long as I like. You can't go anywhere if I forbid you. I can stop you forever if I like. For ever and ever and ever....' She chanted delightedly, hugging her knees.

She is only a child, Hazel reminded herself, struggling for calm. A spoilt unfeeling child. She wants to break my spirit to make me docile, to have me under her thumb like that poor wretched beast on his chain. It makes her feel strong to force me against my will. Or to force him. Because when she is forced into something she has to take it out on, someone. When she is forced it is something dreadful - like being made to marry that baby with the terrible head ... her 'husband', to whom she will have to give heirs if he lives long enough to make them ... remember she is a child, to be humoured, an unfortunate child ...

'But you wouldn't,' she said gently. 'You're too kind.'

Joanna laughed and spun completely round upon her stool.

'I may be,' she conceded happily. 'And then again' - mischief enchanted her - 'I may not,' and she spun again wildly. 'Come and hold the lute!' she commanded suddenly. 'I feel like music.'

Hazel followed her with a sinking heart. This could mean hours. When Joanna was absorbed she had no idea of the passing of time. She couldn't face another night away from Angel, she couldn't, she thought with rising hysteria. She tried desperately to control it. She dug her nails into her palms and closed her eyes.

Something crashed stinging into her face. It was Joanna's hand.

'Who said you could go to sleep!'

Caught off guard she choked on a sob and her own hand flew up to retaliate.

'Ah - now that's better! I don't like meek and mimsy creatures about me. Now for some sport!'

Hazel faced her, blazing.

'Whatever made me think you were like your father!'

Joanna laughed, 'I'm not like my father -my father was a ruddy man, little and timid. I'd make two of him!'

'Your father was a mighty man - and a strong and a brave and a fearless - but you're right, he wasna like you! He wouldna stoop to tormenting underlings! And as for being ruddy,' she went on recklessly, 'he was no more ruddy than you are. Black hair like yours and black eyes like yours - and a wild black spirit too - but that's where the likeness ends.'

'And how do you know that?'

A voice from behind silenced her like a douche of cold water. Both girls turned to see the still figure of the Lady Edith framed in the doorway. Her pallid face was shadowed with something like fear.

Hazel stammered: She did not know what to say. She had already said far too much. And she still trembled from her outburst. She pressed her clenched hands together and shifted from one foot to the other. They were both staring at her now; Lady Edith with apprehension and mistrust, Joanna with a new interest.

'I ask again. What makes you think you know?'

The question was subtly rephrased; it was not only Hazel who had said too much.

Hazel missed her advantage. She groped for an answer and seized on the wrong one.

'There's them-' she faltered. 'Them as just - knows things.'

The silence was deafening. None of them dared to speak.

The Lady Edith was the first to recover. She drew a deep breath and composed herself carefully.

'You are overwrought by separation from your child,' she said. It was as if she were dictating the rules for what they were to think. 'You may go.'

Hazel raised her head slowly, unable to believe what she heard. She had expected - what? Certainly not this.

Lady Edith's cool eyes were averted. 'You may go,' she repeated.

Hazel went quickly, trying not to look at either. Once outside she began to run. Why couldn't she learn to curb her tongue! She would have to leave Buxford now, whether or not she wanted to stay. She heard Joanna's steps behind her.

'Is it true ? Are you really a witch? Sarah says you are!'

Hazel glanced sideways to see her face alight with curiosity, eyes dancing.

'No!' she snapped. 'You shouldna listen to gossip!'

She shook her off and ran on. So Sarah's tongue had been rattling ... she ran faster, biting her lips. She trusted the Lady Edith no further than she would trust an adder. Smooth words and a body in the moat was the way of these people with those who knew too much. She would have to take Angel and go, tonight, before darkness fell, or she would never leave alive. She would manage to feed them both somehow. Since others had been so keen to sell her, why not sell herself? Her body was her own and she if anyone had the right to sell it - not outright, just from time to time, to make enough money to live. No one else had had that right; not even John, though she had allowed it him, poor fool that she was, because of love. And what was the use of love? It didn't shelter a child or fill an empty belly. It didn't bring happiness, either. It was a trap.

She reached her sleeping quarters and rummaged for the homespun Abby had made for her. She could not find it. Someone had been there before her, someone with even less than herself. Kate, perhaps. She shrugged, but a lump formed in her throat. She had wanted it as a remembrance of Abby, knowing Abby to be dead. It seemed she was condemned to keep nothing of the brief happy life with John. Just as in, her first days here when she had hoped against hope to find that she was carrying his child. And her flux had come as it always did, withering her last faint hope.

She knew now the meaning of the dreams that were not dreams. She had prised out of Kate the words she had spoken, and they had proved the key, unlocking the memory. Abby was dead; and Little John too, most likely. It was people she had known, or people who had crossed her path. People in torment, people dying. Their minds somehow got into hers and ran amuck, so that she felt their terrors, their ghastly pain. She shivered. Perhaps this was what being a witch really meant.

'There's them as just knows things.' She had spoken without thought. But extra nipples were not for suckling imps. And dancing round trees and drinking roosters' blood didn't raise the dead. Only she had seen Nanny Webster, she was certain of it. The others had gone on with their meaningless games as if nothing had happened, not knowing her to be there. Only she had known. Nanny, hanged as a witch, had come only to her. And this, if anything, was what it was all about.

If it was a gift it was one she could do without. There was nothing to be gained from it worth swinging for. Though maybe-yes, if she'd known about Jud in time, if she could have somehow warned John....

Why, then he might have sent for her. Instead of being caught, of being betrayed by Little John at breaking point. Instead of being dead . . .

But he was not dead. If he were she would have known. It was she who was betrayed. He had simply walked away and left her behind.

The If s and Why's tore at her like hungry animals. She pushed them to the back of her mind and hurried on in search of Angel.

She found him where she expected to, making puddings in the ashes of the cooking fire with the other uncounted children of the household. She left him squatting on the hearth and searched for food to take with her. There would be lean days until she found customers. Until she found a home. She took a pie and two fresh loaves and tied them up in a square of linen. No use to carry more meat because it would not keep. Bread was better. You could soak that and eat it even after many days, however hard it became.

She took a last look around the familiar kitchen. There would be lean days, miserable days. But so there had been here. She would like a penny for every time she had cried herself to sleep in the nook behind the fire. And nights when she had ached to feel somebody's arms around her. There would be arms enough now. What if they were only to hold her still - they were arms just the same. The touch of another human being in some kind of warmth. And they would pay. She and Angel would belong to themselves at last. He was grinning up at her from the wood ash. Munching a piece of charcoal with his few small teeth. She stooped to pick him up.

A shadow blacked out the sunset glow that streamed in through the doorway.

'Well - if it isn't our Hazel!'

Her heart went bang in spite of her. A message - after all this time! But no - she knew that voice. She stiffened, turning slowly. The doorway was filled with three ragged figures and a quantity of iron pots.

5

The autumn dusk hung blue among the gaunt spires of the Abbey. Mist rose from the river and shrouded its environs in the ghost of a moat. In the ruined refectory a huddle of figures pressed close around the fire for warmth.

'To get in - and out again - and not be seen or heard. It's not going to be easy,' said the Patch. 'Any of you specialists got any ideas?'

Spider wagged his head. 'Not in my line,' he said, regretfully.

The others looked at each other, and then back at the newcomer. A woman said, 'And you got to find someone in there without rousing the house?'

The big man nodded, his hand on the shoulder of the Patch, who was leaning against his knee like a devoted dog.

'Hm-mm,' the speaker watched him calculatingly, 'might be a way as I knows of - at a price. Not easy come by, like he says. But I reckon as I could get it. If you want.'

She waited, expectant. The man did not answer her, but stared broodingly into the embers. She reached across and poked him with her stick. 'You,' she prompted, 'do you want it or don't you?'

'What-' he focused on her from a distance and she could tell that he had not been listening. 'Want what?' 'Never mind what,' she said irritably. 'No questions asked or answered if you want rny help. Now, do you?'

The man passed a hand over his face in a gesture of infinite weariness. 'Yes,' he said without interest. 'Yes…. whatever you can do.'

She looked at him piercingly, trying to assess his resources. 'That'd have to be worth my while-'

'Shame on you!' The Patch tried to rise but was firmly held to the ground.

'It will be worth your while.'

'In that case,' said Bent Meg, 'leave it to me. Be there tomorrow night when the moon goes down. And I'll take the money now.'

6

Tim Kettle's weather-beaten face lit with pleasure.

'If it isn't our Hazel,' he repeated. 'As I live and breathe!' He lowered his voice confidentially. 'Did you have the babby, Hazel ? Have you got it yet - can I see?'

Hazel backed away, her suspicions unallayed by the unexpected warmth of his greeting.

'What do you want?' she asked defensively. 'Where's Joan?'

She tried to see past him, half expecting Joan to jump at her with a knife.

'I come with the pots,' said Tim. 'Where's the babby, Hazel? I only wants to see 'un - 'tis much mine as yourn, remember.'

It was, of course; she had not considered it until now. And it wasn't Tim's fault he had arrived at the wrong moment. Reluctantly she picked up the little boy and carried him over. Blue eyes looked into blue eyes, and a small head drooped shyly onto her shoulder. A grubby thumb found its way into his mouth.

'Looks well enough,' said Tim grudgingly. 'Is it a boy or a coopie-down ?'

'A boy,' she said, and Tim beamed. Touched, she added, 'He looks like you.'

It had only a nodding acquaintance with the truth. Angel was sleek and well fed by contrast with his ragged brothers tagging behind the pots. She missed the youngest. She asked again, 'Where's Joan?'

Tim hesitated, his pleasure dimmed. 'Her's dead.'

'Oh, no !' What could she say? 'What was it, the plague?' He shook his head. 'Reckon as 'twere that tooth of hern. Near out of her mind with it she were, and all green stuff coming out of her ear. Head come up like a pumpkin, it did, and her burning like a torch and shivering and sweating all at the same time. Well, I didn' know what to do for her, see ... and then she were dead.'

He raised bewildered eyes to Hazel's as if even now he couldn't understand what had happened to him. Why he had suddenly found himself alone in a world that had always been shared. A big soft stupid loud-mouthed woman had filled his life. And now it was empty; he was lost.

'Had to bury her out in the woods, just me and the boys. Ate her sins, I did, but then - well, didn't know no prayers like, not like a proper funeral. I just says "God help you, girl" and then we fills her in. I didn't have no money, see, to get it done right.' He looked at Hazel anxiously, pleading to be absolved from his sin of omission. 'You reckon she knowed it weren't proper?'

She shook her head. 'If she did she'd understand. She knew you never had much to spend.' She searched in vain for words of comfort. At last she offered, 'I'm sorry, Tim.' Tim mumbled something, face averted. It came to Hazel that he was weeping. She would not have believed it, that Tim, so tough and unfeeling, could weep for his wife. She felt her own throat constrict. Best not to ask about the youngest child. Unable to cope without Joan, he must have been desperate.

Tim pulled himself together abruptly. He dragged a sleeve across his nose, sniffing noisily. He said with forced cheerfulness, 'And what about you? What you'm doing here - I heard tell that you'd married Black John?'

The name sent a sensation through her like the raw edge of a burn. She glanced about her nervously. Tim was rattling on, '. . . rich man he was once, so I've heard. House and lands and all till he went to the wars. When he came back - nothing. Gates barred - mind, there's been others like that, turned outlaw like him. Only they do say he's different from the rest.'

Clearly his tone invited comment. She said from the desert inside her, 'He's no different. Robber, murderer - common thief. What's different about that?'

Tim looked at her knowingly, eyes narrowed, 'Left you, did he?'

Tight-lipped, she said, 'They don't know about me here. I dunna want them to.'

'I'll not tell.' He hesitated, then blundered on impulsively, 'Come with me, Hazel! There's just me and the boys now and we'm all one family. There'll never be nothing for you with the likes of him, no hardship ain't never going to make him one of us. I allus did like you, Hazel. That's why I - well - what else could I do? - me wanting you so bad and you so high and mighty, like - and seemed like it was the only chance I'd ever have. Come with us, with your own sort, you don't want him-'

'But I do!'

It was wrung from her. She had not meant to say it. With Tim trying to pull her away she clung more stubbornly than ever.

'But he ain't never coming back to you, Hazel! Folks like him don't care nothing for the likes of us, dispossessed or no. Their lands is everything to them, take 'em away and all they can think of is getting them back. People's nothing to them, only to kick to one side if they gets in the way.'

Hazel in her anguish turned away from him. She had been glad in an odd way to see Tim, a familiar face in her world of strangers. But now she wished he had never come.

'I canna,' she sobbed.

Clumsily, Tim tried to take her in his arms. Gestures of affection were foreign to him but he wanted to help her grief. He wanted her, too, and did not know how to achieve his want. For the first time in his life he was at a loss. He said helplessly, 'We could be happy, Hazel. We'm all of a kind.' He cast about for something with which to attract her. 'Remember how we used to roast nuts in the fire? And the birds - how we used to charm the birds ? And the little foxes-'

Hazel struggled free, 'Let me be, Tim! Go away - I dunna want you!'

He stared for a moment in anger. Then he released her and picked up his pots. Cuffing the boys who stood gaping, he turned and stumped off down the path.

She heard them go and wished she could have been less rough. He, too, had his pain. He was lost without Joan. And he had small hopes of replacing her, poor ugly little man with his stubby frame and his two runny-nosed kids. He had no life to offer a woman. She knew she was mean and selfish to withold her help from Angel's father and brothers who so badly needed it. She ought to go after them, catch them up, take Angel and make them 'all one family'. But she could not.

She stood and watched them out of sight although she felt still further diminished by their going. It had been good to feel wanted, needed, if only by Tim Kettle. Poor Tim. She had never understood about him and Joan from the time she had seen them fighting on that first day. Such a child, she had been, so shocked and uncomprehending. She knew now that the brawling was as much a part of their life as the laughter that followed it. And she could no more replace Joan for Tim than he could make her forget John.

She rationalised her refusal while the tears dried on her face and Angel scrambled down from her arms. But the truth was deeper and simpler even than that.

'I couldna,' she said aloud; and then mechanically, without

thinking, corrected herself, 'Could not.' She was treading her chosen path in any case.

She remained at the kitchen door long after they had gone. Dusk gathered in the corners. Angel came back and tugged at her skirt. Still she stood there, undecided. Seeing Tim had brought back to her the roughness of the world outside. She had lived too long in shelter. She had forgotten. And once she broke away from here she could never come back.

She looked down at the little boy swinging on a handful of her skirt. He was well fed now; housed and safe. It was unfair to drag him through the wet wild woods. But dare she stay here with the Lady Edith's hand against her? With one part of herself she longed to be free, to go out into the world and search for John ... Seeing Tim had done that to her too - put her back in his camp and ready to stand by him as before. The more cautious part reminded her that if he still lived, this was the only place in which he knew where to find her.

She leaned down to rescue something that Angel was trying to stuff into his mouth. The next moment she was staring in disbelief at a huge purple stone that glowed like blood in the light from the fire. A stone that was set in a heavy gold ring, so large that it fitted her thumb.

Life began to stir in the kitchens behind, preparations for the evening meal. She gathered her skirts and ran, down the path, across the yards, out through the postern gate. She ran until she was gasping for breath, until she made out in the dusk three distant figures on the road that led to the village. Still she ran, calling to them to stop, calling breathlessly.

'Tim, wait! Tim Kettle - come back - tell me where you got this ring!'

Tim made a gesture as if to shake her off, but he stood still and waited just the same. As she came up with him, panting, he said, 'Changed your mind then, have you?' Then he saw the ring in her hand and his expression changed, 'Where did you find that?'

Hazel stopped, her sides heaving. 'That's what I come to ask you!'

They stared at each other. Then Hazel said, 'The baby had it - I thought you must have dropped it.'

Tim shook his head slowly. Hazel's heart sank.

'But I was sure - it wasna there before you came. It must have been you!'

Tim laughed, 'You think I'd have a thing like that and not make money on it? You'm dafter than I thought!'

'But - but Tim -' She sank down on a stone to get her breath; as she pushed back the tumbled hair from her face the ring slipped from her thumb and rolled to the ground.

As quick as a squirrel, the elder boy pounced upon it. Tim cuffed him and made a grab himself, but the boy danced out of reach.

'It's mine!' he shouted. 'I found it!'

'It's never!'

'It is! I found it - you missed it and I found it after - it's mine!'

'You lie!'

'It's mine, I picked it out of the mud!'

'Where?' put in Hazel, desperately. 'Where?'

'Never you mind,' retorted Tim. 'If he found it, 'tis mine!'

'It dunna matter whose it is,' said Hazel beseechingly, 'just tell me where you found it - please!'

'Nowheres around here,' Tim told her. ' 'Tain't no good for you to ask. You wouldn't be no wiser if I told you. Anyways it was miles away from here.'

'Where?'

'You wouldn't know if I told you,' he repeated testily. 'I been down the West Country all this last few months.' 'The West Country,' breathed Hazel. She looked up, 'Tim - could you take me there ?'

"Tisn't no good to go back there now,' said Tim. 'All cleared away it'll be by now. No pickings left for anyone but the crows.'

She steeled herself. 'What was it, Tim?' she asked. 'What was it you saw?'

Tim sat down beside her. 'Shove up,' he said. 'It was what I wouldn't want to see again. All dead men and horses, like there'd been a battle or summat. Bad it were, dead and dying and all heaped up together. Like nobody cared. And there was these villagers, helping themselves to what they could find. So I thought, why not me? After all they was done for- they got no more use for it. And it helped to feed me and the kids. But I didn't know that varmint had that ring-' He stopped and looked into her face, 'Why, was it his?'

She nodded, her hands pressed to her mouth. The dead and dying, all heaped together. She took a grip on herself.

'Tim, will you take me there?'

'Now, Hazel, you dunna want-'

'He isna dead, I know he isna dead!'

'And if he is?'

'If he is,' she said slowly, 'and if you've took me there, then I'll stay with you. And I'll do for you -what you want.'

It was a fair exchange, she thought; that's what John would have said.

Tim grinned at her wryly, 'And if he ain't?'

She looked at him helplessly. She could not answer for that.

'He ain't no good to you,' he reminded her.' You know he ain't.'

'No,' she said quickly, to stop him saying more. But she wanted him to understand. 'You canna tell your heart where to fall. It drops like a bird from the air and lights on dung if it's a mind to.'

Tim sighed. 'Get you back,' he said, pulling her to her feet. 'I'll be back this way day after tomorrow. I'll be outside the postern gate at sunrise. And I'll take you there.'

She walked back slowly through the twilight, thinking. She was at peace now, with her mind made up. Another day was not long to wait, although it seemed intolerable. It would give her time to prepare, and she could surely survive that long. She was going at last to find John, and she knew in her heart that he still lived. She thought of what Tim had said about him; he had been right in his limited way - but what could he know of the pressures that had turned John rogue? When everything from your infancy was sacrificed to the ownership of land, and then it was snatched from you - what was there left to you? An iron creed of human sacrifice - for nothing. She was glad of her time at Buxford if it had only taught her that.

She thought briefly of the girl she was deserting. But Joanna was beautiful and rich and would always find those to care for her. While John ... She wanted to find him now, when he had need of her, to give him her love and her warmth before it was too late. And if he died before she could reach him-

She could not think of it yet. But if he did ... then she would keep her promise to Tim Kettle. It was only fair. And he, of all men, would approve the justice of that.

She awoke in the certainty that something had awakened her.

It was still dark. The house was silent. She looked at Angel: he was sound asleep. She had meant to awake before dawn, to be down at the postern gate well before sunrise; and yet - the feeling was uneasy on her mind that something had disturbed her. She lay very still, holding her breath, trying to penetrate the hush that lay on the house.

She disentangled herself from the baby, careful not to wake him. She had smuggled him into her quarters without leave; if he woke in a strange place and cried ...

Barefoot she crept along the gallery and peered over the screen. She could see nothing, hear no sound but the soft 'tock' of the machine that stood above the fireplace in the Great Hall. It told the time, they said, like an hour glass. But even if she could see, it would not help her. She did not know how to read it.

She stood looking over, leaning down, uncertain what to do. She had little idea of how long she had been asleep. It might be nearly dawn. If she meant to go ...

Moving very quietly, she stole down the main staircase and felt her way across the Great Hall to the passage that led to the kitchens. A faint, sickening odour hung on the air, lying like a veil over the unnatural stillness, over the silence that had awakened her. Cautiously she made her way along the passage.

'Sesamie, sesamie,' her bare feet whispered rhythmically over the stones, 'sesamie, sesamie de laponie....'

Where had those words come from to drift into her mind at this moment? She had heard them somewhere, sometime. The smell too was known to her. Or something of it was. There was a nauseating sweetness - and something else like the incense in a church - and under that-

Her footsteps slowed. 'Sesamie, ses-am-ie-ee...

It was coming from the kitchen, seeping like evil under the door. The undersmell was of burning. Burning flesh - burning meat, she told herself firmly, something forgotten by the cooks. And she leaned her weight against the door.

As it creaked slowly open the smell engulfed her. Her stomach somersaulted as she recognised it. The smell that arose from a stake-fire. A gallows fire. The acrid unforgettable smell of burning bone.

And then she saw it.

At first she made out only five points of light, greenish blue, wavering and flickering like candle flames. But they gave no light. Five candles would have illuminated most of this kitchen. These did nothing.

She was drawn unwillingly towards them. She was near enough to touch when she discerned the dim shape of a hand;

the grey flesh shrunken into strings, the outstretched fingers burning like ghastly tapers in the gloom. She felt her legs turn to water. She stared at the Hand of Glory as though paralysed.

The Croppers! How could she have forgotten them - and Angel slept unguarded in the room upstairs-

Something moved behind her. She was not alone. Her head whipped round. A figure loomed dark and dreadful in the shadows - Hal Cropper! A scream built up in her throat and froze to death - 'Presto - the house is theirs ...' She must somehow break the spell - put out the flames. In desperation she seized a pitcher from the table and flung the contents.

'Be still, for God's sake -you'll wake the house!'

The voice was not Hal Cropper's. She stood still. The figure stood taller, broader - a name formed and jerked itself free of her in a sob-

'Sh-sh ... Mistress Ash-'

She groped her way towards him. Even without seeing, she knew. Unbelievably, unmistakably. 'It's all right,' said Black John.

Then a voice shrilled, 'Thieves - thieves in the house!'

The cry rang through the silent halls, footsteps thundered along the floors overhead, fists pounded on doors, arousing the sleepers.

'Christus! A trap!'

She ran towards him - their fingers touched-

But there were other hands that caught her.

Suddenly the kitchen was a blaze of light, a hubbub of voices, a confusion of blows and noise. Lights appeared from nowhere, people from everywhere. She was violently seized from behind and roughly pinioned. She jerked and twisted to free herself but her arm was being wrenched from its socket. Sweating with pain she had to give in.

John was being borne to the ground. Three men were grappling with him while a fourth tried to kick him senseless.

They'll never hold him, she thought, with agonised pride. But they did.

As the light fell on his face she saw why. Among the new marks of battle a still angry scar had broken open and was pouring blood into his eyes. He lashed out wildly, blindly. But at last, still fighting, he was dragged away.

Hazel called on her last desperate ounce of strength to follow him. A heavy blow felled her. She lay weeping helplessly as he vanished from her sight.

And now a new uproar had broken out. Someone else, it seemed, had been laid by the heels. She heard a woman's voice cursing raucously, a man's booming over it.

'. . . no Christian granny with a right to be here needs to hide in a linen press-'

'You'll be sorry for this-'

'No doubt, no doubt! Meantime you can cool your heels along of this one!'

She was hauled to her feet and thrust before her captor down a blind confusion of corridors, sobbing and struggling through a part of the house she had never seen before. They were taking her to the dungeons - they couldn't, they couldn't! Joanna would miss her - Joanna would get her out! But Joanna was capricious and people disappeared into dungeons never to be seen again. And Angel! What would become of Angel? She fought and kicked at the man who held her while a massive grid in the floor was raised. She could hear the other captive doing the same. It was no use - no use - the pair of them were flung through the opening to fall together in a heap at the foot of a flight of steps.

For a moment they both lay stunned, defeated. Then they disentangled their limbs and sat up on the damp chill of the floor. The darkness was total, except for a faint light seeping through the grille at the head of the stairs. They peered at each other in the gloom. A low unpleasant laugh came from the other woman.

'Weil, well, well, if that isn't neat! Two birds with one stone,' said Mother Cropper.

7

Her first thought was, She can't touch Angel while she's locked in here. Then she remembered.

'Where's Hal?' she demanded sharply.

'Hal?' The other woman's tone changed and she seemed to recoil into herself. 'Where's Hal, did you say? And who should know better than you - a son for a son, that's what he said!' Her voice rose to a cracked wailing note. 'Oh, my Hal, my Hal! My only one!' Her tone hardened and her eyes glinted viciously in the darkness. 'I swore I'd have him for that! I told him - I knew he didn't take no heed. But we can bide our time who have the power. We can read the minds of them as we want to read. I knew when you came back. And when I heard you calling to him, calling night and day, I knew I only had to wait.'

Oh God, thought Hazel, oh, John, John, John - why didn't you tell me! I could have warned you what she was.

'Wonder what they'll do with him,' Mother Cropper was saying with relish. 'Hanging - or burning, perhaps? Or maybe they'll think up something just for him - he's no favourite of the Lord Eustace's, you know. But there, whatever it is you'll know, won't you? You'll be able to share it with him, won't you? Down to the last drop of blood ...'

She knows, thought Hazel. She knows - that dreadful gift, it comes from her. Fury and hatred boiled up in her.

'I'll see you get the same! You'll suffer everything my mother suffered, and if I get the pain with you I'll enjoy it, you hear me! I'm going to tell them what you are - I'll tell them everything-'

Mother Cropper's voice cut across hers, cold and implacable. 'Oh, no, my dear. You're not going to tell them anything. Don't say you've forgotten so soon . . .' Hazel's ravings stopped in mid-syllable. She felt her mouth go dry. 'I don't think you're going to tell anyone anything, are you? Go on, say you're not,' Mother Cropper said coaxingly. 'Just try.'

Hazel's throat constricted. Words screamed and whirled around in her head but nothing came out of her mouth. Mother Cropper went on, 'That's better, now we shall get on famously. You really should have known better than to try crossing me. By the way,' she added conversationally, 'have you seen the black dog lately?' She leaned forward, her face so close that the air was tainted by her breath. 'No?' with a sudden change of tone she seized Hazel by the shoulders and whirled her around, 'Look there! In the corner - and what's that he's got? Isn't that your baby?'

Hazel tried not to look but she was powerless to resist. The sulphurous yellow eyes blazed from the hulking dark shape; the hackles were raised, fangs bared, jaws snapping as it savaged something between its forepaws-

She covered her face. Reason told her it could not be so. Angel was safe upstairs - and yet she was sure she heard him cry-

Her mind said it was not so, but all her senses protested against it. And then her mind shut off and told her nothing.

Sunrise sent a stream of light between the mullions and across the broad bed. Joanna struggled to the surface of sleep and pushed unavailingly at the weight of the deerhounds sprawled upon the furs.

'Leda, Cygnus - get off!' She heaved at them with arms and legs.

Leda raised her head and sighed gustily, then she subsided. Cygnus remained ostentatiously asleep.

'Hazel, take them off!'

She waited for the answering footfall from the anteroom, but none came. She sat up.

'Hazel?'

Still no answer. Only Jester, the monkey, confined in his night quarters, chittered hopefully in the expectation of release.

Joanna sat still. She felt deserted. For the first time in her life she was alone and it was strangely disturbing. So often she had wished for solitude, for a privacy denied her by position. Now without warning she had it. And it alarmed her.

She wriggled free of the sleeping hounds and crept towards the door. If that Hazel was over-sleeping! But there was no one in the ante-room; no shabby velvet bundle trying to conceal a smuggled child. She went to the outer door and peeped out. Even the lad assigned to sleep across the threshold was not to be seen. She listened. She could hear no morning bustle of servants going about the business of the house. But somewhere not far away a baby voice babbled and whimpered by turns.

Something was wrong.

Her stomach tightened. Hastily she snatched up a robe and dropped it over her head. She turned to the bed, an indeterminate heap of snoring fur, and clapped her hands together.

' Cygnus! Leda - come!'

She delivered a resounding thwack on the nearest flank and Cygnus poured himself onto the floor. He yawned prodigiously and settled down to enjoy a leisurely scratch.

'Come on!' Her foot caught him off balance and sent him sprawling. He picked himself up and wagged amiably after her. Leda, sensing his departure, loped gracefully from the bed and padded behind them. But it was Cygnus she followed, not Joanna. She frisked up to him and playfully gnawed at his ear.

They broke into a wild romp along the gallery, racing madly ahead and careering clumsily back again, blundering against her legs, tripping and rolling over each other like puppies.

'Much good you are to me!' scolded Joanna. 'A robber could cut my throat before you noticed him.'

At the head of the spiral that led down to the kitchens she found the source of the voice. Small, sturdy and flaxen haired - Hazel's child. He stood unsteadily on the brink of a precipice that twisted down and away from him, drawn by hunger yet daunted by the mechanics of the journey, one thumb jammed up to the knuckles in his mouth while the other hand searched vaguely for something to hold on to.

The madcap rush of the hounds unsteadied him and only Joanna's instinctive grab stopped him hurtling to his death.

'What are you doing here without your mother?'

The little boy stared at her solemnly. Then he grinned, and held up his arms. She picked him up, clumsily, treading on her skirt, and held him distastefully as his sticky fingers plucked at her hair. Kitchen's the place for you, she thought; and to go down the back way was not such a bad idea. Somewhere down here she would find the servants; she could tell by the smells.

The squirming baby was heavy in her arms that had never lifted anything heavier than a lute. She tried balancing him on her hip as she had seen his mother do but her frame was undeveloped and he slipped off. Finally she wrapped him in a fold of her robe and managed tolerably well. She leaned her free hand against the wall of the stairwell and was preparing to make the descent when a commotion broke out in the Hall below her.

'Give me a decent death!'

The voice roared and echoed around the walls. She stopped.

Turned. Crept to the gallery screen and looked down through the carving.

The Great Flail was suddenly filled with people. All of them were guards except for three - her mother, Lord Eustace, and a man she did not know. He was darkly massive and looked as if he had just staggered from a battlefield. His hair and beard were bloody and unkempt and his hands were tied with rope.

'Sweet Jesus!' his bound fists demanded justice from the table like a crash of thunder. 'You sit at my board, you enjoy my wife - do you think you owe me nothing!'

Lord Eustace gave an order and the guards withdrew to the far end of the hall. He leaned forward across the table,

'You know as well as I that you must hang. Nothing else can be considered.'

'Men of our standing do not hang, cousin! A soldier expects to die - but with honour and by steel -'

'You had that choice. You should have died in battle at Pengerran.'

'But the rope is for the common thief, for scum-'

'By all accounts, my lord, you have earned yourself that merit.'

It was her mother who spoke. Joanna caught her breath.

'Be silent, woman! Take yourself off.'

Pale and unmoved as always, the Lady Edith looked from one to the other. 'Am I to go? I think not. The matter concerns me closely since you both aspire to my bed.'

The laugh that cut her short was scathing.

'I know of better beds. Do not flatter yourself, madam, you go with the land!'

Lady Edith turned away, an ugly mottled flush creeping up her sallow cheek as the two men shared the joke at her expense. The dark man stopped laughing. He said, 'Such things are not personal, madam. If I am churlish it comes of living too long like a wolf.' He jabbed a look of hatred at Eustace. 'But the fact remains that you and I were sold to join these lands together.'

She looked back at him across her shoulder. Joanna could not see her face.

'Well I remember it,' she said. 'I must have been six years old, you a mere babe just beginning to talk. I had been promised a doll - a mannikin most beautiful, I remember; you, I don't know what. But I recall how you fought and screamed and kicked the priest. "Say Yes," they said, "and then you may go and play."' She turned back and a wry smile pulled at her faded mouth. 'Even then you did not want me.'

Eustace shifted restlessly in his chair.

'Is there more to be said? Leave matters as they stand.

One nameless outlaw hangs in obscurity; and when in the fullness of time I come to join you in the Elysian Fields we can fight it out at our leisure while your blood inherits in my name. The estates will come to your Cornish brat, since our lady wife did you a service she has signally failed to do me.' His voice had an ugly edge to it.

Lady Edith squared her shoulders. 'I continue to try, my lord,' she said acidly.

'No doubt you do!' said the black-haired man with asperity. He turned to Eustace, 'And if some day she should succeed-'

'- Joanna will of course be disinherited. It's the chance you take. As you say, 1 owe you something.' He looked about him with insolent satisfaction, 'I suggest you accept that chance in payment - since it is all you are offered. Be reasonable, cousin. To grant what you ask, to behead you as befits nobility, would be tantamount to admitting your claim. It could start an uprising, provoke a bloodbath - and we'd all be the losers. Harry takes the land and likely all our heads go with it; now, how say you?'

'How say I, how say I?' The man paced in agitation. 'What can I say, what choice is open to me?'

'None,' agreed Eustace smoothly, 'so let it be amicably understood. One or other of our children will succeed - and more probably yours than mine.' He whacked his thigh in a sudden gust of laughter. 'But you'll never know which! Amusing, when you think of it. Something to take your mind off the gallows-'

'I'll kill you first!'

He launched himself at Eustace who went down like a felled ox under the impact of his two bound hands. The long table overturned with a crash, Edith jumped clear with a surprising agility as the guards came clattering up the length of the hall to the rescue, and in the pandemonium that ensued Joanna slipped away unnoticed.

Her mind was filled with the image of the man who had levelled against Eustace eyes that mirrored her own. Dizzying words swam into her mind, 'Your father was a mighty man, a strong and a brave and a fearless....' Hazel knew about this! What did she know - and how? She, Joanna, must find out. Hazel should be sent for, and at once. Something bad was afoot, something dangerous - but where was Hazel?

She took a firm grip on the baby and made her way down the spiral to the kitchens.

A hush fell as she entered. Everyone was suddenly too busy to talk. No one made obeisance as they did when she accompanied her mother. She set down the struggling baby, straightened her rumpled robe and said as firmly as she could muster, 'Send Hazel to me!'

For a moment nobody moved. Then a woman kneading dough knocked flour from her hands, and as if by afterthought, fell to kneading it again. Two kitchen maids exchanged looks and disappeared into the buttery. The little scullion on the treadmill redoubled his efforts, whistling nervously. The baby set up a wail: silently, almost furtively, a young woman picked him up and clamped him to her breast.

Joanna felt her face begin to burn. 'Madam my mother shall hear of this!' She heard her own voice grow shrill in her effort to make it imperious. 'You shall all be whipped for disobedience. And - and Hazel for deserting her post!'

Still no one answered her. Beside herself with rage and frustration, she turned to storm through to the Great Hall. Old Sarah blocked her way.

'Not so fast, my pretty!'

'How dare you!' She tried to shake off the restraining hand. 'I go where I please!'

'Not now, you don't.' Sarah, old and tough, held her fast. 'I got my orders from the Lord Eustace.'

There was a disquieting note of triumph in the tone. Almost, thought Joanna with surprise, as if she were glad ... In the tail of her eye she saw two women tittering in a corner. She turned and glared. They did not flinch but stared calmly back at her. They no longer feared her: a prickle of alarm ran along the edges of her nerves. What did they know? She pulled herself together.

'From the Lord Eustace?' she said scathingly, tossing her head with a fine show of arrogance. 'And what orders would he see fit to give to you, concerning me?'

The horny hand tightened its grip on her arm. 'From the Lord Eustace,' repeated Sarah, unabashed.' I'm to take you to your room and keep you there.'

'I am not dressed.' She wrestled to maintain her calm above a rising panic. 'Send Hazel to me!'

'You won't see Hazel again.' This time the note of relish was unmistakable. 'She's under the Tower.'

'Under the Tower-' Then it was worse, far worse, than she had expected. Hazel was imprisoned - and her only offence was that she knew too much. What might her own fate be, once her door was slammed and barred ...? It was not to be thought of! But who was there to help her - certainly no one here. Her mother? Powerless, probably, and clearly she did not care. But then, she might not know what was afoot. If she could be reached, could be pleaded with ... Desperately she tried wheedling Sarah as she had in her baby years. 'Come, my old Sarahkins, you'll get Hazel back for me? They gave her to me, you know, and she'll spoil down there. We shall tell Madam my mother, you shall take a message from me-'

Sarah cut her short, 'I'll come and help you dress.'

It was hopeless, then. She felt herself thrust roughly towards the stairwell. Her mind raced as she plodded with deliberate slowness up the stairs. She needed time to think, to plan, and every step took her further into danger.

'I want Hazel, ' she whined, playing for time. She pouted, letting her body go slack, making it difficult for Sarah to push her ahead.

'You'll be in the one Tower,' retorted Sarah with ugly satisfaction, 'her at the bottom and you at the top. There's a pretty kettle of fish.' She felt a spiteful nip on her arm and realised despairingly that Sarah hated her. 'Now stand up straight and walk properly, can't you!'

Useless then to look for help to Sarah. Eustace had chosen her well to become her gaoler. Eustace - he had never been her friend. And she had never known the reason until now. Tomorrow her father was to die at his hands, and after tomorrow ... A wave of terror engulfed her, drowned her and receded, leaving her cold. Something inside her shivered, then shrank, then tightened itself like a bowstring. Her fate might be sealed in Eustace's eyes but she was not to be led meekly to the slaughter! Here on the stairs she had Sarah at a disadvantage. Without warning she sank her teeth into the hand that held her arm.

'You vixen!' gasped Sarah, and withdrew the hand to suck it.

Joanna seized the moment. Ruthlessly she lunged at the old woman, plunging her backwards down the terrifying spiral.

Then picking up her skirts she raced up the remaining stairs and fled like a doe across the gallery and down on the far side. She saw herself in deadly peril and spent no more time on thought. She knew who she was, and what she was. And what she had to do.

Tim Kettle was growing uneasy. The sun had been up for an hour or more. He could hear sounds of life from within the walls, but no one had come to unbar the postern gate. And there was no sign of Hazel.

He could hardly believe that she had changed her mind. Something must have happened to delay her. Or perhaps she was inside, just waiting for the gate to open and let her out. He would give it a bit longer.

He sent the boys off with the last of the pots and settled down to wait. It was unusual for the gates to be closed as late in the day as this. Someone inside would get his ears lopped for forgetting his duty. He pulled a long strand of timothy grass and chewed on it thoughtfully, lying on the turf. After a while he got up again and began pacing up and down under the wall. He did not want to be noticed loitering here by the gate. Tinkers had a bad reputation and his motives might be suspect. He thought of going back to the village. Then he remembered that he had told the boys to meet him here. And besides, he wanted to know about Hazel.

He had noticed on a previous call that at one point the stables backed on to the outer wall. If he made his way along there, if he listened ...

'Ss-sst!'

He stopped dead.

'Hazel?'

'You down there - you, tinker, or whatever you are!'

He looked about him. Looked up. Saw a flurry of movement in the branches of a tree just within the wall. 'Hazel - is that you, what you'm doing up there?'

A face looked out, young and vivid. But it was not Hazel's.

'I'll come to the end of the branch. Catch me!'

He had no time to argue. A moment later they were sprawled together on the grass as the girl's sudden weight caught him off guard. She was up on her feet in an instant and pulling at his hand.

'You've got to get me away from here - they'll kill me if they catch me!'

'Here, hold on a minute,' Tim was not one to be rushed. 'Who the Hell are you - and what have you done?'

'I've done nothing. And who I am is none of your business. If you won't help me I must go alone.' With a toss of her head she turned and started running.

Tim hurried after her, 'Here, hang on, hang on a minute!' He caught her arm and snatched her back. 'You help me and I might help you. What's up in there's what I want to know? You come over the wall for your own reasons - but why ain't the gates been opened?'

The girl looked at him. She was very young, and under that bravado very frightened. He said, more gently, 'Look, I ain't about to hurt you nor stop you running away. Like I said, I'll likely help you if you help me. But I come to fetch Hazel and she ain't come out. And now the gates is locked.' The girl looked at him suspiciously. 'Hazel, did you say?'

'That's right. You know where she is?'

'Yes, yes, I know! Let me go' - she was tugging distractedly to free herself - 'let me go and I'll tell you. I've got to get away from here before they see me. If they catch me they'll put me in the Tower with her-'

'In the Tower!'

Tim stood still. His grip on the girl's wrist tightened like a vice. He had no words to express what he felt at that moment. He would have done anything to save Hazel, to take her away with him. But he was one poor tinker of stunted growth against an army of men. He looked at the girl whose eyes were wild with fear.

'Bloody Hell!' he said. 'Let's get out of here!'

He muddied her face and clothes and took away her shoes; then he tore a strip from the skirt of her gown to cover her conspicuous black hair.

'You'll have to do,' he said. 'Come we meets the boys you'll have some pots to carry. And you'd best learn to walk with your head down - not stuck in the air like Lady High and Mighty. Who are you, anyway?'

She hesitated, biting her lip. 'Call me Joan,' she said.

Tim stared straight ahead of him to where he could see two small figures hauling a handcart. With them was a stooped old woman leaning heavily on a stick.

'Well, well, well,' cackled Bent Meg as they drew level. 'And what have we here - a little one in need of Meg's protection?'

'One of mine,' Tim grinned, but his tone brooked no argument. 'From the other side the blanket, as you might say.'

'Oh, well,' returned Meg without interest. 'It's all one to me today - I've other fish to fry this morning.'

'Oh-ah,' said Tim, preparing to move on. 'Here -no, you don't!' he rebuked the girl about to climb onto the cart. 'Cart is for pots, not kids. You walk like the rest.' She daggered him with a look, but she obeyed.

'Yes, indeed,' Meg was determined to have her say. 'I've got a bone to pick with Mother Cropper after last night. If I buys her help for a friend, as you might say, I expects that friend to come home safe and sound. 'Tis only natural. And if he don't, then I wants to know why. And if, so to speak, she's let him walk into a trap - why, then she might find as some of her little secrets wasn't secret anymore.' She winked and grimaced, and nodded her satisfaction. 'Open my mouth like the parish oven I could, if I had a mind. So you keep an eye open, tinker. Come you sees they're hanging a witch - you'll know who's put her there!' and she nodded and winked and bobbed her way up the hill.

Tim took little notice of what she said. Old women's quarrels were of no interest to him. He wanted to be away from this place; and he was beginning already to regret taking on the strange girl who had abruptly burst into tears and was lagging behind the rest.

The Lady Edith sat biting her elegant nails. She wished she had dealt with that girl of Joanna's more promptly. She wished that Joanna herself were less like her father; wild and wilful as she was, she would bring them all into peril one day. She wished that Pengerran had stayed in his convenient grave instead of breaking into the house, jolting her emotions and causing an uproar. Above all, she wished that this upheaval were over and life could return to its normal smooth routine.

But apart from all this, she wished she knew how the girl had come by her knowledge. There might be others involved, a plot to be uncovered. There could be no doubt that it was she who had let him in. No doubt that there was, or had been, something between them. And Pengerran, with all said and done, was her wedded lord. Not that she was jealous - such coarse emotions were confined to the lower orders. But what more might the creature confess to - given the right persuasion?

Wisdom told her to leave her underground in the well-named oubliette, to leave her and forget her as if she had never been. But curiosity gnawed.

Presently she left her embroidery frame and went over to the window. Below her across the sunny lawns she could see Eustace practising archery at the butts.

'Come here,' she beckoned to a maid-in-waiting, 'I wish you to carry a message to my husband.'

The turnkey came clanking along the passage overhead and stopped at the grille below which the two women sat in darkness. Iron grated against iron as the key was jabbed into the lock and the reluctant tumblers were forced to move. The man crouched and peered down, his hand shading his eyes, squinting in an effort to decipher the shapes in the blackness.

'You down there,' he called, 'you're wanted for questioning!'

A figure started up the steps.

'Not you, granny' - he pushed her back - 'there's a charge of witchcraft against you.'

'Witchcraft!' The woman sounded surprised. 'Got it the wrong way about, haven't you? I mean, that's the one that's been trafficking with Satan, sitting down there. Been calling on him for help this last hour, she has. Only now he's tied her tongue to keep her quiet - and none too soon for my liking. The things she's been saying - enough to make a Christian woman's hair curl!'

'Can't help about that,' he crossed himself perfunctorily. 'I got my orders. It's the young one the Lady Edith wants to see.'

'Well, I wish you joy,' said the woman sagely. 'Wouldn't be in your shoes and that's a fact.' She wagged her head and folded her arms across her skinny bosom. 'I wouldn't be the one to take her into the presence! I'd sooner stay down here,' and she seated herself on the steps to give weight to her words.

The man hesitated in spite of himself. 'What's that supposed to mean?'

'Well, now,' she lowered her Voice, 'have you had a good look at her? I mean, a good look?'

He shrugged. 'All look the same come they've been down there a week.'

'Well, you take my advice - for your own sake. Go on, you get a torch and have a proper look. I shan't run away.'

He laughed unpleasantly, 'No fear of that.' The clang of the iron grille echoed through the stones as he slammed it down on her. Presently he was back with a light.

'Well?' he prompted.

'Just you look down here.'

He held the torch high and leaned down, holding his breath against the smell. At the foot of the steps he could see the woman crouching over a girl who sat on the stinking floor with a face as empty of expression as a mill pond. She offered no resistance as the woman opened her bodice to display her breasts.

'Look at that,' she triumphed, 'as witchmarked as ever you saw! And see' - she inflicted a vicious pinch - 'she feels no pain, that's a certain proof.'

The girl's lips parted but no sound came out. She turned her face towards the woman as if bewildered, and slowly tried to pull her clothing together. She formed her arms into a cradle and a large tear rolled down her face.

'Mad as a March hare!' said the woman confidentially. 'That's what comes of meddling with demons. Can't speak a Christian word, to save her soul -just makes noises like an animal.'

The turnkey drew back. There was something more down there than he had bargained for. At that moment the girl looked up. The light from his torch bounced back from her dilated pupils like the red glow of an animal's eyes at night.

'Jesus!' he muttered, and slammed the grille on both of them. As he hurried away he could hear the woman's voice whining, 'Don't leave me alone with her, I'm feared! Don't leave me, as a Christian man, have pity ...'

The Lady Edith was ushered into her husband's presence and made her customary obeisance. His face told her instantly that his mood was sour.

'Yes, yes,' he said testily. 'What is it now?'

He had not done well at the butts. The fracas this morning had upset his aim.

'The girl, my lord-'

'I thought I granted you leave to deal with her.'

'Indeed, and I thank you. But there is a complication. It seems she cannot speak. Moreover, she now stands accused of witchcraft. A matter, I think, for the Church's authority.'

Eustace pulled a strand of his sandy beard into his mouth and chewed on it. 'She cannot speak, you say?'

'She is struck dumb.' She smiled faintly. 'By the Devil, they would have us believe. It appears she is quite mad.' 'By whom is she accused?'

'By the old woman -who is herself accused by another.' 'A pretty nest of vipers.' He leaned back in his chair. Edith lowered her head and waited. After a moment a look of satisfaction spread over his face. 'Let it not be said that I infringe the prerogative of Mother Church. They shall be handed over to her ministers. They can try the pair of them and string them up.'

8

The tumbril swayed and rumbled over the cobbles, jostled on all sides by those who had come to see the spectacle.

His head still throbbed from the hammering it had taken and his eyes were parched by lack of sleep. His mouth was dry too. He had been offered neither food nor water since yesterday. But that was no hardship; an empty stomach was best for what he was about to face. He was going to his maker unshriven, for what it was worth. He did not care. If there was anything beyond death he did not want it. He had had enough.

There was only one thought that still disturbed him. It was that in his disastrous attempt to retrieve Hazel, he might have endangered her life. He had no way of knowing, no way of finding out. He would die not knowing.

There was no possibility of escape this time. When they had bound him, he had blown his sides to stretch the ropes as a horse blows his sides against the girths, but a glance was enough to tell him that the effort had been wasted. Even free and armed with a knife he would have been hard put to it to escape through such a throng, and the crowd that had once laughed at his sallies was howling now for his blood. He could see them everywhere, choking the main street so that time and time again the cart was brought to a standstill, filling every side street, hanging from windows of upper storeys, clambering up trees for a better view. Sellers of water and hot pies fought their way between the bodies, trays held aloft as they shouted their wares. The town had turned out as for a public holiday. He had not thought his ignoble death to be such an attraction.

As by slow stages they reached the place of execution, he saw a second cart approaching from the direction of the church, converging on the green by the crossroads where the gallows had been set up. In it he could discern three figures. One stood upright, holding aloft a tall cross. Behind were huddled two formless bundles that might have been anything. At its approach the women in the crowd set up a cry, 'The witches! The witches!'

They shrieked like maniacs, tearing their hair, and the men caught the infection from them and shouted in response. Of the two women in the cart, still sodden from their ducking, the water still streaming from their clothes and hair, only one made any response. Struggling to her feet she railed back, screaming her impotent rage at her tormentors. The other remained unmoving, with bowed head.

Poor wretches, he thought dispassionately, they would have a worse end than this. The dog-tongs had been fetched from the church and were being brought to red-heat in a brazier of coals. The one who was on her feet stared at them in dread and then began fighting frantically against her bonds.

'Confess!' a voice demanded. 'Confess to your sins!'

'No - no!' she cried, incoherent in her terror as her clothing was ripped away. 'Her over there - not me, not me!' but she was dragged from the cart and over to the brazier.

'Don't worry, granny - her turn's next!' they assured her. 'Now confess!'

She gave a piercing scream as the hot metal touched her skin. At the sound, the other figure raised its head, and recognition stabbed him.

He stared at her. She seemed to be coming out of some sort of trance. Her movements were slow, as if drugged. She looked in bewilderment at the cords tying her hands as if she had only just discovered they were there.

'Hazel!'

Her head came round, her blank eyes slowly coming into focus.

'John - the water ... I held on like you said ...' she was still wandering. She looked about her as if trying to understand what she saw. The woman writhing on the ground screamed again. Her eyes filled with horror. 'Oh, dunna-'

The torturer turned his attention to her and as he moved towards her a whimper escaped her like that of a frightened child. 'No -no ...' she backed away, shaking her head. The man grinned.

There was a guard on either side of John in the tumbril, but both were absorbed in the spectacle. Not for nothing was he muscled like a blacksmith. He strained on the stretched ropes and felt a sinew tear but after that he was out of them. He seized the two from behind and slammed their heads together, and as they reeled from the blow was over the side and into the cart with Hazel. The man with the cross turned to intervene and was lifted bodily and hurled towards the brazier, his cross wrenched from his hands and swung like a club round the heads of the bystanders.

Before they could recover John had pulled Hazel to her feet. He thought briefly of escape, but it was hopeless. They were hemmed in on all sides. His escapade had won them only a moment. But a moment was all he needed.

In Hazel's twilit world the clouds were clearing, her stunned mind coming to life.

'John!' she buried her face against him. 'Dunna let them burn me!'

'Sh-sh,' he soothed her, stroking her back. 'They shan't

touch you.' There was no way out. The crowd that had loved them would only be content with their blood. 'It's all right,' he assured her, and felt her relax. 'I'm here. Look at me ...' She raised her face, tremulous, trusting. 'Mistress Ash ...' he whispered, and bent his head to kiss her.

It was over in an instant. He hooked his iron fist under her jaw and gave one mighty wrench. There was a sickening crunch and her head lolled helpless on its broken neck.

He stared at her numbly, at the sudden radiance fading from her face, the single tear already drying on her cheek. It was all I could do, my chuck ... He stood gripping her in his terrible grasp, her body that was suddenly heavy in his arms, incapable of further action, immobilised by an agony he had not known about.

A roar of anguish built up inside him, tore loose and went bellowing round the square, the last despairing cry of a wounded animal.

It checked the advance of Tim Kettle, chilling him as he battered his way through the crush. His stubby body was spewed forth just as Black John raised his head. Their eyes met full and what Tim saw there sent him blundering back the way he had come.

It penetrated the walls to the Lady Edith, who turned pale. 'My lord, this is unseemly,' she protested, imagining that the cry had been extracted by torture.

Her husband shrugged. 'It is the end of our problems,' he said.

It reached faintly the ears of the last of the Pengerrans, where she waited in the greenwood by a battered tinker's cart. 'That is my father,' she thought, wrestling with a new and strange emotion. 'Someday I will avenge his blood!' She wept painfully as she had never wept before, while a small grubby boy tried vainly to console her.

It acted like a signal to the mob. With an answering howl they flung themselves forward, and what had been an ordinary barbarous execution turned into a bloodbath. They were unable to wrench Hazel's body from his arms until they had severed his hold with an axe. He felt it as one heavy blow among many. Only the dizzying of his head and the hot gush of blood told him what was done. Her body seemed to go from his piecemeal, and in his delirium he fancied he saw her face swing past him at the end of her long drowned hair.... but the eyes were calm and unaware, the lips still curved towards a smile .... if it was really so, she did not know.

They used the dog-tongs on him as he knew they would. He had cheated them of their prey and must pay the price.

They had learned their lesson about tying him and this time they broke his shin-bones with the head of the axe. He lay helplessly sweating while they brought the tongs to white-heat, feeling them burn through skin, through muscle, through the stench of his own entrails ... Tyburn must be like this ... Hearing between the waves of blackness someone screaming and knowing it must be him ... while fire and lightning shrieked up his spine as the tongs seared through to bone.

The only clear thought his mind could make was, They can't do this to Hazel.

Then he reached the level of pain beyond which the brain can register no more. And at last, long after he had forgotten to hope for it, death let him go.

CODA

The men who build motorways sometimes turn up strange things. The stone that was unearthed near Buxford, on the site of the intersection of the old road, baffled them.

It looked like a milestone and was obviously of some antiquity. But the marks on it were indecipherable, partly through age and partly because the writer was unlettered, and when it was finished only he could read it.

What he meant it to say was,

HAZEL

BELOVED OF JOHN 1546

Tim Kettle put it there.

Made in the USA
Las Vegas, NV
09 August 2021